Dead Air

Also by Deborah Shlian

FICTION

Rabbit in the Moon

Nursery (Re-released as Double Illusion)

Wednesday's Child

NONFICTION

Self-Help Handbook of Symptoms and Treatments

Women in Medicine and Management: A Mentoring Guide

New Frontiers in Healthcare Management:

MBAs Evolving in the Business of Medicine

Also by Linda Reid

FICTION

Where Angels Fear to Tread (aka Yolanda Pascal)

NONFICTION

Collaboration Across the Disciplines in Health Care
(aka Yolanda Reid Chassiakos, co-Editor)

DEAD AIR

A Novel

Deborah Shlian
&
Linda Reid

IPSWICH, MASSACHUSETTS

FIRST EDITION

This book is a work of fiction. Names, characters, places, and incidents either are the products of the author's imagination or are used fictitiously. Any resemblance to actual events or locales or persons, living or dead, is entirely coincidental.

ISBN: 978-1-933515-50-2

Published in the United States of America by Oceanview Publishing, Ipswich, Massachusetts
www.oceanviewpub.com

2 4 6 8 10 9 7 5 3 1

PRINTED IN THE UNITED STATES OF AMERICA

For our parents

Joseph and Evelyn Matchar

and

E.G. and Effie Stassinopoulos

Acknowledgments

Dead Air is a work of fiction, but the setting is authentic, and the premise is frighteningly plausible. In addition to our own experiences as medical directors at university student health services and as principal investigators in medical research, we drew on the expertise of Dr. Warren Strauss, Dr. Jonathan Hayes, Dr. Joel Shlian, Dr. Steve Singer, and Steve Tiplitsky. Special appreciation to Alice Suna, Steve Manton and E.G. Stassinopoulos, avid thriller fans who tirelessly read and critiqued our manuscript.

Thanks also go to Bob and Pat Gussin, Susan Greger, John Cheesman, Maryglenn McCombs, and Susan Hayes from Oceanview Publishing who all helped to launch this first of the Sammy Greene thriller series. And to George Foster for another beautiful cover.

Finally, thanks to our spouses, Joel Shlian and Anastasios Chassiakos, for their unfailing love and support.

Deborah Shlian and Linda Reid

"If you really want to reform American higher education, start by burning the buildings and hanging the professors."

—H. L. Mencken

"The greatest good to the greatest number
is the measure of right and wrong."

—Jeremy Bentham: Volume X of *Works* (1830)

"America's research universities today rest
on unstable and shifting ground."

— Sergio Vest, President of MIT,
to a White House panel, May 1992

Dead Air

Prologue

Ellsford University, Nitshi Institute
Locked Lab
July 1995

Cacophonous shrieks and squeals of ten pigtail macaques ricocheted off the walls of the soundproofed fourth-floor lab. One small, scanty-haired monkey rocked back and forth, hitting the outer wire-mesh barrier of her enclosure, her silver neck collar clanging against metal like a prisoner's cowbell. The animal peeled back its gums in a yellow-toothed grimace and reached out its paw as if pleading for help.

"Damn near human, huh?" Lila Raymond had just wheeled her housekeeping cart into the room. The "Danger, Infected Animals" sign kept her at a cautious distance, but as she moved alongside an empty cage, she asked the handler, "Where's the big guy?"

"Didn't make it."

The plump cleaning lady shook her head. Night after night for the past eighteen months she'd seen the macaques grow thinner and weaker until most were gone.

The handler shrugged. Not his responsibility. Lila knew he was just hired help. Though if rumors were true, not for much longer. A guy on the day shift claimed that with animal rights activists screaming bloody murder, the medical director planned to terminate the project.

For a few moments the monkey struggled to squeeze its body

through the bars, then with a small, pitiful yelp, withdrew, exhausted, against the back of the cage.

"Poor creature. Guess she don't like being here." *Who could blame her*, Lila thought, noting the placard on the wire mesh marked "Placebo." Lila didn't know what the word meant, but she did know one thing: every one of the monkeys in that same group had long since died.

Ellsford University
Orientation Week
July 1995

The alarm roused her from a deep sleep. Lucy Peters reached for the snooze button, then, realizing she'd already squandered her nine bonus minutes, forced herself awake.

Her eyes stung, assaulted by a ray of bright sunshine from a crack in the window blinds. Ten after eight.

It didn't seem possible. She'd crashed on the lumpy mattress only three hours before. Learning her way around the small New England campus, registering for classes, sorority rush, meeting new friends — especially one handsome sophomore who'd made her forget her old boyfriend in Sioux City — orientation week at Ellsford University left little time for sleep.

She heard voices from the hallway just outside her dorm room. Better hurry or she'd lose the competition for the communal showers. She threw back the covers and stumbled to the closet for her floral print robe — her parents' going away present. Not her style, but then parents are parents.

As she tied the belt around her narrow waist and wiggled her feet into matching slippers, she flashed an image of her father's furrowed brow and her mother's forced smile when she'd announced her choice of a small New England campus over Iowa State. Lucy hoped they could hear her across the miles. "I'm eighteen now, making my own choices, and doing just fine."

In fact, she'd just made an important decision. Later that morning she'd tell the doctor in Student Health she'd join his study. Mom and Dad always preached that in this world you needed to give back. Energized by the sense of purpose, Lucy grabbed her towel and headed down the hallway.

Ellsford University
First quarter
September 21, 1995

Sergio Pinez barely felt the steel point of the butterfly pierce the skin of his forearm. Less than a bee sting. Just like last time.

He shut his eyes while the gloved doctor removed several vials of blood. Sergio despised needles, only agreeing to all this because they claimed he had no choice. Something about new requirements for freshmen. According to the doctor, college campuses were plagued by outbreaks of measles and mumps. Anyone who hadn't received a booster since childhood had to be vaccinated. He'd gotten the shot two months ago during summer orientation, so now he was back for tests. Actually the second set in two weeks.

"To make sure you've developed antibodies — that's immunity — to these viruses. Otherwise we won't know if the vaccine is working."

Sergio didn't completely understand the doctor's explanation, but if it was all part of college life, so be it. Ellsford University had been his dream school since he'd first heard about it from his high school band teacher. Nestled in the hills of Vermont, Ellsford's two-hundred-and-fifty-wooded-acre campus boasted a top law school, a renowned medical center, and an impressive humanities program. A world away from 124th Street in Spanish Harlem.

"Terrific music department. With your outstanding talent on the flute, you have a real shot."

A ticket to a future.

Two years later, after a perfect audition, he'd won the coveted spot in the freshman class.

"All right. One more and you're all set."

Sergio closed his eyes even more tightly. "Good."

Pulling a syringe from his pocket, the doctor removed its plastic cap and injected clear fluid into the boy's vein. "That's it."

Sergio exhaled. By the time he'd opened his eyes, the doctor had extracted the butterfly cannula and was placing a small Band-Aid over the site. "We'll need you back in eight weeks for a blood test."

"More blood? Do you have to?"

The doctor's smile was reassuring. "Absolutely."

"I don't know my practice schedule yet." Unlike his family physician who'd performed a few cursory taps on his chest and knees, filled out the form, and sent him on his way, this doctor probed his history and prodded his body for almost an hour. But then Dr. Ortiz had delivered Sergio. There was nothing he didn't know about him. Especially after his last visit.

"Six p.m." The doctor checked his pocket calendar, then wrote the date on a blank prescription. "November sixteenth. Here in Student Health. The clinic will be closed, but I'll meet you at the entrance and let you in."

"I'm just a freshman. How come I rate special service?" Sergio asked as he sat up on the exam table.

The doctor patted the boy on his shoulder. "Students are our number one priority here at EU."

Sergio hopped off the table. "Thanks." He extended his hand. "I'm glad I came here."

Ten minutes later, headed off toward the music building, Sergio Pinez had no idea how truly wrong that decision had been.

The doctor reviewed the entries for S.P., Patient #14, before closing the file and shutting down his PC.

7/1/95 Viral culture: negative; Anti-HIV antibodies: negative; Polymerase chain reaction assay: negative

7/5/95 Vaccination administered. Batch #25497

9/7/95 Anti-HIV antibodies: positive (ELISA and confirmatory Western blot), T4 cell subsets: helper/suppressor ratio 1.2, Absolute helper cells 680, White blood cell count 8,700, 76% segs, 22% lymphs, Platelets adequate, Hemoglobin 14, Chem panel normal

9/21/95 Intravenous challenge administered. Lab repeated. Return: 11/22/95.

That next visit would be critical, the doctor knew. The difference between success and failure. Life or death.

CHAPTER ONE

NOVEMBER 16, 1995
THURSDAY MORNING

From the last row, Sammy Greene watched the professor pace the stage of the tiered lecture hall. He seemed mesmerized by the piece of chalk he tossed up and down in his left hand like a tennis ball. Though no science fan, the freckle-faced junior had to admit that Professor Barton Conrad possessed a true gift. For three months, he'd pushed and prodded the two-hundred-plus undergrads who packed his gateway class, until even Sammy, a communications major, had begun to appreciate the elegance of genetics.

"Consider, for a moment, an amplifier powerful enough to convert the inaudible whir of butterfly wings into the roar of a seven forty-seven." Conrad pointed to a plastic model of a double helix balanced on the edge of the demonstration lab bench. "That's what a new tool called PCR routinely does to the tiniest piece of this DNA molecule."

Slouching against the blackboard, he looked up toward the back row. "What, by the way, is PCR?"

Several hands rose, but most students remained hunched over open books, studiously avoiding eye contact. Sammy, fearing her bright red curly mop of hair — her best and worst feature — might be a target, kept her head up, but slid her five foot slender frame a little lower in her seat. If Conrad called on her today, she'd be *ahf tzoris* as her late Grandma Rose, who'd taught her Yiddish, would say. Last minute prepping for her campus radio show had trumped reading the assigned material.

"Mr. Stanton, could you enlighten us?"

The blond-haired sophomore was a mere three seats from Sammy. Better him than me, she thought. She breathed a sigh of relief as Stanton flashed his disingenuous smile. "Sorry, didn't catch the question."

Embarrassed titters from his cohorts.

"That's 'cause it wasn't a ball," Conrad parried, aiming a look of disdain at the young man he knew to be one of the university's star hoopsters and one of his least promising science students. "The answer is polymerase chain reaction. PCR. You might be surprised to know a jock like you discovered it."

"Cool. Did he play basketball?"

"No. Kary Mullis is a surfer — among his other hobbies." Conrad resumed his pacing as he delivered a two-minute lecture on the eccentric inventor and the discovery that revolutionized biology.

"While winding through the mountains of northern California in his Honda Civic, Mullis envisioned a way to copy a single fragment of DNA in a chain reaction so gracefully simple, it makes Mother Nature's work seem tacky."

"Like a biological Xerox machine," a girl in the middle of the class volunteered.

"Probably a pre-med," Sammy grumbled under her breath.

"Not a bad analogy, Miss Novak, though slightly misleading. PCR cranks out copies of DNA, not one by one, but in an exponential fashion."

The young woman's head bobbed up and down to show off her understanding. "Twice the genetic material each cycle?"

Definitely a pre-med.

"Exactly, and invaluable to researchers who require relatively large quantities of DNA," Conrad responded, "or to someone who needs to know if a given gene sequence is present in a test sample of DNA."

"Haven't they used that technique to find murderers?" Sammy interjected, her interest piqued.

"And in some cases, convict them." Conrad added with a hint of irony. "With PCR, law enforcement labs can make an identification from the DNA in dried saliva left on a cigarette butt, a licked envelope, even a single hair. Basically any bodily fluid or tissue can be analyzed—bone chips, bloodstains, or semen. Imagine if Sherlock Holmes—"

"Is this on the midterm?" Bud Stanton interrupted.

"Let's just say this, Mr. Stanton. You're going to need to know this material and then some to pass my class. You in the game?"

Stanton favored Conrad with a polite smile and a barely perceptible nod. "Double or nothing," the athlete mumbled just loudly enough for the few students nearby to hear.

Conrad glanced at the overhead clock. "Then match game begins Monday, folks. Remember to bring two blue books and a couple of number two pencils for the exam. I'm afraid I'm late for a meeting," he said, collecting his lecture notes from his desk and heading for the door. "Any last-minute questions, come by my office from three to four tomorrow. After that, you're on your own." At the door, he turned to the class, "Oh, and good luck," his eyes focused on Stanton, "to all of you."

Conrad disappeared before Stanton's smile slid into a menacing sneer.

FRIDAY. NOVEMBER 17, 1995
1:00P.M.

"All I remember is the pain." After a few moments, the tremulous voice choked back a sob. "I couldn't tell anyone. Ever."

"Talking about it helps," Sammy answered gently. "You've done nothing to be ashamed of." She nodded and gave a thumbs up signal at the engineer's window across from her rickety stool. For Sammy, these few hours hosting her own daily campus radio broadcast were a welcome respite from the challenge of required science and math courses. Sammy had worked the graveyard shift, midnight to six a.m., for six months to stir up buzz for her talk show *The Hot Line* and to finally land the prime afternoon spot. Now it was the most listened-to program on the Ellsford campus — if not St. Charlesbury itself.

"We were friends," the caller explained. "I never thought he'd do something like that."

"It wasn't your fault," Sammy reassured her again. "Tell us what happened."

"We had a couple beers, that's all. He was going to crash at my place for a few hours, you know."

"Mmm." Sammy encouraged vocally, as she scribbled notes on her station log, and cast a pleased eye at the bank of telephone lights blinking invitingly off to her side.

"I thought he just wanted to sleep. And then. And then." The caller could no longer hold back her tears. "He attacked me! I tried to fight, but he was so big. There was nothing I could do!" Her crying filled the cramped room.

"I know," came the soothing response. "It's okay." Sammy paused, "Did you call the police?"

The voice sounded terrified. "I-I couldn't. I c-can't."

Sammy shook her head, but continued, "It's hard, I understand. Maybe calling our campus support group at the Rape Crisis Center can help." Reaching off to her left, she grabbed a scrap of paper. "Campus extension forty-eight twenty-four," she read. "Forty-eight twenty-four, twenty-four hours a day. Thanks so much for sharing with us." Before the woman could respond, Sammy clicked off the connection.

"Sex, Lies, and Date Rape, today on *The Hot Line*, Ellsford station W-E-L-L." She punched another of the blinking phone buttons. "Hello, you're on the air."

"This is Jeff."

"Yeah, Jeff, go ahead."

"It's all bullsh —"

Sammy managed to hit the buzzer before her caller completed the word. “Keep it clean,” she warned.

“Okay. How come it’s ‘yes’ until the morning? Then she changes her mind.”

“We’re all allowed to change our minds. That’s no excuse.”

“After we had sex? The fucking bit — ?”

Sammy’s fingers leaped for the “off” button, but her reflexes couldn’t prevent the expletive from going out over the air. Glancing at the window into the producer’s booth, she winced at the angry face staring back at her. Program Director Lawrence Dupree had his limits — and obscenities crossed the line. Ellsford University was still a bastion of New England conservatism. Though she had chosen the Vermont campus to get far away from painful memories of home, it was hard to deny her roots. Sammy was well aware that her New York–bred tart tongue was a constant irritation to Larry. As she clicked for the next caller, she hoped he wouldn’t fly off the handle at the slipup this time.

“Sammy?”

“You got me. Who are you?”

“Doesn’t matter.” The male voice was brusque.

“Okay. What’s on your mind?”

The caller cleared his throat. “They like it, you know.”

Sammy was incredulous. “They like it?”

“Sure. She fought for a while, but then she just relaxed and let it happen, you know.”

“You’re telling me you raped somebody?”

The caller hesitated. “Wasn’t rape. I just had to push a little, you know. We still see each other. We’re friends.”

Sammy shook her head in disgust. “Sounds like rape in my book. I’d have nailed your *batzim* to the wall. If your ‘friend’ is listening, that number for the Rape Crisis Center again is forty-eight twenty-four. Call them. You need help.”

She clicked off. A glance at the clock showed enough time for one more call.

“You’re on the air.”

"You're all sinners!"

Sammy couldn't be sure if the high-pitched agitated voice was male or female.

"Violating God's word and God's law! You're going to burn in hell!"

Sammy adopted a mocking tone. "For what?"

"The sin of fornication. You will face the wrath of God and die a thousand deaths of the horrible plague! AIDS will—"

Sammy severed the connection. Her own tolerance for on-air invective was nonexistent. "I think it's about time for a little less passion and a little more compassion. That's *my* kind of religion."

She looked over at the program director as he simulated pulling a knife across his throat. "Well, it looks like our time's up. Stay cool, and we'll see you again tomorrow—on *The Hot Line*."

No sooner had she clicked off her mike than the studio door burst open to admit Larry Dupree. Sammy threw up her hands. "I know. I know."

"Ah can't keep doing this, Sammy, ah just can't," he drawled in his Mississippi accent. "Potty mouths and lunatics. Next, you'll be getting death threats."

Sammy nudged her delicate features into a calculated pout. "Hey, it's not like I'm Rush Limbaugh or Howard Stern."

"Is that what ahm supposed to tell the dean? After your shenanigans last year, you know he'd like to can this show. The board of regents doesn't take kindly to controversy."

"Tell the dean and the board we're exercising our first amendment rights *and* our religious freedom."

"Religious freedom?"

"Sure, free expression is America's secular religion. My job is to protect those rights—and give them a forum."

The program director shook his head. "Sammy, you are some piece of work."

"I'll take that as a compliment." Gathering her papers, Sammy eased her tiny frame off her stool, and turned to Larry who hadn't moved. "Hey, stop looking so worried."

"That's *my* job!"

"Okay then, let's set up a seven-second delay. That should give me enough time to cut off the kooks."

Larry nodded at the engineer's booth. "Brian's working on it. Maybe by next week. But until then," he added firmly, "do something a little less controversial, okay? How 'bout a story on that teaching award? Or those hydroponic veggies they're growing in the greenhouse?"

"Even aggie shows talk about manure. It's part of life, if you get my drift."

"Well, y'all'll be standing deep in it if you don't tone it down. If you get *my* drift."

Sammy refused to acknowledge the warning as she headed out the studio.

"Going to the greenhouse?"

"Going to hell," she retorted. "I've got an afternoon rendezvous with the Reverend Taft."

"Gawd, Sammy, please be careful."

"*Halevai!*"

"And what in hell does that mean?" The tall, lanky southerner was as much a foreigner to Yiddish as to Yankee.

Already at the door, Sammy turned and tossed Larry an ironic smile, "Loose translation: 'the saints preserve us.'"

He'd been sitting there, feet dangling over the precipice of the university clock tower for nearly twenty minutes, not clear how he got there or why. But then he hadn't been certain of much since — since when? He wasn't sure. He couldn't seem to remember anything except the recurrent nightmares. Tormenting him. Invading his thoughts. He'd hardly slept at all in two weeks.

A sudden lancing pain pierced his temples. He grabbed his skull. What was happening to him?

Fifty feet below his perch, campus life proceeded at its usual frenetic pace. Everyone rushing: to classes, to meetings, to parties. No time to stand still — even for an instant. He closed his eyes, seeking solace. Deep breaths. That girl in his psych class had shown him how to do it. Progressive relaxation. Another inhalation. It seemed to help. What was her name?

The thunderous clang of the two o'clock hour resonated within him, sending out tendrils of pain. It felt as if his head would burst.

"Look! Someone's in the clock tower."

In the courtyard below, a crowd quickly gathered around the student pointing up.

"Wait! Don't jump! We'll get help!"

Help? He'd told them something was wrong, but nobody believed him. Now it was too late. No one could help him. All those voices, shouting, screaming. He wanted them to shut up, to leave him alone. Just a few precious moments. Alone.

"He's going to jump! God, somebody stop him!"

Easing himself to the very edge of the precipice, he pushed off, feet first, toward the bosom of the crowd. His final expression was a gentle smile. Soon it would be over. Finally the pain and the nightmares would stop.

Forever.

Sammy strode across campus, ignoring her twinges of guilt. Yes, she'd failed to tell her boss at the station that she'd been tipped off about an animal rights protest organized by the Very Reverend Calvin Taft for that afternoon. At best, Larry would send someone to accompany her; at worst, he'd forbid her going. She didn't want either scenario. Taft was *her* story.

By the time she entered the university's biology building, the demonstration was in full swing. She followed the rising sound of chants and claps to where Taft and more than two dozen rabid followers were trying to push past a harried-looking lab tech guarding the entrance to the animal studies unit.

"I'm warning you!" the tech shouted." The police'll be here any minute!"

A chorus of curses erupted from the mob.

"Murderers!"

"Killers"

"Death Dealers!"

Jockeying for a good position amidst placards and fists, Sammy raised her microphone above the heads of the protesters in front of her, shielding her small tape recorder under her left arm. The reporter in her loved to watch people react. The tilt of a head, a wrinkled brow, a downturned lip, a not-quite-guileless grin. She studied any gesture that might belie the speaker's words — what Sammy liked to call the "story within the story." Observing the faces of these kids, she was fascinated and horrified by the ardor she saw there. She knew it was a testament to the power of their leader.

Taft turned to his flock. "The hand of the abuser does not threaten us. We have come to rescue these poor suffering souls from your inhuman treatment."

Right, Sammy thought — *Father Teresa*. She'd run into the Reverend before. Tall and gawky as Ichabod Crane, Taft exuded the arrogance of a man personally chosen to serve God. For more than a decade the charismatic evangelist had led the Traditional Values Coalition, a vocal group of religious extremists. And for most of that time, Taft had been no more than back-page news copy, crisscrossing the country advocating his fundamentalist version of morality to local cable TV and after-midnight talk radio audiences.

But with the malaise triggered across the country by last year's economic downturn, his message had begun to resonate. Not only religious kooks listened to his florid speeches. Taft had tapped into a frustrated segment of society that grew day by day: weary workers falling behind as they struggled for a piece of the American dream. God would stand by their side and give them hope. From the past year's donations alone, Taft's coalition now boasted a multimillion-dollar war chest.

Taft targeted colleges and universities as "dens of iniquity," promoting rallies against abortion, gay rights, and recently, animal research. What worried Sammy most was that so many students seemed persuaded by his hateful rhetoric.

Reaching into her purse, she grabbed her Nikon One Touch

and snapped shots of the demonstrators. She'd track them down for interviews later.

The flash caught Taft unaware. For a moment he stared in her direction. Even from the distance, Sammy was struck by the power in his dark eyes, an expression she'd seen at last year's abortion protests — rage saturated with hatred that seemed just a fraction away from an explosion of violence. Then he had led a mob through the medical school, painting hate messages on the walls of the GYN clinic where poor women came for abortions. One nurse ended up in the ICU with a head injury, but after hospital bills were quietly paid, no one pressed charges. Sammy never did discover the name of the anonymous benefactor, though she had strong suspicions.

Now she took a deep breath, unconsciously anticipating trouble.

"Chill out man!" the tech snapped. "They're just animals."

"You're the animals!" retorted a conservatively dressed protester to Sammy's left.

A boy with a military-style crew cut shoved the tech to the ground, "Let's get 'em!"

The mob pressed forward, pushing open the door and storming into the laboratory where the pigtail macaques were boarded.

Sammy stopped to help the tech who was on the ground, moaning. Blood oozed from a cut on his forehead. "It looks as though it's just superficial," she told him as she helped him sit up. She handed him a Kleenex from her purse.

"I'm okay," he said, "but these people are nuts. Don't they know our work saves lives?" Sounds of crashing cages and breaking glass brought him to his feet. "Jesus, they're letting them out," he screamed. "The monkeys!"

Sammy turned to where he pointed. Taft stood to one side, nodding approval as several of his group unlatched the animal cages. The injured tech started to run from one cage to the other, trying to prevent the jailbreak, but he was outnumbered by the violent horde. Several monkeys, now free, joined the melee, providing a chattering chorus amid the shouting.

Sammy watched the tech lunge for one tiny pigtail whose silver collar glistened in the morning sunlight. In a flying tackle, two of the protesters pounced on the hapless lab worker, and the frightened primate leapt into the arms of the youth with the crew cut.

"Ow!" Sucking his bleeding hand, the flat-topped youth dropped the squirming animal, which scampered off into the crowd.

Sammy witnessed one of the protesters fly backward onto a lab table, victim of a well-placed accidental kick from the struggling technician.

"Freeze!"

As three more protesters lunged in revenge, Sammy heard a whistle behind her.

"I said, all of you, freeze!"

A balding, pot-bellied policeman with a bushy salt-and-pepper mustache stood at the door to the lab. He was flanked by a corps of younger deputies. Sammy recognized Gus Pappajohn, campus police chief, and his cavalry, and stepped aside to make way.

"Don't anybody move," Pappajohn barked. He pointed at Sammy. "That means you too, Greene."

The deputies moved in to corral the protesters while Pappajohn bestowed a withering glare at the reporter. "Where angels go —"

Sammy responded with a tense smile.

The chief of police shook his head. "Greene, haven't you graduated yet?"

"Less than two years, Sergeant."

"May they go ever so quickly." Pappajohn's Boston accent held a trace of his Greek roots. A member of Boston's finest for over twenty-five years before taking two bullets in the gut, he was forced to accept early retirement, and moved up the coast to Ellsford. He hadn't counted on the climate being quite so harsh. In a weary voice, he added, "You want to tell me about it?"

"Look, this isn't *my* show." She scanned the gathered protesters for their leader.

"What's wrong, officer?" Reverend Taft appeared at the lab entrance as if he'd just arrived on the scene.

How did he get back there? Sammy wondered.

Pappajohn's expression grew more dour. "Good. Another one of my favorite people. Join the party."

While the deputies helped the tech round up the monkeys, Taft surveyed the damage with an unconvincing look of shock. "My heavens, what is going on here?" He nodded at the injured protester, who clutched his abdomen. "This is what happens when a university allows innocent animals to be used for experiments."

Members of Taft's flock joined in a chorus of assent. "They must pay for their sins!"

"Fuck you!" screamed the tech whose head wound now sprouted fresh blood. "You'll all pay for this!"

"All right. I'm not about to play judge and jury here," Pappajohn answered. "We'll talk about it at the station." He turned to his men and pointed to the tech. "Get this guy to the hospital ER, ship any injured kids to Student Health, and move the rest of 'em out."

Pappajohn draped one arm over the Reverend's shoulders. "Okay, let's go." He nodded at Sammy, who was inching toward the door. "You too, Greene. "

Damn. Larry Dupree was not going to be happy about this. Not one bit.

"Special interests are taking over our campus!" Barton Conrad slammed his fist on the end table, startling several bored colleagues. "One of these days, you'll wake up and find you've paid too high a price for their support. And you can kiss your precious academic freedom good-bye!"

The science professor poured his second glass of sherry and swigged it down in one gulp. A log in the oak-paneled fireplace sparked and snapped, the crackle an emphatic coda to his impassioned outburst. In the flickering light Conrad appeared far older than his forty-two years.

Seated nearby, Dean Hamilton Jeffries pushed his poker at the embers with tense, staccato strokes. "I understand your concern, Connie," Jeffries answered. "But we've taken every precaution to ensure that no financial contribution will interfere with the work we do here. Even the Nitshi Corporation has a written hands-off policy."

"Have we read the fine print?" Conrad wondered aloud, ignoring his colleagues' smirks.

"No one's asking you to sleep with the devil." Jeffries responded.

"Not in so many words. But it does seem that the more money we bring in from industry grants, the happier *we* are."

Jeffries adopted a tone of frigid politeness. "You are probably aware that federal grant funding for research is down forty percent this year. Tuition increases can't even touch our needs." He glared at the professor. "Just how do you propose we pay your salary, Connie?"

"All I'm saying is there's no such thing as a free lunch."

"Except at our Friday faculty meetings," injected Bill Osborne, professor of psychology, triggering a round of laughter. He filled his sherry glass and passed the decanter to his neighbor in the circle of faculty.

Friday afternoon gatherings at the chancellor's home were a once a month tradition at Ellsford University — ever since Thomas Ellsford, Jr., had founded the private institution some eighty years earlier. Over the years, the catered luncheons had become a reluctant obligation — especially for junior faculty out to impress those elders who would award tenure, a lifetime of job security. The tasty fare compensated for the stultifying atmosphere and obsequious conversation. Today, though, Conrad's outburst was livening up the late meal and après sherry hour.

In deference to old-fashioned manners, everyone now stood when Chancellor Reginald Ellsford entered the study. In his arms he held a bronze plaque.

"Sorry I'm late, gentlemen and ladies. A little business to attend to. Thank you for waiting." He took his place in the throne-like chair beside the fireplace. Conrad refilled his sherry glass and found an empty space on the couch as the group nestled back down into their seats.

The Chancellor continued. "I don't have to tell you that outstanding teaching has always been top priority on this campus. So, it is my great pleasure to bestow this year's Ellsford Award for Excellence in Teaching to—" Pausing, he squinted at the engraved letters "to Dr. Burton Conrad." He looked up and scanned the room until he saw Conrad. Acknowledging him with a nod, he added, "It's an honor to have you at Ellsford University."

Polite faculty applause broke out as the chancellor rose and displayed the bronze plaque.

"Well done, Connie!"

"Right on."

Conrad summoned a tenuous smile and slowly stood, unsteady from multiple drinks. The chancellor met him halfway, shook his hand, and gave him a pat on the back. Face flushed, Conrad muttered a quiet "thanks." After a short pause, he took a deep breath, deciding to use this moment to further express his concerns. "We're on the verge of—"

"I'm afraid I can't stay," the Chancellor interrupted. "Business calls." He smiled and pointedly adjusted his Rolex. "See you all next month."

The cue for the meeting's dissolution given, the others stood up as well, gathering overcoats, papers, and grabbing last-minute snacks from the half-eaten platters of pâté and crackers.

As most of the group filed out, Conrad remained in the center of the room, irritated that his audience had been stolen from him by his hesitation.

"Saved by the bell," Bill Osborne whispered in his ear.

Conrad turned to his friend and colleague. "Always the politician."

Though Conrad's tone was obviously sarcastic, Osborne merely shrugged. In fact, he did affect a rather patrician air. His herringbone sports coat, impeccable blue button-down, pinpoint Oxford shirt, red silk tie, sleek black tassel loafers, and heavy silver ID bracelet were a fashion contrast to the threadbare tweed blazer, shiny corduroy trousers, and rubber-soled Rockports that Conrad wore.

"We're both too old to play the part of perpetual grad student," Osborne said. "Personally, I want tenure." He winked at Conrad. "Thought you did too."

Conrad ambled over to the couch and reached for his sherry glass, emptying it once again. "So did I." He held the plaque to the lamplight, noting that under the inscription "Ellsford Award for Excellence in Teaching," his name had been misspelled.

"So why threaten to flunk our star forward?" Osborne asked.

"Where'd you hear that?"

"On the news. Campus radio, yesterday afternoon. Some female talk-show host."

"Wonderful," Conrad snorted. "Truth is, if Bud Stanton doesn't pass Monday's midterm, no more basketball."

Osborne shook his head. "Death wish."

"What's that supposed to mean?"

"It means that if you don't pass Stanton, EU can't beat Duke. Which means otherwise generous alumni will think twice before writing their usual fat checks."

"Stanton doesn't know a chromosome from a hole in the wall."

"And last semester he knew diddly about the superego."

"You passed him anyway?"

"Don't act naïve, Connie. Whether you know one bloody thing about psychology or genetics doesn't matter in the least. What matters is how you play the game."

Conrad poured himself another drink. "And what if they ask you to take a fall?"

Osborne frowned. "Meaning?"

"To throw the g—" Conrad started to answer, then caught the unfriendly eye of Dean Jeffries who was heading toward them. "Call me tonight and I'll explain," he whispered.

"Okay," Osborne nodded. "I'm flying to New York tonight. My flight gets in at eight. I'll call from the hotel."

"Dr. Jeffries!" Conrad recognized the high-pitched whine of Edwin Houk. The anemic junior history professor pulled the reluctant dean back to the middle of the room before he'd had an opportunity to reach Conrad. "Two of my students — our students — are up for a Rhodes. Quite an honor for us at Ellsford, wouldn't you say?"

Osborne turned back to Conrad with a barely concealed smirk. "Subtlety was never Houk's strong suit."

"He's a shoo-in for tenure."

"You could be, too. With your publications," Osborne nodded at the plaque by Conrad's glass, "and that."

"That." Conrad took a large sip.

Osborne's tone reflected exasperation. "Come on, Connie. Have you thought about what'll happen if you're denied tenure here, too?"

Conrad stared into his empty glass. "I suppose I'll have to find another job."

"You're not exactly a kid anymore."

Conrad tossed him an indignant look.

"Anywhere you apply will need references. They'll ask EU if you're a team player." He pointed to Dean Jeffries. "Speaking of which, we'd better do our bit to butter up the dean. Want to go save him from Houk?"

Conrad waived the offer. "I can't."

Osborne shrugged. "Suit yourself." He turned back to his friend with one last warning. "Look, Connie, don't be so self-righteous. You could end up committing academic suicide."

Student Health was just a few buildings away, but policy required paramedics to deliver the injured riot victims by ambulance — even those with minor injuries.

"ID?" A nurse near the entrance accepted the plastic card. "Luther Abbott. Freshman."

"Have you been seen here before?"

"Just for my shots."

"Good, then you've had your tetanus booster." The nurse examined the back of his right hand.

"Darn monkey practically bit my arm off."

The wound wasn't deep, but there was a one-inch tear just below his wrist on the surface of his skin.

"Look, it's still bleeding!" Luther said. "I ought to sue the university!"

"Uh-huh." She tried to sound noncommittal. The last thing she wanted was involvement in some legal action. Bad enough she had to sign the incident report.

"Will I need stitches?"

"Animal bites like this are never closed. Too much chance for infection to spread," she explained. "You'll probably need antibiotics, though." She instructed the paramedics to put the gurney in the treatment room. Then she told her assistant to start irrigating the wound with normal saline under pressure. "Doctor'll be with you in a minute." She handed the youth a clipboard. "Fill out this questionnaire in the meantime. Dr. Palmer requires it for his patients."

4:30 P.M.

Upset by the faculty meeting, Conrad sought solitude and sanctuary in his tiny office. He stared vacantly through the window, its stained glass filtering early evening light onto his cluttered desk. Multicolored leaves from restless maples, oaks, and elms, shades of scarlet and maroon, blending with crimson and amber blanketed the meadow beyond the genetics building. Fall had stayed longer than usual this year, but there was a frail quality to this magnificent quilt, its brilliance all too transient. In a few weeks the covers would be a sterile white.

Laughter and shouts from students on the walk, calling out plans for midterm cram sessions jolted Conrad back to his world. He reached in his drawer for his pipe. If only midterms were the hardest thing faced in life. If only life could freeze at those halcyon days.

"Sorry I'm late."

The voice sounded familiar. Conrad looked up. Standing in the doorway was a young woman with short, curly copper-colored hair surrounding a heart shaped freckled face. Not quite five feet tall, in a bulky green wool sweater over black tights and mid-calf black leather boots, she appeared almost elfin. Only the heavy New York accent shattered the image of puckish innocence.

"Excuse me?" *She always sat in the back, didn't she?*

"I know you said office hours were over by four, but, um, I got tied up," Sammy repressed a chuckle. "Anyway, I'm glad you're still here."

His tone was sardonic. "One of the few. It's Friday afternoon." He pointed to a ratty chair across from him. "Have a seat, Ms., um?"

"Greene. Sammy. I'm taking your Bio one-o-one this semester."

"Ah, yes." Conrad eased himself back in his chair with a polite smile. "What can I do for you, Samantha?" The sherry was diffusing through to his shaking hand as he raised it to light his pipe.

"It's Sammy — not short for Samantha. My parents were looking for something different."

"Sadly, I'm not the first Barton in my family." Conrad said. "Did you bring your textbook?"

"Nope, just this." Sammy grabbed a mini-notebook and tape recorder from her purse, and placed them on the desk.

Conrad's eyes narrowed. "You with the *Eagle*? They can't get one story straight."

"No, I'm here about the Ellsford Teaching Award." Sammy smiled at the professor. "Well deserved, for sure."

His reddened eyes traveled to the plaque he'd placed on the windowsill. The edges were already tarnished, he noted without surprise. He shifted in his chair. "Okay. What do you want to know?"

"Well, let's see." She flipped open the notebook. "You've been here — ?"

"Six years." Conrad chewed on his pipe.

"Like some of our undergrads," Sammy said. With so many required courses filled, it often took more than four years to graduate.

Conrad's eyes sought out a four-color brochure among a stack of papers on his desk. He pulled it from the pile and showed it to her. *Recruiter's Guide to Ellsford.*

"Yeah, I've seen it."

Conrad squinted to read one of the pitches. "'Teaching is the mission of Ellsford University'. Sounds good," he said, his voice filled with disdain. "But once your checks clear, teaching is no longer a priority." He bit the end of his pipe. "No, what really counts here is something more quantitative."

"Such as?"

"Articles, papers, books, for a start. There are forty thousand separate journals in the sciences alone; new articles are turned out every two minutes. That's almost three thousand every twenty-four hours." His laugh was bitter. "More and more people writing more and more articles that fewer and fewer read. And I'm not even going to talk about the trees."

"We have three Nobel laureates on this campus. Surely their research is important."

"Three among dozens of second- and third-rate hackers who will never come up with an important finding. Yet they fight for grants to fund mediocre work to produce yet another worthless paper. Quantity, not quality. Publish or perish. The overwhelming function of research is to get books and articles you wrote on your résumé for promotion and tenure."

"You're up for tenure this year, aren't you?"

"I'm up for it. Now we'll have to see what the Tenure Committee thinks." Puffing on his pipe, he studied the chipped plaster on the ceiling and ruminated. "Ah, tenure. The ultimate protection from accountability. Freedom to —" He stopped himself, turned back to her and chuckled, "to be incompetent."

"You sound so cynical."

"Cynical? No, just realistic. The system is skewed to reward research. The best teacher in the world is known only in the perimeter of his campus; a mediocre researcher is known around the world." Conrad shivered, trying to ward off a wave of vertigo. "Open your eyes. And I mean wide open. Disguised in the garb of academic excellence is a community of malcontents and thieves."

She smiled at him. "I've got to hand it to you. You've got chutzpah. "

His mind wasn't working clearly anymore. "Meaning?"

"Yiddish word. Nerve. Like cojones," she explained.

"I know that. I mean, what are you referring to?"

"Not kissing ass like the rest of the junior faculty." Sammy's bright eyes bore into his. "Bud Stanton."

Her intelligent features blended into a reddish blur. Conrad dropped his gaze to his hands clenched in his lap. The sherry wouldn't loosen its grip. "You work for the campus radio station?"

Sammy nodded at her tape recorder, "Yeah, I host a talk show."

Conrad tried to control his rising anger. Tight lipped, his voice was icy, "Yes, well, it's late, Ms. — Sammy and, as you can see, I'm in my cups just now. Perhaps we should reschedule." He rose unsteadily, clutching the edge of his desk for support.

"Well, the award should help get you tenure," Sammy ventured.

Conrad eyed her coldly. "The Ellsford Teaching Award is hardly a prize to cherish."

"Sorry?"

Conrad moved toward the door with measured steps, careening like a moth toward extinction. Halfway there, he turned back to Sammy with a pained smile. "Everybody knows it's the kiss of death." With that he stumbled from the office, slamming the door behind him.

"Another one? Christ, that makes two in two months."

"Don't worry. Nobody suspects a thing. Suicide among college students isn't so rare. Even here at EU. Four or five manage to do it each year. Not to mention the hundreds who think about it."

"What about the autopsy?"

They both knew that in cases of unexpected death, the law required an official medical examiner's report.

"Everything's been taken care of. Just like last time. You'll get the specimens you need tonight. The official report will be in the coroner's computer system by Monday. Cause of death — suicide."

"And the body?"

"On its way back to the grieving family tomorrow. Along with the Student Health Service records that his general practitioner requested."

"You're not serious?"

"Relax. They've already been doctored."

"That's not funny."

"Sorry."

"What does the chart show?"

"We're covered. Long history of depression. Grades down, girlfriend left him. That sort of thing."

"You sure like to live dangerously."

"Trust me. No one'll figure this as anything more than a crop of crazy kids." A pause. "So what's the problem?"

"I don't know. These side effects. If we're producing some kind of dementia, maybe we should suspend our work for a while, find out why."

"Let me remind you just how much is at stake here."

"If I can make a few adjustments. Recheck the original data. Maybe we stopped the animal studies too soon."

"You said yourself that even if the vaccine worked perfectly in monkeys, you couldn't be sure it'd work in humans."

"I know, but—"

"No buts, doctor. Any hint of a problem and the FDA will cancel our Phase III trials for good. Not to mention the scandal when the Human Subjects Committee finds out what you're up to. Besides, you're assuming the problem is yours. Maybe college life *was* too stressful for these kids and they checked out on their own. You'd have stopped the most important work since Salk for no reason."

"I don't know."

"Come on. Think of this as a temporary setback. Two bad outcomes, twenty successes. Pretty good stats, I'd say. And by this time next year you'll have enough proof that this vaccine works to beat your French competitor to the marketplace. You and I, my dear doctor, will be richer than we've ever dreamed."

5:15 P.M.

Through Conrad's office window, Sammy watched the professor stagger across the meadow. She had no idea what she'd said to upset him. She shook her head. Damn. Monday's show down the tubes. Maybe she ought to switch to Larry's greenhouse story.

"Jesus, there you are. I've been looking all over."

Sammy spun around to face Reed Wyndham. Not handsome in the classic sense, Reed was good looking in his own way. Deep violet eyes, a well-formed mouth, strong jawline, and thick waves of sandy hair all added to his appeal. Definitely an attractive guy, Sammy thought — even in his rumpled hospital whites.

Now his eyes were red-rimmed from fatigue and pulsating with obvious annoyance. "Is it too much to ask that you meet me *when* and *where* we'd arranged? Thank goodness I found Larry still at the station. He told me where you might be."

"Look, I got caught up on a story."

"What does that mean?"

"What do you mean 'what does that mean?'"

"You're telling me you've got a hot story, so I can't count on you?"

"I would have called."

His lips registered doubt. After eight months of dating, they both knew that keeping schedules was not one of Sammy's strong suits.

Sammy's jaw tightened. Why couldn't Reed understand the drive she felt to be a journalist. She was just as ambitious as he was. "You have your work. I have mine, doctor."

Her passion softened his irritation. "Doctor-in-training," he corrected. "I've still got seven months of med school to go." He held out his arms in surrender. "I'm sorry. I've been on call for twelve hours straight. I'm totally beat."

"Then go home and go to bed." Still peeved, she pulled back from his embrace.

"I was hoping you'd join me."

Sammy had turned to focus on the Ellsford Teaching Award abandoned on the windowsill.

"Earth to Greene!"

"Huh?"

"I'm offering you a full apology *and* my body."

"Oh, sure," she said, distracted, "but not tonight." With one backward glance at the plaque, she slid through his outstretched arms, allowing him only a quick peck on the cheek. "Rain check, okay? I really have some work to do."

Before he could protest, Sammy sped out the door, leaving a confused Reed alone in Conrad's office, shaking his head.

Sammy cajoled a stack pass from an old boyfriend working the night desk at the Virginia Ellsford Barrington Library. She clambered up the narrow staircase to a dark, dusty corner of the fifth floor. Scanning the overstuffed bookshelves, she finally located the loosely bound newspapers piled in mounds on the floor. The topmost issues of the *Ellsford Eagle* dated from the 1920s and '30's. She glared at the stacks, then closed her eyes, conjuring up an image of Bubbe Rose chiding and lecturing her teenage charge. *Never give up.*

Sammy smiled, acknowledging the vision of the wise old woman. *Yes, Grandma, your counsel has gotten me this far. But you know, it means I'm going to be here the whole* farkakte *night.*

9:30 P.M.

"Thanks for coming at this late hour, Reed."

"No problem, sir."

Fiftyish, tall, graying hair with pale gray eyes to match, Dr. Marcus Palmer was chief of immunology and Reed's preceptor for his last quarter of medical school. Reed had been lucky to land this rotation with one of the top professors at EU Medical, luckier still that the man who was known for his aloof manner had taken him under his wing, encouraging him to apply for a prestigious residency at Mass. General. So even if Reed had objected to jumping out of a warm bed, he'd never let on.

Palmer flashed a plastic badge to the armed guard seated in front of a large U-shaped bank of TV monitors. "Dr. Wyndham is with me."

The guard merely nodded.

It was only the second time Reed had been inside the Nitshi Research Institute, a modern four-story glass-and-steel structure planted imposingly on a hillside just at the north edge of the Ellsford campus. He recalled the controversy three years earlier when Nitshi Corporation, the Japanese drug conglomerate, had funded the construction. Protesters were concerned that the university might be forging an unholy alliance with an aggressive international pharmaceutical corporation eager to establish a stronghold in the United States.

To the board of regents, the chancellor pleaded financial necessity. With government grant funds providing less and less economic support, he'd explained, EU would be forced to take a backseat in science to major research centers like Harvard, Stanford, and MIT whose international reputations guaranteed first-pick for limited grants. The institute was touted as a positive example of the new spirit of scientific cooperation for the global community of the new millennium less than a decade ahead.

But the protesters remained undeterred. So much so that one demonstration led to a riot, resulting in a dozen injured students and police. It had been several months before calm returned to EU. Today, the Nitshi Research Institute's bucolic setting belied past tempests. The hillside grounds once trampled by rioters were lush with overgrowth; the air once choking with tear gas was scented with pine. Ellsford graduate students in biology and chemistry worked side by side with visiting fellows from renowned Japanese research programs. Everything Dean Jeffries had promised, Reed mused, had come to pass—Japanese and Americans together stretching the horizons of science and technology, freely sharing their information and discoveries.

That is, on floors one through three.

The fourth floor was off limits to everyone but a select few. Dr. Palmer led Reed to an elevator marked PRIVATE and placed his plastic card face up, the magnetic code instructing the car to travel straight to the top, bypassing the other floors.

When the doors slid open, Reed struggled not to gawk. He'd toured the first three floors with a group of medical students some months earlier, more than a little impressed with the quality of the labs. But to get access to *this*—something out of a science-fiction movie. The titanium-plated walls resembled the corridors of the *Starship Enterprise*.

A shutter snapped. "Welcome Dr. Palmer." Reed spun around, stunned. The voice of the tiny silver robot facing him was part Bart Simpson, part Elmer Fudd.

"Hello, CARL." Palmer explained that the acronym stood for Computer Aided Robotics for Learning. "Carl is state of the art—complete with infrared scanners for short distances, sonar for longer, lasers, TV cameras, the works."

"Your guest will need a pass." A tray emerged from within the machine. "Place your right hand here," the robot commanded Reed. Within moments, his prints had been copied and processed. "Reed Wyndham, fourth-year medical student, Ellsford University Medical School, 3304 Menlo Avenue, Apartment number 2B, phone number: 617-555-9748. Social security number: 555-03-1806."

"How—?" Reed blurted, as seconds later, a plastic card similar to Palmer's appeared on the tray.

"Keep it with you at all times. Follow me, sir," Carl lisped.

The robot turned, gliding silently along a labyrinth of white tiled corridors, negotiating corners with programmed ease. They passed a couple of Asian men in lab coats who nodded to Palmer. Must be developing new drugs in this area, Reed guessed. No wonder it was restricted. That kind of research demanded utmost confidentiality and security, explaining all the miniature TV cameras hanging from the ceilings.

Finally, the corridor forked two ways. From a passage to the right came the low hum of machinery. Pointing the other way, a single sign read in English and Japanese: PATHOLOGY.

The robot stopped at the door, but Palmer ushered Reed inside a fluorescent-lit, formaldehyde-smelling room lined with counters, shelves, and sinks. A long soapstone table stood in the center on which lay the newly deceased body of a young olive-skinned man.

"Sir?" Reed ventured.

"Yes?"

"May I ask why *we're* doing this post?" He'd been told the dead man was an undergrad who committed suicide. Reed knew that Palmer had been a pathologist before turning to immunology and research, but it seemed unusual for him to be performing the autopsy. "I mean, instead of the coroner."

"Long story," the silver-haired professor smiled easily. "Bottom line, this is one of my HIV-positive patients. Frankly, the ME would just as soon we do the post here. Don't worry, it's all very official. Your first one?"

"Third." Reed replied. "The others were — older."

Palmer reached into one of the lockers lining the far wall and handed Reed shoe covers, a plastic apron, and rubber gloves. "You'll need these too," he said, adding a mask and goggles.

Palmer snapped on surgical gloves, and stepped up to the table.

Reed took his place on the opposite side, facing Palmer. He adjusted the overhead light, its beam bathing the nude body stretched before them in a rectangle of iridescence. He couldn't help thinking how vulnerable the boy appeared. By the fourth year of medical school, Reed had seen his share of death, but had never overcome his overwhelming sense of sadness at facing mortality in one so young. Perhaps it was simply the reminder that even at twenty-five he himself was not immortal. This case, though, seemed doubly poignant. Did the knowledge that his diagnosis carried an ominous prognosis lead the young man to take his own life? The fresh venipuncture marks on both arms made him wonder if he'd seen Palmer recently. The massive head wound and obvious limb fractures were signs of a painful end. Such a tragedy.

"Ready?"

Reed nodded.

With his gloved left hand providing traction, Palmer made the typical Y-shaped autopsy incision from the points of each shoulder to the middle of the chest and then down to the pubic bone.

Reed handed him a pair of branch cutters to cut the ribs, clipping all of them from the diaphragm right up to the clavicle.

Palmer pointed to several large rib fractures. "No doubt they were sustained in the fall."

Reed watched his preceptor remove the breastbone. It lifted off easily, like a box top, exposing the entire chest cavity.

"Heart and lungs look good on gross," Palmer reported. "Of course, the microscopic will be telling." Tying off the carotid artery, he removed the whole chest block — heart, lungs, trachea, bronchi — laying them out on separate trays on a steel cart and covering them with a towel.

"Want blood cultures?" Reed asked, anticipating the nod. He had a long syringe ready for the former pathologist to insert in the sac around the boy's heart, drawing a large tube of blood for the lab.

Palmer next tackled the abdomen. He pulled out the intestine, coiled round and round the belly like a large serpent. "Liver and spleen seem untouched by disease," he noted. "Hand me a couple syringes." With Reed's help, he took various fluids for testing, placing them in separately labeled specimen bottles. Then, returning to the organs laid out on the trays, he took multiple samples from each for microscopic examination.

"Just the head now and we're through." Palmer began reflecting back the scalp. Despite the fact that the skull had been crushed by the fall, he needed to use the power vibrating saw to cut through to the brain. Once exposed, he lifted it out and plopped it into a pan. Wielding a long bladed knife similar to a butcher's, he made serial cuts for future review. It was all very efficient, requiring little conversation. Just as well, Reed thought. Even after working with Palmer for the past two months, he still felt awkward around him.

Less than an hour later, Palmer began proficiently wrapping up the procedure. Reed stood by, wondering how best to help. "Should I make any notes in the chart?" he asked, picking up the victim's file from the counter and flipping through to the last page.

Palmer jerked it from his hand. "No!" he snapped. Then in a more reasonable tone, "No, it's uh, I'll do it. I need to sign the report anyway. And you, my boy," he said, placing a collegial arm over Reed's shoulder and pushing him toward the door, "need to get some shut-eye. I expect to see you for rounds bright and early tomorrow morning." Palmer pressed a button mounted on the wall, adding with a rare warm smile, "You've been a big help."

Seconds later, the silver robot appeared at the entrance to the autopsy room. "You rang?"

"Please escort Dr. Wyndham out, Carl."

"After me, doctor."

Reed followed the machine through the tiled maze, back to the elevator where he relinquished his plastic pass as requested. All the way down to the lobby, he reveled in the praise he'd received.

You've been a big help.

Not much, but significant, coming from a man who rarely gave compliments. He'd have to keep on his toes. And just maybe, he'd get that recommendation he needed for a choice residency.

That thought alone was enough to extinguish any notion that something odd just occurred on the fourth floor of the Nitshi Research Institute.

At least two hours before the autopsy was complete, the medical examiner's computer system had been accessed and a final certified report filed: Sergio Pinez, EU freshman, cause of death: multiple blunt trauma; manner of death: suicide (jumped from height).

9:40 P.M.

Sammy rubbed her weary eyes and tried to suppress a yawn. Hours of searching had turned up an incomplete collection of campus newspapers from her freshman year. She was hoping the story she remembered was in one of the survivors she'd scattered on the dust-streaked library floor.

The faded type blurred into the stained yellow newsprint made the articles difficult to read. Still, she struggled on.

Her growling stomach reminded Sammy that she'd barely eaten that day—just an English muffin before morning class and an apple at noon. It was now after nine-thirty. She massaged her neck and shoulders and did a few graceful stretches, secure from prying eyes in her distant stack hideaway. Another large pile of newspapers awaited her search and she briefly debated the prospect of giving up for the night. Journalism won out over dinner, however, and she dove into the next set of papers.

Minutes later, she found it. Barely legible, portions of the article were destroyed by a large water stain. But enough remained to refresh her memory of the event early in her freshman year. Professor Yitashi Nakamura, a respected Japanese-American microbiologist had been found dead in his office on North Campus from a self-inflicted gunshot wound.

A police investigation concluded that Nakamura, who had been herded into one of the U.S. internment camps that imprisoned Japanese-Americans during World War II, suffered from delayed post-traumatic stress syndrome leading to depression and, ultimately, suicide. The gun, a .22 semiautomatic, with five remaining bullets was clutched in his hand. And, Sammy noted with a shudder, on the floor by his desk, broken and bent, lay the bronze Ellsford Teaching Award he'd received the day before. Survived by his wife and two grown children, the article stated that Mrs. Nakamura planned to return permanently to Kyoto, her husband's birthplace.

Sammy made a Xerox copy of the article, checked the campus directory, then grabbed her purse, threw on her jacket, and hurried from the library in the direction of Professor Conrad's home. Running at top speed, she reached his two-story Queen Anne near South Campus in less than twenty minutes.

It looked as though someone had begun a badly needed renovation, then abruptly stopped. A light coat of fresh yellow paint only partially covered the white primer underneath, the fish scale siding on the upstairs turret was coming apart. The shutters were drawn with no light visible through the windows. She leaned against the newel post on the broad front porch to catch her breath, then knocked firmly on the splintered door.

Sammy strained to listen for footsteps, but heard nothing. She knocked even more loudly.

Still no response.

Glancing at her watch, she frowned and began shuffling down the front steps, almost missing the faint "Who is it?" from behind the door.

"Professor. Please, I have to talk to you. It's Sammy."

The door slowly opened a crack, held in place by a rusty chain. Conrad's bloodshot eye met hers. "Not short for Samantha. I know." His tone was unwelcoming. "What do you want?"

"May I come in for a second? There's something I'd like to ask you."

The door remained chained. "So you can broadcast more of my secrets on campus radio?"

"Fair enough. What if we just talk for a few minutes 'off the record'?"

"Is there such a thing?"

"With me, yes." Sammy looked openly and intently at the professor's disheveled visage.

"Oh, all right, come in." Peering behind her into the darkness, Conrad unhooked the chain and hurried her inside. He latched the door closed as soon as she entered. In the dim hall, she could see he was wearing an old sweat suit, socks, and no shoes.

"Thanks. Hope I didn't wake you."

He led her to the front room. "Couldn't sleep."

Conrad switched on a table lamp, illuminating a cozy, eclectic, and thoroughly chaotic living area. A small French provincial patterned sofa, two mismatched leather armchairs, and an oak rolltop desk filled most of the room. On the far wall were bookshelves tightly packed with science textbooks while several lopsided piles of research journals lay on the scuffed oak wood floors, yellow Post-its flagging areas of interest.

A few photographs of Conrad and a dark-haired woman were also displayed. Sailing, skin diving, hiking, the attractive couple always smiling, holding each other in a warm embrace. The woman must be his wife, Sammy presumed, wondering why he still kept her picture when everyone on campus knew she'd left him for another professor nearly a year ago.

Without waiting for an invitation to sit, Sammy created a place for herself on the sofa between a stack of books, opposite from Conrad's chair by the rolltop desk. She draped her jacket on the sofa arm and rummaged in her oversize handbag amidst her tape recorder, notebook, makeup, and pens before finally extracting the Xerox copy. "Look at this," she said, handing it to Conrad as she laid her purse on the hardwood floor.

"Just a minute." He reached for his reading glasses. "I need my specs." Scanning the story, his face paled. "Why are you showing me this?" He shoved the article back at her.

"You knew him?"

Conrad's response was guarded. "He was a very well-respected professor."

"You didn't answer my question."

"Yes." His expression was neutral.

Sammy stared directly into his stony face. "They say he killed himself."

"Yes." Conrad didn't blink.

"Why?"

His tone was wary. "Why ask *me*?"

She tapped the article. "Look at this. Paragraph after paragraph of praise and eulogies. Hundreds of publications. Over thirty scientific awards. Not only a full professor with tenure, but the guy brings in millions of dollars a year in federal grants to the university. He's about to be crowned king of Ellsford — and he kills himself. Why?"

"People have personal demons."

"Married over forty years and a new grandfather." She looked at

Conrad again. "His wife says in the article that they were planning a second honeymoon."

Conrad snapped back. "What makes you think I've got an answer?"

"Because of what you said back in your office about the teaching award. You were trying to tell me something."

For a second, Conrad's eyes drifted to a brown envelope on the desktop next to his computer. He seemed about to say something, but stopped himself. "I was speaking metaphorically. And drunk."

"That's it? Nothing else?"

"That's it. Just the intoxicated ramblings of a weary man," he said. "I've learned that sometimes it's better to let sleeping dogs lie." He looked at her and his tone turned cold. "Stay as far away from this as you can." With a glance at the window near the front door, Conrad rose from his chair, indicating that the interview was over.

"That sounds like a threat."

"Just a warning."

She reached for her jacket, letting her eyes fall on the envelope. It was addressed to Dean Jeffries and marked CONFIDENTIAL.

Conrad stood by the front door. As she approached, he opened it carefully, peering into the moonlit darkness, then added firmly, "Now good night, Sammy." He hesitated for a second before adding a softer, "And — take care."

"Thanks. You too."

As she left, Sammy was pleased to see the professor's smile. For just a moment, he resembled the carefree man in his vacation photos. It was an image she wanted to remember him by. And would.

Sammy walked all the way across campus in the crisp autumn air before realizing she'd forgotten her purse. She debated briefly about going back, but eleven o'clock might be too late to disturb the professor again. No matter, Sammy thought. It would give her a perfect excuse to return tomorrow and see if Conrad was in a sunnier and more open frame of mind. Good thing she kept a spare set of keys at the station.

11:20 P.M.

"Dammit, Sammy, must y'all make a megola out of every assignment?" Larry Dupree drawled.

"I think the word you're looking for is megillah," Sammy corrected the program director as the two sat in the tiny station office planning the next week's program schedule.

A smile dawned on Larry's dour face. "Oh yeah, like Magilla Gorilla."

Groaning, Sammy returned to the business at hand. "I'm figuring a week-long series'll do. 'The Death of Education.' 'Sell out or Get out' for Part One."

Frustrated, Larry interrupted, "This was supposed to be a simple piece. 'Professor wins teaching award.' Three minutes at most. Just filler. Now you want to do an in-depth review of everything that's wrong with higher education?"

"I'm telling you. There's more here than meets the eye."

"What meets the eye is all we can put on the air. Look, Sammy, you're good, real good. But the second responsibility of the media is to get the facts."

"And the first?"

He threw her a glare. "The first is to get the proof."

"Pappajohn called you again?" More a statement than a question.

Larry nodded. "Apparently you've made some unsubstantiated allegations against Reverend Taft. *Again.*"

"Unsubstantiated?" Sammy sputtered. "I saw Taft instigate that riot. And that's a fact!" she added with emphasis.

"Evidently none of the other witnesses agree with your version."

"'Witnesses?'" She snorted, "More like doppelgängers for the Reverend."

"Sergeant Pappajohn says—"

Sammy rolled her eyes. "That old codger would say anything to keep his sinecure."

Larry exhaled. "Look, Sammy, we almost lost our license last year when you blamed Taft for that anti-abortion violence. Ah don't want to have to face another lawsuit for slander."

"A journalist can't take the easy road."

"No one would ever accuse you of that," Larry agreed. "Certainly not our attorneys. Or don't you remember the fancy legal footwork that barely extricated this station from a budget-busting court battle?"

"I don't think we should've backed down," protested Sammy. "Not then and not now."

"Sammy, we're journalists, not missionaries." He held up his hand. "We're not going to change the world here. So unless you've got some hard proof, Reverend Taft is a dead issue. Understand?"

Grudgingly, Sammy nodded. *But I won't give up*, she thought. As soon as she developed today's snapshots, she'd track down a few of those reluctant "witnesses" and confront them.

"Now, as far as the case of the Perfidious Professor and the Corrupt College—"

"I'll have the proof. I'm almost there. I think we've got enough to go on from my sources."

"Well, ah don't. A psycho professor that shot himself three years ago and another one that's killing himself by—" he brought a cup-shaped hand to his mouth, "don't qualify for me. You come back with something concrete, and we'll talk about it. Besides, we've got something else more urgent for Monday's show."

Sammy looked up from her papers with concern. "What?"

"A student suicide."

"My God, who?"

"Sergio Pinez, a freshman."

"Why does that name sound familiar?"

"Music major from New York." Larry checked his notes. "Flute player. Apparently couldn't hack the pressure—first time away from home. Jumped off the bell tower this afternoon. Splat! Pronounced at 2:42 p.m. Take it you were still playing cops and robbers with Sergeant Pappajohn at the station."

Sammy looked stricken.

Larry continued matter-of-factly, "So we kill everything else for Monday and do the whole show on the kid. Family, friends, teachers. Ah think you should also get one of those health workers to come on and do a little counseling about suicide. Might stop any copycat jumpers from getting ideas."

Stabbed by a cruel, fleeting memory, Sammy grew pale. *Stop her.*

"Uh, sure. I'll get on it right away," she stammered, trying to push away memories of long ago, the jumble of images she desperately wanted to forget. That, and the silence.

In her memory, the silence had frightened her more than the black casket that rested, its lid shut tight, in the middle of the dimly lit funeral hall.

She was alone.

Slowly she crept toward it, her heart hammering against her chest, willing the coffin to burst open with a cry from within. She wanted to save her, to bring her back to life. She was almost seven. She should have been able to—

My fault.

All she could hear were their whispers just beyond the room.

Such a pity

So much to live for.

Poor child.

Selfish, if you ask me.

A single tear descended to her chin. Warm memories of comforting arms around her as she'd once buried her face against smooth skin smelling of Shalimar and felt at peace. And at home. Kneeling beside the closed casket, she laid her head upon the cold box and cried.

My fault.

Sammy put her hands over her ears now, willing the voices to stop. "I'm sorry."

"Sorry about what?"

"Oh, uh, nothing." Sammy shook her head, refusing to share her nightmare.

Larry looked at her oddly. "You sure you're okay?"

Wiping away the tear, she replied, "Yeah. Fine. Just fine."

• • •

You have reached 617-555-9748. I'm not able to come to the phone right now. That means I'm either on call or sound asleep. However, if you leave a message at the beep, I promise to get back to you one of these days." Beep!

"Well, you missed your chance, Wyndham. I was just thinking about coming by to keep you warm. But if you're already asleep, I'll see you tomorrow."

Before hanging up, Sammy added, "By the way, I left my purse at Professor Conrad's house and I've got to go over there and pick it up before I come over. But I'll be there. So, save me a bagel, will you? Beep!"

"Bingo," Barton Conrad said softly. "I've found you."

He continued staring at his computer monitor for a long time, perversely pleased by what he'd just uncovered. On the screen in black and white was the verification he'd been seeking. No doubt now that he had to tell someone.

He checked his Timex: just past eleven p.m. Not that late. Heart pounding, he lifted the receiver and dialed each number by heart. Both calls took under five minutes, but once he completed them, he felt exhausted by the effort. He shuffled over to the sofa, threw some books and papers on the floor, and lay down. Seconds later, he sank into a deep, alcohol enhanced slumber.

"I'm afraid we may have some problems."

"I don't want to hear them. Just take care of it."

"Okay, boss."

"And I mean permanently this time. Understand?"

"Sure, boss." the caller replied, though the connection had already been severed.

CHAPTER TWO

Saturday

Sammy awoke at six thirty the next morning, bounced out of bed, and threw open her window. One of the privileges of being a junior or senior at Ellsford was no longer living in the dorms. No more roommates to answer to, community bathrooms to fight over, blaring rap to complain about. Her studio apartment was one of a cluster of prefabricated faux brick dwellings reserved for upperclassmen located on the western side of campus. It was just a six-hundred-square-foot box on the third floor, but the spectacular view of the Ellsford estate made up for the cramped quarters and the utilitarian decor.

From her window, she could view the majestic Gothic university buildings dotting the rolling meadows, the ultramodern Nitshi Institute atop the hills to the north, and the stately Victorian homes where many of the faculty lived along South Campus. At its easternmost edge, EU ended where the city of St. Charlesbury, Vermont began. It was a typical New England small town whose eight thousand inhabitants tolerated Ellsford students in the same cool, dubious manner they suffered "the summah people" — those wealthy East Coast vacationers who summered there. Just like the tourists, the university population supplied substantial revenue to local coffers.

A bright morning sky reflected an impossible blue with a clarity Sammy had never known or even imagined in the polluted skies above the New York of her childhood. She inhaled deeply of fresh Vermont air.

Wonderful.

The sun had just come up, long shadows retreating from streets and walkways, over the trees and rooftops like the outgoing tide. The fact that the temperature was near freezing and that she wore nothing more than her minilength Ellsford U. nightshirt didn't faze Sammy. She loved this time of day — crisp and new, filled with possibilities. An early riser since childhood, she never understood people who stayed huddled in bed until all hours. Such a waste of opportunities, as Grandma Rose used to say.

Breakfast with Reed was usually one of those morning treats. This morning, however, she had to make a stop first. She planned to follow up with Conrad. Perhaps if she confronted the professor before breakfast, he'd be too hungover to resist her questions. And, she had to retrieve her purse. She needed her tape recorder for the interviews on the suicide kid she'd be doing this afternoon.

Fearing an unwelcome reception, she prepared a thermos of fresh coffee as a peace offering and gesture of goodwill. Then, slipping on faded blue jeans, a green turtleneck sweater, and a pair of black leather Doc Martens, she grabbed her peacoat and headed out the door.

The campus was eerily quiet as she made her way across the quad, the only sound the crackle of tawny autumn leaves beneath her energetic stride. Reaching the law school, she stopped to admire its ivy-colored ribbed vaulting and pointed arches. It was said that Thomas Ellsford, Jr., founded the university just so his son would not have to travel to Boston to study law. Whether apocryphal or not, the law complex was probably the most beautiful spot at EU, nestled in the bosom of a soft meadow spangled with dandelions in the warmer months. It was a favorite place for students, including Sammy herself, to sit and read. Just behind the law library stood the chancellor's home where today Reginald, a fifth generation Ellsford, resided.

Farther along, she passed the music building, an unpleasant reminder of yesterday's suicide and her task to interview a few of that poor kid's classmates this afternoon. The bell tower from where he fell now scattered the sun's rays like a yellow daisy on the quad below.

Flowers on the grave.

She shuddered at the memory and sped on. It was too beautiful a morning to think about death.

Within twenty minutes she'd reached South Campus and the walkway that led to Conrad's home. Just as yesterday, the shutters were drawn, the pale yellow house still. She hesitated for a moment, wondering even as she climbed the front steps whether she really ought to wake him. The front door was locked. Several knocks produced no response. About to retreat, she was surprised to see the side window slightly raised, the shutters open.

Frowning, she bent down and whispered through the crack, "Professor. It's Sammy. May I come in?"

No answer. She tried calling more loudly. Still nothing.

Now what? She considered leaving, but her purse was in there.

Repeating his name, she slowly eased the window open and leaned in just enough to peek into the living room. The shutters were drawn, the table lamp turned off. It was difficult to distinguish beyond shapes and shadows, but she recognized Conrad still in his sweat suit, lying supine on the sofa, his head angled slightly to his left. One arm was folded against his chest, the other hung down, fingertips just brushing the floor. It seemed an uncomfortable position for sleep, but recalling how much he'd imbibed last night, Sammy guessed he was feeling no pain.

Clearing her throat, she tentatively called out his name to avoid startling him awake.

He didn't move.

She pushed the window open so that she could climb inside, placing the thermos of hot coffee down on the floor. "Professor Conrad!" she repeated more loudly. "Sorry to intrude, but—"

The slackness of his jaw made Sammy edge closer. "I thought maybe—" She flipped on the hall light.

Something was terribly wrong. Even in shadow, the professor's skin appeared a shade too pale. And it looked like—like blood splattered on the patterned sofa.

"Professor!"

Sammy stumbled into the living room and touched his dangling left wrist. It was cold. Frantically, she pressed her fingers against his neck, feeling for a pulse. There was none. She moved his chin toward her and as she did, his jaw opened wide, exposing a ragged, round hole in the roof of his mouth. She gasped in horror. The back of his head had been blown off. Blood soaked into the cushion where his head lay.

Sammy stepped away in revulsion, almost tripping over a gun lying on the floor. Next to it she saw a note, just a half sheet of computer paper with the typed message: *No use*. C.

It can't be happening. Not again! she thought.

"Wake-up, dammit! Wake up, please!"

But he didn't rise up. Sammy was trembling all over.

My fault!

In an instant the years rolled back and she recalled the image of her mother lying on the daybed. Not quite seven, Sammy had come home from school one day to discover her, still warm, but long past life. On the end table she'd found an empty bottle of pills and a note, scribbled in her mother's neat hand, *Sorry. I tried.*

Sammy never cried that day so long ago. Even at the funeral hall as she knelt beside her mother's coffin. Her father had not come. He'd already moved to Los Angeles, and was living with his new fiancée. Bubbe Rose would become both grandma and mother now—seeding Sammy's tongue with Yiddish idioms, her soul with Jewish guilt.

Over the years, Sammy strove to appear unflappable, self-assured, tough. Keeping all her emotions bottled up, the paragon of self-control.

But, yesterday, news of a student's suicide had created a tiny chink in her reservoir of unresolved feelings. Today, finding Conrad's lifeless body had broken the dam. The child within her wept as she could never remember weeping.

When she was done, she wiped the tears from her cheek, picked up the cordless phone from the end table by the couch, and calmly dialed the campus police.

Luther Abbott was exhausted. The throbbing in his hand had kept him awake all night. He'd been told to elevate it, but how was he supposed to accomplish that and still sleep?

"Blasted chimp!" He unwrapped the loose gauze dressing and examined his wrist.

"Lucky that monkey didn't injure any tendons or joints," the doctor in Student Health had declared yesterday as he cleaned the wound. "I'd have to put you in the hospital on IV antibiotics. This way you can go home on oral medication."

Now Luther was taking pills four times a day, though the angry red color of the skin surrounding the bite suggested they might not be doing any good. He extracted a bottle of aspirin from the drawer beside his bed. A couple of these, he thought, should do the trick. He rubbed his flattop. Might even help the headache just forcing its way into his consciousness.

He didn't have time to be sick, darn it. Today he had to crack the books for Monday's midterms. And tomorrow he'd attend Reverend Taft's Sunday service. In the afternoon the Reverend's group would be planning the next campus mission of the Youth Crusade. He had to be there. After his outstanding performance in the last demonstration, they'd made him a group leader.

He chugged down his pink antibiotic along with two aspirins and a prayer. God will look out for his soldiers. I will not be sick, he vowed. And that's that.

But as he returned the aspirin bottle to the drawer, Luther Abbottt had no idea he was soon to be sicker than he'd ever been in his life.

After alerting Campus Police, Sammy gently set the cordless phone back in its cradle and walked over to the front door, unlocking it as the dispatcher had requested. She returned to Conrad's desk and sat down, turning for a moment to look at the body. From this distance, she could almost convince herself he was peacefully asleep. But the jarring image of the professor last night, anxious and upset, flashed into her mind.

The Ellsford Teaching Award is the kiss of death.

Ironic.

She turned from the body and felt a twinge in her heart as she scanned the cluttered desktop. Folders, envelopes, scientific journals, and papers were scattered in disordered piles over every available surface. A small bin on one end masqueraded as an outbox where several stamped bills waited to be mailed.

Sammy remembered the large brown envelope addressed to Dean Jeffries that had lain on top. Marked CONFIDENTIAL, it must have been important to Conrad. She searched through the pile of letters. It wasn't there. Curious, she examined the open desk drawers, but found only more reports and journals, all dealing with molecular genetics.

She tugged at the lower left-hand drawer. It was locked. The center drawer was jammed with thumbtacks, paper clips, and rubber bands. Conrad had also accumulated a collection of pens, many sporting the advertising of hotels far away from St. Charlesbury's row of homey bed and breakfasts. Fumbling her way through, her hand closed around a small glass object at the back of the compartment. Guiltily, she extracted what turned out to be a bottle with a #12 printed on the label. Inside were two white tablets. Quickly, she slipped the bottle into her pocket and resumed her search.

Where was that envelope? Conrad couldn't have mailed it last night. Not in his drunken state. One last pull at the locked drawer proved futile. She briefly considered prying it open, but the police would arrive soon. She didn't want to be caught breaking and entering.

Her roving eyes came to rest on the sleeping computer screen of Conrad's Macintosh. Without thinking, she reached in back and turned it on, the pinging and whirring soon ending with the familiar heading of a file folder and its contents. What had Conrad been working on before he died? She sat, stunned at the answer. On the screen, under the folder heading "Games," a ready-to-be-played version of "Hangman" opened.

The jangle from the desk phone startled her and she jumped.

A second ring.

She stretched her hand toward the sound, then stopped.

The stillness of the house magnified the shrill third ring. What should she do? Her hand hung motionless.

Before she could respond to a fourth ring, Conrad's answering machine intervened. A ghostly voice spoke from the box: "You've reached the machine. You know what to do, and I'll get back to you." The machine beeped.

"Osborne here. Hey, guy, I'm worried about you. Let's talk, okay?"

Too late.

For a long time, Sammy sat quietly as the machine clicked and whirred back into ready mode. Finally, noticing an orange button lighting the outlet chain at her feet, she closed the "Games" file, and kicked the button off with her toe, darkening the computer screen.

Conrad's silent guardian once again, Sammy thought as she leaned forward and buried her face in her hands.

As graceful as a gazelle, Bud Stanton leapt four feet and deposited the ball into the basket. In the same seemingly effortless way, he'd fed countless layups and jumpers to the net this season, leading the previously unlucky Ellsford Eagles to first place in the Northeast NCAA conference.

"Not bad."

The six-foot-seven sophomore pivoted to face husky Lefty Grizzard who'd just entered the empty gym. "Didn't expect to see you here today, Coach."

"Me either. Thought you'd be studying. Conrad gives killer exams."

Stanton shrugged and turned back toward the basket. "Yeah, well, I'm not worried." He fired a three-point jumper from thirty feet. It sank easily.

Grizzard eyed his star hoopster warily. Cheating was not something he encouraged, even if a coveted playoff berth was at stake. He asked firmly, “Then why don’t you tell me how come?”

Stanton’s expression was pure innocence. Cradling the ball, he said smoothly, “It’s taken care of.”

A flare of anger crossed Grizzard’s face. He kept his voice even. “You want to explain that?”

“I just called in some markers.” Stanton’s eyes twinkled. “Don’t worry, Coach. I’m not about to get my hands dirty.” He threw a backboard shot which found its target, then held up his hands in a “you’ll see” gesture. “Everything’s gonna work out.”

The player’s nonchalance irritated Grizzard even more. “I don’t want to hear that bullshit,” he shouted, “You don’t do nuthin’ here without clearing it with me. Understand?”

Stanton backed off. “Okay, okay, everything’s cool.”

“It better be.” Grizzard growled, poking his finger into the athlete’s chest. “Because if I find out you crossed the line, asshole, mark my words. I’ll hang you out to dry.”

“Don’t touch that!”

Startled, Sammy jumped up from the desk chair to face an irritated Gus Pappajohn. Standing in the middle of the living room, he seemed like some enormous, lumbering, brown bear — his five-foot-ten, two-hundred-seventy-five-pound, beer-bellied hulk barely covered by a bulky wool sweater, stretched over a pair of baggy corduroys. His unshaven face suggested he’d been dragged out of bed. His grumpy mood confirmed he wasn’t happy about it.

“What a sight to wake up to.” His gaze traveled from Sammy to Conrad’s body. “What is it with you, Greene? For a pint-sized package, you’re sure a bundle of sore ass.”

“The Yiddish term is *tzoris*,” she returned, adding wryly. “Nice to see you again, too.”

“I thought all you college kids slept in on Saturday.”

She allowed herself a half-smile. “I like to be an early bird.”

Pappajohn grunted as he slipped on a pair of latex gloves. "Worms are my job, Greene. What are you doing here?"

"My job, Sergeant. I'm a reporter."

The ex-cop scrutinized her. "So what's the story this time?"

"I don't know. I came too late." She paused to force down an uninvited sob that surprised her, then manufactured a smile. "I guess things got a bit too much for him."

"Bit too much of this." Pappajohn picked up one of two empty wine bottles from the floor by Conrad's feet and eyed the label. "Good year."

"The gun and the note are over there." Sammy pointed as Pappajohn began examining the head wound. "Thought you might want to check for fingerprints, maybe take some pictures." She remembered Conrad's lecture on PCR and added, "Maybe call in forensics people for a DNA match?"

Pappajohn gave her a weary look and ambled slowly around the couch, noting the cluttered desk. "You haven't answered my question."

"Which one?"

Sitting back onto the edge, arms crossed, he turned to face her, his gaze less than friendly. "Goes without saying you're a magnet for trouble."

Sammy felt the color rise in her cheeks. Pappajohn's attitude was getting irritating. She knew he didn't like her. She felt the same way about him. The man might have been a hot shot Boston detective once, but as far as she was concerned, he'd really done a lousy job tracking down last year's campus rioters, and she hadn't been afraid to say so—on the air. If it almost cost him his job, it wasn't her fault. "What was the question again?"

"What in blue blazes are you doing here?"

"Uh, I came to interview Professor Conrad."

Sammy's hesitation was not lost on the detective. "At seven o'clock Saturday morning? Must be some story."

"The Ellsford Teaching Award. It's a great honor. He won."

Pappajohn pulled a couple of Rolaids from his pocket and popped them one at a time into his mouth.

"You know, you'd be better off if you laid off the moussaka."

"And you'd be better off if you laid off the bullshit." Pappajohn wasn't smiling.

Sammy tried to maintain a confident demeanor. Her mind raced to find a plausible explanation for her presence. Conrad's midnight paranoia may have been the ravings of a depressed man, but if he had stumbled onto an academic conspiracy at Ellsford, it could involve even the campus police.

She stepped back toward the large armchair, stopping herself just before her hands touched the armrest. Frozen, she looked up at the sergeant. "May I sit here?"

Pappajohn waved a hand. "Sit." He continued to glare at her.

Sammy took a deep breath, hoping her story would sound convincing. "Look, I really did come to talk to him about the award. He said he had something to do this weekend and this was the only time we could meet. I've got a Monday deadline. We were going to do a show about the award — you know, testimonials, students of his, colleagues — that's all there is to it."

"That's all there is to it," Pappajohn mocked. "So, how'd you manage to get into the house? Seeing that the professor over here was already dead and the house was locked."

"He *was* dead!" Sammy asserted. "The side window was open. I saw him lying on the couch and I —" She shuddered, thinking about it now. "I only came in when I called out and he didn't answer."

"Listen to me, Greene." Pappajohn leaned toward her with steely eyes. She could smell the onion on his breath. "This poker game's out of your league. You'd be smart to keep your nose out of it."

A uniformed emergency medical technician knocked on the door "Sarge?"

Pappajohn waved him in. "Over here, Dan. He's all yours." He looked over at Conrad's body for a moment. "Got a camera?"

"Yeah, in the van."

Pappajohn nodded. "Good. Grab a few shots, then take him out."

So Pappajohn wasn't going to call forensics. Sammy knew better than to comment.

The campus cop kept silent while the young tech left and returned with a Polaroid Spectra to snap pictures of the dead man. A skinny companion with sloped shoulders wheeled in a gurney. Together, they matter-of-factly approached the body and aligned the transport bed.

"Third suicide this month," Dan said.

With a sidelong glance at Sammy, Pappajohn joked, "Popped himself with a .22 just to avoid talking to her."

Sammy's outward bravado couldn't drown out her inner voice.

My fault.

As the EMT reached under Conrad's shoulders to lift him, the professor's arms dangled stiffly. For a moment, Conrad's head hung lopsided in the tech's sling. His lifeless brown eyes stared directly at Sammy.

Pleading eyes.

Accusing eyes.

Dead eyes.

Like her mother's.

My fault.

"L-look, I'd b-better go," Sammy stuttered, grabbing her purse.

"Well, don't wander too far from campus," Pappajohn said.

Sammy barely heard the warning. Pale and shaken, she stumbled past the gurney and dashed from the house.

A gloved hand reached into the wire-mesh cage, trying vainly to grab the baby pigtail macaque by its silver collar.

"Hey, what are you doing?" the tech demanded.

"I'm afraid this little one's gotta be quarantined." The man in white overalls pulled a university form from his back pocket. "Incident report."

"Shit." The tech touched his forehead where a short row of

stitches brought the jagged edges of the wound he'd received yesterday into neat apposition. "Damn that Reverend Taft. He's nothing but trouble." He pointed to the monkey. "She didn't mean to bite that kid. He provoked her."

The man shrugged. "All I know is I gotta get her outta here." He reached into the cage once again, but the primate bobbed and weaved against the bars. "Can you give me a hand?"

Reluctantly, the tech held out his arms. Without hesitation, the animal came forward, grasping the tech's neck with human-like fingers.

"She really likes you."

"Yeah." The tech helped place the pigtail in a small portable cage. "What's going to happen now?"

The man threw a canvas cover over the top of the pen, ignoring the monkey's howls of terror. "That's up to the boss." His reply was deliberately noncommittal. Fact was, he had orders to dispose of the macaque before the day was done.

Outwardly, Sammy appeared calm.

She didn't let her guard down until she was halfway across campus. She'd run the distance in record time, her legs pounding the frozen ground with angry determination, her mind chanting the mantra, *I'm in control, I'm in control* to the rhythm of her feet.

As she ran, she looked around. Everything was just the same, the sights and sounds of campus as familiar to her now as hours before. Perhaps nothing had happened. But, of course, it had. Out of breath, Sammy collapsed on the dewy grass under a grove of large oak trees.

Why did death always seem to follow her? From the day her mother had passed away, it had haunted her with memories and guilt. Now it was Conrad.

My fault.

Sure, Conrad had been depressed. Drunk and depressed. A lethal combination. It had nothing to do with her. Just a horrible coincidence. Still, she couldn't shake a feeling that the sessions with him yesterday had something to do with his passing.

Inner protests couldn't ease her growing anxiety. She didn't want to lose control again. Maybe the relaxation exercises she'd learned in psychology class would help. Students held hands and closed their eyes — tried to visualize a peaceful mountain spring. The trickling water, the lullaby of the gurgle.

She almost giggled at the memory. Struggling to picture what the group leader was suggesting, her senses kept coming back to the moist left hand of her neighbor to the right. The poor kid was so nervous, his hands drenched with perspiration. After class, she'd gone over to talk to him. A freshman, not quite used to "new age" teaching methods. She remembered his soft voice and shy smile. And his name.

She sat bolt upright. Sergio Pinez. His name was Sergio Pinez! The boy who killed himself.

She dropped her head to her hands. Again. Another soul she had touched was gone.

Pappajohn remained in the empty Conrad house for a long time after Sammy ran out. He walked from room to room just as she had done, making a cursory survey of the surroundings, orienting himself to the scene. He was convinced there was no mystery to the professor's death, but he'd be damned if some college kid was going to tell the university honchos that he hadn't done his job.

Satisfied, he went out to his car and returned with a forensic kit. Slipping on a new pair of latex gloves, he carefully placed the typed note and the gun in separate evidence bags. He selected several strands of brown hair he found on the sofa — no doubt belonging to the victim.

Then he dusted a few areas for prints, including the windowsill and the front door, discovering several partials, certain the lab would identify them as belonging to either Conrad or Greene. Good thing hers were on file — ever since he'd hauled her down to the station after last year's anti-abortion demonstrations. His stomach twisted, recalling the grief she'd caused him then.

Still gloved, he wandered over to the cluttered desk and sat down in front of the Macintosh. Pappajohn was a PC man, but he knew enough about computers to appreciate the elegance of the Apple operating system. He flipped the "on" switch and waited for the smiling face to appear on the screen, indicating that all was well with the hard disk.

He double clicked the icon to view the computer's contents. Under applications he found "E-net," an online network that allowed Ellsford University computer users to talk to each other. Pappajohn could access the system on his own PC. It enabled him to work at home and download information from anywhere on campus through his modem.

After staring at the screen for a few minutes, Pappajohn began searching files. Within minutes he located the access log for the past month, still intact in the E-net folder. Several entries dated back to the beginning of November, but only one to last night. Exactly three minutes after eleven. That must have been just before Conrad died. Pappajohn double clicked, expecting an answer to his question, but a message appeared: "This document requires the proper access. Continue or Quit?"

Pappajohn frowned. Without the correct access code, he couldn't review the log. Fortunately, all campus-linked E-net codes were recorded in the registrar's office. As campus police chief, he could insist on a copy. He'd just have to wait until Monday when the bureaucrats were back at work.

He keyed in "Quit" and shut down the computer. Slipping off the latex gloves, he gathered up his forensic kit, walked out the front door, and locked it behind him.

"Where the hell have you been?"

Startled, Sammy looked up, the blurry white form standing over her slowly coming into focus. "Oh, God. Reed. I'm sorry."

Reed Wyndham was dressed in a stained hospital work uniform, a grim reminder of the brutal battles beyond this oasis of grass and trees. Like Pappajohn, a soldier of misfortune, to whom death was no stranger. And like Pappajohn, angry with her.

Sammy stood up slowly. "You wouldn't believe what happened."

He held up a hand. "Don't. No more excuses. I don't want to hear it. It's always some crisis or another. You seem to think I'm never busy, that I have no responsibilities." He brushed back an unruly blond lock from his brow. "I'm a fourth year med student. I'm at the beck and call of everybody up the ladder from interns to residents to junior faculty to people like Marcus Palmer. They all expect me to be there when they snap their fingers."

Sammy took a deep breath and interrupted with a firm voice. "Look, I know that, but if you'd just let me explain." Surely he'd understand when he knew the facts. "I had to stop by Professor Conrad's for—"

"I can't afford to jump up and down for you anymore, Sammy." He fixed her with a look of exasperation. "You knew I had rounds at eight. At seven thirty, I called your room. No answer. I figured you were on your way, so I waited. By the time I finally did get to the hospital, I was twenty minutes late and caught hell from Palmer. And you know what the worst part was?"

Sammy started to reply, but was steamrolled by Reed's tirade.

"The worst part was that I was worried about you. Maybe you were mugged on your way to my place or—" he shook his head, "or you were in some kind of trouble, so I asked a buddy to cover for me and started running around campus like a goddammed chicken trying to find you." He let out a long exhale. "And you, you were on some stupid story about some stupid teacher."

Sammy fought to control her own temper, though her emerald green eyes radiated frustration. "If you'd only listen for a second, you'd—"

"Forget it. It's not important. *I'm* not important. You broadcast that bulletin loud and clear."

"That's not fair!"

His tone shifted to a fatalistic calm. "So I think you should find someone who is important, Sammy. For you. Maybe someone like that brilliant Professor Conrad."

Sammy's hands were shaking, her face red with anger.

Reed didn't linger. "I've got to get back to the hospital. Patients are waiting. For *me*."

She considered going after him, then acknowledged the futility, leaned back wearily onto the bark of the giant oak tree, and watched him disappear.

Once again, she was alone.

"Awesome."

Lucy Peters turned to face her sorority sister. She'd been trying on clothes all morning, hoping to select just the right outfit for the Midterm Madness party that night. Right now she wore a turquoise tank top that accented her eyes and another pair of attributes. "Think so?"

Anne Sumner nodded. "Chris'll be blown away."

"I hope so." Christopher Oken was a sophomore from Philadelphia, and probably the coolest guy Lucy had ever known. They'd been seeing each other every weekend since they'd met four months earlier. Compared to the revolving-door social life common among freshmen, theirs was considered a long-term relationship. Lucy hoped Anne would be lucky enough to find someone so special. "Who're you bringing?"

"Mike's got a chemistry exam on Monday, so I'm taking Ron. Of course, if I had a hunk like Chris, I'd go out on both."

Lucy laughed as she stepped out of her jeans. "You sure like to take chances, don't you?"

Anne flipped open her purse to show her sorority sister a color assortment of condoms. "Thirty-one flavors. AIDS isn't in my game plan."

Lucy nodded in agreement. "You're telling me. You can't be too careful." She wound a gold choker around her neck and reached under her hair to latch it.

"Hey, what's that?" Anne pointed to an elevated, quarter-sized pink circle on Lucy's chest.

Lucy checked the mirror. The spot looked so big. "I don't know." She touched it gingerly with one finger.

"Does it hurt?"

"No."

"Itch?"

"No." Lucy rubbed the area. It didn't change. "I never noticed it before."

"Love bite?" Anne teased.

A sudden fear gripped Lucy. Could she have caught some venereal disease? That would be really rank!

Anne would know. She was so experienced. Lucy ventured, "You don't think it's something like, uh—?

"Like what?"

"Herpes," Lucy whispered.

Anne laughed. "No way."

"How do you know?"

"Let's just say I'm from California." Anne bestowed Lucy with an innocent smile. "Relax, it's probably nothing. If you're that worried, why not stop by Student Health?"

"I thought they were closed."

"I mean Monday. Just cover it with a little foundation and it won't even show." Anne consulted her watch. "Shit, I've got to pick up my dress from the cleaners before noon. Catch you later."

"Sure." Lucy barely noticed her friend's departure. She was still staring into the mirror with a worried frown. Anne was right. It was probably nothing. She touched the pink circle with disgust. Just something to make her look gross.

As she reached for her makeup, her eyes fell on a business card lying on her bureau. Should she give that nice doctor a call? Didn't he say he was available any time for an emergency? Day or night?

And with a big date with Chris only hours away, this was an emergency.

• • •

The Student Health building stood deathly silent, the air still and heavily scented with disinfectant. An infirmary for ghosts, Sammy thought, as she tiptoed by the empty, darkened exam rooms, toward the nursing center. A single swatch of light came from the triage office where an on-duty nurse took student phone calls about medical problems when the clinic was closed.

"Hello." Sammy stuck her head in the door.

Nurse Lorraine Matthews was busy on the phone. A doughy, gray-haired woman, one could easily imagine her gathering a frightened student to her ample-sized bosom to offer solace. The embodiment of *in loco parentis*, in the place of a parent, Sammy thought, smiling.

The nurse raised a finger in greeting and nodded at Sammy, mouthing the words "just a minute." Sammy entered and took a seat near the bank of phones.

"Uh-huh, uh-huh. Well, the Student Counseling Center has a support group. Yes, every Tuesday, depression. Uh-huh. That's the number. Okay, and remember, call us if you think things are getting worse. Yeah, bye."

The nurse put down the phone, shaking her head. "It's been like that all morning."

Sammy arched an eyebrow. "Like what?"

Nurse Matthews pointed to the lit lines. "The suicide. Students are really upset. I've referred at least ten over to the Counseling Center. Those are just the ones that called."

"Well, then, maybe our show will help," Sammy offered.

The nurse agreed. "We've got to reach out to these kids in the next few days." She held up a finger again, as she turned to pick up another call. "Just a second. Student Health Service, Nurse Matthews. What can I do for you, Jeff? Uh-huh. It's pretty rough, I know. No, you can't blame yourself. Sure, uh-huh. It sounds like you tried."

I tried to help her.

No one could help her.

"So what're you planning to do on your show?" The nurse's matter-of-fact voice, finally off the phone, brought Sammy back to the present.

"Sorry. We're planning a memorial for the guy—for Sergio. We'll have remembrances from his friends, teachers, classmates." Sammy looked away for a moment. "And we're thinking about getting a counselor to talk about suicide."

"Sounds perfect," the nurse said.

"Would you like to be on the air?"

"Monday afternoon? Impossible. Monday and Friday are our busiest days. I'm covering triage." Nurse Matthews's face brightened. "But, look, we've got somebody terrific we can send over—a med student working with us who's got a great bedside manner—and he's not that much older than the students. He'd be perfect."

"Great. How do I contact him?"

"I'll give you his number. Hold on." The nurse nodded at the blinking phone lines and reached for one of the buttons as she picked up the phone.

"Student Health Service, Nurse Matthews. Yes, Lucy, uh-huh." She scribbled the name down on the almost filled call-in log. "Where's the rash? How long? Any fever? Well it's probably nothing to worry about, we can see you on Monday. I'm sure it can wait. If you— Who? Dr. Palmer? Okay, just hold on a second, I'll put you right through."

Matthews quickly picked up the receiver of a red phone off to one side and dialed a number. When the party answered, she patched Lucy through, then returned to the next blinking line.

"Student Health Service, Nurse Matthews. Yes, uh, what can I do for you, Tim? Uh-huh. I know, it's terrible, but talking helps."

The phones didn't show any sign of letting up. Sammy was growing restless. The whole morning was gone and there was still much too much to do. She motioned to the nurse and quietly rose from her chair.

"Just a minute." Matthews put her caller on hold and looked up at Sammy.

"I'm going to have to go," Sammy apologized.

The nurse shrugged. "I really thought we'd have more time to talk." She scribbled a name and number on a loose Post-it note and handed it to Sammy as she punched her caller back on the line. "Give him a call. He can help you with your show."

It was only after Sammy had left the building that she examined the Post-it. The telephone number was all too familiar. Frustrated, she tossed it into a nearby trash can and trudged off.

As the note settled among discarded greasy fast-food wrappers, only the name remained visible in Nurse Matthews's delicate script: Reed Wyndham.

Marcus Palmer peered down the barrels of his binocular microscope and rechecked the tissue specimen from Sergio Pinez's brain. He had to be sure. "Damn," he muttered, refocusing to a higher power. Just as he had in the last case, Palmer observed nodular collections of so-called "microglial cells" scattered throughout the boy's gray matter; and small, poorly defined areas of demyelination surrounding the veins of his white matter. With these destructive changes in his brain tissue, Sergio had probably experienced memory loss, confusion, and dementia for weeks. Poor kid. If he hadn't been driven to suicide, his lethal sub-acute encephalitis would have inexorably progressed to coma and death. There was no treatment for this complication.

Damn. Palmer carefully recorded his findings in the experimental log. The viral studies were still pending, but the results wouldn't change what he now acknowledged. Despite the apparent immunity of the majority of subjects thus far, at least twice, his vaccine had failed. Patient #12 and patient #14 were dead.

Damn, damn, damn.

Palmer knew he had only two choices. He could go to the Human Subjects Committee, stop the project, and review the original animal work. Perhaps after months of study, he'd get permission to repeat the experiment. But the ensuing investigation might uncover the fact that he'd deviated from the original approved protocol. He would lose his tenure and be banished from the university in professional disgrace.

His second option was to continue his work, and say nothing. It was possible that both suicides were coincidental, that the two students were simply depressed. Coming forward with these data now would end his work, his life, for no reason at all.

Palmer rose and walked to his window. Gazing out at the view overlooking the gentle slope of North Campus, he was stirred, as always, by its serenity. *Ironic*, he thought. Only in such a cloistered setting could this experiment take place — blessed by grant money, lax official university oversight, and the unquestioning trust of the subjects themselves. He watched now as young men and women, cheeks flushed by the cold, hurried along the crisscrossing walkways — laughing, talking, utterly oblivious to their potential danger should any of them be selected for his study.

For a long time, he remained there, weighing his choices. Then, with more than a slight twinge of guilt, he returned to his desk, closing the ledger just as the telephone began to ring.

A smorgasbord of Mozart piano concertos, Paganini violin caprices, and Wagnerian opera arias wafted from various practice rooms, mingling into a discordant soup that was not at all to Sammy's more modern taste. She hurried down the hallway of the music school, stifling the impulse to cover her ears.

"This day's already a complete bust," she muttered to herself. None of the students she'd interviewed so far had much to say about Sergio. They were all saddened by his death, but no one admitted to knowing him all that well. Quiet, loner type. Quite the cliché.

She knocked at yet another door without much enthusiasm. "Excuse me." Sammy smiled at the slim black man with shoulder-length dreadlocks and a tuba wrapped around his neck who opened the door. "I'm Sammy Greene. I work for W-E-L-L."

"Yeah, I know, mon. *The Hot Line*. I listen to your program."

His lilting accent was Jamaican, she noted, as she entered the closet-sized cubbyhole. There was barely room for his enormous instrument.

The musician extended a hand. "C. C. Marone."

Sammy reached over the music stand to shake it. "I'm interviewing students who knew Sergio Pinez."

Marone looked slightly disappointed, shrugged, and turned back toward his music. "Sergio was not into the social scene."

"So I gather."

Nodding, C.C. blew a series of darkly resonant notes, ranging from velvety softness to a low growl.

"Quite a range."

"Surprising, eh?" The young musician tapped his tuba and winked. "For a baby this big." He hiked the instrument up until it almost completely covered his slight body. "Takes good teeth and plenty of wind."

"Beg your pardon?"

"To play it well. You need to have good teeth and plenty of wind."

Sammy chuckled as she grabbed a pen and notepad from her purse. "Did you know Sergio well?"

"No. Only from orchestra. He was a flautist."

Sammy appeared puzzled.

"Flutes sit with the piccolos near the front. Tubas and trombones, we're herded to the back."

"Oh. Was he good?"

"An artist, mon. A Jean-Pierre Rampal."

Sammy wrote the name on her pad for future reference. Larry would know who that was. He listened to Bach a lot. "Any idea why Sergio might have killed himself?"

C.C. shook his locks. "He was very quiet. We only had the music together."

Sammy felt growing frustration. "Did he have *any* friends?"

"We only had the music," C.C. repeated. Another low growl emanated from his tuba. His eyes avoided hers. "Perhaps you might ask his roommate."

Finally a connection. Sammy's pen was poised. "What's the name?"

C.C. hesitated for a moment, as if trying to remember. "Lloyd Fletcher."

"You know where I can find him?"

"Yeah." He opened the door and pointed down the hall. "Orchestra practice will be over soon."

Sammy slipped her notepad into her purse and stepped outside the room. "Thanks. You've been a help."

"Not to Sergio," C.C. said softly. "I should not have talked to you."

Before Sammy could question why, the door closed in her face.

"It's done."

"You removed the bugs?"

"Every last one."

"And the envelope?"

"Yes."

"Anyone see you?"

"Not a chance. We took extra precautions."

"That's what I'm paying for."

"And the other situation?"

"Keeping an eye on it."

"That's good. Very good."

The man on the other end knew better than to respond. He merely smiled and gently replaced the receiver.

Lloyd Fletcher played piccolo like an angel. Sammy entered the wings of the rehearsal hall just as the musician began his solo. His eyes were closed, his body swaying in rhythm to his haunting tune. For the few moments he played, Sammy had the sensation of being transported to another world — a world where all those lost were waiting once again with open arms. The rap of the conductor's baton on the music stand signaling the end of rehearsal jarred Sammy from her trance. She opened her eyes to see the musicians packing up their instruments and sheet music to make room for the next class. Fletcher alone lingered, staring at the empty chair beside his.

Sammy had reached his seat before he noticed her. "Lloyd Fletcher?"

He turned slowly and nodded.

"Sammy Greene. I work for W-E-L-L."

Fletcher's dark, sad eyes were magnified by the thick lenses of his clear plastic frames. His face was a mask of pain and confusion. "Sorry?"

"W-E-L-L. It's the campus radio station," she explained. "Can I ask you a few questions?"

Lloyd frowned and started to place his piccolo in his case. "About what?"

"Your roommate. Sergio Pinez."

Lloyd snapped his case shut. He hesitated a moment before finally motioning her to follow.

As she walked beside him, Sammy observed how tall and stocky he was, built more like a linebacker than a musician. A handsome man, he had dark curly hair, dark eyes, rugged features. Yet his fingers were thin and delicate, like his instrument.

They moved silently down the labyrinthine halls of the music building. Few students acknowledged Lloyd's presence, though Sammy got one or two nods or greetings. At a small practice room on the opposite end from C. C. Marone's, Lloyd waved her inside, shutting the door behind her. He still had not spoken and Sammy felt uncomfortable opening the conversation. Prying into people's private tragedies was the downside of her job. It was so much easier to chase down corrupt public figures like the Very Reverend "Shaft." She cleared her throat. "Uh, I'm really sorry about Sergio."

Fletcher nodded, his eyes welling up with tears. "Thanks."

"Are you all right?" she asked.

Lloyd swallowed, then nodded again.

"Would you like some water?"

A shake of the head.

"I know it must be hard to talk about him, but you seem to be the only one on campus that knew him very well. I'd like to try to understand why he did what he did."

"Why?" The question was barely audible.

"We'd like to . . . to . . ." Sammy stumbled over the words, "a memorial on Monday. We'd like to do a memorial for Sergio. A way for everyone at Ellsford to remember. A way to let everyone show that his life mattered."

Lloyd's expression was a mixture of anger and anguish. "It mattered."

"Oh, no, no, I didn't mean—" *Put your foot in it again, Greene.* "I know. He was very special."

"Yeah."

"I mean, I'm sure—" *Shut up, Greene, you're digging it deeper.* "Okay, you're right," she said. "I'm sorry. Maybe if I can start over. How about if I listen, and you talk?"

Lloyd gazed down at his hands. "What do you want to know?"

"Well, how did you come to be roommates? I mean, you're an upperclassman, aren't you?"

"Fifth year senior. I asked him. Met him last summer in P-town, and thought we'd get along." He looked off at the corner. "We did—"

P-town. Provincetown. The penny dropped. The Cape Cod resort was well known as a favorite beach destination for gays and lesbians. Lloyd and Sergio may have been more than roommates. Sammy blushed, embarrassed by her insensitivity.

Lloyd seemed oblivious as he continued his reverie. "Kind of a shy boy. I remember the first time we met. It isn't often that I find someone who enjoys tackling Paganini concertos as much as I do. We rehearsed the third and fourth sonatas for two weeks. I've never had a partner quite as talented. Did you know that Sergio was a composer?"

Sammy shook her head.

"He would ad lib these passages, 'Variations on a Theme by—', you know, that would wrap themselves around your soul. Brilliant. We'd spend every evening working on his new concerto. He'd just finished two new movements last week."

"Sounds like things were going great. What happened?"

"I honestly don't know."

"Was he upset about anything?"

Lloyd looked directly at her when he answered. "You mean about being queer?"

Sammy still wasn't comfortable with that activist word. "Uh, yeah."

"On the record?"

Sammy raised an eyebrow. "No? Okay." She put down her pencil.

"It was harder for him," Lloyd said. "Macho culture. Not as accepting. He only came out to a few of us. Maybe I pushed him too hard to do more."

"His family didn't know?"

"No way. They're Catholic. It's a mortal sin." Lloyd's eyes filled with tears once again. "And now—"

Sammy pulled a Kleenex from her purse and handed it to the musician. He took it and crumpled it angrily in his hands.

"That's what our society demands." His tone was bitter. "Better dead than gay. That's why we have to come out. We have to fight, we have to let them know we're here. Next to them, their neighbors, their friends. We have a right to be accepted as ourselves."

Sammy nodded. "It seems horribly unfair. Do you think that's why—?"

Lloyd shrugged his shoulders. "I don't know. I thought talking to Bill was helping him."

"Bill?"

"Bill Osborne in the psych department. He helped me out last year, so I sent Sergio to see him. Thought maybe it might help him too."

Sammy picked up her pencil again and jotted down "Bill Osborne."

Osborne here. Hey, guy, I'm worried about you. Let's talk, okay?

That's why the name sounded familiar, she thought, remembering Osborne's voice on Conrad's answer machine. She definitely needed to talk with the psychologist for background.

"He seemed to be getting better," Lloyd was saying. "Then just this past week, it's like, it's like he lost himself." He dabbed at his eyes with the Kleenex. "And we lost him."

Sammy patted Lloyd's arm gently. After a moment, he met her eyes with renewed enthusiasm. "You know, you can do something for him that I don't think he would have minded."

"Sure."

Lloyd rifled through his piccolo case and pulled out a cassette tape from one drawer. "You can play his concerto. As a memorial. On the record."

Sammy smiled. "I think that would be very nice."

"That's right, Senator. Off the record?" Reverend Taft shifted the phone to his other ear and rubbed his neck as he leaned back in his fine-tooled, high-back leather chair. Cradling the receiver against his shoulder, he made a church house with his fingertips. "Yes, sir. The publicity we got on the animal rights protest should help fill the coffers at tomorrow's sermon."

He placed a hand over the receiver as an assistant entered the room carrying a fresh pot of coffee. "What's up?"

The short, stocky man pointed to the empty mug on the cedar desk.

Taft shook his head. He made a point of limiting his caffeine intake to one cup every morning. Anything more he considered a sin. "No doubt about it, Senator," he said, returning his attention to the call. "We should be well set for next November."

The assistant stuffed a few papers from the out-box under one arm and ambled out with the coffee pot in the other, loitering only for a moment to attach a beetle-sized eavesdropping device to the undersurface of Taft's desk. At the door, he stopped to wave to his boss who was too busy talking to notice.

• • •

From the music building, Sammy headed straight for the phone booth on the quad and dialed Bill Osborne's campus office. She needed a clearer picture of Sergio and his problems. On the record.

The line was busy. Irritated, she hung up, then dialed again. A sudden thought occurred to her. Since this Osborne was a shrink, maybe *he* would come on the show and talk about suicide. If so, she wouldn't have to eat crow and ask Reed.

After five rings, a recorded message told her the psychology professor was attending a conference in New York until Tuesday; anyone with an emergency should contact Student Health. Sammy dropped the phone back in the cradle, disappointed.

Her second call was equally unproductive. In no uncertain terms, the medical examiner's clerk informed her that only physicians or authorized family members could access autopsy reports. Hanging up, she realized that if she wanted the official cause of death for Sergio and Conrad, she'd better figure out a less direct way to get the information.

She checked her Swatch. Almost five. She'd never make it to the campus photo shop before closing. The roll of film from Friday's demonstration was burning a hole in her pocket. Maybe someone she shot could finger Taft as the instigator. Doubtful, she knew from her experience last year, but certainly worth a try. Now, she'd have to wait until after the show on Monday to drop off the pictures.

The show. A whole day's work for nothing. The little she got on Sergio was off the record. And Larry would never buy filling the whole hour with the poor kid's music. She could get away with ten or fifteen minutes maybe, but then she needed some hard news and commentary. About suicide prevention. Not music. And she didn't think that Reed would be in a forgiving mood. Frustrated, she inhaled deeply, and trudged off, away from the music building, toward her apartment.

Bud Stanton wrapped his towel tightly around his buttocks and stepped into the steamy main locker room. He winced as the lingering odor of ammonia and wintergreen assailed his nostrils.

"Hey, dude, quit dripping on my ass," chided left guard Lamar Washington when the star hoopster ambled by.

"Thought you were used to it," Stanton snickered, flipping off the towel and flicking it at his teammate.

Washington grabbed a damp sweatshirt from the bench and went after Stanton. The two men sparred like dueling swordsmen, spurred on by the gathering cheering squad of basketball players drawn to the fight.

Stanton seemed to be losing the advantage when the gravely voice of Coach Lefty Grizzard echoed through the cavernous locker room.

"All right, girls, party's over." He clapped his hands and the group scattered. "Stanton, get your bare-assed butt over here now." He waved toward a small windowed cubicle behind the lockers.

Stanton rewrapped the towel and, tossing a final glare at Lamar, sauntered over to the coach's office.

Grizzard shut the door behind his star forward and walked casually to his tattered armchair. He sat back, struck a match, and lit a thick cigar, all the while studying Stanton through narrowed eyes.

The player leaned against the back wall, conscious of his minimally clothed condition — and proud of it.

Finally, Grizzard spoke. "You're lucky, ain't you, boy?"

"Sometimes," Stanton answered warily.

"Here you were, about to say good-bye to," the Coach waved a hand "all this. And now, everything turns out just the way you wanted."

"Excuse me?" His tone was innocent.

Grizzard pulled another puff from his cigar, slowly rolling the smoke on his tongue. "Professor Conrad is dead," he announced, waiting for a reaction.

"Dead?" No surprise appeared on the hoopster's face.

"Police found him this morning. Killed himself."

"Suicide." It was not a question.

Grizzard sent another smoky cloud into the air. "That's the word."

"How 'bout that." Stanton spoke too softly for the coach to hear.

"So, looks like you'll be able to play out the season after all."

"Yeah." Stanton allowed himself a broad smile. "I told you not to worry."

Grizzard arched an eyebrow. "Yeah, you did." With a suspicious glare, he added, "You want to explain how you knew not to worry?"

Stanton shrugged. "Like you said, Coach, just lucky, I guess." He rolled his eyes toward the ceiling.

Grizzard looked up to see only cracked plaster, then back to the athlete with a frown.

Stanton stood up, rubbing his hands. "Listen, it's kinda cold. Could I get dressed?"

"Go on," Grizzard snapped. "Get outta here."

As Stanton headed back to the locker room, Grizzard leaned back in his chair and, brows knitted, watched a ring of smoke rise up to the flaking ceiling.

Blue deepened against a descending sky. The sun set over the treetops on West Campus, casting figurelike shadows along the university walkways. The afternoon's breeze had turned into an evening chill, and Sammy bundled her peacoat tightly around her.

Wandering past a kiosk plastered with posters announcing campus activities, one caught her eye. A notice about Sunday's eight a.m. sermon at the St. Charlesbury Church of God proclaimed: "The Very Reverend Calvin Taft discusses Sin, Suicide and Family Values." Sammy made a mental note to set her alarm for seven the next morning. A title like that would certainly pack them in. She intended to get a good seat for that show.

So complete was her concentration at that moment that she had no idea she was being observed. Had been followed, in fact, since she'd left her apartment that morning.

• • •

Pappajohn half-listened to the six o'clock news while dining on two-day-old moussaka from a scratched plastic container. Bits of ground lamb crumbled onto his shirt and lap, a few eggplant particles clung to the bristles of his bushy salt and pepper mustache. He made no effort to brush them off as he chewed. His own cooking couldn't compare to Effie's magic with food, but in the five years since her passing he'd learned some of her recipes well enough to get by. On the arm of his naugahyde lounge chair was a plate containing a few sugar-drowned slices of baklava that had begun to stiffen around the edges.

His beer was warm, but he didn't care. He barely tasted it. Since the discovery of the professor's body that morning, Pappajohn had been in foul spirits. The third suicide in two months. So much for a quiet retirement. Things were getting a bit too hot for his liking. Dean Jeffries had his dander up, and the board of regents was breathing down his neck. And to top it off, he had that radio reporter snooping around. Nosy college kid stirring things up. She was gonna be trouble. He could just feel it. Deep in his gut.

He grabbed a couple of Rolaids, washed them down with the beer. The leftover moussaka went into the trash. Damn that girl. Reminded him of his own daughter. Anastasia was also capable of bringing out the worst in him. Always challenging, never content to leave things be. Maybe that's why they hadn't talked in over a year. He plopped back in his chair and turned back to the TV.

"We'll go live now to Cambridge with Nolan Rickey."

"Thank you, Tim. The death toll on our streets hit a record high today. An off-duty, twenty-year police veteran, Jermaine Lavond was shot and killed by two armed robbers. Lavond was shopping next door in Kim's Market when he saw the alleged felons running from the Harvard Street branch of the Bank of Boston. Though he didn't have his gun, Lavond still went after them. Both men fired at him. Two bullets hit Lavond in the chest. He died at the scene. A bag of stolen money was later recovered several blocks away with about five thousand dollars in it. The good samaritan leaves a wife and three children. He was forty-five years old. Back to you, Tim."

The anchor's tone was somber. "That makes sixteen peace officers killed this year. Mayor Hamel has appointed a police commission to look into this new wave of violence."

Jermaine Lavond.

Pappajohn remembered the boy — that's what he was then — fresh out of the academy. Bright, hard-working kid. First in his family to go to college. First in his family to be a cop. Getting on the force back in those days was almost impossible for a young black kid. Getting out alive was even harder. But Lavond was a good man and a good cop. Shit.

Pappajohn took a hefty swig of his beer, closed his eyes and tried to picture himself thirty years before when he'd first put on his uniform. That tall, black-haired, swarthy young man had cared back then — actually wanted to change the world. It didn't matter that the pay was lousy, the hours worse. The work had been its own reward — the good feeling that came when he'd dropped exhausted into bed each night, knowing that he'd given it his best.

With the idealism of youth, Pappajohn had volunteered for the toughest assignments in Boston's South End. He was what they called a "street dog" — out there pounding the pavements — getting rid of the pimps and pushers, the addicts, the johns, cleaning up the neighborhoods so kids like Ana could have a future. He'd received many awards and commendations by the time he started going undercover. He moved Effie and Ana from the city to Newton, but thugs and scum were still there.

He swiveled the end table photo of his wife to face him. Her brown eyes twinkled up at him. Her smile still warmed his heart. Effie had always been supportive — even though it meant rewarming his dinner most nights. Like many cop wives, she learned to go it alone — even the day she drove herself to the hospital to hear the news that her body was riddled with cancer, had six months at most to live. She had the moussaka waiting for him when he came through the door at ten p.m., smiled as she relayed what the doctor had said, insisted he continue his work, no matter what. His eyes filled with tears as he kissed the photo and whispered softly, "*S'agapo*."

She'd been gone less than three months when he began his last investigation. He'd discovered a couple of narcotics officers squirreling away part of the take from their drug busts, then selling the stuff on the street. He and Chief Donovan set up a sting to catch the bastards. But this time his gut failed him. Maybe it was Effie's death.

Chief Donovan was in it up to his eyeballs. The sting was a setup that caught Pappajohn unaware. He could still taste the fear as he stood cornered in the alley, staring down the barrel of his own revolver.

"It's a new world. Honesty doesn't pay the bills these days," Donovan had growled. "You're a shmuck if you think you can change the way it is. You gotta look out for yourself."

Even now, Pappajohn remembered the hopelessness, almost welcomed the two bullets exploding in his gut. But as Donovan turned away, leaving him for dead, Pappajohn found the strength to kick the chief's leg, throwing him off center just enough to make him drop the gun. Pappajohn grabbed it and got off three rounds before passing out. Weeks later, an Internal Affairs investigation had cleared Pappajohn of the chief's death, calling it "a righteous shoot." A grand jury brought indictments against the two foot boys on the take, but Pappajohn's protests that the corruption may have spread even further fell on deaf ears.

Pappajohn wasn't surprised when the commissioner himself stopped by his hospital bed and urged him to consider early retirement. The force would no longer be safe for a "stool-pigeon" with "sharks" still at-large. Pappajohn agreed. The job would never have been the same after that. He'd had enough. Besides, there was nothing to keep him in Boston. Ana always blamed him for "abandoning" her mother when she was sick, and had left for California soon after Effie's death.

A month later, he spotted the ad in the *Globe*: "Chief of Police for small Ivy League college in quiet Vermont village." Perfect for him to escape and recover. Two months after his hospital discharge, he closed up the house, packed a few belongings in his Chevy Nova, and drove the 180 miles to St. Charlesbury, Vermont.

His new home was a tiny cottage in town, next to the campus. A simple wooden structure built almost a hundred years ago and largely unmodified since. The landlord was one of the "summah people" who'd bought several places to rent out, keeping the nicest for himself and his family. Pappajohn mailed his rent check to an address in Connecticut every month and expected nothing in return but running water and a roof over his head.

"—precipitation."

The TV weatherman was waving his arms over a satellite map of the northeastern United States, New England's outline hidden by white cloud formations. "—light flurries tonight, but we could get up to five inches accumulation by mid-morning."

Terrific, Pappajohn thought. He'd have to get out the chains for the car. Couldn't remember exactly where he'd stowed them in the cluttered shed in the back. He rose from his chair, clicked off the TV, then walked to the kitchen and dumped the empty beer bottle into the trash can.

As Pappajohn reentered the den, the screen saver on his computer was throwing up an intriguing pattern of shapes and colors. Random regularity. There was a beauty and logic to that world.

Reluctantly, he clicked his mouse and the magic world disappeared.

Replaced by a file named "Taft."

Whitney Houston sang softly in the background while Sammy worked at her desk. As the announcer came on with the news brief, Sammy checked her watch. Eight p.m. She'd skipped dinner to review her interview notes from that afternoon. Stretching, she suppressed a yawn, drained by the emotional twists and turns of the horrible day. Finding Conrad, sparring with Pappajohn, and then fighting with Reed. It was all too much.

Recalling Reed's pained expression, she felt a rush of guilt. She should've called, she knew, but everything had happened so fast. If only he'd let her explain, maybe for once he'd understand. About her work. About her life.

When they'd first met at a party last spring, she'd assumed the differences in their background and upbringing made any notion of a relationship a non-issue. "Let me guess," she'd said, trying to size up the blond-haired, New Hampshire native, "you attended boarding school somewhere in New England, spend summers in Hyannis, buy drawers of cashmere sweaters from Brooks Brothers. Your father's a senior partner in a fancy downtown law firm. Am I right?"

Reed's laughter had been contagious. "Actually, Dad's in banking." He'd smiled at the perky redhead. "And I'm allergic to wool. How about you?"

"Strictly New York Jewish, went to PS 125, waitressed at a local deli most summers, searched for bargains with Grandma Rose at Macy's."

"Sounds like a lot more fun."

She'd looked for ridicule, but his lavender eyes were guileless. Turned out she'd been completely wrong about him. He'd rejected pressure to enter the family business and impressed her with his dedication to medicine. And Reed found her spunk "cute." Sammy had been called many things, but never cute. To her surprise, she'd liked it.

So they'd been attracted to one another, had been dating steadily. That is, as steadily as both their busy schedules would allow. Once a week at best, occasionally time together on weekends. He'd shared the exhilaration of sailing at the Cape, she'd introduced him to bagels and cream cheese. They'd eased into intimacy like two friends might, three months after meeting. Over a ruined dinner of chicken soup and brisket, Reed had told her she was special. Sammy'd thrown her arms around him and he hadn't let go.

Being with him was fun; it felt good, and nice. With AIDS around, other choices could be dangerous. What she had with Reed was probably not tenure track, but for now at least, the comfortable aspects of a risk-free, steady relationship neutralized the lack of earth-shaking passion.

Michael Bolton sang "Don't Make Me Wait for Love," and she promised herself to talk with Reed again tomorrow.

"Here is Kenny G playing "Silhouette" from his *Live* album — how sweet it is." Sammy had to agree with the DJ as she listened to the deliciously mellow sounds emerging from the alto sax. The piece ended and the audience went wild with applause. Sammy wondered whether Sergio Pinez would have found that kind of fame as C.C. had predicted. So sad for the boy, she thought, trying to imagine what it must have been like for him, the depth of his pain. Unable to deal with his life, driven to the brink of despair.

She held the cassette with his concerto in her hands, running over the label with her fingers. This really belonged with his family.

She jotted down plans to visit the registrar's office Monday morning and get his class list. And maybe, she could even swing a trip to New York next weekend to check out his home. She smiled broadly at the thought. For almost a year, she'd been looking for a chance to get back to civilization. A chance to revisit roots. Sergio's and hers.

She sat up, frustrated. A half hour to fill. Larry wanted to do something to help the other students. Looks like she was back to suicide counseling and prevention. And Reed. How would she get him to go along with this one?

She flipped the cassette around in her hands, deciding to escape with Sergio's music.

Where was her tape recorder?

Her purse. That was what had started the day, after all — the excuse to return to Conrad's home. Fishing it out, she realized the machine was still set on voice activated. She hit "rewind". When the tape was ready, Sammy's finger hovered over the "play" button for a few moments, afraid of what she might hear. If she pressed it, Conrad could die once again. But she *had* to know. She took a long, deep breath, then clicked the machine on.

Conrad's voice came through clearly. "So, what makes you think I've got an answer?"

Her voice was next. "Because of what you said about the teaching award."

Friday night's interview. Momentarily relieved, she fast-forwarded a bit.

Conrad was speaking again. "I've learned that sometimes it's better to let sleeping dogs lie. Stay as far away from this as you can."

Sammy slowly inched the tape forward and pressed the "Play" button. This time, all she heard was static.

After a few moments, the tape crackled and Conrad's voice rasped, "Who's there?"

Silence. And more static.

Conrad's voice, louder, "I said, who's there?"

Sammy heard only sounds of movement. She thought she recognized a door opening. "Wadda ya want?" Conrad's speech slurred by alcohol.

Another stretch of static and then Sammy recognized the sound of a door slam.

"What . . .going . . ."

". . . is it?"

"Give . . . me . . ."

Bursts of static made it impossible to understand the jumbled spurts of words, but Sammy thought she could distinguish at least one voice besides Conrad's on the tape. She couldn't be sure, but the tones were clearly angry.

". . . bye . . ."

Something from Conrad, several minutes of static, then just dead air. A few beats later, her own voice broke in: "Sorry to intrude, but—I thought maybe—" followed by an audible gasp and "Professor Conrad!"

Sammy clicked off the recorder, upset by the memory of her discovery, renewing her feelings of helplessness. Poor Professor Conrad. His last words were buried in an avalanche of static. She could only make out that he had had one or more visitors. Surprise visitors. Friends? Or—?

The Ellsford Teaching Award is the kiss of death.

She shuddered at the thought. Better not to let her imagination get the best of her. Shaking her head, she stood and walked to the window. For a moment she simply stared out at the velvety layers of darkness, then closed the drapes. She grabbed her notebook and jotted a few words. Another task for Monday. She'd hit up Brian at the station to see if he could enhance the sound.

Monday was going to be a very busy day.

CHAPTER THREE

SUNDAY
7:25 A.M.

Reed Wyndham was beyond exhaustion. In addition to his regular hospital night call schedule, Dr. Palmer expected him to work in Student Health several times a week as well as help with the immunology research at the Nitshi Institute. His call-room bed was barely slept in. No matter that it was Sunday. Just another morning to face with almost no sleep.

Close to seven thirty, he still hadn't finished checking lab results for Palmer's AIDS patients. Case discussion rounds started promptly at eight.

"Okay, and the CD4 count? That low? Well, thanks." Frowning, he hung up the phone, entering the results in the chart. A tap on the shoulder and he spun around, startled.

"Can I buy you breakfast?" Sammy offered a bag of bagels and a conciliatory smile.

He turned back to his work without responding.

"Sesame, rye, wheat, and," she grimaced, "I even got you blueberry."

Still no response.

"So, you're not going to talk to me?"

Reed continued recording results, his silence a clear signal that he was still angry.

"You didn't mean it yesterday when you said we were through, did you?" It was Sammy's plaintive tone that made Reed turn and take a measured look at the pixie face that had been slowly claiming his heart for months, knowing that underneath lay a passionate, but complicated soul that could—and often did—drive him to distraction.

"What is it you want from me?" he finally asked. "From us?"

Sammy drew in a deep breath. "I don't know."

"Well at least that's an honest answer," he said. "But after all this time together, I thought we had something special."

"Of course we do. We—"

Reed held up a hand to cut off her protest. "Not special enough to deserve your full attention."

"Now that's not fair. We both have lots to do—"

"True, but I'm at the bottom of *your* to-do list."

"That's what I came by to explain." Her green eyes appealed to him. "About yesterday."

Glancing at his watch, Reed interrupted. "You've got five minutes. I can't be late for rounds," he said, adding pointedly, "again."

In breathless spurts, Sammy quickly explained what had happened the day before. "Conrad, my biology professor. He, uh. I went to get my purse. I left it there Friday evening. On my way to your place Saturday morning, I found him, lying on his couch. Shot. Dead."

Reed's expression switched to concern. "Jesus, what happened?"

"Suicide. He left a note. Pappajohn thinks the guy had too much to drink, got depressed and," Sammy fought back an unwelcome gasp. "I had no choice. I found him. I had to call the cops. I had to wait. I tried to tell you. I'm really sorry."

Reed reached for her hand. "I'm sorry, too," he said. "Are you okay?"

"Honestly, I'm not sure. I keep wondering if there was something I missed when I talked to Conrad, maybe some way I could have—"

"Prevented his suicide?" Reed shook his head. "Don't you think that's a lot of responsibility to put on yourself? You hardly knew the guy."

"But are there some signs or clues that people should know about? Maybe I couldn't help Conrad, but if I knew what to look for—" Sammy said. "I was talking with Nurse Matthews in Student Health. She thinks we need to reach out to the campus. In fact, she suggested I talk with you about doing our show."

"I see." Reed's eyes narrowed, "So if Matthews hadn't recommended me, you wouldn't be here now with your bagels and apologies?"

Sammy produced a genuinely hurt expression. "I really do want to make us work," she said. "How could I know that you'd be the expert Matthews felt could best relate to students?"

Aware that Sammy had dodged the question, but too tired to resist her wiles, Reed exhaled a sigh. "Oh, all right. What time's the show?"

Sammy smiled, triumphant. "It starts at one, but come by the station a half hour earlier so we can prepare. You'll talk about suicide prevention for about ten minutes, then we'll take phone calls and you can counsel the kids." She leaned closer to give him a kiss.

He pulled back, checking his watch. "Jeez. It's after eight. I'm late."

Sammy pulled him closer to her lips. "As always, you can blame me."

The man pushed his reading glasses down along the bridge of his nose. Settling back into the soft upholstery of the leather armchair, he studied the pages. So here was the proof Barton Conrad claimed to have found. Proof that would make even the most extreme skeptic believe. Proof that would guarantee his undoing—not to mention Ellsford University's. He frowned, lost in thought.

Thank goodness they'd had the foresight to plant listening devices. Barely a word had been spoken within Connie's home or office that wasn't overheard. Satisfied, he placed the printed pages back in the manila folder. It was all such a nasty business. But, what other choice did he have?

Embers shifting on the hearth made him look up. He was close enough to the fire's warmth, yet he still felt chilled. For a long time, he simply sat there, staring into the flames. Then, with the agility of a man half his age, he rose from the chair and squatted before the fireplace, laying the manila folder on the logs, waiting until its edge ignited. Seconds later, consumed by flames, the folder began its evolution into ash.

"There's a religious war going on in this country," Reverend Calvin Taft thundered from the podium of the St. Charlesbury Church of God. Dressed in a winter-white linen suit with gold blazer buttons, the pewter-haired preacher was an imposing figure, carefully modulating his voice to make each point.

"We're at a cultural Armageddon, as critical a test for us as the Cold War was," he screamed into his microphone, "for this is a war for the very soul of America."

The speaker was awash in cheers and applause by his enthusiastic audience.

"Barbarians are taking over our cities. It is no longer safe to walk our streets. These forces of evil seek to destroy the foundations of America and American greatness."

Appreciative murmurs echoed from the listeners below.

"They wish to destroy the church, the family. They wish to destroy God!" Taft pointed a ringed index finger of accusation at his audience. "You know who they are. Feminists, gays, lesbians, abortionists, atheists, agnostics—all agents of Satan!"

From her pew in the crowded sanctuary, Sammy observed the Reverend. Like a brilliant musician, Taft played the audience. His range was as wide as C.C. Marone's—from velvety lows to bellowing highs. A virtuoso performance. The emotional rush she felt was undeniable. The man was amazing—and dangerous. Setting himself up as the final arbiter of morality; manipulating so many souls.

"The child is being born and they say it's okay to kill it," the preacher was shouting.

"Murderers! Devils!" sang his chorus.

"Radical feminists are taking over the Senate, homosexuals are infiltrating the military. We have leaders who would put women in combat and gays in the Cabinet."

"Blasphemers!"

Someone waved a placard that read "Family rights forever, gay rights never." The *Y* in gay was written with a pink triangle.

Sammy shuddered, recalling late night chats with Grandma Rose. As a teenager, she'd often stay up past two a.m. studying, then head downstairs for a snack. Sometimes Rose would be there, her gaze lost in the ripples of a large glass of chamomile tea. Remembering, vowing never to forget. Grandma Rose escaped Poland in 1939, but the vivid pictures she painted of her country's descent into hell resonated with Sammy as she watched the spectacle before her.

"They would take God and the Bible from our schoolchildren," the Reverend warned. "And replace them with condoms, sex, and AIDS!"

"Atheist demons!" Caught up in the passion of the moment, a familiar sibilant voice was especially loud.

Sammy recognized Luther Abbott in front of her from the animal rights protest and made a mental note to stop him after the service for an interview.

"And if they cannot kill our children through fornication and sodomy, they will force them into the ultimate sin against God: suicide. They will be handed the weapons to kill themselves and close the path to heaven for eternity."

Sammy fought to suppress her anger. *Her* God would always open his arms for troubled souls like Sergio, Professor Conrad, her mother.

"It is time we awaken America to their wicked agenda. Our nation must return to its Christian roots or we will continue to legalize sodomy, slaughter innocent babies, destroy the souls of her children, squander her God-given resources, and sink into oblivion."

"Never! Never! Never!" The frenzy intensified.

"Those who argue that this is a free country are absolutely right. Free to spread the Word of God, to fight for moral purity!" Taft raised his arms like a crucified Christ. "To fight Satan for America and for God! Ladies and gentlemen, if we do not succeed, then it is America that will be committing suicide and we will all, every one of us, end up at the gates of hell!"

A rising chorus of amens. Energized by their leader's words, some jumped to their feet and began moving down the aisles.

"Sit down, good people, sit down," said the Reverend. As if about to share a secret, he lowered his voice. "Remember, our agenda is God's agenda, and God is patient and wise."

The crowd returned to their seats, mumbling assent. Sammy unclenched her fists and sat back.

"Like an avenging army, we must carefully plan our strategy." The evangelist seemed to catch Luther's eye as he smiled. Luther sat up straighter. "This afternoon we will organize the next campus mission of the Youth Crusade. These wonderful young people will form the core of our program to create a Christian America in the schools and homes. And, by supporting Christian candidates running for office, we will slowly spread God's word to the government — to America itself." He looked over the crowd. "Can we do this?" he queried his flock.

A resounding. "Yes! Yes! Yes!" came the answer.

"We must! It is God's Will!" Taft closed his eyes for a dramatic moment, then opened them again and spoke softly. "We will not be ignored. We will win — for America and for God!"

Taft's "Amen" was almost drowned out by the raucous cheers.

But Sammy could only hear Grandma Rose weeping.

Even before the choir sounded its last "Hallelujah!" the hall began emptying. Somehow word had spread through the congregation that instead of the predicted snow, it was pouring outside. Hammering down from an iron gray sky, the rain came in driving spikes. Rivulets dripped from the umbrellas of the few worshippers who had thought to carry them to the church service.

"Damn," Sammy cursed, as she stepped into a puddle, losing sight of Luther Abbott. Like some apparition, he had melted into the crowd drifting away from the church. Through the torrent, she couldn't tell where he'd gone. She was just about to give up when someone tapped her on the shoulder.

"Heard about the Crusade planning meeting?"

Sammy spun around to see a young brunette about her age dressed in a hooded raincoat and carrying an umbrella with the blue and gold Ellsford colors. The girl must have figured her for a fellow Youth Crusader, Sammy thought, grateful that her campus fame was limited to radio. She pulled her coat collar up to cover her cheeks and shrugged.

The girl continued brightly, "The Reverend canceled it. The back of the rectory's leaking." She looked up at the gray sky. "All this rain."

Sammy responded with a noncommittal "Yeah."

"You got all your stuff for Wednesday's march, didn't you?"

Sammy nodded, refusing to reveal her ignorance.

"Good. Show up a few minutes early for final instructions."

Smiling, the girl offered the shelter of her umbrella, but Sammy declined, shaking her wet mop of red curls. "I'm already soaked," she explained. "Besides," she said, pointing in the opposite direction, "I could use the extra library time. One more midterm to go."

"Good luck. See you Wednesday."

As the girl started to walk away, Sammy called after her. "What happens if it rains?"

The girl laughed. "If it rains, Nitshi Day will be a disaster anyway."

Huddled together under a black umbrella, two men — one short and stocky, the other taller, mustachioed, and less willing to put up with the discomfort of their assignment — stood watching as Sammy waved good-bye. When she headed west across the humanities quad, they followed — the taller man complaining that he was cold and wet and none too happy. Only his companion's terse reminder of the consequences of failure terminated his laments.

• • •

Sammy didn't really have to study — there were already rumors that with Conrad's death, her last exam would be postponed, if not cancelled altogether. But, to escape the inquisitive Youth Crusader, it seemed as good an excuse as any. She headed toward the library until she was sure the girl was out of sight, then turned south across campus to the radio station. Truth was, she had plenty of homework for Monday's show.

Longhaired DJ Skip Hogan was finishing up his Sunday spot *Heavy Metal Thunder* out of Studio B. Otherwise, the station was dark and deserted. Fire-colored shadows played across the hallway as Sammy quietly inched her way past the red "On Air" sign to her desk in the back office. Outside, the wind had picked up again, splashing rain against the windowpanes. The sound of thunder rumbled in the distance.

Throwing her soggy peacoat over her chair, Sammy kicked off her black boots and poured herself a cup of hot chamomile tea from the electric teakettle on the windowsill. She pulled out several cassettes from her purse, checked them carefully for water damage, and popped the last cassette out of her slightly damp recorder. Thankfully, it, too, was dry. She didn't want to lose the interviews from which she'd draw the sound bites for tomorrow's introductory piece.

Sammy rummaged through her cluttered desk and located several box-like tapes that resembled old eight tracks. Juggling the carts, her notepapers, her cassettes, and her half-empty cup of tea, she moved into the editing room, eager to get started. Scanning the material on her cassettes, selecting the best passages from her interviews, then editing them onto the carts enveloped by her narrative track would take several hours.

The rain was still coming down in buckets when she finished the preliminary edit of the five-minute introduction almost three hours later. It opened with an excerpt of Sergio's haunting music and ended with a touching poem read with a wavering voice by his roommate, Lloyd. After reviewing it, she sat quietly, moved by the memorial.

"Not bad."

Sammy whirled around to face a dripping Larry Dupree. "Didn't hear you trickle in."

"Glad to see my staff doesn't punch a time clock."

"Neither rain nor snow —"

Larry nodded, removing his raincoat. "Rain, anyway. Ah feel like ah'm home in the Louisiana bayou."

"So, what brings you here tonight?"

Ignoring her, Larry plunked down on a rickety chair. "Just wanted to go over the schedule for this week," he said, pulling out a tattered notebook. "Knew you'd be working."

"God, I'm turning into a radio wonk," she moaned.

"Join the club." He checked his notes. "Set for tomorrow?"

"Pretty much. You heard the intro piece. Next we'll interview our expert on suicide. Then we go to the phones."

"Who'd you get for the expert?"

Sammy hesitated. "He was highly recommended by Student Health."

Larry waited expectantly.

"Reed Wyndham's had lots of experience working with students on mental health issues."

The program director raised his eyebrows. "That the Reed you're datin'?"

"Uh, not at this moment," Sammy answered semitruthfully. "He's serving as a counselor for troubled students at Student Health, and he's a top fourth-year medical student."

"Okay, okay, I'm sure he's very qualified," Larry chuckled, adding, "And, of course, you'll be there to hold his hand."

Sammy answered tersely. "Yeah. I'll be there."

"Good. What about the professor?"

"Conrad? What do you mean?"

"You going to talk about his death?"

"We'll have to. But I haven't been able to track down his people yet. I was thinking I'd hit the dean's office tomorrow, maybe interview some of his colleagues or students if I have time. The funeral's Tuesday. I thought I'd get more then."

"So you want to save Tuesday for Conrad."

"Or Wednesday, so I can get a chance to talk to—"

"Nope. Can't. Remember? Wednesday we're doing a remote for the Nitshi party outside the institute."

Sammy groaned. "Oh, right. Nitshi Day." How could she have forgotten? The station's plans to report live on the midday ceremonies and subsequent celebrations had been set weeks ago.

Larry continued from his notes. "You'll cover the speeches at noon by the chancellor and Nitshi President Ishida. Our booth will be across from the grandstand, with your hookup there. Gary will cover the parade at one and Roger will report from the carnival."

Sammy didn't hear the rest of Larry's recitation. Her thoughts had turned back to her cryptic conversation with the Youth Crusader. It was obvious that Reverend Taft had plans to disrupt the activities. Perhaps she should say something about it to Larry. But Larry had already leaned on her for jumping to conclusions where Taft was concerned. No, better not to say anything yet. Whatever the Reverend had in mind, at least she'd be there to find out.

CHAPTER FOUR

MONDAY

When Sammy sauntered into the registrar's office at five to nine, only one student stood in line ahead of her. She recognized Chuck Lambert, president of Gamma Tau, EU's "animal house." A Beverly Hills brat from his Guess sweats to his Gucci loafers, rumor had it that the blond surfer would have flunked out long ago if his father had not endowed a chair at the university.

"You know you can't drop a class after the third week," the middle-aged woman at the desk was explaining. Tall, thin, all hard angles, she was one of the many locals employed by EU.

"Practicum in Art. It's just a three-credit class," Chuck argued. "My pre-law classes are real tough." He pointed to the pile of textbooks in his overstuffed backpack. "I don't have time to play with toothpicks and tissue paper."

"Take an incomplete."

"You have my transcript. I'm maxed out."

"Should have thought of that before." No sympathy was offered from the other side of the desk.

Chuck flashed his best counterfeit smile. "Come on, Mrs. Teicher. What harm can it do?"

"Sorry. I don't make the rules, I just enforce them."

"I can see we're getting nowhere." Lambert zipped up his backpack and angrily slung it over his shoulder. "I guess my father'll just have to have a talk with the chancellor."

Mrs. Teicher refused to be intimidated. "Be my guest." When he'd gone, she shook her head. "Always an angle, that one. If you ask me, you kids all get too much coddling."

"College can be pretty stressful," Sammy offered, "especially around midterms."

"Whatever." Her voice tightened suspiciously. "You want to drop a class, too?"

"No, I work for the campus radio station," Sammy explained. "We're doing today's show on suicide. I guess you know about Sergio Pinez."

The woman's expression softened. "Now there was a nice young man. A real pity."

"You knew Sergio?"

"Scholarship students are required to work ten hours a week on campus. Sergio put his time in here. He was so polite, always followed the rules," Mrs. Teicher said. "He invited me and my husband to one of his concerts last month. A real talent."

"So I've heard. Listen, Mrs. Teicher, I've talked to some of Sergio's teachers in the music school, but I wanted to get a few comments from others on campus. Could I get a copy of his class schedule?"

The tall woman thought a moment, then responded. "I don't see what harm it would do." She typed a few lines on her desk computer, keyed in the printer, and a few minutes later handed Sammy a printout.

Perusing the list of classes, Sammy noted that except for Psych, Sergio's courses were all in the music school: Advanced Composition, Ear Training, Musicianship, Orchestra, Pop Music USA. Twenty-one credits. The kid carried a heavy load.

"Thanks," she said, checking her watch: nine fifteen. Psych 101 was due to start at ten. She had little hope that the professor would remember Sergio. It was an intro course with over two hundred students. Cakewalk class for general education requirements. As she left the office, she planned her strategy. She'd skip the prof and try to find the teaching assistant who just might recall the shy freshman, then ditch the lecture and swing around to Dean Jeffries's office. After that she had to head over to the radio station. Still a lot to prepare before her show at one.

The line barely moved. It coiled around the foyer of the Student Health clinic like a snake, its tail lengthening every few minutes.

"I'm gonna miss my midterm," one student complained.

"Tell the nurse. Maybe they'll let you go first," suggested Lucy Peters, who stood just ahead of the girl, waiting her turn.

"Naw, that's okay." The girl leaned over and lowered her voice. "I'm not ready for the Physics test anyway. I'll just get an excuse from the doctor. Another week to study, maybe I can pull a D."

Lucy nodded. She wasn't exactly prepared for her exams today either. Too much partying this weekend. She smiled, thinking of her hours with Chris. The time had passed too quickly. She'd never been so happy. She wanted to spend every minute with him — to be with him forever. Forever, she mused. Christopher Oken. Mrs. Christopher Oken. Lucy Oken.

"Lucy Peters!" Nurse Matthews strode into the foyer and read her name from a clipboard.

Lucy raised her hand.

"Come on in here," the buxom nurse summoned. "Dr. Palmer will see you now."

Lucy stepped out of line, temporarily destroying the uniform contour of the snake.

"Aren't you lucky?" the girl behind her remarked.

"I, uh." Lucy was surprised and slightly embarrassed by the obvious special treatment.

"Miss Peters called ahead for an appointment," the nurse intervened. "If the rest of you kids would do that instead of just dropping in, we wouldn't have such long waits."

Lucy scurried behind the nurse, trying to ignore the groans and grumbles. She followed her into an alcove off the foyer where Dr. Palmer routinely saw his patients.

"What are we here for today, dear?" the nurse asked, smiling for the first time.

Lucy smiled back. There was warmth and sympathy in the woman's hazel eyes. "My rash. I called Saturday."

"Oh yes." Nurse Matthews remembered the call.

"It's probably nothing." Lucy felt sheepish. "It's really not that big. Dr. Palmer said to come in."

"Better safe than sorry." The nurse gave Lucy's shoulder a comforting squeeze. Opening a door to one of the patient rooms, she pointed to a gown lying on the examination table. "One size fits nobody," she chuckled. "Undress from the waist up, then have a seat. Doctor will be with you in a minute."

Sammy dashed into the dean's suite of offices a few minutes after ten. Talking to Sergio's teaching assistant, unfortunately, hadn't been particularly productive.

Panting, she pushed open the oak doors and took a moment to catch her breath. *Nice digs*, she thought as she examined the lushly appointed anteroom. The thick maroon carpet and wood paneling represented a stark contrast to the institutional decor of most Ellsford classrooms.

Jeffries's secretary looked up casually when Sammy approached. The nameplate on her desk read: Mrs. Cook.

"Hello. I'm Sammy Greene."

Mrs. Cook slid the Ben Franklin half-frames farther down her aquiline nose and gave Sammy a perfunctory smile. "Yes?" An antique clock on the wall chimed the half hour.

Sammy pressed on, "I need to speak with Dean Jeffries."

"Do you have an appointment?"

"Well, no, but—"

"I'm afraid you'll have to talk to your student advisor. Dean Jeffries isn't able to meet with students directly."

"Sorry," Sammy corrected, "it's not a student issue. I'm here as a reporter for campus radio. I wanted to talk to him about Professor Conrad."

Mrs. Cook remained unmoved. "The dean's comment has already been released to the press." She handed a typewritten memo to Sammy. "Here's a copy. It's the only statement he plans to make."

Sammy skimmed it quickly. The usual public relations white was — "great teacher, great scientist, great loss." She looked back at Jeffries's gatekeeper. "This says nothing about Ellsford's sacrifice of teachers for dollars. Professor Conrad was a victim of—"

"I'm sorry, Ms. Greene," Mrs. Cook's tone was icy, "Dean Jeffries is unavailable. I'm afraid you'll have to leave." The secretary turned back to her computer terminal, dismissing Sammy with a curt nod.

Sammy remained at the desk. The great oak doors to her left creaked open and Dean Jeffries ambled out, followed by a tall, fifty-something Asian man with a warm smile.

"Everything's taken care of, we'll be all set by Wednesday at noon," the dean said, stepping aside to make room for his guest.

"I have no doubt," the man replied, in softly accented English. "We're grateful for your cooperation."

The dean leaned over to his secretary with nary a glance at Sammy. "Margaret, could you call for Mr. Ishida's car, please?"

Nodding, Mrs. Cook picked up the phone.

As the dean turned back to Ishida, Sammy decided to make her move. She leaned over to the secretary and spoke loudly, "So when we broadcast that special interests are influencing academic decisions at Ellsford, you won't have any official comment, is that right?"

As she expected, the dean quickly reappeared at her shoulder.

"Sammy Greene," Mrs. Cook told her boss.

"I'll see you in just a moment, Ms. Greene." He pointed to the adjacent chamber. "Wait inside. I'll be right with you."

While Sammy strolled into his office, the dean crossed over to a frowning Ishida and explained sotto voce, "The beer industry's been a sponsor of our Homecoming Day. We may have to reevaluate the health implications for our students. Anyway, I'll look forward to seeing you Wednesday."

Ishida nodded and shook the dean's hand, as a uniformed chauffeur appeared at the door. "I, too, Hamilton. I, too."

The moment Ishida left, Jeffries marched over to his office door with a forced smile.

"Tenure Committee at eleven," the secretary reminded, shutting the door behind her.

Jeffries inner sanctum was spacious, wood paneled, and decorated in an understated fashion: Oriental rug over distressed parquet, antique brass lamp on an oversized oak desk. The large black leather armchair facing the desk bore a decal of the Ellsford University logo on its back. Behind the desk, a beveled leaded-glass window filtered a variegated view of the EU campus. The rain had just stopped, leaving droplets clinging to leaves like iridescent jewels.

On the far wall, a row of Perma-Plaqued diplomas and awards documented Jeffries's ascent through the academic hierarchy: B.S., summa cum laude from Stanford, Ph.D. in Biology from Harvard. Next to these were photos with colleagues and friends including several with past U.S. presidents and world leaders, and just below, a row of bookshelves filled with leather-bound copies of Shakespeare and Chaucer.

Sammy took in the room at a glance, then regarded the dean for a moment. Jeffries was a man to whom the passing years had been more than generous. Though the date of his college graduation clearly put him in his sixth decade, he had the unwrinkled face of someone closer to forty. A small man, he wore his still-dark hair in a conservative style that matched the traditional cut of his dark suit —the only pretension, a gold chain and Phi Beta Kappa key. But for all his academic credentials, Jeffries was known primarily as a superb fund-raiser, bringing in enough money over the years to ensure his tenure as Dean of the College of Arts and Sciences.

"Thank you for seeing me, sir."

Jeffries waved at the armchair across from his desk. "Sit down, Ms. Greene. Your reputation has preceded you."

Sammy couldn't resist a smile. "Sorry, but I had to talk to you about Professor Conrad. We've planned a memorial on today's show." She pressed the record button on her tape player.

Jeffries's eyes narrowed. "Professor Conrad was a gifted teacher and scientist," he said quickly. "We'll all miss him very much."

"Yes, I know." Sammy tapped the press release. "But I've also heard that he wasn't going to get tenure. The question then is why?"

Jeffries cleared his throat. "Now wait. That's not true. The Tenure Committee doesn't make its final decisions 'til December. They're still reviewing publications and student evaluations." A genial smile. "We do take those into account, you know."

Sammy nodded politely. "What other criteria do they use to evaluate professors — money they bring in, perhaps? Grants?"

"I'm afraid I can't discuss specifics. All I can say is that Connie was a superb teacher and researcher — even back in his Berkeley days."

"You knew him from before?"

"Connie was a graduate student. I chaired his department at Berkeley."

"Genetics?"

"Biology. Genetics was a division. Anyway, he was a tiger even then — bibliography a mile long. Hundreds of citations. And his work was good. Not the factory output that passes for research nowadays."

"Beg your pardon?"

"The current penchant for writing five papers from one experiment to pad your publications when it's really five different versions of the same work."

"So you brought Professor Conrad here to Ellsford after he graduated?"

" Not exactly. Connie went over to Stanford as a junior professor working under Yitashi Nakamura."

"The late Professor Nakamura?"

"Yes. I brought Yitashi to Ellsford, and he recruited Connie a couple of years later."

"Why'd he leave Stanford?"

"I offered him a laboratory he couldn't refuse. Yitashi always —"

"No, I meant Professor Conrad."

"Oh." Jeffries checked his watch and added almost offhandedly, "He didn't get tenure."

Surprised, Sammy stumbled for her next question. She flipped through her notebook. "I talked to Professor Conrad the day before he died. He seemed to feel that Ellsford was focusing more on bringing in grants and churning out papers than teaching students —" She left the thought hanging.

"That was his mantra at Stanford too. But I'm afraid the days of the ivory tower are long gone," Jeffries said. "Your tuition doesn't cover a tenth of the expenses of running this university. To provide teaching services for our students without raising fees, we need to find funding from other sources." He chuckled, "As I'm sure you'll agree."

Sammy forced a smile.

"So, we've got to provide services to all our sponsors. They help support our facilities and laboratories, and we produce research. The result — everybody wins. Our fund of knowledge is advanced, and you get the benefit of the best scientists as teachers."

Sammy had heard this official explanation before. The dean didn't make it sound any more convincing. She pursed her lips. "I guess you have to buy the company line to get tenure."

Jeffries was not amused. "I can't speak for Stanford."

"And here?"

The robotic tone returned. "We believe and support academic freedom. The committee evaluates many criteria."

"Who's on the committee?"

"The committee consists of six professors from the College of Arts and Sciences. It changes every year."

Sammy waited.

Jeffries shook his head. "I can't give out the names. After they make their recommendations, I review their comments and forward my opinion to the chancellor."

Sammy frowned, puzzled, "You mean you have the final say?"

"I don't often go against the committee, but I can."

"And with Professor Conrad?"

Jeffries folded his hands over his blotter. "The question, my dear, is now academic." Consulting his watch once again, he rose slowly. "I'm afraid our time is up, Ms. Greene. Let me show you out."

The firmness in his voice was persuasive. Sammy gathered her things and inched toward the door. As she opened it, she added an afterthought. "By the way, the last time I saw him, Professor Conrad asked me to give you a brown envelope, but I forgot to take it with me when I left. Did he get it to you?"

The dean looked at her and shrugged, "No. Sorry. I'm afraid not." He smiled politely and closed the door.

Alone in the exam room, Lucy removed her blouse and bra and stopped to appraise her rash in the wall mirror. The elevated pink circle on her chest hadn't grown since Saturday, but then it hadn't gotten any smaller either. And it still looked gross. Hurrying to cover up, she slipped on the ill-fitting, coarse paper gown just as Dr. Palmer walked in carrying her chart.

"Good morning, Miss Peters."

Always so formal. Not that he wasn't nice. Lucy just wished Dr. Palmer would smile once in a while — like Nurse Matthews.

"Hi." Spying the empty blood specimen vials and syringe tucked into the pocket of his long white coat, she asked sheepishly, "You won't need to stick me today, will you, Dr. Palmer?"

Palmer ignored the question. Instead he turned to a clean page in her medical record and began to write as he documented her symptoms. "When did you first notice the rash?"

"Saturday. Actually my friend Anne pointed it out to me. She —"

"So you hadn't noticed it before?"

"No."

"It isn't painful?"

"No?"

"Any itching?"

"No." The same questions Anne had posed.

"How have you been feeling generally?"

"Well, I haven't really had much of an appetite," Lucy admitted. "And I guess I haven't been sleeping much."

"Oh, why's that?"

Lucy grew shy. How could she tell him about Chris? Can't eat, can't sleep, can't keep my mind on anything but Christopher Oken. "Well, I, uh. It's probably because uh, because I have a new boyfriend." There. She said it.

Dr. Palmer looked at her for the first time. His gaze seemed stern. "Are you having sex with him?"

Lucy reddened. "Yes," she whispered, after a moment. The same fear experienced talking to Anne on Saturday now gripped her. She blurted out, "You don't think this is VD, do you, Dr. Palmer? We . . . we used protection." Oh God, this was so embarrassing, but who else could she ask?

To her dismay, Palmer only mumbled a noncommittal "Hmm." He stretched on a pair of latex gloves and began feeling her neck, then under her chin. "This hurt?"

"No." She fought back a rising sense of fear.

He mashed under her armpits.

She winced. "That hurts a little."

"Hmm." Again.

He next had her lie down and palpated her abdomen. "Have you been running a fever?"

"I don't think so. I don't have a thermometer."

Palmer pulled down the front of the gown just far enough to examine the pink circle. Frowning, he pushed, probed, and measured its diameter with a ruler. Lucy was certain from the doctor's expression that something was terribly wrong. *Oh God, it's VD.*

"What is it? What's the matter?" Her voice quavered.

Palmer's response was not reassuring. "Probably nothing serious, but I'd like to do some tests."

A lead weight hit her in the stomach. "What kind of tests?"

Palmer replaced the paper gown and patted Lucy's arm

gently — the gesture somehow not as encouraging as Nurse Matthews's. "Nothing to worry about. We'll have you in and out of the hospital in no time."

"Hospital?" Overwhelmed by terror, Lucy struggled to stem the flow of tears.

"But I have midterms and —" she gulped air.

Palmer handed her a box of Kleenex. "Forget about midterms for the moment. This is more important." He picked up the wall telephone and dialed a four-digit extension. "Dr. Palmer here. I have a patient for admission. I'd like you to escort her." He listened, nodding. "Yes, that's right. You know the procedure."

Replacing the receiver, he turned back to Lucy who was dabbing her eyes with a tissue. "One of my assistants will get you settled. In the meantime, why don't you give me the names of your professors? I'll take care of canceling your exams."

"You mean postponing them?" she sniffled.

"Yes, of course." Palmer conceded with a thin smile as he headed for the door. "Oh, and if you'll give me the name of your boyfriend and roommate, I'll make sure they know where to find you."

"Dr. Palmer?"

He stopped and faced her. "Yes?"

"Thank you." Her eyes were trusting through her tears.

Palmer's smile tightened and his voice cracked as he turned away with a crisp, "You're welcome."

Moments later, Palmer stood on the other side of the exam room, his smile replaced by an agonized look that reflected inner turmoil. *What had he done? What else could he do?*

He stared at Lucy's chart, knowing the answer. The truth was, he'd already made his choice. He had started down this path. There was no turning back.

1:00 P.M.

"Where's the cart?" Sammy anxiously rummaged through a pile of eight tracks and papers, scattering several on the floor of the studio booth. "*Chaleria!*" she cursed in Yiddish. "Where did I put it?"

Accustomed to Sammy's frenetic preshow ritual, Larry reacted with amused detachment. "Which cart?"

"Those interviews I spliced last night. They were cued up and ready to go. How am I supposed to do this *farkakte* show if I can't find the stupid cart?" She shuffled through the pile of tapes once more.

Reed entered amid the chaos. "Calm and in control as usual, I see."

"It's five minutes to air," Sammy snapped, not bothering to suspend her search to properly greet him.

"Hi, yourself. Pleasure to be here."

Ignoring him, Sammy shouted toward the engineer's booth. From behind the glass, Brian McKernan was taking a final draw on a cigarette before starting the show. "Did you touch my carts? They were right here!"

The engineer shook his head, then put his arms over his head in mock terror while Larry failed to stifle a grin.

"Actually, I had to change my entire schedule to do this, but how could I turn down a chance to help out my very best friend?" Reed was saying while Sammy, in a growing state of panic, muttered to herself.

"There it is!" Spotting the elusive cart, she grabbed it and spun around triumphantly to face Reed. "Well, don't just stand there." Her finger pointed to a rickety chrome-and-vinyl stool. It was set up close to an enormous desk microphone which, rumor had it, antedated the "temporary" World War II building that housed the campus station. "Hurry."

While Reed ambled over to the stool, Sammy tossed the tape to Larry, who left the booth and raced to the engineer on the other side of the glass partition. Larry nodded as Brian grabbed the tape and shoved it in the player.

The clock on the wall flashed thirty seconds to air.

Sammy shuffled her papers and pulled Reed down next to her. "Come on, sit."

Lowering himself onto the stool, a loud squeak echoed off the walls of the tiny booth. "Sorry."

"Try not to jiggle around too much," Sammy advised, focusing on the DJ in Studio B just beyond Brian's room who was ending his midday show. "This Wednesday, live from the plaza grounds outside the Nitshi Research Institute. W-E-L-L will bring you full coverage of all the festivities, including the Nitshi Day Parade."

When the announcement was over, the DJ signed off, then rose and packed up his records. Sitting next to Brian, Larry faced a bank of phones with paper and pencil in hand, waiting to screen incoming calls.

Now the second hand swept up to twelve. Sammy nodded at Brian, who hit the button to play the introductory tape.

Instead of the bulletin sounds of her standard intro, strains of gentle, haunting music wafted through the speakers. Sammy closed her eyes for a moment, drawn into the magical world of Sergio's composition.

With the timing instincts of a professional, she opened her eyes just as Brian faded down the music into background and gave her cue.

"Good afternoon. This is *The Hot Line*. I'm Sammy Greene," she began. "The beautiful piece you just heard was written by an Ellsford student, Sergio Pinez. It was the last piece of music he ever wrote. On Friday, Sergio jumped from the clock tower in the quad to his death."

She motioned for Brian to bring up the music once more. After a moment, she continued. "Suicide is a major cause of death among young people. It's become the second leading cause of death behind accidents. Suicide painfully touches us all." She paused. "As most of you know by now, this past weekend, Ellsford lost two of its best and brightest, freshman Sergio Pinez and Professor Barton Conrad."

She nodded to Brian who started a second tape with eulogies from friends and faculty.

"Sergio was an artist. A Jean-Pierre Rampal."

"A real talent."

"It isn't often that you find someone who enjoys tackling Paganini concertos as much as I do. We rehearsed the third and fourth sonatas for two weeks. I've never had a partner quite as talented."

In the background, the concerto continued as Lloyd Fletcher spoke. "He would ad lib these passages, 'Variations on a Theme by—' you know, that would wrap themselves around your soul. Brilliant."

Again, Sammy nodded to the engineer, who stopped the tapes. Sammy leaned into the mike. "Students and faculty across campus have expressed shock and sadness." She looked down at her notes. "In a written statement, Dean Jeffries called these losses 'tragedies not only for the individuals and their families, but for everyone in the Ellsford community.'

"We'd like to talk to you today about your feelings. We want to hear from you, so we've opened our phone lines for call-ins. The number is five-five-five-WELL. On campus, just dial ninety-three fifty-five."

She turned to Reed. "With us today from Student Health Services is fourth-year medical student Reed Wyndham. He'll help guide us through this difficult subject. Reed, welcome."

Reed frowned. "Sorry it's under these circumstances."

"Yes," Sammy quickly agreed. "Let me start with why. Why do people kill themselves?"

"Trying to find the answer to that question is a lot like trying to find out what causes us to fall in love or what causes war," Reed began. "Suicide is a complex behavior. We do know that there's no one stressful event, no one biological marker that can explain it. It's always a combination of many factors."

Sammy pursed her lips and checked her notes. "Are all people who commit suicide mentally ill?"

"Some are, but not most. Some people may be okay until something pushes them over the edge."

"Like?"

"Alcohol or drug abuse. The risk of suicide among people

who've been hospitalized for alcoholism is three to four percent. And depression. Once someone has had an episode of major depression, his or her risk of suicide jumps to fifteen percent."

"How do you know if someone's depressed? You know, versus just being sad."

"Good question. You see, not everybody who's got the blues is depressed."

"How do you tell the difference?"

"Sometimes it's a matter of degree. But with depression you've often got headaches, sleep disturbances, body aches and pains, trouble concentrating or making decisions, muddled thoughts, poor appetite, loss of interest in activities that used to be fun."

"What about fatigue?"

"That too," Reed acknowledged. "Depressed individuals say they wake up more tired than they were when they went to bed or that they run out of steam early in the day."

"So how do you treat depression?"

"Counseling helps. And, in some cases, drugs — medicines can work miracles by correcting a chemical imbalance that may be an underlying cause."

"If depression's curable, then why —?" Sammy left the question hanging.

Reed shrugged. "A lot of people aren't comfortable asking for help. There's still a stigma attached to counseling. For one reason or another, they may be afraid to talk about what's bothering them."

Sammy nodded, thinking of poor Sergio.

"Each year in the United States, thirty thousand people die by their own hand. The vast majority had at least one thing in common: they saw a physician within a few months of killing themselves."

"Like the doctors at Student Health and Counseling?"

"Absolutely. Outside of family and close friends, the person most likely to have talked to a potential suicide is that person's doctor."

Sammy made a mental note to find out if Sergio had seen a medical doctor on campus shortly before his death.

"But, all of us can help. If you've got a friend or a roommate who's depressed, and talks about suicide and death, don't ignore it. Stay with them until they get help," Reed warned.

"Where do you go for help?"

"A family doctor, a clergyman, any trained professional. At EU, you can call Student Health every day from eight a.m. to eight p.m. at five-five-five-HLTH, or go to the ER when we're closed. Someone trained will take it from there."

"Thanks, Reed." Sammy looked up at Larry who was motioning that their first caller was ready. "Let's take a call now." Three lines were blinking, holding. She pressed the speaker button on the telephone in front of her. "Hello, you're on the air."

"Hi."

"Hi." Sammy kept her tone warm. "What's on your mind?"

"Well, a coupl'a years ago in high school, Dale killed himself," the caller began. "We were like friends. You know, like, if only I'd done something, you know? But, like I didn't know." His voice cracked.

"That's why we're talking about this today."

Reed interjected, "You can't feel responsible. I've got to make that point. It's one thing to recognize a problem and try to help, but the bottom line is people who kill themselves make that choice. It's not your fault if they succeed."

Reed allowed himself a side-glance at Sammy, who seemed intent on her notes.

The caller's voice brightened a bit, "Yeah, hey, thanks."

"Hello, you're on the air."

Sammy's distorted voice echoed out of overhead speakers in the Student Health Service as one student finally heard her name called. "Urgent care. Right!" she grumbled. "I've been waiting two and a half hours. Some urgent care."

Grabbing her books and coat, she stood just in time to prevent the nurse practitioner from calling the next student in line. "I'm here. Wait! I'm here." She climbed carefully over the outstretched legs of her neighbors as she wended her way through the crowded hall to the nurse's exam room, looking angrily at the empty corridor down which Lucy had been led hours before.

"I've been listening to you, man, and I don't know what the big deal is. This is a free country. If someone wants to kill himself, it should be his decision."

"You make a good point," Reed said, deciding to turn what might have seemed a hostile call to his advantage. "A lot of people think suicide is a rational choice, especially when you're very sick. But, even people with terminal illnesses generally change their minds after they get counseling or treatment." Terminal illnesses, like AIDS, Reed thought sadly.

"Besides," he quickly added, "don't forget, a decision to commit suicide affects other people. No one lives in a vacuum."

"Thanks for calling." Sammy hit the next phone button. "You're on the air."

This time the voice on the line was tentative: "My, uh, my aunt and my grandfather both committed suicide. Does it run in families?"

Reed waited for Sammy's segue. It didn't come. He finally stepped in. "Another good question. And a great myth," he added. "The confusing aspect of this myth is that some families have more than one suicide in their history and it does seem to run in the family. That does not mean that suicidal behavior is predetermined by genetics. Rather, once a suicide occurs in the family, other family members are at higher risk for committing suicide."

"Why?" The girl's voice was shaking.

"The suicide victim leaves a legacy that includes permission to choose suicide as an escape from painful life experiences. But, remember," Reed said gently, "suicide is an individual choice. It's not inevitable and it's not passed along from one generation to the next like eye color or height."

Bud Stanton briskly ran the comb through his hair and slipped it into his back pocket just as the cheerleader knocked. He strode across the spacious living room of his dorm suite and opened the door with a grunt, motioning the attractive woman to enter.

"Hey, Bud." She planted a wet kiss on his lips.

He returned the kiss. As he inched his hands down her back, the phone chimed and he pulled away. "Couch is yours, babe." He nodded at the cushioned sofa next to the expensive stereo system, walked over and picked up the cordless phone. "Yeah?"

The girl settled down amidst the soft pillows and reached for the remote control.

"About two thousand bucks, yeah." Stanton cradled the phone between his shoulder and neck and headed to his fridge for two beers. "Not this week."

The cheerleader clicked the power button and the radio speakers hissed on.

"You said there isn't one reason for suicide. But that's not true," the caller was asserting. "Everyone knows the real reason."

Sammy sat up. The voice on the phone was male, agitated, and vaguely familiar. "And what is the real reason?" she challenged.

"The breakdown of family values, the loss of religion in this country."

Sammy tried to place the emotion-filled speaker as he started to hyperventilate.

"If the Ellsford administration spent less time condoning promiscuity and perverted sexual acts and more time teaching God's word, Sergio Pinez and Professor Conrad would never have committed this terrible sin. They're atheist demons and they deserve to burn in h—!"

Bingo. Sammy cut the connection just as she recognized the caller. Luther Abbottt of Taft's Youth Crusade. "Thanks to the Ayatollah for taking the time to call our show," Sammy quickly added. She glared at Larry through the window, who gave her an apologetic shrug.

"You know," Reed interjected, "religion and family are mechanisms for social cohesion. But neither lagging church attendance nor changes in sexual behavior have shown to have any real correlation with the rising rate of suicide among young people. Fact is, it's just harder to be young today."

Sammy smiled at Reed for saving the moment. The phone lit up again. "You're on the air."

Frowning, the Reverend Taft turned down the volume of his radio to speak to his assistant. "I didn't like that. I didn't like that at all."

The assistant nodded. "I admit it was a little overdone."

Taft's voice was icy. "The kid sounded downright hysterical. Makes us look like fools."

"I'll talk to him; tell him to tone it down."

"Why not take him off the front lines for a while?" Taft suggested. "Let him do a little bit of studying. We've got others who can do the job."

The assistant nodded again, and hurriedly left the room. Taft leaned back in his chair and turned the volume up once more.

"Well, in the late 1950s," Reed explained, "experts began using a technique called a psychological autopsy."

"What's that?" asked Sammy.

"Medical records and extensive interviews with survivors are used to build a portrait of the individual's personality and reasons for committing suicide. Sometimes they can even reconstruct a person's final days."

"No kidding." What would they say about Professor Conrad, Sammy wondered. "So you can go back and piece together why someone committed suicide?"

"And hopefully learn to prevent future attempts of people in similar circumstances. By the way, they've found that attempters and completers are different groups."

"Completers?"

"People who succeed. The majority of people who attempt suicide are female, while most of those who complete are male. Often it's their first attempt. Men are also less likely to see a mental health professional. Like I said before, they go to their primary-care doctors instead."

"What else did they find?"

"People tend to take their lives when they feel they've lost all hope or have completely failed at something."

Sammy frowned, "You mean as long as they have some hope, they won't?" Poor Sergio must have felt so alone.

"That's right. Depressed people will cling to any hope that—"

Sammy recalled her interview with the dean. The tenure decisions weren't due for another month. Sergio was one thing, but why did Conrad give up so early?

"Then if things fall through, they'll turn their rage inward against themselves." Reed stopped and looked at Sammy.

"Uh, if that's true, why wouldn't Professor Conrad wait until after the Tenure Committee made its decision before he—?" she blurted.

"I don't know," Reed admitted. "It doesn't fit the profile. But, then again, when you're dealing with people, research doesn't always have the answer."

"Then maybe we've got to look a little harder and find out what really happened and why," Sammy said sharply, as a phone light came on. "Hello, you're on the air."

Disgusted, Gus Pappajohn snapped the "off" switch on the office radio. Wonderful! Bad enough to have a couple of suicides to deal with. Now Nosy Nellie implies this could be something more. If she starts asking questions, or, worse, gets others asking questions.

Feeling the burning in his stomach rise up his gullet, Pappajohn reached for a roll of antacids. This would go over real big with senior administration and the board of regents. So much for his quiet, cushy job.

"And remember, always call for help." Reed finished.

Clicking off the caller, Sammy smiled. "Thanks, Reed, for coming and all your excellent advice. We'd like to close our show today with a memorial to a friend. The finale from Sergio Pinez's final concerto." A glance at the clock indicated she was almost out of time. "Join us tomorrow on *The Hot Line*. 'Til then." She motioned to Brian to start the tape.

Sammy flipped off the mike switches, as Sergio's haunting notes came over the speaker. Reed listened intently. The music was soothing and calm. *So unlike the poor young man's last days.*

Sammy eased over to him, wrapping her arms around his neck.

"Mmm." Reed smiled. "I like how you say thank you."

"Well, you were terrific. Really."

"So, how 'bout we go over to my place and finish that thought?"

"Wish I could, but I've got a million things—"

"Uh-huh."

"Look, it's a crazy week. I promise, after Wednesday, I'll make it up to you. Really." Sammy gave him a warm kiss. "Promise."

Larry sprang through the studio door. "Great show, y'all. Just great."

"Thanks," Reed said. "I enjoyed—"

Larry nodded and quickly turned to Sammy. "Let's plan for tomorrow in my office in five."

"Aye, aye," Sammy replied, as Larry rushed off. She shrugged at Reed. "Story of my life."

"Wednesday, huh?"

"I'll try," Sammy said. "Listen, can you do me a favor?"

Reed's eyes narrowed.

"Nothing big. Can you get a copy of Conrad's autopsy report for me?"

"Uh, I don't know. Maybe. Why?"

Her expression was earnest. "Research."

Reed raised his hands in a gesture of exasperation and surrender. "Oh, all right. You know I can't turn down those eyes."

"And," Sammy fished in her purse for a moment, then brought out the pill bottle from Conrad's home and showed Reed the two tablets, "know what these are?"

"No, why?"

"When you have a chance, can you find out?"

"Where'd you get the bottle?"

She looked around before whispering, "Conrad's study."

Reed's reply was a very loud "What?"

"Shhh."

"Are you crazy?"

"No, just curious."

"I'm not going to say it, Sammy."

Sammy patted him on the shoulder. "Don't worry. I'm always careful. I'm just doing my job."

A lone fluorescent lamp fastened precariously above the engineer's board flickered, bathing the cluttered room off the main studio in an eerie light. Balancing a warm pizza in one hand, Sammy carefully stepped between snaking wires and boxes of old records and eight-track cartridges. Egg cartons paneling the walls and industrial carpeting dulled external sound, so that when she reached Brian McKernan and wrapped her free arm around his broad shoulders, his lighted Marlboro nearly fell from his lips.

The bearded grad student pulled off his padded headphones. "Christ, Sammy, you scared the crap out of—" His chubby face broke into a grin as he saw the pizza. "Mmm. What took you so long?"

"Luigi's during midterms?"

Brian sniffed at the air. "I smell anchovies."

"With your smoking, I don't see how you can smell anything." Sammy made a face and brushed at her sweater. "I'll have to do laundry tonight."

The engineer deposited the half-smoked cigarette in a can of Mountain Dew. "If I didn't smoke, I'd be fat."

Sammy surveyed the countertop, littered with soda cans, fast-food cartons, and Snickers wrappers, then the white polo shirt that stretched like a drum over Brian's ample stomach. It was stained with the remnants of some ancient meal. "You got room for this?"

"Always." Brian pushed a stained wiring schematic diagram to one side, clearing some counter space for the dish. He eagerly opened the box and pulled off a slice drowned in cheese. While negotiating his first large bite, Brian failed to notice that the "everything" on the pizza was sliding down the front of his shirt.

"Should I get you a bib?"

"Nah," Brian said sheepishly as he saw the tomato sauce flowing toward his lap. "Some people wear stuff tie-dyed. I go for 'pie-dyed.'" Grinning, he scooped up the ingredients with two fingers and popped them into his mouth.

Sammy rolled her eyes and stifled a groan. "Just make sure this stays clean. Okay?" She pulled the cassette from her purse and placed it on a shelf above the desk.

"Your wish is my demand." Brian was not entirely joking. "What is it?"

"An interview I did last week. Parts of it didn't quite — You think you could enhance the sound?"

"If anybody can. Phone tape?"

"No, live." She felt a momentary pang of irony. "The recorder was in my purse, so some stuff didn't come out too clear."

Brian raised an eyebrow. "Off the record, eh?"

Sammy nodded. "Way off."

Brian wiped his fingers on his jeans and examined the cassette. "Conversation is a lot trickier than music." He checked his watch and frowned. "I've got to jerry wire the board in Studio B tonight. Even whispers send the VU meters into the red zone." He pulled a pen from the nerd pack in his shirt pocket and labeled the cassette "Greene." "When I'm done, I'll come back here and give it a try."

Sammy gave Brian a friendly pat on the shoulders. "You're a real mensch."

Brian responded with an aw-shucks look and a shrug, "You're not so bad yourself." Eyes twinkling, he opened his mouth wide and folded in a second brimming piece of pizza.

Reed grabbed the report as the machine ejected it. He didn't want anyone to know he was using the hospital fax — especially Palmer.

Sometimes he wondered how he let Sammy talk him into these things — though he had to admit, the radio show today had served a good purpose. He hoped at least one kid would consider alternatives before doing anything foolish. Yeah, the show had actually turned out to be one of Sammy's better ideas.

This, on the other hand, was another story. He slipped the fax into his lab coat and walked briskly toward the men's room. Inside a locked stall, he removed it and skimmed over the computerized autopsy report:

> Date of report: 21 November
> Time of report: 3:00 p.m.
> Name of decedent: Barton Edward Conrad
> Age: 42
> Profession: Professor, Ellsford University
> Time of death: Postmortem hypostasis puts death at somewhere between midnight and two a.m.
> No outward physical evidence of struggle
> A detailed description of the route the .22-caliber bullet traversed and the trauma produced in the mouth and brain.
> Internal organ assessment otherwise normal.

Reed skipped to the lab report near the bottom of the page:

> Paraffin test: positive on left hand
> Toxicology Screen: Blood alcohol concentration .15. Legal limit: .08.

And the final verdict:

> Cause of death: Gunshot wound with perforation of skull and brain
> Manner of death: Suicide

There it was in black and white. The bullet had effectively destroyed all of Conrad's vital centers. Once he pulled the trigger, nothing could save him. Suicide. Just as the cops suspected. Sammy's overactive imagination had struck out. Drunk and depressed, Conrad had put a gun to his head.

Reed reached in his pocket for the pill bottle Sammy had given him earlier and held it up to the light. No doubt this would be another wild-goose chase, but he'd promised to take the vial to the pharmacy right after the show. Reed's high-pitched beeper began an insistent echo off the lavatory tiles, confirming that the page operator's access to medical staff included every corner of the hospital. He checked the number. It was the emergency room. Reed flushed the john for effect before rushing from the stall. Racing down the hall, he returned the pill bottle to the side pocket of his lab coat where he'd already replaced the autopsy report. Sammy's request would have to wait.

"Code blue, emergency room, code blue," blared the hospital intercom as he neared the ER's double doors.

Anne Sumner hung up the phone, looked at her sorority sister, Jenny Claris, and threw up her hands. "That was Dr. Palmer. It's okay. Lucy went home."

Jenny raised an eyebrow. "Why? What happened?"

"Chickenpox." Anne frowned.

"It's not contagious?"

"He says not if you've had it."

Jenny looked relieved. "So why'd she go home?"

"I guess to keep from exposing students who haven't. You never know."

"I wish she'd told us."

Anne shrugged. "We were in class all day. She probably had to rush to catch her train."

"Does Chris know?" Jenny asked, referring to Lucy's boyfriend.

"Dr. Palmer said he'd call him. He's also getting her excused from exams."

"Wow, that's nice."

"Yeah, Lucy said he was great."

Jenny giggled, "Lucky girl." They both knew that Lucy's mind hadn't been focused on schoolwork lately. "Got her number in Iowa?"

"Somewhere. I'll have to dig it out."

"Say hi from me."

"I'll call later this week." Anne said. "Two midterms to go. If I don't hit the books, I'll need a doctor's excuse myself."

Carl Brewster was as close to a true Vermonter as anyone Sammy had met since coming to EU. "Seventh-generation St. Charlesbury on both sides of the house, if you please," he told her. His family had run the country store and post office for most of that time.

In the 1960s, Brewster opened a photo shop just on the edge of campus to cater to the college crowd. His advice to the students then was the same as now: get off drugs and join the Masons. When he turned seventy-five, his sons urged him to retire. He agreed to let them run the store and the post office, but insisted on managing the photo business — as an amateur photographer, he enjoyed dabbling in the darkroom.

The first few times Sammy had come into the place, she couldn't pull more than "Nope" and "Yup" from the eighty-year-old. He possessed the laconic canniness of those legendary Green Mountain folk who directed lost flatlanders into back-road oblivion. Lately, though, he'd loosened up and Sammy found him to be a friendly, if still not particularly loquacious sort.

"How's life, Mr. Brewster?"

The old man had his back to her, but in an accent thick enough to chop wood with, replied, "Can't complain, Miss Greene."

Sammy found his down-to-earth attitude refreshing. "Wish most of the people I run into felt that way."

Brewster turned, his ever-present corncob pipe clenched between his teeth. "That's what's wrong with you young'uns today. Too much complainin'." Although the words were serious, the robin's egg blue eyes twinkled.

Sammy pointed to a photo of a craggy, bearded man on the far wall. "That a new one?"

Brewster had the entire shop filled with his photographs. Most were Currier and Ives shots of covered bridges, quaint, steepled nineteenth-century towns, serpentine country roads, dazzling winter landscapes. A few were portraits of independent-minded Vermonters like this one. The man with a chest-length beard resembled an Old Testament prophet. Sammy didn't recognize the machine he was working on.

"Yup. Took it last month at the Ellsford Museum. That's Godfrey Dunn demonstrating pump-log boring."

"Pump-log boring?"

"Somethin' you New York folks wouldn't know about, that's for sure." Brewster explained that before plastic pipe was widely available, wood was the cheapest Vermont material for making water pipes. A pump log was a hollowed-out timber through which water flowed from outdoor springs and was pumped indoors. "After cutting the right size trees, Dunn hollows them out with a long-handled auger, sharpens one log end like a pencil, and indents the other to fit its neighbor."

"Presto! A pump log." Sammy was fascinated.

"Not so easy," Brewster advised. "Ordinary person could well go wrong. If the borer forgets to remove the wood shavings inside the opening, when the auger freezes in the clogged hole, the only way to fix it is to chop the log apart to free the tool." Brewster pointed to the photo of his old friend. "Dunn was the best pump logger there was. Doing it with his dad since he was seventeen."

Sammy studied the man in the picture, now appreciating the history.

"So, what can I do for you, Miss Greene? I'm a might busy this morning."

Sammy didn't argue, though no one else was in the shop. She

found the roll of film in her purse and placed it on the counter. "I'd like these developed as soon as possible."

Brewster shook his head. "You New Yorkers are always in a hurry." Reminding her that New York and Vermont were miles and worlds apart.

"I need them for a story I'm reporting."

Brewster had already turned his back on her. "All right. They'll be ready first thing tomorrow mornin'. That soon enough?"

Sammy smiled as she watched the old man tack up yet another photo, this one a black-and-white family portrait. "Thank you, Mr. Brewster. That'll be just fine."

Outside the photo shop, Sammy blew hot breath on her ungloved hands and turned up the collar of her peacoat. Yesterday's rain had stopped, but the air was biting. Even her nostrils tingled from the cold.

Hands stuffed in her pockets, Sammy stepped off the curb. She was midway across the narrow street when she saw it out of the corner of her eye — a late model Ford hurtling toward her at breakneck speed.

"What the —?"

The mustachioed driver seemed to be staring directly at her. She momentarily froze, then, off to one side, she heard a high-pitched scream.

In a second, the car's chrome bumper was less than ten feet away. Afraid she wouldn't make it across, she started to run back, but her feet gave way. Sliding the last few feet as the car sped by her, she rolled into the gutter by the roadside.

Sammy heard the brakes squeal, felt the wind from the car's rear fender careen past her. Shaking, she lifted her head to observe its disappearing outline, but saw only the faces of Carl Brewster and a few frantic passersby standing above her.

"You all right?" Carl helped her to her feet.

She took a shaky breath. "I think so." Her legs were weak as she tried to stand, but, thankfully, she felt no pain.

Once upright, she turned to Carl with concern. "What happened? Did you see that car?" She surveyed the gathered observers. "Anybody?"

One shrugged.

Another suggested, "Green Chevy?"

"Black Toyota."

"Dark blue."

The witnesses argued among themselves.

Carl helped brush off her coat and whispered calmly. "Blue Ford Taurus."

"Get a license?" Sammy asked.

"Nope. Too busy watchin' you."

Sammy tried to recall the sequence of events. Stepped off the curb. Saw the car coming. The driver seemed to look at her. Then? "I, uh, guess I slipped."

"Seems so." Carl agreed. "Midwinter rain here's worse than snow. A good old-fashioned gullywasher can make ice as slick as deer guts on a doorknob."

Sammy almost laughed at the old man's colorful metaphor. "Thank God I got lucky."

Stepped off the curb. Saw the car coming. The driver seemed to look at her. Then. Then what?

A crazy, diabolical thought peeked through an empty corner of her mind.

"Yup. Got to be more careful next time," the old man was saying.

Yup, she agreed to herself, shooing the thought away. Mr. Brewster was right. It was simply a close call. Nothing sinister.

Still, she was lucky she hadn't been killed. Smiling at the Vermonter, she said, "I will, I promise."

It wasn't just Luther Abbott's hand that throbbed. Now the pain racked his whole body, making it impossible to concentrate on his English midterm: *Discuss the symbols that Hemingway uses in the* Old Man and the Sea *to develop the Christian theme.*

Christian theme? Luther's thoughts became disconnected snatches: the fisherman and the boy. Christ and his disciples. Christ and Reverend Taft.

The outline of the words in his blue book blurred as he placed his hands on either side of his head, squeezing the ache into submission.

Can't think!

Hurts too much!

Try!

His hand seemed to drift off the page.

Help me!

"Are you all right?" The proctor was shaking him.

"Call Dr. Palmer — Student Health." Abbott barely got the words out before he lost consciousness and toppled forward onto the floor.

Frosted earth reflected an almost-full moon, making glittering jewels of the meadow just beyond the law library. Sammy watched the digging for some time before she wondered what the man was doing there. His back to her, she could see that he was tall and strong; he seemed to lift each spadeful of dirt effortlessly. Slowly, he began to disappear from sight, although the pile of dirt continued to grow higher. Then he hopped out, pushed what looked like a large sack into the hole, and jumped in again.

Curious now, Sammy ventured from behind the tree where she'd been hiding. Cautiously, silently, she edged forward, until she was less than a foot away. Jesus! The man was digging a grave!

Horrified, yet needing verification, she peered in. Narrow, but deep, the hole already contained a body. Sammy's heart pounded with fear. She couldn't see the victim's face — the man blocked her view.

She stepped backward, a frozen twig cracked loudly beneath her feet. The man spun around and stared directly at her. She gasped as she saw his fiery eyes and large black mustache. Instead of anger at being caught, the man smiled at her, his hideous grin widening like some horrific jack-o-lantern carved from ear to ear. Laughing, he moved aside just enough so that she could view the face lying in the dirt.

Oh God, no! No! Her screams drowned out his maniacal laughter as she gazed down onto her own frozen face.

She was the victim!

She held up her hands, hoping to erase the terrifying image, as her screams and the howling wind merged in an agony of pain.

It was the wind rattling against her bedroom windowpane that finally woke her from her nightmare.

Her eyelids fluttered open. The room was pitch black. The luminescent face of the clock radio by her bed read 4:00 a.m. She lay in the darkness, shaking.

Just a dream. Just a dream.

Not until the next morning did she finally remember where she'd seen the mustachioed face before. The image came back to her with sudden clarity. It was the driver of the car that had almost run her down.

CHAPTER FIVE

Tuesday

Snow predicted for Sunday arrived Tuesday morning.

Great soft flakes kissed cheeks, then fluttered down to the bottom of the pit sunk deep within the earth, creating a fluffy comforter of snow. Several hundred mourners — mostly Ellsford faculty, administration, and students — formed a silent wall beside the open grave, watching Barton Conrad's casket lowered onto that blanket of white.

"We are gathered here . . ."

Sammy stood among them, off to one side, listening to the minister's eulogy. The chill wind whipped up his words, carrying them into the heavens where Conrad, she surmised, might at this moment be angrily arguing policy with Saint Peter.

"God's will . . . the Lord giveth and the Lord taketh . . ."

Ironic, Sammy thought, since Conrad had taken his own life.

". . . and whosoever liveth and believeth in me shall never die."

Faith. Her mother had none in man or God. Conrad, too, had seemed too cynical to be religious. If they had been, would that belief have kept them alive as Luther Abbott suggested yesterday?

"Untimely death . . ."

"Eternal hope . . ."

Sammy frowned. Why did Conrad give up when he should still have had hope? Dean Jeffries admitted the issue of tenure hadn't been settled yet.

"A tragedy we can't explain."

Reed said that people don't commit suicide until they feel all hope is lost. It just didn't figure.

"Ashes to ashes, dust to dust," the minister intoned, throwing a handful of soil atop the polished coffin with a final "amen."

"Amen," the mourners echoed.

The graveside service concluded. Chancellor Ellsford, his face creased with concern, walked up alongside a somber Dean Jeffries to pay his respects. Among the sad-faced groups of students, Sammy recognized a few other administrators and faculty. Even Coach Grizzard and Bud Stanton had come. If only Conrad had known how many people cared about his life.

Sammy watched each in turn step forward to throw a flower on the casket.

Flowers on the grave.

She blinked back tears as the scene stirred old, painful memories.

Barely seven, she was too young to be responsible, but in Sammy's mind, her mother's death had been her fault. If only she'd been a better child, if only she hadn't cried so much when Daddy left, if only she'd gotten home earlier.

They hadn't let her go to the cemetery—just the funeral parlor. Later, after she'd begged Grandma Rose, they'd visited her mother's grave together, bringing flowers—even though it wasn't Jewish custom. Her mother had loved roses. She'd laid the petals on the ground so carefully, one by one.

Sammy fought to control long-suppressed emotions as she observed today's procession. Near the end of the line, a dark-haired woman stopped for a moment and bowed her head. When she looked up again, Sammy recognized the face she'd seen in pictures on the professor's wall: Mrs. Conrad. Or rather, the ex-Mrs. Conrad. Dressed in black, her face, while as pretty as Sammy remembered, was not smiling now. Tears streaked down her cheeks and her body seemed to shake with silent sobs—more a grieving widow than a woman who had left her husband for another man. Not what Sammy would have expected. As she watched, a tall man in a trench coat took the crying woman's arm, and led her to a parked Volvo station wagon. Sammy put the ex-wife on her mental list of people she planned to contact later that day.

"I suppose I should have seen this coming," a voice nearby confided to Chancellor Ellsford. "Those who commit suicide are the forgotten tragedies, tortured souls who die of loneliness and broken hearts, ultimately destroyed by inattention."

Sammy edged closer to eavesdrop on the chancellor and his well-dressed companion.

"Come on now, Bill, you of all people shouldn't engage in self-recriminations. Conrad was depressed, yes. But inattention? You were there for him." The chancellor conferred an avuncular pat on the back. "Always."

"I certainly tried," the man acknowledged, brushing off a few snowflakes that had settled on his cashmere coat. "If only the conference had been another weekend. I called Connie from New York the morning he—" the man's voice cracked and he coughed to clear his throat.

Hey, guy, I'm worried about you. Let's talk, okay?

Sammy recognized the deep voice she'd heard on Conrad's answer machine: Professor Bill Osborne.

"You did all you could, Bill. Remember that. I'll see you tomorrow." The chancellor turned to several faculty rushing forward to shake his hand and deliver obsequious greetings.

So she wasn't the only one who felt responsible, Sammy thought as Osborne broke from the cluster and set off briskly for the parking area. "Excuse me, sir." She waved at the psychology professor.

Osborne spun around. Close up he was not so handsome as well-groomed. Barely six feet and trim, his face had strong, chiseled features: broad brow, cleft chin, and the straight nose of a Roman senator. Gray hair, now displacing black, was professionally styled, strategically hiding a nearly bald pate. "Yes?"

"Professor, my name is Sammy Greene. I'm a student here."

Osborne's smile was tentative, though his hazel eyes radiated warmth. "What can I do for you?"

"I couldn't help overhearing what you said to Chancellor Ellsford. About your call to Dr. Conrad."

The patrician forehead creased in puzzlement.

"I was doing a piece on the Ellsford Teaching Award for W-E-L-L."

A glimmer of recognition. "Ah, yes, Greene. Station W-E-L-L. *The Hot Line*."

"Right."

Osborne's smile widened. "I listen to your program whenever I get a chance. Helps me keep a pulse on student concerns. You do a great job."

Sammy was pleased; the compliment felt genuine. She quickly explained how she'd come to interview the genetics professor.

"So Connie was going to do your show?" Osborne appeared bemused. "That would've shaken up," he nodded at the administrators a few yards away, "some old soldiers around here. Shame he didn't get a chance to talk to you."

"Actually, we had a pretty good interview Friday night." Sammy looked off for a moment, reliving the sad memory, then returned, resuming a professional tone. "Anyway, I went back to his house Saturday morning to clear up a couple of things and found him —" She didn't finish the sentence. "Your call came while I was waiting for the campus police."

"I'm sorry." Osborne's tone was filled with concern. "That must've been terrible."

"Yeah," Sammy said. "You think maybe I could talk to you? I mean, I have a few questions."

"For your show?"

"No," she replied honestly, "for myself."

"Of course." Osborne adjusted the heavy, silver ID bracelet embracing his left wrist. "I have a one-hour graduate seminar at five this evening. Why don't you stop by the classroom around six? We can talk then."

"Thanks. I'll be there."

As he walked away, Sammy felt a strange sensation of comfort. Osborne had such kind, *haimish* eyes, drawing you in for a figurative hug. No wonder Sergio had trusted the man with his secret. She looked forward to talking with him again tonight.

"My, my, if it isn't the queen of talk radio."

Sammy jumped, startled. She hadn't sensed Gus Pappajohn sneak up behind her. The policeman wore a heavy wool overcoat, unbuttoned. Beneath it, Sammy noticed a sober, navy blue pinstripe suit — simply cut, but neat. On his feet were his regulation wing tips, spit-shined as always. It was the first time she'd seen him out of uniform and not clothed in a manner designed to claim a spot on Mr. Blackwell's worst-dressed list. *Must be his day off*. "Something bothering you, Sergeant?"

Pappajohn scowled and his mustache flared. "*You* bother me, young lady. I heard your radio show yesterday."

"Gee, I didn't know you were a fan."

"How could you be so irresponsible?" Pappajohn snapped.

"I think we helped a lot of troubled students."

The cop continued to glare. "You know what I mean. How do you come off saying Conrad couldn't have killed himself?"

Sammy held up a hand. "Wait a minute. I didn't say that. I just said he didn't fit the profile Reed — Dr. Wyndham — had outlined." She knew she shouldn't have blurted that over the air, but Pappajohn's confrontational approach made her angry.

The cop pointed a beefy forefinger at her. "I've known you long enough to understand the way your mind works."

"And how is that?"

"Devious." He breathed a white cloud of condensation in her face.

"What does that mean?" Sammy tried to maintain a mask of defensive calm, but she was quickly losing control.

"It means, Greene, you don't care who you hurt — as long as you get a story — even the wrong one." He caught her eyes in a hammerlock, held them for several moments, then growled, "Just tell me one thing."

"What's that?"

"If the good professor didn't kill himself, who did? And why?"

"How should I know? I'm not the detective."

"Glad you understand that." Pappajohn turned his attention to Dean Jeffries signaling him from across the cemetery. "Now keep it that way," he added coldly, acknowledging the dean with a wave. "Good day, Greene."

"Same to you," Sammy muttered between clenched teeth as Pappajohn lumbered off.

"We got the pictures."

"And the negatives?"

The tall mustachioed man handed them across the desk. "Everything."

After a moment of inspection, there was a sigh. "A nice likeness."

The shorter of the two men was clearly embarrassed. "I was caught up in the front. I never saw the camera."

"Think she'll remember you?"

Peter Lang shook his head. "Not a chance."

"You're sure?" The tone was ominous.

A long pause preceded his response. "No."

"Well, then, you know what you have to do."

"We'll take care of it," Lang promised.

The man behind the desk nodded. "See that you do. And this time," he said staring at both henchmen, "don't leave any loose ends."

Lucy struggled to relax, but she'd never been a hospital patient before. Everything about this place frightened her — so high tech and sterile. And so quiet. Only the gentle background hum of machinery invaded the silence.

The nurse who'd checked her in had called the private suite a laminar flow room — something about the continuous flow of filtered air passing from one end to the other. Everyone entering wore masks and gloves. "Just precautionary," she'd explained, though Lucy didn't understand why. All she had was a dumb rash, for God's sake. Even the fever she spiked this afternoon was a mere two points above normal. She felt fine. Why the IV? The nurse said to ask Dr. Palmer. He could answer all her questions.

Lucy sighed. When she saw Dr. Palmer again, she would ask. She wanted to know exactly what was happening to her.

It was just as well that Luther Abbott didn't know what was happening to him. He'd been comatose since Monday and, judging from his clinical course, it was unlikely he'd last another day.

"— increased cefuroxime. His T cells are down to seventy-four."

"A most unfortunate situation, Doctor."

Palmer gently closed Luther's medical chart and sat staring at the metal cover.

"Letting the baby monkey live was very unwise."

Palmer flinched. "I had to learn the virulence of the virus in offspring of infected subjects."

"Obviously, it persists."

Palmer studied the patient whose only breaths were fueled by the rhythm of the respirator. Snaking plastic tubing connected him to an IVAC dripping a steady beat of clear fluid; the fingers of the boy's hand fell open like the petals of a fading bloom. Palmer shook his head. How could he have foreseen the demonstration or the fact that the monkey would bite Abbott? "Yes, now I know."

"Is there anything else to be done, Doctor?"

"No," Palmer replied wearily, "all we can do is keep him as comfortable as possible."

"And the monkey?"

"She's been taken care of."

The man nodded. "Good. We appreciate effective conclusions."

Palmer's eyes remained frozen on the flattening curves of the brain-wave monitor. No question, it would all be over soon.

• • •

Sammy may have had the last word, but she had to admit, Pappa-john's question was a fair one. Right now, it was instinct telling her Conrad's death wasn't suicide, her reporter's sense of a story within a story. She hadn't really tried to address the obvious conclusion: if the professor hadn't killed himself, who did? And why?

Granted, Conrad may have been iconoclastic, argumentative, and irritating. But so were many of the professors she'd run across — especially those with tenure. So why single out Conrad? What about him could have been so upsetting — or threatening — that someone would want to —

Trudging back toward campus, she wondered if her approach to the mystery had been all wrong. No matter how Conrad died, Sammy was sure he'd been very disturbed about something at Ells-ford. A motive for murder, perhaps?

Sometimes it's better to let sleeping dogs lie. Stay as far away from this as you can.

What exactly was behind Conrad's warning? He'd talked about the sacrificial fate of teaching at EU, his disdain for the university — and the Ellsford Teaching Award. And, oh, yes, the death of poor Professor Nakamura. Or rather, he *hadn't* talked about Nakamura. He'd looked off at something on his desk and switched gears right away. The brown envelope. Gone by morning. Could it have some-thing to do with Nakamura?

She stopped in her tracks. Come to think of it, that was another suicide that didn't fit Reed's profile. If the news article was accurate, Nakamura seemed the epitome of happy success and achievement, personally and professionally. Why kill himself? She'd give anything to know what was in that envelope marked CONFIDENTIAL. And where it was? Had the dean lied about not re-ceiving it?

Just ahead, a bluebird perched on a branch ribbed with crystal frost, its sapphire wings and reddish-orange breast a brave splash of color against the gray of early winter. Sammy crept closer, but the bird flew away — as elusive as the answers to her questions. She stepped back on the path, shaking her head. To come so close.

Preoccupied, she hadn't realized she was within a block of Conrad's home. Maybe taking a second look at where he lived and worked would provide a clue about the man — and his dangerous secrets. The vintage Queen Anne seemed like an abandoned dowager, her shroud a thin blanket of newly fallen snow. Sammy carefully negotiated the slippery front steps to the wooden entry. Hesitating, she turned the knob, but the door was locked.

Fresh flakes of snow swirled around her as Sammy gave a furtive glance around. Seeing no one, she slipped out her plastic student ID, sliding the card between the door and the jamb. Several attempts to unlatch the door failed. She rummaged in her purse for her Swiss Army knife and nervously aimed for the lock. In a few minutes, the door creaked open to admit her to the musty hall.

She flipped on the light, casting a bright patch across the floor, illuminating the living room where just a few days ago she'd discovered Conrad lying dead on his sofa. Now the room was a mute tableau. Everything remained as she'd found it then, except, of course, for his body. She took several deep breaths, hoping to calm herself. *Get a grip.* A good reporter checks her emotions at the door.

Sammy tiptoed up the wooden staircase to the second floor. Two small bedrooms at the end of the narrow dark hallway were vacant, save for some empty unmarked cartons and a few crumpled blank sheets of computer paper. The large master bedroom overlooking the campus, however, was filled with an antique four-poster, a beautiful armoire, even a writing desk in one corner. Here the old house appeared in better shape than the living room or the outside. All the original oak floors had been stripped and re-stained so they sparkled, the light beige paint on the walls appeared fresh, the curtains and matching bed ruffles, new. Someone had paid attention to detail. Probably Mrs. Conrad before she ran off with her lover.

The layer of dust on the windowsill indicated that the professor did not share his ex-wife's housekeeping skills. Sammy gazed out the locked window at the expanse of white below. The snowfall had slowed again so that beyond a single path of her own footsteps, she could see traces of Puhawtney Creek as a brown vein winding through marble. Far in the distance, she could barely make out the university clock tower from which poor Sergio had fallen to his death. Squinting, she could convince herself the clock hands were pointing up to noon. *Ask not for whom the bell tolls*. She waited for the chimes, but heard nothing except the whisper of falling snow.

After a moment, she turned away. The bed was still made, of course. Conrad had taken his last breath on the sofa downstairs. Sammy walked over to a large wardrobe and tentatively opened its creaking door. Only a few pairs of slacks, two corduroy jackets, and several button-down shirts hung on real wooden hangers — the typical professorial uniform. A drawer at the wardrobe's base contained a jumbled heap of white boxer shorts and cotton socks.

The adjacent bathroom was also devoid of female paraphernalia. Sammy found a worn toothbrush in a stained water glass on the cracked sink, a rusted razor, a nearly empty shaving cream can, and several shards of soap by the bathtub. The medicine cabinet contained only a leather dop kit, a box of Actifed, a bottle of Motrin, and some Band-Aids. Shaking her head, she had to acknowledge that she'd found nothing unusual in any of these rooms.

Back downstairs, she wandered through a sparsely furnished dining room and a bright country kitchen with wood countertops and appliances in the off-white manufacturers call "almond." The sink was filled with dirty dishes — strings of red sauce and spaghetti. Remnants of Conrad's last meal, she guessed, looking away. Privacy destroyed as completely as life. Feeling guilty, she took a quick peek in the refrigerator where she found the spaghetti moldering in a plastic container along with several unopened bottles of beer and wine. The professor obviously kept himself well supplied, she noted sadly.

A squeal. Or was it a squeak? Startled, she bumped the back of her head on the freezer door as she pulled out of the fridge. It sounded like the stairs. Or even the front door. She froze, afraid to take another breath.

Did I close the front door? Is someone in the house?

Heart hammering, she gently shut the refrigerator and remained perfectly still, straining to coax sound from the silence. For several seconds she waited, but there was nothing. Nothing except the wind and snow. She breathed normally again.

Must've been my imagination.

Trepidation mixed with curiosity as she crept into the lit hall, half expecting to see a figure among the shadows. The front door was shut.

I'm sure I closed it.

She paused. Again silence.

Before her was the living room. She shuddered, recalling the scene she'd stumbled into last Saturday. The clutter of books, journals, and papers scattered through the room and on Conrad's desk had already begun to accumulate a thin layer of dust.

Sammy walked over to the large desk and slumped into the rickety chair. Almost mechanically, she opened each of the drawers. No sign of the brown envelope. The left lower drawer was still locked. Sammy leaned forward as she reached for her Swiss Army knife. Despite being careful, her tugging produced two bright scratches on the drawer's lock. Inside she found a thick manila folder containing more journal articles, all dealing with arcane aspects of molecular genetics. Sammy jotted down the references, noting that Conrad himself was co-author on two. Most of the papers were several years old and, many, she observed, had Yitashi Nakamura as the final name. That meant something, she remembered. She'd have to ask Reed.

Then she struck her forehead with the flat of her hand. *Oy gevalt*—Reed. She'd promised to call him this morning. He'd be furious.

Concerned, she picked up the cordless phone from its cradle. He was probably at the hospital by now. She'd have to beep him. About to punch in the number, her eyes fell on the redial button. She knew Osborne had called the professor Saturday morning, but what if Conrad had phoned someone Friday night? It was worth a shot.

She hit the button. Seven pulses indicated a local number, and seconds later, she was listening to the greeting from a familiar voice: "This is Hamilton Jeffries. Please leave your message."

HARLEM

The entire church community packed the tiny Iglesia de la Santa Maria. Most had watched Sergio Pinez grow from the shy little *papi* to a handsome nineteen-year-old with musical talent that promised to be his ticket to a better life.

Now all their hopes for him were buried in the closed pine coffin that lay before them. Father Campos struggled for reassuring words about his former altar boy, but was unable to console Sergio's family who sat, shoulders sagging, faces streaked with tears, in the front pew.

At sixteen, Maria Pinez was the closest in age to her brother. In her arms, she clutched Sergio's first flute, as if willing it to play a comforting tune. José Pinez sat stiffly, stone faced, his fourteen-year-old hands fingering the knife hidden in his pocket. The younger children seemed equally shaken, little Felicia stroking the hair of her doll with a comforting pat. As the priest began talking about eternal life in heaven, Lupe Pinez burst into loud sobs. Raoul Pinez turned from his children and pulled his wife closer into his arms. "*¿Parqué, dios?*" she wailed. "*¿Por qué m'hijo?*"

In the back of the crowded church, Dr. Ortiz stood off to one side, alone, knowing that no answer would ever really satisfy the grieving woman. Still, as the boy's family doctor, he felt a duty to try to ease her pain. When all the services and prayers were over, Lupe would come to him once again with her questions. This time, he needed to be ready with some answers. The university promised to send a copy of Sergio's medical records this week. As soon as they arrived, he'd study them, and hoped he'd discover *porqué*.

So Conrad had phoned Dean Jeffries the night he died — apparently on the dean's private line. Sammy wasn't surprised. She'd felt Jeffries had been less than forthright when they talked yesterday.

Although her first impulse was to go to Blair Hall and confront the dean, Sammy realized the call itself meant nothing.

Frustrated, Sammy replaced the folder and slammed the drawer shut. She dialed the hospital page number with one hand and slipped the phone under her chin. While she waited for the operator, she flipped through Conrad's Rolodex absentmindedly, considering several possible scenarios.

If Conrad never mailed the envelope to the dean, and it wasn't in the house, perhaps he'd stashed it somewhere for safekeeping.

Or, maybe it had been taken. From the tape recording she now knew that someone had been here after her visit Friday night. She recalled Conrad fastening the chain before she left and warning her to be careful. Saturday morning the door had been locked, the chain unbroken. So, whoever had come by, Conrad had let in. Someone Conrad knew and trusted. Who, she wondered. And what had they argued about? Were the contents of the envelope a motive for murder?

"Hello."

The voice of the hospital operator interrupted speculation. "I'm sorry, Dr. Wyndham doesn't answer his page. Would you like to leave a message?"

"No. No, thanks." Sammy hung up the receiver and saw that the Rolodex had fallen open to a familiar name and address: Karen Conrad.

Sammy added the information to her notes, and checking her Swatch, decided to visit the professor's ex-wife that afternoon. First stop, however, was Conrad's office at the genetics building.

Sammy flicked off the hall light and slowly nudged the front door open. The snow had tapered to a few sprinkles, so she now had a clear view of the yard to the street. Closing the door behind her, she started carefully down the steps, then froze when she spotted two more rows of footsteps beside the gullies left by her own feet as she'd entered. Both sets traveled up the stairs and ended at the front door. Propelled by fear, she made a dash for the street, hurrying down several blocks before the sight of a group of students frolicking in the freshly fallen snow gave her cover to resume a normal pace.

Still, she couldn't resist the occasional backward glance to reassure herself that she wasn't being followed.

The neighbor who called Campus Police never saw the tall man with a mustache. She only reported a frizzy-haired redhead hurrying from the Conrad residence shortly after eleven.

"Thanks for stopping by, Gus," Coach Grizzard said.

Pappajohn hung his overcoat on a peg by the door. "You had something to tell me?"

"Take a load off," Grizzard pointed to the chair in front of his desk. He pulled out a cheap American cigar from his top drawer, clenched it between his front teeth, and lit a match to the other end. "Smoke?"

"No. Thanks." Pappajohn sat down impatiently as Grizzard took a deep puff.

"Probably wondering what's on my mind." The coach blew out a curtain of smoky haze.

Pappajohn nodded, trying to keep from grimacing at the stench. The man didn't know from good cigars.

"Bud Stanton."

Pappajohn acknowledged the name. But the connection? "Yeah."

"It stinks. Something stinks."

Pappajohn couldn't hide a look of amusement as he eyed the foul cigar. He resisted the obvious comment and returned a noncommittal "What?"

"Stanton's an A-one forward. But, let's just say he's not the best in the brains department."

"So? You're going to the finals this year."

"With him. But if he hadn't passed his courses—"

"He passed?"

Grizzard shrugged. "We'll never know. Dean Jeffries waived most of his midterms. Of course," the coach added, "I'm not about to look a gift horse in the mouth."

Pappajohn waited.

"Maybe I'm off base, but Stanton was having a real hard time in bio."

Pappajohn raised an eyebrow. "Conrad's bio?"

"Yup. Dean couldn't budge the professor." He waggled his hand sideways. "So, the big exam's Monday. Three to one, it would have been a knockout. Now, all of a sudden, Conrad croaks and everybody gets to sail through — even Stanton."

"You suggesting the kid had something to do with Conrad's death?"

"I ain't suggesting nothing. I just know that Stanton was parading his ass around here Saturday like the fix was in. Before any of the rest of us even knew the guy was dead." The coach launched a few more cloudy puffs to underscore his point.

First Greene, now Grizzard. Paranoid imaginations. Pappajohn did not hide his irritation. "Seems to me that Stanton could've maybe worked out something with Conrad. You know, extra credit, a paper, maybe even tutoring. The faculty bends over backward to help our athletes."

"Not Conrad. Stanton was up against the wall. That exam was going to kill him."

Pappajohn eased up from his chair and slid on his overcoat. "Well, thanks for letting me know."

"You gonna look into it?"

Do I have a choice? Pappajohn mused, nodding toward the coach. "Yeah. I'll look into it." He gathered his scarf and headed for the door. "I'll get back to you when I get something."

If I get something.

The door to Conrad's campus office was unlocked. Sammy stepped inside, quietly shutting it behind her. Last time she'd been here, she'd focused on the grumbling professor. Now she took a moment to study the room itself. If not for the rainbow of light streaming through the stained-glass window just behind the wooden desk, the spartan cubicle would have been stifling. The furnishings were Victorian and austere, the room was dark and devoid of personal touches. Sammy saw no photographs, posters, or *chatchkes* among the dusty books and papers.

Propped on the floor in one musty corner were Conrad's diplomas and certificates. Sammy stooped down and flipped through the frames: B.S. in biology from Wisconsin, Ph.D. in biology from Berkeley, Member of the American Association for the Advancement of Science, Phi Beta Kappa. Barton Conrad was brilliant and accomplished. Standing, she noticed the Ellsford Teaching Award, still posing on the windowsill. Dear God, why did he throw his life away?

Abruptly, she turned from the window and back to Conrad's desktop. Unlike the one in his living room, this was uncluttered—only a few recent genetics journals stacked neatly beside the Macintosh—an identical twin to his home computer. Except for some loose paper clips and a couple of Bic pens, the two drawers were likewise devoid of disorder. Unless someone had cleaned up, it seemed that Conrad did his serious work at home.

Sammy sat down in the swivel chair behind the desk and flipped on the computer switch at the back of the monitor. The familiar ping sound came on; the computer started whirring as it booted up and the screen took on the familiar gray glow.

A look at the hard disk directory was not particularly illuminating. Sammy scrolled up and down, examining the file titles. Most referred to Ellsford administrative subjects, lecture summaries, course outlines, and research papers.

Sammy stopped and double clicked on a folder labeled "Nakamura." The window came up empty. Apparently, Conrad had erased its contents.

Continuing to explore the files, her attention was drawn to a folder labeled "Osborne." Not surprising, she figured, given that they were friends. Inside the folder was a single document, which appeared to be random notes: a few dates and times—perhaps when he'd met with the psychologist—and a list of scientific articles. No titles, just journals, volumes, and pages. Next to one he'd asterisked "see Darsee and Summerlin." Sammy had no idea what that referenced, but she copied the names down anyway.

"What are you doing?"

Startled, Sammy looked up to see a young, neatly dressed woman leaning against the door. She was carrying several manila folders filled with blue memorandum paper. Must be a departmental secretary.

Sammy adopted her most convincing smile. "I, uh, Dr. Osborne asked me to pull up references for a project he and Professor Conrad were working on." Smoothly, she reached behind to turn off the computer.

"Not there!" the secretary snapped. "You turn it off from the master switch." She pointed at a row of plugs on the floor. "Down there, by your feet."

"Oh." Sammy pushed the floor switch off with her toe. "I didn't know."

"Professor Conrad would've killed you," the secretary explained. "He always used the floor switch. Said he hated wasting time with the individual switches, turning them on one by one. This way, zap, and everything was ready to go."

"Sorry, I forgot." Sammy stood and folded her notepad into her purse. "Anyway, I got what we needed. Thanks." Shaking her head, she walked out of the room alongside the woman, "Sad, isn't it?"

The secretary agreed. "Yeah. I mean, he wasn't exactly Mr. Nice-to-be-around, but it's not like we wanted him gone, you know? At least I don't think so," she added in a half-joking manner. "You're lucky, you know."

"Yeah?" Sammy cast a glance toward the outside door in the distance. Only a few more steps. "How come?"

"You work for Osborne. Now there's a nice guy."

"Yeah." Sammy waved and made her way quickly to the door.

The door cracked opened with Sammy's first knock.

"Yes?" Karen Conrad had changed from her dark suit into a pair of gray wool slacks and a light blue silk blouse. Framed in the doorway with her long brown hair unclasped, falling in waves on her shoulders, she looked more like the happy woman in the photos Sammy had seen in her ex-husband's home. Her tears were gone, her makeup reapplied. Her smile, however, was tentative. "Can I help you?" she asked in a soft English accent.

"My name is Sammy Greene. I'm a student at Ellsford," Sammy explained. "I also work for the campus radio station W-E-L-L. Would you have a moment."

"This really isn't a good time." Karen moved to shut the door.

"I know. I'm sorry. I saw you at the funeral." Sammy's smile was full of sympathy. "I took Professor Conrad's bio class. He was a wonderful teacher."

Karen nodded. "Yes. He was." She paused, then opened the door wider to let Sammy in. Stepping aside, she waved her hand toward the brightly lit foyer. "Come, I was just about to have tea."

She led Sammy to a sunny sitting room filled with potted plants and comfortable pastel-colored furniture. Sammy settled on a loveseat while Karen poured brewed Darjeeling from a white china pot. Her hand — and her voice — were steady.

"I was one of his students myself, you know," Karen said, taking a seat opposite Sammy. "I came to Berkeley after my third year at Christchurch."

"Christchurch?"

"Christchurch College, Oxford. Barton was one of my first American professors. Rather different than what I'd expected." Karen sipped her tea. "Still, I took a fancy to his unusual approach. Science as politics — the politics of science."

Conrad hadn't changed much over the years, Sammy thought.

Karen leaned back on the sofa, her eyes twinkling. "Barton would get particularly passionate on Friday nights."

Sammy's eyebrows shot up at the unexpected admission. "Uh, with you," she stammered.

"Oh, dear, no." Karen laughed gently. "I meant Friday night discussion sessions at Yitashi's house."

"Yitashi Nakamura?"

"A group of us would gather at his home each Friday and chat."

"About science."

"World affairs, politics, movies, music, philosophy." Karen smiled at the memory. "Barton and Yitashi used to go at it like two samurai. Fight to the death."

In response to Sammy's raised eyebrow, she added. "Figuratively speaking. But, they were quite close in their own way. Wise father and prodigal son. I recall once they were talking about individual rights versus family obligations. Barton was ever the cowboy, stridently in favor of a self-based ethical system. Yitashi argued about the moral virtues of family loyalty over individualism."

"Who won?"

"We all did. It was a most stimulating evening."

"You sound as if you still—" Sammy searched for the right word and tense, "care about him."

"Life with Barton was always a challenge. An adventure."

"So what happened?"

Karen gazed off in the corner. "When Dr. Nakamura died, Barton was devastated. As if he had lost his father all over again." She looked back at Sammy. "Not long after that he began drinking. Barton needed a full-time nurse and mother more than he needed a wife and lover. I simply couldn't do the job any longer."

Sammy asked, "How long have you been divorced?"

"Separated, six months. I guess it's not a secret. The EU grapevine is better than the tabloids. I had a brief . . . relationship . . . with a sociology professor."

The man with the Volvo, Sammy speculated.

"The affair was over before it really began. Foolish," Karen admitted. "I suppose it was my way of letting Barton know we had a problem. Otherwise he'd just bury himself in his work. He hated confrontation." She paused a moment before adding, "at least with me."

"Uh, you'll have to excuse me for this question, but did Professor Conrad ever seem like . . . did he ever talk about wanting to . . ." Sammy struggled, "to kill himself?"

Karen took a long sip of her tea before answering. "Intentionally? No. Yes. Maybe. Not when he was sober."

"And when he wasn't?"

The pause was even longer until Karen whispered "Yes." She forced a smile. "But, I never believed he'd truly do it. He was an angry man, but never the sort to give up." She looked down at her empty teacup. "It's funny. If anything, I would've thought he'd have something more to live for."

"What do you mean?"

Sammy could see the start of tears as Karen fumbled in her pocket for a tissue. "Sorry. It's just that we'd been talking—seeing each other once in a while, now and then. Things were going well enough between us that we were planning a joint Thanksgiving holiday to—" Karen spoke between sniffles, "to see if we could get back together."

Pappajohn exited Dean Jeffries's office and consulted his watch. He still had a few minutes to swing by the medical examiner's office before lunch. Time to get a few answers. Unfortunately, the dean's secretary flagged him down as he headed for the outer door.

"Sergeant, wait."

He turned and she handed him a piece of paper.

"Message from your office. There's been a break-in."

Pappajohn frowned. "Where?"

"Professor Conrad's house. This morning."

Pappajohn swallowed a Greek oath. No chance he'd make it to the coroner's now. Irritated, he walked back toward the secretary's desk. "Can I use your phone?"

"Try line three. They said the burglar was a young woman. With red hair."

Pappajohn groaned silently. Greene. *There goes my lunch hour, too.*

• • •

After leaving Karen Conrad, Sammy hurried toward midcampus, her mind in turmoil. The astonishing news of a possible reconciliation between the professor and his wife was an even stronger reason why suicide didn't fit the picture. Conrad had kept his wife's bedroom pristine — and ready. Why would a man who obviously still cared about her, who had a good chance of winning her back, go and throw it all away?

He was an angry man, but never the sort to give up.

Karen's words. If she was right, suicide made even less sense.

On the other hand, Conrad apparently hadn't felt close enough to share his disturbing concerns about the university. Karen seemed genuinely surprised that her husband might have discovered some campus scandal, and she claimed to know nothing about a brown envelope.

Sammy arrived at the musty campus police office and passed purposefully through the swinging gates to a large wood-paneled desk. On its polished surface was a brass placard that read INFORMATION. The twenty-something bleached blonde seated behind the desk was busy applying a second coat of red nail polish to claw-length acrylics as she chatted on the phone cradled between her neck and shoulder. Sammy couldn't resist a furtive glance beyond her at the empty glass booth that was Pappajohn's office. When the cat's away — she cleared her throat.

"Just a minute," the blonde whispered into the phone. Placing the receiver on the desk, she tossed Sammy an irritated glare.

Sammy's voice exuded calm authority. "I'd like to see the file on Professor Barton Conrad."

The clerk lazily replaced her minipaint brush. "What?"

Sammy enunciated very slowly. "Con-rad, Barton Conrad. He committed suicide a few days ago. I'd like to see the report on his death."

"Why?"

"It's public record, isn't it?"

"Well, now, I don't know." The woman stared at a nail as if the answer might be found in the bright enamel.

Sammy pressed on. "You are familiar with the Freedom of Information Act?"

"Listen, Tony, I better call you back." The blonde hung up the receiver and turned to Sammy. "What are you, a law student?"

"Concerned citizen."

The woman shrugged. "Everybody's at lunch. I'll have to ask one of the regulars. I'm just a temp."

Sammy took a chance. "I'm sure it's just in the files." She nodded at the large black file cabinets that lined the back wall of the anteroom. "I'll save you the trouble." She took a few steps toward her goal.

"Maybe I should page Chief Pappajohn," the clerk said, picking up the phone.

Sammy froze and kept her voice even. "I wouldn't. Not on Tuesdays. He's lunching with the chancellor."

"Yeah, so?"

Sammy examined her watch. "They should be starting on the lobster tails by now. So, knowing the chief as well as I do, I know he hates being disturbed when he's," she patted her stomach, "doing important business."

Sammy leaned closer and spoke conspiratorially. "All I want is a quick look at the report. I won't even ask for a copy. And you won't need to fill out a request."

That seemed to clinch it. The temp replaced the receiver. This was a woman who had better things to do with her time. "Oh, all right, but hurry up." She waved her freshly manicured hand toward the back wall.

Sammy scurried over to the cabinets and scanned for the "C" drawer. She opened one labeled "B-C" and started rifling through the files. Calley, Canteras, Connors, Conrad. Sammy pulled out a manila folder and spread it open atop the drawer. She caught a glimpse of the clerk's reflection in the glass, relieved to see that the young woman had resumed her nail repair.

The folder contained only a simple police report of the death, with segments of it still incomplete. Sammy pursed her lips in frustration as she skimmed the meager data: Barton Conrad, age 42, Professor. Found at home, 8:13 a.m. No sign of forced entry prior to discovery by Sammy Greene, Ellsford University student. Probable cause of death: self-inflicted gunshot wound.

Pictures, fingerprints, and paraffin testing were pending. Okay. But no ballistics confirmation. Just a description of the weapon printed sloppily at the top of the second page: 22-caliber semiautomatic. The gun's registration number 72674. Sammy's eyes widened. What a horrible coincidence. 7-26-74 was the date of her birth. Shuddering, Sammy quickly closed the folder and replaced it alphabetically among the files.

Her eyes fell on the adjacent drawer labeled "N-O." The letters reminded her of another suicide—Dr. Nakamura. Sammy glanced back at the clerk who had now turned away to dry her nails at the window heater vent. Taking advantage of the woman's distraction, Sammy opened the drawer. Finding the folder, she pulled it out and opened it to the first page.

Sammy skimmed the death report, a standard printed form, dated September 6, her freshman year. Its edges were already yellowed. Most of the *e*'s looked like *o*'s, Sammy noted, the *n*'s like *r*'s. The information must have been typed in by an inconsistent typewriter. Or typist.

Decedent: Yitashi Nakamura
Age: 67
Occupation: Professor
Circumstances of death: found in his campus office, 8:21 a.m., single .22-caliber bullet to the right temple
Cause of death: Suicide (self-inflicted gunshot to head)

Sammy stood there for a few moments, disappointed. Nothing she hadn't already learned from the newspaper article. No witnesses. No doubts. Cut and dried. Case closed.

Appended to the report were two pages. One listed Nakamura's personal belongings, returned to his family. Nothing of note—a watch, his suit, underclothes, loose change.

The other sheet was an official descriptive report of the suicide weapon: .22-caliber semiautomatic, registered to Nakamura. Sammy froze, staring numbly at the report. The serial number for the gun was also 72674. The same number as the gun that killed Conrad. Same gun?

The jangling ring of the phone startled Sammy. She checked the clerk's reflection in the glass.

"Campus Police," the woman answered wearily. After a brief pause, Sammy heard a brisker, "Uh-huh. Sure. I'll hold."

The clerk's staccato rhythm of nails clacked on her desk, echoing through the empty office. Sammy frowned. The call sounded official. Better not press her luck. She started to close the folder when her eyes caught the signature at the bottom of the page. The investigating officer on the case was Chief Costas Pappajohn. Very interesting.

"Hello, Chief."

Uh-oh. The clerk's voice jarred Sammy into action. She stuffed the file back into its place and pushed the drawer shut with one hand, then hurried toward the door.

"Sure, right away. It'll be ready." The clerk's phone demeanor was now all business.

Sammy didn't stop to listen. She waved a casual thanks to the woman, as she strode through the gate, trying to keep her pace even and relaxed. She was pushing open the exit door when she heard the clerk add, "By the way, there was somebody here who wanted to see one of your files. Connors or something."

Sammy didn't stop to hear the rest of the conversation. She broke into a run the moment she stepped outside. The freezing wind led her to turtle into the upturned collar of her peacoat, a vain attempt to keep warm. Bundled and buried with her collar blinders, she missed the mustachioed man who came around the building corner and headed inside.

• • •

Sammy knocked on the thick door and eased it open. It gave a piercing screech as its lower edge scraped the uneven linoleum floor. With an apologetic "sorry," she tiptoed into the smoky room.

Brian flipped off his headphones and turned to her with a broad smile.

"It's my do-it-yourself alarm system," he joked. "That way nobody catches me by surprise."

Sammy surveyed the shabby engineer's studio. "And to think the Athletic Department just got a new gym."

Brian shrugged. "We don't bring in millions of dollars in alumni donations." He reached for a half-smoked cigarette and took a few quick puffs in succession. Tapping her cassette tape, which rested at the top of one of the many piles on his counter, he added. "Nothing yet. Haven't had too much time."

"That's okay," Sammy said, her sincerity feigned.

Brian wasn't fooled. "The new wiring took a lot longer than I figured," he explained. "Then Larry hit me up to do these promos. I promise I'll get to it tonight. Okay?"

Sammy produced her warmest smile, as she waved a good-bye. "Okay. Call me when you're done." Out the door, she stuck her head back in, and added, "Thanks."

Sammy walked down to her desk and plopped into her chair. Reaching for her pocket notebook, she opened it to a middle page where she found Karen Conrad's phone number.

The widow didn't answer. Sammy left an urgent message for Karen to call her. Maybe she would know how Barton Conrad had gotten hold of Yitashi Nakamura's gun.

2:00 P.M.

"Join us tomorrow on *The Hot Line*. This is Sammy Greene." Sammy clicked off her microphone switch and leaned back on her stool. Her moment of rest was brief, as Larry entered the studio from the engineer's booth.

"Not bad. For a five thousand watt station."

Sammy smiled. "Damned by faint praise, eh?"

Larry studied his hands for a moment.

"Uh-oh. What's up?"

"You tell me."

"I know that tone. Evidently, I've done something I'm supposed to be sorry for."

Larry remained silent.

"Really, I haven't had time to get into mischief today. Unless you call attending a funeral a problem." Of course, she didn't mention breaking into the professor's home and office, her scam at the campus police station, or her visit with Mrs. Conrad, but it was hardly possible he'd found out about any of that. Yet.

Larry sighed. "Actually, it was yesterday."

"Yesterday?"

"Your conversation with Dean Jeffries."

What in the world? "I just asked for a few quotes about Professor Conrad. What's wrong with that?"

"You never said you planned to broadcast the fact that special interests influence academic decisions at Ellsford?"

"Well, sure, I might have said something like that to his secretary," Sammy acknowledged. "But she wouldn't let me see him without an appointment, and I needed an in."

"That got you in, all right. In his craw. Last night ah had to listen to a twenty-minute lecture on our journalists making unsubstantiated allegations."

"You'd be surprised what's going on."

Larry held up a hand. "Got the proof?"

Sammy hesitated. Should she mention the tape?

The lanky southerner sighed. "Ah have told y'all before, never leave your tookies flapping in the breeze."

"That's *toochas*, and I'll thank you not to cast aspersions on my body parts."

Larry threw up his hands and paced the room. "Look Sammy, you know as well as ah that this station is subsidized by the university. Why go out of your way to antagonize the hand that feeds us?"

"Okay, so I was fishing a little yesterday. But the way Jeffries reacted, you know I must have touched a nerve."

He stopped pacing and faced Sammy once again. "All ah know is that you irritated a very important advocate. The dean's always been on our side."

"Well, doesn't that tell you something?"

Larry's expression was a mixture of pain and frustration.

Sammy decided she should play some of her hand. "What if I told you that Conrad had placed a call to Jeffries the night he died? On the dean's private line no less."

An eyebrow went up. "Where'd you learn that?"

Not eager to add trespassing to her growing list of sins, she shook her head and merely said. "I'm protecting a source."

Larry appealed to the ceiling for relief. "Fine, okay, so he called the dean. What does that prove?"

"You know Conrad was onto something, Larry, and it had to do with special interests right here. The last night I saw him, the man was afraid for his life."

"The man was drunk as a skunk."

"He was sober enough to warn me away that night. But not before I saw an envelope addressed to the dean lying on his desk. Next morning, the envelope was gone. When I interviewed Jeffries yesterday about Conrad, he said he never got it. And he never mentioned that he'd talked to Conrad Friday night."

Another sigh. "Maybe he didn't."

"How's that?"

"Your source said Conrad placed a call to the dean. Maybe he didn't actually talk to Jeffries. Doesn't he have a service, a machine?"

That stopped Sammy cold. She hadn't considered the possibility that Conrad hadn't gotten through.

Larry began advancing a possible scenario, "Here's a guy who's four sheets to the wind, paranoid, and self-destructive. He starts tossing off crazy thoughts to a journalist, so why not to the dean? Two hours later, he wakes up and changes his mind. He destroys the envelope himself." Larry shrugged. "What've you got?"

Without the envelope, *bupkas*, Sammy thought. Nothing. If only Brian could finish working on that tape. She shuffled the papers in front of her, gathered them under her arm, and rose.

"Look, Sammy, ah have stood behind you as much as ah can. But if ah have to choose between supporting our shows or you, you know which way ah have to go. Y'all may have a death wish, but ah don't."

Sammy eased her way to the door, her expression weary. "I don't have a death wish, Larry." She added, before leaving the room, "And I don't think Conrad did either."

Pappajohn's detour to the Conrad home had been a waste of time.

Almost.

The doors and windows were all locked now. He'd used his master key to enter and survey the inside. Nothing appeared touched. The neighbor wasn't much help either. She'd only seen a redhead walking down the front stairs.

"I'm not a busybody, officer. I couldn't tell you if the girl went inside."

So even if it had been Greene — and Pappajohn had no doubt that it was — he had no evidence a crime had been committed.

Still, the trip had meant putting off his stop at the medical examiner's office. The afternoon was already shot with meetings for Nitshi Day security. Now he'd have to see the coroner after the Nitshi event tomorrow.

Frustrated, Pappajohn decided to use the remaining ten minutes of his lunch hour to review Conrad's computer files again. The registrar never questioned his need for the professor's code and password and once inside the Macintosh system, he'd located the E-net folder, this time typing in "21,8752" and "gene?human" following the prompt. After a moment, the computer screen flashed up the message: "File deleted."

As an amateur hacker, he was surprised, but not stymied. As long as new data had not been overwritten on the same sector, there was still a chance to recover the old file. He scanned the applications folder until he located "Guardian," a data-recovery utility. Following the "help" menu, step-by-step, he slowly restored the original to the hard disk. The process took longer than he expected. He was twenty minutes behind schedule before he finished. He would barely make it to the Nitshi offices in time.

Quickly, he grabbed a blank floppy from Conrad's messy desktop, copied the file, then raced outside to his rusty Land Cruiser. After work he could peruse the data at his leisure.

Sammy rushed to her desk phone and lifted the receiver on the fifth ring.

"Miss Greene?"

"Mrs. Conrad?"

Karen responded in her soft English accent. "You asked me to ring you up?"

"Yes, thanks. I had one more question." Sammy settled into her chair and caught her breath before continuing. "Did Professor Conrad keep a gun at home?"

Karen gasped. "I didn't know he had any ammunition."

"So he had the gun. From Professor Nakamura."

Clearly shaken, Karen's voice was unsteady. "Look, you must understand. Barton was a strict proponent of gun control. After Yitachi killed himself, Barton was a different man."

"That must have been so hard."

"It destroyed him almost as much as it destroyed Yitachi's family."

"I'm sorry."

"I think it was Mimiko — Mrs. Nakamura — who ended up giving him the gun."

"Why?"

"I don't know. I guess she didn't want it around. Would you?"

"And he kept it?"

Karen's voice was tinged with anger. "Yes. Some kind of perverse memorial for the death of his mentor and friend."

"Did he ever use it? Play with it?"

Karen was vehement. "Never. He never touched it. Always kept it sitting on his bookshelf, propping up one of his books. Said that was the perfect place for it."

"Oh?"

"Yes. Holding up the Bible."

Sammy said nothing for a moment. Then, she asked, "Um, would you know how I might reach Mrs. Nakamura?" Sammy recalled the newspaper article reporting her move to Kyoto.

"As a matter of fact, she'll be in New York this weekend. If you call me on Thursday, I can get you the name of the hotel where she'll be staying."

Sammy brightened. She'd been considering a trip to the Big Apple. If she could meet Mrs. Nakamura in person, perhaps she could learn something to tie the two deaths together. "I'll do that. And thanks for taking the time to tell me what you know."

Sammy barely heard Karen's tearful whisper, "I didn't know he had ammunition."

Taking a giant bite of cold pastitsio, Pappajohn waited for his computer to boot up. The food landed like a lump of coal into his empty, churning stomach and he reached for an antacid chaser to ease the burning. All he'd had all day were too many cups of coffee. Absentmindedly, his eyes fell to his bottom right desk drawer and the unopened box of expensive Havana cigars he'd secreted there when he'd quit smoking. *That's* a real cigar, he remembered fondly.

Forcing his eyes back to the screen, he watched the directory unfold to a list of recently created files. Wiping an oily hand on his slacks, he grabbed the floppy disk, keyed in a few instructions, and waited for the data to be converted from Mac OS 7.1 to IBM DOS. The cigar box beckoned, and he found himself reaching for it before stopping himself and kicking the drawer shut, disgusted. Another bite of pastitsio would have to do.

The computer finally signaled "Task Completed." With his free hand, he typed in two words and sat back once again to wait. The response was immediate. The screen filled with data. Pastitsio and cigars forgotten, he leaned forward to scroll and review with a sense of urgency he hadn't felt this morning. After ten minutes, he switched on his printer and instructed the data transfer to begin. Within seconds, the file contents began filling the paper.

When the grating noise ended, he severed the connection and shut down his computer. Satisfied, he tore the printout off the roll and stuffed it in his pocket, pausing only to grab the last dripping piece of the casserole with his free hand before speeding out the door.

"Sorry, Miss Greene. I gave those pictures to your boyfriend."

Sammy looked at Mr. Brewster with surprise. "My boyfriend?" Why would Reed pick up the pictures?

"Eh yup. And if you don't mind my saying so," the shopkeeper quipped, "he's quite a rude young man."

That didn't sound like Reed at all. Sammy frowned, "What did he look like?"

Brewster thought for a minute. "Can't say that I really noticed. Had a busy morning. Fellow didn't want to wait his turn. I remember that."

Sammy grew impatient. "A tall sandy blond with dark blue, almost purple eyes?"

"Tall, I think so. I didn't catch the eyes, mind you, but this one definitely did not have light hair." The old man rubbed his stubbly chin. "Matter of fact, it was black — same as his mustache."

"Mustache?" Sammy's heart began to pound as fear squeezed her chest. The man in her dream. "Oh my God." The man who tried to run her down! Feeling lightheaded, she grabbed onto the counter for support.

"You all right, Miss Greene?" Brewster had started to come around to her side, but she held up a hand.

"Yeah, I'm okay." Despite her attempt at bravado, she was shaking.

"How 'bout a glass of fresh apple cider?" Brewster filled a mug from a pewter pitcher and held it out for her. "I can warm it up."

"No, thanks. This is fine." She took a sip of the tart drink. It was smooth and soothing. She looked at the shopkeeper, "Mr. Brewster, that wasn't my boyfriend."

A frown crossed his furrowed brow. "He wasn't? Why'd he pick up the pictures then? And how'd he know they were here?"

"Because he saw me yesterday. I think that's the guy who tried to run me down."

The old man registered surprise. "The accident?"

"That's what he wanted it to look like," Sammy theorized. She'd finally stopped shaking. "But, believe me, Mr. Brewster, that was no accident."

"Why would someone try to hurt you?"

Why? Now that was the million-dollar question. Sammy had no idea. But since the pictures were of Taft and his protesters, she felt certain the good Reverend had to be involved. "I don't know," she responded. *But I intend to find out.*

Who's there?

Silence, then static.

Brian McKernan's nicotine-stained fingers skittered over the keys and levers of the graphic equalizer. Earlier he'd transferred Sammy's cassette to quarter-inch tape. Now he adjusted each frequency bandwidth, attempting to minimize the hiss and enhance the quality of the recorded conversation. He replayed the tape and the static became: *It's*—

Brian couldn't make out the next word. He ran the tape back and forth a few times, to no avail. Frustrated, he moved forward, planning to return and enhance the dialogue later.

I said, who's there? This voice was easy to hear.

Brian recognized rustling sounds—movement?—and then a door opening.

Wadda ya want? The loud voice again. Slurred. Someone had been on quite a bender, Brian thought as he moved on to another stretch of static. By adjusting the tracks, he was able to identify the words.

Then—*need to talk.*

After a few beats, the door slammed shut.

The engineer stopped the tape and removed his earphones. He rubbed his temples with two fists. His shoulders were aching. He'd been sitting hunched over the board for more than two hours and was only a third through the recording. No way he'd finish today. And he still had several commercials to put on carts for this week's radio shows.

He pulled a pack of Marlboros from his shirt pocket, removed the last one, and lit it. Drawing hard on the cigarette, he blew smoke into the air. What the heck was Sammy up to now? He liked the feisty redhead — even when she handed him assignments he hardly had time for. Still, after hearing only part of the tape, he couldn't shake the feeling that this time she might be sticking her nose into something sinister. Whoever she'd been talking to at the start of the conversation had been very specific.

I've learned that sometimes it's better to let sleeping dogs lie. Stay as far away from this as you can.

Rewinding the reel, he shook his head. No question. Those words came through loud and clear.

5:45 P.M.

At five forty-five, Sammy slipped into the psychology conference room and took an empty chair at the oak table. Dr. Osborne acknowledged her entrance with a nod, then returned his attention to the young man seated to his left.

"Mr. Stevens brings up a very interesting question," Osborne continued. "Why should scientific fraud be any more immoral than fraud in industry, politics, or even marriage?" The psychology professor searched the faces of the five young men and three young women attending his graduate seminar. The students all wore jeans and sweatshirts. Osborne, however, was nattily dressed in a three-piece suit and Gucci loafers.

"Because," an attractive Hispanic student was ready with an answer, "fraud in the other areas isn't as critical to our lives."

Osborne raised an eyebrow. "How so?"

"Well, scientists confirm theories by setting up tests."

"Experiments," Osborne suggested.

The Hispanic student nodded. "If the theory is wrong, the tests won't work, so you develop new theories. But when experimental results are faked, you won't find out if a theory is right or wrong, maybe for a long time. If a medicine will cure, if a power plant is safe, if a plane will fly." Her face reddened with passion, "People could die."

"She's right," another student remarked. "Fraud in science kills the meaning of science."

"If that's true, why would scientists betray their principles?" an earnest blonde in a tight turtleneck challenged.

"Come on," a long-haired young man sitting beside her responded, "The three *F*'s: Fame, Fortune and Faculty appointments."

Another student broke in through the chuckles. "We all know how competitive scientific research is; the pressure to produce so many papers in so many years. Publish or perish. The system's bound to tempt some of us."

"Yeah, you're right," still another agreed. "In academia at least, cheating is an evolved and often highly adaptive trait."

The comment evoked a round of appreciative laughter from her classmates.

"Psychology meets anthropology," Osborne summarized. "Sounds like a good way to end class for the day." He checked his course syllabus. "Next time, let's review the Solomon Asch experiment. Oh, and by the way, anyone who wants to submit final papers on disk is welcome to do so. No sense in wasting trees."

"PC or Mac?" someone asked.

"Either. I'm bi-literate." Osborne shrugged good-naturedly. He waited for the group to file out before joining Sammy.

"Lively discussion," she remarked.

"Yes, grad seminars tend to develop a life of their own." He shifted his weight slightly and scratched his chin, apparently lost in some deep thought, then abruptly turned to her, "How about adjourning to Rodolfo's? I'm starved, and we can have that chat you requested. My treat."

"Sounds great."

They left the office and walked the three blocks from the Psych building to the only serious Italian restaurant in St. Charlesbury. The owners were third-generation Romans whose flair for risotto and saltimbocca more than made up for their restaurant's utilitarian atmosphere. And Rodolfo's was just pricey enough to guarantee that EU students didn't frequent the establishment — especially on weeknights. The few patrons present when they walked in were university staff and St. Charlesbury locals who sat in cozy, candlelit booths and spoke in soft tones.

"So nice to see you again, Professor Osborne." Rodolfo himself escorted them to their seats, then rattled off the evening's specials.

"Can you order?" Sammy asked. "I'm afraid anything beyond basic pasta and pizza is out of my league."

"Sure." Osborne quickly scanned the menu. "For the lady, the nodino di vitello. For myself, the risotto con porcini and a small carafe of your house red wine."

Rodolfo nodded his approval and disappeared into the kitchen. Seconds later he reappeared with a big bowl of pinzimonio. Osborne offered Sammy the Italian crudités with balsamic vinaigrette, then took a few for himself. Between bites, Sammy found herself sharing her feelings about Sergio's death with the psychologist.

"I guess I took it as hard as anyone, and I never really knew him. He was so young." She fidgeted, trying to articulate her thoughts. "I know I'm overreacting — being unprofessional. I mean, if you want to be a good journalist, you can't get involved."

Osborne stopped chewing and stared at her. His eyes softened as he seemed to search for an appropriate response. "You're a human being. You can't help but get involved."

"I suppose. But it's even worse when you get involved and you can't do anything." Sammy took another bite of her antipasto. "Like Professor Conrad. If I'd only realized that he was in that much trouble. I keep thinking, I might've been able to help."

"Blaming yourself?"

"I guess."

"How could you have known what he was going to do? Did he say something was wrong?"

He didn't have to, Sammy thought as she recalled Conrad's alcoholic indulgence that night. And the warning. Just the rambling of a depressed and paranoid mind? She was about to ask Osborne for his opinion when Rodolfo reappeared with the entrees and wine. The owner poured a small amount for Osborne who sniffed, then sipped the Chianti before declaring it "delicious."

Rodolfo filled both glasses, then left them to "buon apetito."

Osborne took a sip, leaned back and continued, "Sorry, you were saying?"

Conrad. She shook her head. She knew the answer. "I know there's nothing I could've done. But I feel like I should have —" She left the sentence unfinished.

"'Should' is a word we learn not to use in psychology. It's still a struggle. Even for me."

"With all your training?"

"Psychotherapeutic training is an ongoing process. Inappropriate guilt isn't limited to our patients," Osborne said, focusing his attention on his main course.

They ate in silence, accompanied by "Al di la" from a ceiling-mounted stereo speaker. Sammy's veal chop was very tender, the green peppers the perfect complement. She hadn't realized how hungry she was. Osborne made his way resolutely through a mountain of smooth textured, pork laced rice, ate most of the crudités, and refilled his wineglass twice. "Tell me," he said finally, wiping his mouth, "how did you get interested in radio?"

Sammy pushed her plate aside. "Actually I want to be a journalist. Radio just happens to be today's medium. It's the best way to get information to the most people."

"I see. And why journalism?"

Sammy thought for a moment. "I guess I've always felt the need to understand."

"Understand?"

"How things happen, why they happen."

"And what things happened to you that you haven't been able to understand?"

Sammy's throat closed. The words came slowly. "I, uh. My mother's death. She killed herself. I was seven." Sammy swallowed a burning lump. "The truth is, I thought I was over it — I hadn't had the nightmares for years and then these suicides on campus brought it all back. I never understood why she did it."

"And why you survived?"

Sammy was stunned. "Yeah. Silly, huh?"

Osborne's eyes were full of sympathy, his voice gentle. "Not silly at all. It's only natural to feel that way. We call it 'survivors' guilt.' " He explained how family left behind often blame themselves for staying alive when their loved one chose to die. "But that's the point, Sammy. *They* chose to die. Ultimately it was their decision, not yours."

"I hear you, but it's still hard to accept." She found herself recounting her visit that afternoon with Karen Conrad and the surprising news of reconciliation.

The information seemed to astonish Osborne as well. "Perhaps she was engaging in a bit of wishful thinking," he offered.

"I don't think so. But then it doesn't all make sense." She presented her theory that the professor couldn't have killed himself because he didn't fit the typical profile.

"Typical profile. You sound like one of my grad students." Osborne's smile was tolerant. "Psychology, I'm afraid, is not an exact science. Despite all our attempts to categorize and profile individuals, they are just that — individuals — each with a unique set of needs and motivations. I think I knew Connie as well as anyone and, much as I hate to admit it, my efforts to pull him out of his depression failed."

Rodolfo appeared again, this time with a tray of desserts. Osborne selected the tiramisu. Sammy declined the sweets. They both ordered cappuccino.

Sammy waited for the coffees before asking, "So the fact that his tenure wasn't decided yet wouldn't have precluded his killing himself?"

Osborne shook his head. "Fear of failure is sometimes more frightening than failure itself. Connie set very high standards for himself."

"And those around him, I hear."

"Yes. And he was very unforgiving. Especially to himself. Unfortunately, the Connie I knew had a self-destructive personality." Osborne took a bite of his tiramisu. "Look, Sammy, it's not unusual for someone who has experienced suicide in a close relative or friend to feel obsessed with the need to explain the act in others as well. It's a way of working through those feelings of guilt I was talking about before."

She considered his words, reluctantly acknowledging their truth. There was guilt inside her, so buried, so denied, that she could not or would not face all these years. "You think I need a shrink?"

Osborne's laugh was warm. "A little counseling couldn't hurt." He finished the tiramisu in one final forkful. "I'd be happy to make myself available, if you'd like."

"That's very kind."

"Not at all. It's my job. I have regular hours at Student Counseling." He motioned Rudolfo over for the check and paid the bill.

"If you're serious, I might just take you up on your offer."

"Fine," Osborne said, getting up. "I'll tell my scheduling clerk to expect your call."

7:00 P.M.

"Yeah?" A well-endowed blonde in a tight T-shirt and cutoffs answered Pappajohn's knock. He recognized her as a member of the Ellsford cheerleading squad.

"Sergeant Pappajohn, campus police." He held out his badge. She didn't bother to inspect it.

"You have a peephole and a chain." He stepped into the spacious living room. "You ought to be more careful about opening that door to strangers." How these college kids could be so oblivious to potential danger was a constant amazement to the ex-street cop.

The blonde ignored his warning, leaving the door unlatched behind him.

"This Bud Stanton's place?"

"Yeah."

"Is he in?" Pappajohn scanned the room. The girl seemed to be alone. From where he stood, he could see a bedroom off to one side, a small kitchen and dining area off to the other. Not your typical dorm accommodation. Obviously one of the perks of a basketball star.

"He's out with the team." She smiled, displaying two rows of perfect white teeth. "You know—partying."

"Partying?"

"Yeah. They're going to the playoffs now for sure." The girl walked over to the cushioned sofa in the middle of the room and settled down on the pillows like a kitten marking off its territory. She'd been watching TV and now turned the volume back up—some insipid sitcom with a laugh track.

"I heard he was having trouble with bio," Pappajohn said over the ersatz giggles.

Engaged in the boob tube, the girl didn't reply.

"I heard he was headed for an F."

Still no response.

Pappajohn saw the remote on the glass coffee table in front of the sofa and, reaching over, punched "Mute."

"Hey!" she protested.

"As I was saying, I thought he was going to flunk."

Irritated, she grabbed for the remote. "He'll pass." She searched the buttons to turn on the sound.

"Professor Conrad dying like that must have been a real lucky break for your boyfriend," Pappajohn said casually.

The blonde lowered the remote to her lap and looked up at him, eyes narrowed. "What do you mean?"

Pappajohn shrugged. "Nothing. I just heard Conrad wasn't planning to give him a break. And then—" He smiled, leaving the sentence unfinished.

Her tone was unfriendly. "Is Bud in some kind of trouble?"

"Should he be?"

She didn't answer for a few moments, then turned back to the TV with a shrug and flicked on the sound. "I don't know. I only see him at the games and like on weekends."

"You don't live together?"

"Coach doesn't allow it. Says it breaks an athlete's concentration."

"Coach ought to put a similar ban on TV," Pappajohn muttered to himself. The raucous laughter from the show was enough to irritate anyone. "You know when he's coming back?" he asked.

"Knowing Bud, it'll probably be late."

"Mind if I look around?"

"Suit yourself." She clicked up the volume another notch.

Pappajohn moved toward the bedroom. He strolled through the suite, taking inventory, not sure what he was looking for—some clue as to whether Stanton had any involvement with Conrad's death. He looked in the bedroom. There was a double bed, unmade, with white, Ellsford University-issue sheets. A walnut bureau, its drawers hanging open, revealed only rumpled socks, shirts, and underwear. Several tarnished trophies sat on its dusty surface amidst framed photos of Stanton alone and with other players. High school pictures, the sergeant surmised. There was less grit to Stanton's cocky grin.

The large closet was crammed with T-shirts and jeans and at least a dozen brand-name athletic shoes of different styles. Pappajohn wondered how many were gifts from eager advertisers. The rest of the closet held assorted sports equipment, most of it well worn. In the back was a paper file box, unlabeled.

Pappajohn peeked inside and pulled out one torn piece of crumpled yellowed paper. He unfolded it, smoothing it out on his knee. A list of numbers from 78 to 84 with adjacent letters, ABBCEBD remained on the fragment. Probably an old test answer key. Pappajohn pocketed the fragment, shaking his head. Impossible to trace the exam by now, but it could be useful when he talked to the boy himself.

Sighing, he wandered into the kitchen area. The tiny cooking space, small refrigerator, and a chipped porcelain sink were luxurious by dorm standards. There was also a counter with two barstools that served as a table and opened into the living room. Except for some leftover pizza, a half-finished carton of milk, and a six-pack of Coors, Pappajohn found the fridge empty — typical college diet. He scanned the notes and papers mounted on the refrigerator door next to the phone. A shopping list included chili dogs, fried chicken, beer, and more beer.

The other notes seemed to be reminders about this practice or that party. Nothing helpful. About to turn away, he noticed a folded sheet of paper held up by a basketball magnet and took a closer look. A few nondescript doodles along with several telephone numbers he recognized as campus exchanges filled corners of the page. Beside each number was a set of initials. He lifted the magnet, slid the paper from the fridge, and turned it over. It was a flyer announcing Reverend Taft's sermon last Sunday. Now that was interesting.

He leaned over the counter and waved the paper a few times in the air to get the cheerleader's attention. "What's this?"

This time she turned down the volume herself. "Just other girls, you know. I mean we're not monogamous or anything," she reported. "He thinks I'll be jealous. Like I care." Her smile was candid. "I get around, too."

Great. Pappajohn grimaced. Hadn't these kids heard about AIDS? Times certainly had changed, and from where he stood, it wasn't a change for the better. He wondered how their parents would react if they knew their children played Russian roulette with their bodies. "Actually, I was interested in the other side of this flyer. It's an announcement for one of Reverend Taft's sermons. Is your, uh, boyfriend involved with Taft's organization?"

She shrugged. "I don't know. Our relationship isn't exactly intellectual." The girl settled back on the sofa and returned to her TV.

Hopeless, Pappajohn slipped the flyer into his pants pocket. Obviously if he wanted more information, he'd have to talk to Stanton himself. But not tonight. He still had to go over the security plans for Nitshi Day. He'd catch up with the kid in a day or two. If there was a Taft connection, it could wait.

"Don't forget to put the chain on," he said as he walked to the door.

"Sure."

Pappajohn stood on the other side of the door and listened for a few moments. Nothing except the raucous laugh track. It was clear the girl had no intention of complying.

Hopeless. He sighed. *Absolutely hopeless*.

9:00 P.M.

There were three messages waiting for Sammy when she returned to her apartment that evening.

One from Larry reminded her to be at the Nitshi demonstration by noon. Brian called to let her know that he'd just begun working on the tape — he'd get back to her later that week. The third message was from Reed. His voice sounded more tired than usual.

"Don't call tonight. I just want to hit the sheets." Sammy was about to click off the machine when Reed came back on. "Oh, and before I forget, I didn't have time to check that pill bottle."

Another beat and Reed added, "I did get the autopsy report on Conrad. The man definitely committed suicide. Talk to you tomorrow."

Sammy rewound the machine, deleting the messages, then plopped onto the sofa, trying to digest the events of the day. What did it all mean? Yesterday, after the radio show, she'd doubted Conrad had killed himself. He hadn't fit the suicide profile — not from what the dean had told her about his chances for tenure. Even his ex-wife had agreed. But now with Reed's message, it seemed she was off base. She closed her eyes, running various scenarios through in her mind. Maybe Dr. Osborne was right. Her own experience with suicide had robbed her of a certain objectivity.

Then there was Professor Nakamura. Another suicide. With the same gun. She thought about what she'd learned that afternoon at the police station. There'd been virtually no investigation. Pappajohn had been the cop on the case; he'd signed the report. Did the Japanese microbiologist really kill himself or had Pappajohn been too lazy to dig? The cop certainly hadn't put himself out last year after the campus anti-abortion riot.

On the other hand, Sammy couldn't forget Conrad's expression when she'd questioned him about Nakamura or his cautioning her to be careful. Not to mention Pappajohn himself warning her to steer clear. *This poker game's out of your league.*

Clear of what? Suppose there really was more to all this? What if Pappajohn wasn't simply a retired cop looking for a regular paycheck with little or no work? What if someone told him not to look too hard into Nakamura's death? What if the deaths of Conrad and Nakamura were somehow related? That thought made her shiver.

Restless, she rose from the sofa, went into the bathroom, and washed her face. Her fatigue was visible in the reflection. She ran a finger through her frizzy copper-colored curls, shaking her head at its self-determination — no matter what, it would never be straight.

The phone's shrill jangle brought her back into the living room. "Yes?" she asked, picking up the receiver on the third ring.

"Miss Greene, this is Mr. Brewster. Sorry to call so late."

"Oh, no, that's okay. What's up?"

"Well, I was working in the darkroom this evening and darned if I didn't find a few of the pictures you'd brought in."

"That's great!"

"Don't get too excited. I'm afraid they're pretty underdeveloped. That's why I must've laid them aside. Probably got interrupted by one of your schoolmates coming in the store. Always in a hurry."

Sammy smiled at the old man's characteristic surliness.

"If you come by tomorrow, you can have them."

"Thanks. By the way, did you notice a man with a mustache in any of the shots?"

"Nope, can't say that I did."

"I appreciate your calling, Mr. Brewster. I'll be there before noon."

"Eh yup."

Hanging up, Sammy walked over to the window and stared out at the velvety layers of darkness. A peaceful facade, but somewhere out there was a man who had tried to run her down. Yesterday, she was willing to consider her near miss an accident. Today, she was certain it was intentional. Why? Obviously the man had followed her to the photo shop and claimed her photos. There must be something — or someone — in the pictures of last week's demonstration worth killing her for. *My God. Could Reverend Taft be behind this?* She always knew he was evil. But was he really capable of murder?

As she settled into bed, she acknowledged that without solid answers, no one would listen to her claims — not Larry Dupree, not Dean Jeffries, not Sergeant Pappajohn, not Reed, probably not even Professor Osborne. She closed her eyes, overwhelmed by exhaustion. Tomorrow, she intended to really start digging.

It took her a long time to fall asleep and when she did, it was a restless slumber punctuated by bad dreams. In the middle of the night, she got up to check that the door and windows were locked.

CHAPTER SIX

WEDNESDAY

Harvey Barnes was hunched over his counter studying the *St. Charlesbury Gazette* and sipping steaming black coffee from a Styrofoam cup. The young pharmacist looked up when he saw Reed. "Jeez, I thought I'd have a few moments of solitude before the stampede."

Reed smiled at his friend. "I'm the one who should complain. I've been up for more than twenty-four hours. You just spent the night in a nice warm bed — with a gorgeous lady, I might add." Reed had been a guest at Harvey's wedding two months earlier. Carolyn Barnes was indeed beautiful.

Harvey leaned back and grinned. "You could drop medicine for a saner profession, you know." He waved his arm at the bright rows of organized medications behind him.

"Too late. I'm in the home stretch," Reed took the pill bottle from his lab coat pocket and placed it on the counter.

"So, what's this?"

"You tell me. My friend asked me to find out what's in there."

Harvey grabbed the vial, uncapped it, and shook out the two tablets into his palm. He held one up, turned it over and over, looking for some kind of telltale marking. "Well, it's not anything on patent," he said. "Could be a generic. Anything specific you were thinking about?"

"Maybe an antidepressant. Something in the barbiturate family."

"Hmm." Harvey frowned at his hand.

Reed knew his friend well. He was smart and he was competitive. The two had taken organic chemistry together—a difficult course that Harvey had aced with ease. "I know you're busy, if you want me to ask someone else—"

Harvey waved away the challenge, never taking his eyes from the mystery white tablets. "Interesting."

"Appreciate your help."

Aware that patients were beginning to push through the open doors, Harvey slid the tablets back into the bottle and stashed it under the counter. "Looks like the rush is on. I'll get on this when my shift ends."

"No hurry."

"Hey, it's fun doing a little research for a change. Counting out pills all day can be a drag," the pharmacist admitted. "If it's a simple ID, I'll have an answer for you tomorrow. If I have to do a chemical analysis, it'll be Friday at the earliest."

"Popping those like candy today aren't you?"

Pappajohn put down his almost empty roll of antacids, and bestowed a grumpy stare upon his gray-haired secretary who'd just returned from a two-week vacation. "Well, don't count on resting now that you're back. Nitshi is turning into a nightmare."

"Don't worry. The rent-a-cops will be here by eight." The secretary pulled out a folded paper and smoothed it out on the desk. "Did you make any changes?"

"Some. I added two or three more stations. They're in red."

Edna frowned. "Don't you think we should have at least four men around the podium?"

"I don't have four men. I'm stretched to the limit already. We've got eight up at North Campus. We're expecting up to two thousand at last count."

The secretary's eyebrows went up. "And the Nitshi Building?"

"They promised their own security. We'll have to live with that."

"The place is a fortress already."

Nodding, Pappajohn looked at his watch impatiently. Seven fifteen. Time for another antacid.

"Mr. Brewster, you're a lifesaver."

The crusty Vermonter accepted the compliment with his usual noncommittal "eh yup" and handed Sammy a pile of black-and-white prints from the animal rights demonstration. Out of the original twenty-four, Brewster had only been able to salvage seven.

Sifting through them, Sammy located a shot of Taft. Her flash had caught the Reverend head-on, and just as she'd been that day, she was struck by the raw fire in his dark eyes. Two black-red orbs floating in the underdeveloped ghostly face.

Sammy drew herself away and skimmed through the other pictures. Brewster had been right — no man with the mustache. Instead there were a couple of views of the lone tech trying to stop the demonstrators and several profile and face-on shots of students she didn't recognize. The exercise wasn't futile, however, because two faces were familiar — the young woman who had leaked plans for Taft's next demonstration to Sammy after the Sunday service and, standing just behind the short, stocky, older-looking fellow was Luther Abbott.

The cadre of campus police and contract security officers crowded into the small office. Pappajohn faced his troops like a drill sergeant. Behind him was a rickety portable blackboard with a roughly drawn facsimile of a campus map.

"The chancellor, Senator Joslin, and Mr. Nitshi. We'll move the crowd around the press area down the brick path to North Campus. We've got cones up to reroute the traffic toward Lot Nine."

The phone on Edna Loomis's desk rang as one of the security officers raised his hand. Pappajohn nodded at the guard.

"You expecting trouble from the Tafties?"

Pappajohn's indigestion was reflected in his expression. "Not with the coverage we've set up, but I want everybody online." He tapped the walkie-talkie on his belt. "Just in case."

"Chief, sorry to bother you."

Pappajohn turned to see Edna standing beside him.

"Call from Senator Joslin's office. Seems he's gotten himself a touch of the flu — won't be flying up after all."

Pappajohn returned to his blackboard. "That should save us about a half hour of hot air. Let's be ready to move them out by quarter to one."

"Reverend, when do we go?"

"Right after Senator Joslin," Taft instructed the placard-carrying group of young men and women. "Move out in front of the press area. Keep the signs facing the cameras. We'll start the chanting slowly and pump up the volume as soon as Ishida gets to the podium. Try drowning him out as much as possible."

"What about the cops?" asked a short-haired girl.

"Let them come after you. Don't resist. Just collapse and let them do all the work. Pappajohn's Boy Scouts'll have trouble carrying anything bigger than a donut."

Several of the students chuckled at Taft's remark. He continued, very seriously. "Remember, no matter what happens, make sure it's on camera. We want a record of their interference with our First Amendment Rights."

The Office of Contracts and Grants was tucked away in the basement of the university library. Inside the newly remodeled space, five full-time and three part-time personnel provided administrative support for all university research projects. Their salaries came from the forty-two cents of indirect costs added to each dollar government and private agencies paid Ellsford University. All excess monies went into the university's general coffers. It was a tidy sum. Each year Ellsford professors managed to bring in well over one hundred million dollars.

Silence greeted Sammy as she pushed through the double doors. Where was everyone? She wandered down several rows of cabinets before she noticed a young man with a ponytail carrying a stack of files. His ID badge read: JON-ERIK SCONYERS, STUDENT ASSISTANT. "Excuse me? Do you work here?"

"Yeah, whatcha need?"

"Well, my T.A. asked me to check sources of private funding for a prospective project."

"Yeah. In what?"

"Molecular genetics."

"You're lucky. We just put everything on computer." He led her to a walled-off cubby and pointed to a PC on the desktop. "All the medical and science contracts and grants since eighty-three. To retrieve the data, just type in the field." He flipped on the screen. "If you need help, holler."

"Thanks." Sammy sat down in front of the computer and typed in "Molecular Genetics" on the keyboard. The word "Searching" appeared in a corner of the screen, followed rapidly by "Forty-five Entries." She called them up. Immediately the screen filled with research projects. Scrolling through, she squinted at the tiny, green luminescent print, most of the titles far beyond her understanding: "Hypothesis for the dual control of CFTR by PKA and ATP," "Effects of MPTP and Gm1 Ganglioside Treatment on TH Immunochemistry of the Squirrel Monkey Putamen," "Triplet Repeat Mutations in Human Disease," "Cloning and Expression of Recombinant Proteins in Bacillus Systems," "Site-directed Mutagensis and DNA Sequencing."

Beside each was the funding source and the name of the researcher. But it was difficult to find, and at this rate, she might be here a while.

Jumping up, Sammy sought out the student assistant still filing away hard copies of old grants. "Excuse me?"

"Yeah?"

"Is there any other way to get to the funding sources besides the field itself?"

The ponytailed student nodded. "Sure. Everything's cross-referenced by government institution, private organization, and principal investigator."

"Oh. Good."

"I did some of the programming myself." Sconyers smiled with obvious pride. "Need help?"

"I think I'm okay now." Returning to the cubby, Sammy quickly keyed in "Conrad, Barton." Within seconds, she was staring at a long list of projects headed by the genetics professor. The most recent seemed to be funded by government agencies like the NIH and NSF. Money for work done three to five years before, however, came mainly from private sources.

She jotted down the names: Biotech Development Corporation, Virology Research Foundation, and NuVax, Inc.—none familiar to her. Beside each she wrote the project title and grant award. Several corresponded to journal articles she'd found at his home. When she was done, she had a list of five grants totaling close to a quarter of a million dollars.

Remembering that Yitashi Nakamura's name had also been on several of the journal articles, she typed in "N-A-K-A-M" and waited for the program to produce his sources of project capital. Not surprising, the same three private companies that funded Conrad had supported Nakamura's work as well. The older scientist had a prodigious output—twenty-three grants over a five-year period, each amounting to more than one hundred thousand dollars. The largest, however, was for one million. Sammy scanned through the scientific jargon until she found the financier: Nitshi Corporation.

Interesting, she thought, tilting back in her chair.

And then she remembered.

She pitched forward onto her feet.

Nitshi Day! Her Swatch read quarter to twelve. Switching off the computer, she hurried out the double doors, and headed toward North Campus. If she raced like crazy, maybe she'd make it in time.

• • •

As Sammy ran, she noticed cars parked along all the side streets leading to North Campus. More than a few had out-of-state license plates — especially New York and Massachusetts. As she got closer, she had to slow for people walking in groups — not only students, but also locals and their families. There were enough youngsters that Sammy surmised the schools let them off for the event.

Yesterday's storm clouds had vanished, along with the little snow that had stuck to the ground, leaving a spectacularly clear fall afternoon, a perfect backdrop for a carnival. Just behind the Nitshi Research Institute were a half dozen game and food booths along with a mini Ferris wheel and a house of mirrors. Facing the striking modern four-story, glass-and-steel structure, a grandstand seated several hundred. It was already filled to capacity, with a large spillover crowd standing in front and around the sides. A small wooden stage with a speaker's podium had been erected in front of the institute. Seated behind the podium were Chancellor Ellsford and a distinguished looking Asian man who seemed vaguely familiar. Several newspaper photojournalists hoisted cameras, while more than one television crew set up equipment nearby.

Sammy scanned the crowd until she located Larry Dupree standing to the right of the platform. Or, rather, pacing.

"For God's sake, Sammy, where have you been? They're going to start any minute."

"Sorry. Tracking down a lead."

Larry rolled his eyes in exasperation. He nodded at the remote set-up where Brian had built a clattertrap collection of boxes and wires perched precariously beside a group of well-dressed, short-haired students.

With the ever-present cigarette drooping from his lips, Brian moved in and handed her a portable microphone and headset. He whispered, "Speaking of leads, I think I've got something for you."

Sammy's face brightened. "The tape? What'd you get?"

"No time to tell you now. I've still got more cleaning up to do, but I should be done by tonight. I'll call when I'm through, and we can meet at the studio." He caught Larry's eye and said more loudly, "Let's go. Ready in five, four, three. We're live."

"Good afternoon, Ladies and Gentlemen," a campus administrator shouted into a squeaking microphone. "Welcome to Ellsford University's celebration of Nitshi Day, sponsored by the Nitshi Corporation. With us today is Nitshi Chief Executive Officer Yoshi Ishida, and—"

Sammy glanced at her Swatch. It was exactly noon.

"—a long and productive cooperative association." Smiling at the guests seated beside him, Chancellor Ellsford eased back to his chair on the podium.

Swallowing a yawn, Sammy spoke softly into her microphone. "That was Chancellor Ellsford who just spoke for about twenty minutes on the cooperative relationship between the university and industry, specifically the Nitshi Corporation. The chancellor stressed that this association would improve research and educational opportunities for Ellsford students and faculty. His speech was met with some resistance from a group of protesters opposed to foreign investment in our colleges." She glanced at the clean-cut group to her right and was startled to recognize the young woman she'd seen outside Taft's service in its midst. She scanned the students for Luther Abbott, but didn't see the angry young man among the crowd.

The hyperactive administrator-announcer had just finished introducing the next speaker and Sammy quickly returned to her report. "In just a minute, we'll be hearing from Nitshi CEO Ishida."

A burst of applause and a few scattered boos signaled the start of Ishida's speech.

He began in soft, clear, and articulate English. "Ladies and Gentlemen. We are pleased to be able to join you today to honor scientists and men of knowledge."

Sammy now recalled where she had seen the handsome Japanese man before. Two long days ago, he was coming out of Dean Jeffries's office.

• • •

Though everything was proceeding surprisingly smoothly, Pappajohn felt his stomach churning. Things were going too well. As he reached in his pocket for a new roll of antacids, his walkie-talkie squawked. It was Edna Loomis from the office.

"Phone call for you, Chief."

"Patch it through," he said, a worried edge to his voice. He knew Edna wouldn't interrupt for anything trivial.

"Sergeant Pappajohn?" The voice was barely audible through the static.

"Speak up. I can't hear you."

A group of marchers next to the grandstand began to shout loudly.

"You Pappajohn?" the caller asked again.

Pappajohn struggled to hear above the growing chanting. "That's right. And who are you?"

"That don't matter. You just need to know there's gonna be trouble today."

"What kind of trouble?" he demanded.

"Just remember the Concord Mall."

Pappajohn froze. The explosion at the Boston shopping center six years ago had killed eight people, including two children. "What the hell—?" he shouted into the speaker. Too late. The connection had been severed. He clicked the button and his secretary came back on the system. "Edna, call the phone company and get that number traced right away."

Before she could respond, he was sending a message to his officers. "Code Red. Phase One Alert."

A tall, dark-haired boy gave the signal. The well-dressed group pulled their placards from behind the grandstand and began marching toward the stage. "L-O-V-E," they chanted in unison. "Let our values endure!" As they formed a ten-deep phalanx around the stage, their shouts grew louder and more strident. "USA for Americans! Foreign interests go home!"

• • •

Pappajohn elbowed his way through the crowd. Caught in the middle of the protestors, he lost sight of his fellow officers closing in on the podium from all sides.

Within seconds, Sammy realized something was seriously wrong. Taft's group had taken center stage, but their shouts were now overpowered by a swarm of gathering policemen focused on evacuating the audience rather than arresting the protesters. One uniformed guard leaped onto the dais and with a few whispered words, urged an alarmed contingent of Ellsford brass to jump off toward the rear.

Sammy was certain that among the panic she heard the word "bomb." Amidst the confusion, she couldn't locate Larry, though she did catch Brian's eye from across the wall of students as she wended her way toward the podium. The engineer had extinguished his cigarette and was frantically waving for her to return to the outskirts of the scurrying audience. She shook her head and pressed on, surrounded by the hysterical screams and shouts from the crowd.

It happened with horrifying speed: an excruciating burst of sound, a blinding sheet of flame, followed by towers of smoke. The podium exploded in a shower of splinters trailing red, white, and blue streamers. Sammy's last memory was of two strong arms pushing her down onto the hard dirt ground.

NITSHI RESEARCH INSTITUTE
FOURTH FLOOR

Though her head felt cottony, Lucy fought sleep. She needed to think. With the shades down, it was impossible to tell exactly what time it was. She only knew it was night because the nurse had just told her so.

Night?

How long had she been here? A few hours? A few days? She couldn't remember. Ever since she'd gotten up and tried to take a walk down the hall, the staff had kept a vigilant eye on her. Every hour on the hour, gloved and masked, they tiptoed in on crepe-soled shoes, their footsteps never disturbing the gentle hum of the laminar flow equipment. Taking vital signs, checking her IV, bringing meals.

"You're too weak," had been Dr. Palmer's explanation.

"But won't I get weaker lying in bed all day?"

Dr. Palmer assured her with a gentle pat on the arm. "You'll get weaker if you don't follow orders." He'd removed a syringe from the pocket of his white coat, plunged the needle point into her IV tubing, and emptied the colorless fluid.

"What's that?"

"Just something to calm you down. I know this is all very strange and I know you're frightened. This will help."

"I'd feel much better if I could just talk to my parents and see my friends."

He'd smiled. "I'm afraid that's not possible. But don't worry. I've called them all, and they know you're in good hands."

She'd returned the doctor's smile — more resigned than convinced.

That had been when? she wondered now. Yesterday? This afternoon? She wasn't sure. All she knew was that she felt terribly alone. Alone and afraid. Looking around her white sterile room, she had the strangest sensation that she wasn't so much in a hospital as a prison.

Sammy's first conscious feeling was the throbbing pain in her head. For a moment she lay still, her eyes squeezed shut, then finally she risked opening them.

"Hello there." Reed smiled down at her.

She tried sitting up, but was assaulted by a wave of dizziness. "My head."

"Whoa, take it easy." Reed gently touched the bandage covering her temple. "It took twelve stitches to close that gash. You suffered a mild concussion."

"Where am I?"

"Ellsford General," Reed reported. "You were injured in the blast."

Blast? She vaguely remembered people running, screams around her, then the sound of a loud explosion. But after that, it was as if a curtain had been dropped over the scene. It was blank.

"You're lucky," Reed added. "The CT scan was normal; no broken bones, no intracranial bleeding."

"Then why was I admitted?"

"Just routine observation. You can check out tomorrow."

Sammy surveyed her private room. It was small, but comfortably decorated—more like a three-star hotel than a hospital, with carpeted floors, curtained windows, even a TV that had been turned on, the sound muted. In the dull light of dusk that filtered through the window, the images flickered silently across the screen like an old kinescope.

"Anyone else hurt?"

"Don't worry about that now. You need to rest."

"Don't baby me, Reed." Her mind conjured a vision of sheets of flames in a web of piercing screams. "What happened?" She pushed herself up on her elbows, ignoring the throbbing in her forehead.

"Evidently a pipe bomb was planted near the podium," Reed explained.

Nitshi Day. She did remember someone yelling about a bomb. That's when pandemonium had broken out.

Reed's voice was reassuring as he guided her back down. "All your people are fine. The cops managed to disperse most of the crowd."

"And the rest?"

"We got about thirty injured, most not too badly," Reed said. "They were treated in the ER and discharged. Including your buddy, Pappajohn."

Another flashback—the campus cop pushing her down, saving her life. "Is he okay?"

"A broken arm, some bruised ribs. The physical injuries aren't bad, but he's taken this pretty hard. Feels responsible for the one . . ." Reed hesitated, "the one who didn't make it."

Sammy sat up quickly now — pain or no pain. "My God. Anybody —?"

"A student. Katie Miller. Protesting with that born-again group."

"How can Pappajohn blame himself?"

"I don't know." Reed shrugged. "But he wanted to leave the hospital and start tracking down the bad guys right away."

The six p.m. local news had just started with a camera pan of the Nitshi Day crowd, followed by a tight shot of Yoshi Ishida speaking. A moment later there was a jostled view of an explosion and the ensuing chaos.

"Turn that up!" Sammy ordered.

Reed clicked the remote.

"Senator Joslin, you canceled your plans to attend today's celebration at Ellsford University due to illness. Your constituents in Vermont are wondering if you could've been the target of the mad bomber."

"An unfortunate coincidence," the senator responded. "But let me say that we will never condone this kind of violence anywhere in this great country. I've already conferred with the university chancellor who promises a full investigation."

"Senator, there's a rumor circulating that you may have ties to Reverend Taft, that —"

Sammy studied the Republican senator as the aristocratic-looking face changed from his usual on-camera Olympian expression to suppressed anger. *Interesting and understandable*. Six months ago the man had barely managed to squelch talk of philandering. Any new scandal could ruin his reelection plans.

"I can only surmise that such rumors are politically motivated. I have never been involved with extremist groups."

Another picture of Nitshi Day flashed across the screen — this time the young Tafties marching toward the stage chanting "Let our values endure!" "USA for Americans!" and "Foreign interests go home."

"Meanwhile, the investigation into the bombing itself has led to speculation that Reverend Taft or at least some member of his right-wing group may be responsible, although the exact motive is unclear. Mr. Grant Stone, assistant director of the FBI was quoted as saying that his organization does plan to question the religious leader and his staff. A spokesman for the Reverend has vehemently denied any involvement in the incident."

"I don't care what he denies." Sammy declared. "It *had* to be Taft."

"How can you be so sure?"

"I knew he planned to disrupt Nitshi Day. I just never—" She grabbed the remote from Reed and clicked off the TV. "Damn him. If only I'd been able to stop him last year after the abortion rights demonstration, this would never have happened."

"Aren't you taking on a little more responsibility than is fair?" Reed asked. "Besides, what could possibly be Taft's motive?"

"The man has always hated Nitshi. Don't you remember the demonstrations he led before the research institute was built?"

"Sure, but there's still a long way from demonstrations to bombing."

Sammy shook her head. "I attended his Sunday sermon. You had to see the man on stage. It was as though he was—" she searched for the appropriate adjective, "possessed. He really believes he's been ordained by God himself to lead mankind into the light."

These forces of evil seek to destroy the foundations of America and American greatness.

"Nitshi represents everything he hates—a foreign corporation trying to control an American university."

"They don't control Ellsford."

"But they do fund a significant amount of research here, don't they?"

"Well, it's true that with so much federal funding gone, the university is becoming more dependent on private sources," Reed conceded. "Big science costs big money."

Sammy nodded, reminded of the millions worth of grants awarded to Professors Nakamura and Conrad by corporate sponsors. "Taft sees himself as some holy crusader fighting the corrupting influence of this major foreign company."

Reed remained unconvinced. "Academics receive industry funding all the time, Sammy. It doesn't necessarily bias their results. If anything, it may positively influence the direction of the work."

"How do you mean?"

"Well, more academics are doing applied research these days."

"Applied?"

"As opposed to basic research," Reed explained. "Some might argue that in a perfect world, academic scientists should only do basic research — say, figuring out the cause of a specific disease — like AIDS — without concern for its treatment. The stark reality is that twelve years and ten billion taxpayers dollars into the AIDS epidemic, there's no cure in sight. On the other hand, applied research could mean the development of a new genetically engineered drug therapy or even a vaccine. In fact, that's what my preceptor, Dr. Palmer, is working on."

"A new drug?"

"No, a vaccine. It's really pretty exciting. He's taking the basic research of people like Giorgi, Shearer, Nakamura and —"

"Yitashi Nakamura?" Sammy interrupted.

"How do you know about him?"

She grabbed her purse that someone had placed on the nightstand by her bed and found the list of article titles she'd copied down that morning. "Take a look." She handed him the paper. "I was doing background on Professor Conrad. According to Dean Jeffries, Nakamura brought Conrad here, so when I looked up his grants, I checked Nakamura's as well. I thought maybe you could explain the research."

Reed examined the titles. "I'd have to see the original papers, but obviously Conrad and Nakamura worked together for a while. At some point it looks like Nakamura did groundbreaking work on cell-mediated immunity or CMI. He felt that the CMI arm of the immune system attacks cells already infected with certain viruses like HIV. That's what led Palmer to his vaccine strategy. So far it's been a success in monkeys, though human trials are still a few years away."

Sammy was half-listening, a thought beginning to churn. "And Conrad?"

"These last published papers indicate that he kept at his original thesis that humoral immunity is the key to protection against the HIV virus. Since the humoral arm of the immune system produces the antibodies that latch onto free-floating viruses, Conrad felt that it should prevent them from infecting cells in the first place."

Although Sammy didn't understand the science, her mind filled with vague connections: Nakamura and Conrad worked together on AIDS-related research, Taft abhorred homosexuality, it was likely a man like Taft would equate AIDS with being gay, and Taft hated Nitshi. "Tell me, does Nitshi fund any AIDS research?"

"Sure. NuVax, Inc. is funding Dr. Palmer's vaccine work. That's why he has a lab in the Nitshi Building."

Sammy perked up at this new information. "NuVax is a Nitshi company?"

"It's one of their subsidiaries."

"What about Biotech Development Corporation and Virology Research Foundation?" Sammy asked, checking the grant sources she'd copied down that morning.

"I'm pretty sure they're Nitshi companies, too."

Could Taft have targeted people working on Nitshi-funded AIDS-related projects? Sammy wondered. Nakamura. Conrad. Could Taft have actually killed them? Reed was right — demonstrations were a far cry from murder. It was too farfetched. And yet, she was convinced that the Reverend was mad. He could certainly be behind the theft of her pictures from the photo shop *and* the attempt to run her down.

If her theory was true, Dr. Palmer might be in danger. She had a fleeting notion to say something to Reed, but let it go. Right now she knew there was still a gaping hole in her hypothesis — like a smile with a missing tooth. Without proof, she was just speculating again. The tape. She needed to contact Brian and find out what he'd learned. Sammy abruptly swung her legs off the bed. "I have to go."

"What are you talking about?"

"There's a story here. I'm a reporter. I need to investigate."

"Why not leave the investigating to the professionals?"

"I *am* a professional."

"And so am I," Reed asserted. "Just because you passed my neurological exam doesn't mean you're in the clear yet." He stood implacably in front of her, a firm arm holding down each of her shoulders. "Any investigating will have to wait until tomorrow. That's an order."

Sensing that arguing would be fruitless, Sammy acquiesced. "All right. You're the doctor."

"Well, I'll just go check on a couple of my other patients. I'm off duty in less than an hour. How about a dinner date? I've always wanted to taste what General serves its customers."

"And I thought it was my charm."

"Oh, that too." He bent down to give her a gentle peck on the cheek.

Brian McKernan absentmindedly flicked an ash into his empty paper cup and glanced up at the clock on the wall of his tiny office in the W-E-L-L studio. Six fifteen. Just one more question to answer and he'd be done. Shame he'd have to wait until tomorrow to share the news with Sammy. Earlier he'd checked with the hospital and learned that she was fine, but would need to stay overnight. He'd left a message on her apartment answering machine to call the minute she got in.

He savored a final drag from his cigarette and dropped the butt into the cup with a half dozen others.

As he waited for Sammy's tape to rewind, he heard a faint noise in the studio beyond his office.

Tap, tap . . . tap, tap . . .

Almost like soft footsteps.

A cold sweat broke out on his scalp and along the back of his neck. "Who's there?"

He thought he heard the noise again, though this time he wasn't certain.

"Who is it?" His heart raced furiously. Everyone had gone home by five. "Larry is that you?"

He rose, stepped carefully over the debris of soda cans, paper cups, and candy wrappers littering the floor around his chair and slowly opened his office door. The studio was empty, lit only by horizontal slats of moonlight through a jalousie window.

He tiptoed in. "Anyone here?" Holding his breath, he listened for a minute.

Tap, tap . . . tap, tap . . .

His heart was thudding in his chest.

Tap, tap . . . tap, tap . . .

He located its source. Someone must have adjusted the window's glass louvers for ventilation. Wind was pushing branches of the old elms outside against the slats. The sound came again.

Tap, tap . . . tap, tap . . .

This is crazy, he thought, walking over to the window. Jumping at strange noises, looking for creatures lurking in the shadows.

Nothing there.

Just tree branches.

His imagination working overtime. Since the bombing that afternoon, he was, understandably, on edge. He readjusted the louvers and fastened the latch shut.

As he listened a minute longer, his muscles gradually relaxed, his heart slowed to its normal pace. He returned to his office, chastising himself for being such a wimp.

He lit a fresh cigarette, put on his earphones, and pressed the play button on the graphic equalizer. By now he was familiar with most of the tape's content.

I've learned that sometimes it's better to let sleeping dogs lie. Stay as far away from this as you can.

Fast forward.

Who's there?

Silence, then: *I said, who's there?*

It's me.

A door opening.

Wadda ya want?

We need to talk and, after a few beats, the sound of the door slamming shut.

What the hell is going on?

Where is it?

Give me the envelope and there won't be trouble.

I don't know what you're talking about.

Here it is.

Sounds of a struggle.

I'm afraid this is good-bye, buddy.

No!

A barely audible pop. Then almost two minutes of dead air and—

That strange sound again. It reminded Brian of something familiar. He backed up again and concentrated.

Ping!

One more time. *Ping!*

"Of course! That's it," Brian laughed. "That's it!"

For a moment Sammy fought the impulse to just lie back and seek the refuge of sleep. But she knew she had to find the energy to get moving before Reed returned. Damn, why didn't he understand? He had his work, she had hers.

Another spasm of dizziness swept over her as she attempted to stand. Sammy sat back on the edge of the bed and tried several calming breaths until the episode passed. Then she took a few measured steps to the closet where her clothes were hanging. The jeans were fine, but her blouse and sweater were sprinkled with bloodstains.

Running a nervous hand through her uncombed red curls, she stared at the somber image reflected in the closet door mirror. Dark smudges on the pale skin beneath her green eyes betrayed exhaustion, but there was more there than fatigue. Fear. That's what she saw. The kind of fear that came with knowing she'd come so close to dying — the second time in three days.

Maybe Reed was right. Maybe she should leave the investigating to the police. The face in the mirror considered his counsel, but just as quickly rejected it. Absolutely not! She would not give in to it. She was a journalist. She had to confront her fear, understand why this was happening, find the story within the story. And she had to do that herself.

Grabbing her clothes and slamming the closet door shut, she began to dress. The process took longer than she'd expected. Her arms and legs felt as if they were moving through molasses, her vision cloudy with streaks of gray. Finally, she slipped into her peacoat, staggered to the door, and opened it just a crack, peering up and down the hall for signs of her boyfriend.

Reed's white coat was heading down the hall away from her. She saw him stop at a room on the far end. After a brief conversation with the two campus cops acting as guards, he was waved in, and disappeared behind the door. A moment later, Pappajohn emerged. His left arm was in a sling, but otherwise he seemed okay. He merely nodded to the guards, then exited via the stairway a few doors down. What was going on in there?

Feigning control and nonchalance, Sammy entered the hall and walked down the tile-floored, pale gray corridor, hurrying past a visitors' area where a woman and teenaged boy sat playing cards. Neither looked up. As she neared the guarded room, she saw two men, dressed in gray overcoats and business suits, approach the campus cops. They flashed some sort of ID, and were immediately admitted. Sammy strolled by the door, hoping to glean a clue about the room's occupant, but the guards' icy expressions discouraged lingering.

She turned the corner and strode confidently past the nurses' station nearest to the elevators. Skimming names listed on the admissions board, she recognized only one of the hospitalized patients. The occupant of the guarded room was Bud Stanton. How was he involved with Taft? Another lead to follow.

"I'm sorry. He's not here." A blonde nurse spoke into the telephone as Sammy stood casually next to another nurse waiting by the elevator doors. "I don't know, sir, you'll have to talk to Dr. Palmer. Yes, sir, I know, but he's gone. Yesterday. No, I don't. Yes, thank you."

Sammy hit the elevator call button as the exasperated nurse hung up the phone. The elevator arrived and as she stepped on, she heard the blonde nurse shout, "Hold it!" Sammy froze, buttressing the door with her hip. Should she make a run for it?

She heard rapid footsteps behind her as she prepared to bolt. The blonde nurse, panting, raced past her into the elevator with a breathless "Thanks!" and moved to the back near her brunette colleague. Sammy eased into the elevator and leaned against the wall to steady herself. That was close.

"Did he call about Abbott again?" the brunette nurse asked her colleague as Sammy watched the floor numbers move downward from seven to two.

The blonde nodded. "It's not my job." She lowered her voice to a whisper. "Once they go to Nitshi—" She shrugged. "I gave him Palmer's number yesterday. He should've called."

"Yeah. Poor kid was looking pretty awful," sighed the brunette.

"They all do." The blonde shook her head as the door opened on the second floor. "I hear the chili's pretty good today," she added. The two nurses stepped off the elevator toward the hospital cafeteria, leaving Sammy standing inside. The smell of cooking wafting into the car made her nauseated, though she hadn't eaten since breakfast. Taking a few slow, deep breaths to stave off the feeling, she punched the lobby button to close the door.

An orderly transporting a young man on a gurney wheeled his load toward the half-open elevator. "Going up?"

Sammy indicated "down" with her thumb.

"I'll wait," he said as the doors snapped shut.

Heart pounding, she rode the rest of the way down alone. What was going on? First Stanton, now Abbott? She wondered if the nurse had meant Luther Abbott. Come to think of it, Sammy didn't recall seeing the young man at the protest today. Was he ill? If he saw Palmer, probably. But why would they send him to Nitshi? It was a research lab. Sammy shook her head. Another question to ask Reed. If he'd still talk to her, she'd wangle an escorted tour of the Nitshi Building tomorrow.

A few seconds later the elevator stopped at the lobby with a slight bounce, the doors slid open, and Sammy stepped out, almost running headlong into Dr. Osborne. Dressed more casually than usual, he wore a red wool V-neck sweater over a button-down cotton shirt and gray wool slacks, his overcoat draped over his arm. "Just the person I wanted to see," he declared.

"Me?"

"The dean asked me to talk with the students who'd been injured in the bombing—see if I could help ease some of the stress. Your name was on the list of patients admitted."

"I, uh, was just discharged."

"I'm certainly glad to see you're on your feet." Osborne slipped his coat back on. "Well, I guess I'm done here. Need a ride home?"

"I, uh, actually, I was going to stop by the radio station first."

Osborne nodded. "No problem," he said, pulling out and jiggling his car keys. "That's on my way, too."

The noise Brian heard earlier was not his imagination. Indeed, two men—one short and stocky, one tall and mustachioed, had jimmied the front door and entered the radio station. They'd hidden from the engineer until he'd returned to his office, then quietly spread a serpentine trail of acetone along the floor. When the stocky man signaled, his partner struck a match and threw it onto the snake, instantly igniting the wood-frame studio.

A piercing cold wind battered Sammy and Osborne as they walked out into the parking lot. Bundling up in their coats, they said little more until they were inside his Lexus 400 SC. Osborne turned the ignition key, gunned the engine, and adjusted the climate control to seventy-five degrees. "It'll be warm in a minute."

"Thanks." Sammy rubbed her hands together and fought back a shiver.

The sleek black car pulled out of the hospital lot onto Campus Drive. At North Campus, barricades blocked part of the road, forcing Osborne to slow down. Sammy peered through the foggy car window. The entire Nitshi Institute was brightly lit — an eerie backdrop to the now empty stage and grandstands. Although it was hard to see from a distance, the bomb had blown off a portion of the speakers' area, including the podium. The whole clearing, still littered with hurriedly discarded food and drink containers, was cordoned off by yellow police tape.

Sammy gasped.

Osborne stopped the car and turned to her. "You okay?" His expression was filled with concern.

"Not bad, considering," Sammy responded, her eyes still frozen on the scene out the window. "I'm one of the lucky ones." Unbidden tears appeared at the corners of her eyes. She wiped them away and cleared her throat. "Sorry."

"It's okay to cry. What happened today was horrendous. For everyone."

"I know, it's just that —" She took a deep breath. "I don't know why I —"

"Survived?" He completed her thought.

She nodded, afraid to speak for fear she might break down. Uncanny the way the psychologist seemed to tap into her innermost feelings. Almost as if he possessed some mysterious sixth sense that pierced her veil of self-deception.

"Look, you've been through a great deal more stress than you realize. I think it would do you some good to talk about it."

"I-I can't." She knew he was right, but —

"Not now. Sure." He stepped on the gas, driving off in the direction of the radio station. "When you're ready."

• • •

Brian felt the smoke before he smelled it. The heat touched his cheek like a lover's gentle kiss — warm at first, then insistent, pressing against his face until the acrid smell of burning acetone filled his nose and lungs and began to smother him.

He yanked off his earphones and grabbed the phone near his desk. Damn. The dial tone was gone. No way to call for help. Maybe he could — Shit! Where'd they put the fire extinguishers? Larry had dutifully held the yearly fire drill just a few weeks before, but like so many of the student staff, Brian never took the thought of death by fire seriously enough to attend. *Stupid, stupid, stupid,* he castigated himself, as his rapid search turned up nothing to help douse the fire. *Fuck it, better get out fast.*

He turned to the thick door only to see caustic yellow fumes seeping in under the jamb. Breathing was getting harder and harder. Grabbing a used napkin to cover his nose and mouth, he reached for the door with a hand. "Ow!" He pulled his burned fingers back, shaking them in the air. The first wave of panic hit. *No way out.*

"Help!" Brian shouted between coughs. Isn't anybody out there? he wondered. Couldn't they see what was happening? Couldn't anyone help?

He yelled "please!" over and over until his voice was scraped raw by his desperation. The sound of flames had become a deafening roar, drowning out his ever-louder screams.

Trapped inside his office, his only hope was to try to escape. He took off one sock and put it over his burned hand like a glove, then unbuttoned his shirt, removed it and held it to his nose and mouth. Slowly, he eased the door into the main studio open, but a wall of fire leapt through the crack and attacked him, setting his pants ablaze. He backed up, pulled off the sock, frantically beating at the flames with his hands.

Staggering wildly around in his office, he stumbled and collapsed back in his chair.

From outside, dimly heard over the hungry crackle of the fire, came the faint sound of sirens.

Hurry! he silently urged, his breathing ragged and weak.

But it was too late. Greedy fingers of flames curled around his body, tightening their grip every second, until they enveloped him in a final blazing embrace.

Anyone seeing him at that last moment would not have recognized the young man at all. Dying, Brian McKernan looked like a burning bundle of rags.

Driving home from the hospital, Pappajohn nursed his growing frustration. Every lead he'd pursued since the bombing had been a dead end. After doing a local sweep, the Nitshi security detail reported finding nothing helpful or unusual. Edna had no luck with the phone trace, none of the Tafties he'd questioned had given him answers, and even Stanton was stonewalling. To top it off, now he had the feds nosing in too. A day from hell. Thanks to Reverend Taft?

Pappajohn shifted his casted arm. His shoulder was already stiff, making driving difficult. Still, he was luckier than Stanton. The boy had lost a couple of fingers and, very likely, his chance for a professional career. Stanton insisted he'd just come to the demonstration for kicks. Quite a loss for a few moments of excitement.

Still, Pappajohn didn't believe the boy was being straight with him. Claimed he appreciated Taft's message — America for Americans — but wasn't involved with the organization. On the other hand, Stanton's answers weren't surprising, what with the coach and those Nitshi people standing guard duty in the hospital room. Maybe the FBI could get more information.

Then there was Conrad. When Pappajohn had broached the subject of the professor's death with the young athlete, he'd fired back that the coach was on his case for nothing. Sure, he'd told *The Hot Line* reporter that Conrad planned to flunk him — that if he couldn't play, Ellsford might lose the national championships. The boy had hoped a public groundswell would lead Conrad to ease up. But that wasn't a crime, was it? No. No, it wasn't.

Damn that Greene. Always sticking her nose where it didn't belong, interfering with —

Pappajohn shook his head. If she hadn't been so close to the podium that afternoon, he might have gotten to the bomb in time. Instead, going for her story put her in the way — in his way — and more than two dozen people had been hurt. One had died.

But of course it wasn't her fault. He should have made sure she and those Tafties had stayed out of trouble. His mistake. It didn't matter that he'd saved so many — including Sammy Greene. As far as he was concerned, he'd fucked things up royally. A broken arm was a small price to pay.

The car radio beeped.

"Yeah?"

"Fire at the campus radio station, Chief. Fire engine on the way."

Christ. Now what? "Roger. Call the hospital," he ordered the dispatcher. "Send an ambulance, just in case. I'm on my way."

Great, Pappajohn thought as he hit the accelerator. *Just great. A day from hell.*

Reed emerged from Bud Stanton's room and leaned against the wall for a moment, overcome by weariness. Every bone in his body ached, every muscle felt on fire. The day had started with such promise, and now, so many lay injured and dead.

He glanced at the closed door to Sammy's hospital room at the end of the corridor. Smiling, he considered how she always managed to keep him off kilter. Passionate and strong-willed, it's what he loved about her. It's also what drove him crazy.

Only three more patients to see, and then he could join her for the evening. The adjacent bed in her room was empty. Happily, he wouldn't have to sleep in the doctors' call room tonight.

Reed pulled out his personal digital assistant to review the latest lab data on his patients just as his beeper went off. A glance at the phone number sunk his hopes. It was the emergency room. He set off for the nurses' station at a gallop to answer the page.

The phone call confirmed his worst suspicions. Another emergency. Second-year ER resident Jim Sullivan wanted him to join an ER team at the scene of a campus fire.

He sighed, thinking his work would keep Sammy waiting for a change.

Dr. Marcus Palmer could not stop his hand from shaking as he placed the slide on the stage of his microscope. He didn't need to focus for more than a second to confirm what he already knew. Luther Abbott had died from a particularly virulent form of AIDS. The brain section contained the same pathology he'd seen in the Pinez boy. Damn. Three new cases in less than a week. Why had everything started to go wrong? And how could he possibly hope to sweep this mess under the rug?

Sergio Pinez had been chosen for the study because of his sexual orientation and his ethnic background. Palmer's sponsor convinced him that the boy's parents were devout, hard-working, no-nonsense, first-generation citizens. They believed in the Catholic Church, respected authority. There was no reason to foresee a challenge to the official cause of death reported by the medical examiner.

And Abbott, luckily, had been abandoned at birth, growing up in foster homes. Only seventeen, he'd been declared an emancipated minor. No family, few, if any, friends. The monkey bite had been a terrible accident—everyone involved agreed. But at least the boy would not be missed.

Lucy Peters, on the other hand, was a different story. Her sheltered background—and virginity—had made her the perfect candidate to test the new vaccine. If she became sexually active, she was probably low risk for the disease, and besides, Palmer expected his vaccine to protect her. Never anticipating that Lucy would get sick, Palmer hadn't worried at all about her friends and family. Now the doctor had to face the fact that Lucy might succumb like the others. And, unlike the others, someone would want to know why.

He returned Abbott's slide to the case beside the other specimens. In a few days, perhaps a week at most, there'd be one labeled "Peters." Damn, damn, damn! How would he explain her death? He could present a thousand arguments in mitigation: at the time it seemed right; the work was a driving obsession—too important to give up; his vaccine would save the world from the scourge of AIDS; if a few innocents died in advancement of that goal, well, it was all for the greater good.

Palmer placed the case in his desk drawer and locked it, knowing these rationalizations might explain but not excuse. Truth was, his project was spiraling sickeningly out of control. He was enmeshed in a web of calculated deception from which he could not escape. He had no choice. Maintaining the lie had become the lesser evil.

"It's on fire!" Sammy shrieked.

Osborne pulled into an adjacent parking lot and stopped the car. A St. Charlesbury fire truck was parked alongside the one-story wood-frame building that housed the campus radio station. The structure was now a blazing inferno. Two firemen were directing a high-pressure water hose toward the flames while two more circled around back looking for possible victims.

Sammy jumped out of the Lexus with Osborne close behind. The air was hot and rich with the smell of burning wood. Two oak trees just behind the studio crackled and split loudly as they turned to ash.

"Oh my God!" Sammy set off toward the fire. A puff of wind blew a shower of sparks at her and she recoiled, brushing at her coat.

"Stay back, Sammy!" Osborne yelled as the fire chief ran toward her.

Shaking her head, she ran in the direction of the burning building again. "Brian! Brian McKernan's in there!" she screamed.

The fire chief caught her by the coat.

She struggled to free herself in vain. "You've got to get him out!"

"Who? The station is closed at night," the fire chief returned.

"Our engineer! He's working tonight."

"You sure?" On seeing her nod, the chief motioned at one of his men.

The fireman quickly approached a window at the side of the building no longer in flames. He hit the frame with his hatchet, splintering the old wood and breaking enough of the glass louvers to allow a thick wall of smoke to escape. The fireman ducked the cloud, coughing and gagging. Taking a deep breath, he shouldered his hatchet again and began smashing at the glass until the open space grew wider. Bending over the sill, he leaned into the room, scanning it with a high powered flashlight.

Sammy and the fire chief ran up and hovered behind him, eyes tearing from the residual smoke.

Sammy gasped at the devastation. What had been the main office and the radio station library was now a charred mass of wood and metal frames.

"Where do you think he might be?" The fire chief asked.

"Uh, h-he usually works in his studio. It's a couple of doors down o-on the right," she said hoarsely.

The corridor beyond the office was still filled with smoke, but no flames were visible from the window.

"I'll have to go in," the fireman stated. Covering his mouth and nose, he climbed into the office and headed off in the direction Sammy had indicated.

Brian had to make it, Sammy prayed as she peered into the smoky blackness. He just had to survive.

Stereo sirens heralded the arrival of a campus police car and an ambulance. Pappajohn and Reed flew out of their vehicles and ran up to the fire chief.

"Jesus, what happened?" Pappajohn asked.

The answer came from the fireman inside. "Looks like there's a body," he reported as he climbed back out of the window.

"God." Tears rolled down Sammy's cheeks.

"Any chance —?" Pappajohn queried, though one look at the charred remnants of the building made the question rhetorical.

The soot-caked firefighter shook his head.

Sammy turned away and stumbled down the grassy knoll to the parking lot. It wasn't possible that Brian was gone. Just some horrible illusion, a cruel trick of her senses. If only he hadn't stayed to work on the tape, he'd be alive. "No, no!" she shouted, breaking out in a blind run.

Two large arms caught her and held her in a firm embrace. She opened her eyes and looked up to see Reed. The medical student's expression was a cross between profound sympathy and parental irritation. "Sammy. Sammy."

Sammy's sobs vibrated against Reed's chest. "I killed him, Reed. I killed him."

"You killed him?" Pappajohn demanded as he walked up to the couple. "Just what do you mean by that?"

Reed answered. "Leave her alone. Can't you see she's upset?"

"Lord have mercy!" The shaken voice belonged to a breathless Larry Dupree. He stood staring at the ruins of his kingdom. "Ah was on the other side of campus."

"Who are you?" the fire chief asked.

"Larry Dupree, program director for the station. Ah just got a call from the dean and ran over as fast as ah—" He turned to Sammy. "Ah thought you were in the hospital."

"She's supposed to be," Reed said.

"I had to see Brian," her voice was quivering. "He was working on a tape."

"He didn't mention any tape to me," Larry stated.

"It was a favor." Sammy could barely control her emotions. "You said you needed proof that Professor Conrad didn't kill himself," she told Larry. To Reed she added, "Remember, I left you a message last week? I'd forgotten my purse at the professor's house."

Reed frowned. "Yeah."

"Well, my tape recorder was in it. I'd brought it for the interview. It's voice activated." She paused before admitting, "It was there overnight."

"You mean you had a tape of what happened when Conrad died?" Pappajohn exploded. "And you never said anything?"

"I didn't know. I didn't remember. I mean, I didn't have very much. Not much of anything."

Pappajohn lowered his voice, but couldn't hide his fury. "What was on the tape?"

She shrugged. "Just my stuff on there and—"

"And what else?" Pappajohn demanded.

"Most of the rest was static. The recorder was under the couch, in my purse." Sammy tried to explain. "I couldn't make out much, so I gave it to Brian. He was going to enhance the sound and see if we could get anything more." She burst into tears once again. "And today, just before the Nitshi remote, he told me he'd learned something."

Osborne, who had been quietly observing the drama until now, asked, "Did he say what?"

"No, he never got a chance."

Two firemen emerged from the rubble, carrying a body bag. They began loading it into the ambulance.

Pappajohn shook his head, anger mixed with frustration. "Looks like he never will."

"It's my fault." Sammy's despair was uncontrollable now.

"Might want to check these out, Chief." A fireman held out several cigarette butts in the palm of his hand.

The fire chief turned to Sammy. "Did your friend smoke?"

"Yes, but—"

"Where'd you find them?" the fire chief asked his man.

"All around the engineering room. On the floor. On the shelves. Ashtrays were full."

"Place was an accident waiting to happen," another fireman declared. "I figure the fella tossed his cigarette. Probably thought it was out. It burns a while, then poof. All this wood—up like a tinderbox."

"We've been trying to get a new building for years." Larry's voice broke. "Ah told Brian he was more likely to quit smoking—" He stopped himself abruptly.

"He wouldn't be dead if it wasn't for me," Sammy whispered again.

"That's not true." Osborne tried to soothe her. "You heard the fireman. It was an accident."

"We won't know anything about anything until the fire chief completes his investigation," Pappajohn said. He turned to Sammy. "I want to see you in my office, Greene."

Osborne draped an arm around Sammy's shoulder and tossed Pappajohn a pointed look. "She's been through enough for one day. Sergeant."

"We all have," Pappajohn conceded.

"She should be in the hospital," Reed added. "She's had a severe concussion."

"Come on, Sergeant," Osborne suggested. "I'm sure that under the circumstances you could postpone your interview."

Pappajohn gave a grudging assent.

"I'll see that Ms. Greene makes it safely home," Osborne promised.

"And I'll see that she stays there," Reed said firmly. "I'm off duty now." There was nothing more he could do for Brian. The ambulance driver would take the body to the morgue.

"That settles it then," Osborne replied. "I'll drop you both off."

Like most parents of Ellsford students who'd seen the Nitshi Day bombing on the evening news, the Peters turned off their TV set and immediately called their daughter's sorority. They prayed that she was not among the students injured. Or worse. But with so many calls flooding the switchboard, Lucy's father didn't get through until almost nine p.m.

Anne Sumner finally picked up the phone. She greeted him warmly. "Hi, Mr. Peters, how's Lucy?"

Frank Peters was stunned. "She's not there?"

"Here? No. I thought Dr. Palmer sent her home," Anne explained. "I haven't seen her since Monday."

"Oh my God," Lucy's father said, his heart pounding as he realized the implications of Anne's response. "Dr. Palmer?"

"What's happened, Frank? Tell me what's happened." A woman's voice in the background, high, tremulous with fear.

Lucy wasn't home, Anne realized. Well then, where was she?

A few seconds later, Frank Peters came back on the line. His voice, though calm, betrayed profound anxiety. "Why did she go to the doctor? What happened?"

"Well, we didn't think it was anything serious," Anne said. "Just a rash. She went to Student Health on Monday, that's all. Dr. Palmer said it was chickenpox, and he didn't want anyone else to catch it, so he told her to go home for a couple of weeks."

"Did she say when she was coming? What flight she was on?"

"No, sir, I didn't see her before she left."

"We're snowed in here since yesterday. But a few flights must've gotten in on Monday. Look, I'm going to call the campus police and report Lucy missing. As soon as the airport reopens, I'll catch the first available plane out. Meantime, can you call us the minute you have news? Any time, day or night, it doesn't matter. Okay?"

"For sure, Mr. Peters."

After he hung up, Frank Peters turned an agonized gaze on his wife's tear-stained face. She could barely whisper the words, "My baby."

"Don't worry," Lucy's father forced himself to say. "I'm sure she's okay. She must have missed the flight Monday and got caught in the snow. She's probably someplace like Chicago waiting 'til the weather clears."

"Then why didn't she call?"

Frank searched for a reason. "Obviously, she thought we'd worry, and she didn't want to upset us." He put one arm around his wife, giving her shoulders a squeeze of reassurance. With his other hand he dialed Vermont directory assistance. The answers didn't seem obvious at all. "Operator, in St. Charlesbury, can I have the number for Ellsford University's Campus Police."

Sammy was strangely subdued on the ride home. When the Lexus finally stopped in front of her building, Osborne suggested she see him in his office the next morning. "I'll call with a time."

Sammy merely nodded as she and Reed stepped out of the car.

"Take care of her," Osborne called to Reed before waving goodbye.

Sammy walked to the entrance trancelike as she fumbled in her purse.

"Here," Reed said, coming up behind her. "Use this." He stuck his spare key in the lock and opened the door, then followed her upstairs and once again used his key to let her into her apartment.

Sammy entered and stood, silently, in the middle of the living room. She veered numbly between belief and disbelief, between wanting to think about what was happening around her and wishing she could shut it all out.

The pulsing beep of her answering machine intruded on these thoughts. She walked over to it and pushed "Play."

"Sammy, this is Brian. I'm so glad you're okay. Listen. Some good news. I'm almost done with the tape. Call me tomorrow and we'll go over it. You won't believe what I found."

Beep.

The second message was also from Brian. "Me again. I figured out that 'ping' at the end of the tape. It's the sound of a computer being turned off."

Beep.

That was it. Brian's last words to her. So alive and yet— She closed her eyes, willing the horror of his death away.

"Dr. Osborne is worried about you," Reed said softly. "And so am I." He came around to face her. "Sammy, I really care about you."

Sammy opened her eyes and stared at him for a long moment, her expression impassive. "But you don't believe me." Her words were spoken in a monotone.

"Believe what?" Reed tried to keep his exasperation in check. "That there's something diabolical happening around here? That Reverend Taft is killing professors and students—right under the noses of the university police?"

"Brian's death was no accident."

"You told me the guy was a chain smoker. The fireman said—"

"I don't care what the fireman said," Sammy insisted. "And Conrad's death was no suicide," she added.

"The medical examiner's report confirmed a self-inflicted gunshot wound."

"Couldn't someone else have shot him?"

"The paraffin test was positive."

"What does that mean?"

"It means he fired the gun."

Sammy mulled that over for a moment. There had to be another explanation. "Well, maybe the murderer put the gun in Conrad's hand and forced him to shoot it," she suggested.

Reed groaned. "He wrote a suicide note for God's sake."

"It was typed on his computer. Anybody could have done it."

"Why? For what possible motive?"

"Listen to me, I know you'll think I'm crazy, but after today's bombing, I started thinking. What if Taft targeted Nitshi people because they fund AIDS-related research."

"Huh?" Reed shook his head. "That's carrying homophobia a little far, don't you think? Anyway, we don't know Taft was responsible for the bombing."

"Well, I'm sure his nose is in there somewhere."

"Even if you're right, what's all this got to do with Conrad?"

"Those articles I found. They had to do with DNA and virus infections. Couldn't somebody use his research to help fight AIDS? Then Taft could—"

"Sammy, molecular genetics is a huge field. Conrad's work was really peripheral to AIDS."

"Well then, how about the list of grants I showed you? If Conrad took money from Nitshi—Taft's latest campaign is 'America First.'"

"First of all," Reed said, "so what? Protesting is one thing, but why in the world would they kill somebody over protectionism?"

Sammy didn't have an answer.

"And secondly," Reed continued, "Conrad's most recent work was supported solely by government grants. U.S. government grants. I did a little research. He only accepted money from corporations while he was working with Nakamura."

"Well, now that you've brought up Nakamura, doesn't it seem funny that both men died the same way—by 'suicide'?"

"A coincidence. You don't know how demanding research work—"

"But Reed, it was the *same* gun."

"I thought his wife explained that. He had the gun around. It makes sense."

Sammy threw up her hands. "You've got an answer for everything, don't you?"

Reed mollified his tone, diagnosing the shrillness in her voice as a sign of hysteria. "Sammy, I'm just worried about you." He put his arms around her, but she resisted when he tried to pull her close. "You've been through one hell of a trauma today. I wanted you in the hospital to rest. Then you go sneaking out, and now there's been another death."

Her temper was skidding dangerously out of control. "Are you going to suggest I had anything to do with it?"

"Of course not!" Reed spread his hands in a gesture of mock helplessness. "I'm suggesting that you're on overload. What happened to your friend Brian is tragic. A tragic accident. If you weren't so exhausted, you'd see that."

Sammy fell silent for a moment and drew a deep breath. "I guess you're right," she acknowledged in a whisper, the last of her energy drained by her outburst. "It has been one *farkakte* day." Reaching forward, she pressed herself into Reed's welcoming embrace.

"Maybe a good night's sleep will put things into perspective."

"Maybe." She didn't sound convinced. "I just wish I knew what Brian learned from that tape."

"Maybe you don't."

"And why not?"

"Because if you *are* right, that kind of curiosity might have killed your professor."

Pappajohn's broken arm made finding a comfortable sleeping position difficult. He had just closed his eyes when the on-duty clerk transferred the long distance call from Sioux City, Iowa, to his home.

"Sergeant Pappajohn?"

"Yeah." *Unbelievable. Now what?*

"I'm Frank Peters. My daughter Lucy is missing."

Pappajohn sat up, turned on his bedside lamp, and tried in vain to clear his head. "What did you say?"

"My daughter, Lucy Peters. She's a freshman. There at Ellsford." Frank Peters quickly explained how he'd called Lucy's sorority house after hearing news of the Nitshi bombing. "My wife and I wanted to know that she was okay. But," the man's voice cracked, "her sorority sister says she was sent home on Monday."

"Sent home? By whom?"

"A Dr. Palmer. In your Student Health. She had the chickenpox."

Chickenpox. What the hell is this, a joke? Pappajohn looked at his bedside clock. Almost midnight. When was this day going to end? "I'm sorry, Mr. Uh—"

"Peters."

"Mr. Peters. I don't understand. What are you worried about again?"

As Peters related what he knew about his daughter, Pappajohn grabbed a pen and wrote down all the particulars. After asking a few more questions, he tried to reassure the worried parents. "All right, Mr. Peters. I'll check on this right away. It's probably just some mix-up. I'm sure she's just fine."

Adding a few more encouraging words, he replaced the receiver, feeling anything but reassured himself. A stab of pain shot through his arm and his stomach burned. He shook out a couple of antacids from the bottle by his bed and chewed them as he stood and walked over to the window.

Staring out into the clear, dark night, he experienced a disturbing sense of dread. Ellsford University was a quiet campus in a sleepy New England town where parents sent their beloved children, secure in the knowledge that nothing extraordinary was supposed to happen to them. Yet that serene image was being undermined by suicide, bombing, fire, and now, missing students.

Why now?

Why indeed.

He turned away from the window knowing only one thing for sure. The possibility of sleep tonight was out of the question.

CHAPTER SEVEN

THURSDAY

"Good morning."

Sammy opened her eyes. "Have you been sitting there all night?"

Reed stretched, uncoiling his long legs from the uncomfortable wicker chair he'd pulled near the bed. "Most of it."

"My own private duty doctor."

"Almost doctor," Reed leaned over and kissed her forehead. "I told you I was worried about you."

"Worried I'd try to escape, you mean."

Not sure she was joking, Reed simply said, "That too."

Sammy peered under the bedcovers and realized she'd slept in her clothes. "Well, at least I see you haven't taken advantage of my vulnerable state."

"And I see the patient's got her sense of humor back." Reed smiled. "You were talking in your sleep."

Sammy's face clouded. "It was—I guess it was a dream." She shuddered at the memory, still vivid in her mind.

"Want to share?"

Sammy closed her eyes for a long moment, then opened them again. "No, I don't remember it."

Reed flicked his watch. The LCD digits read 6:45. "Jeez, I'd better get going. I've got to shower and change before rounds. Dr. Palmer's a stickler for punctuality." He was still wearing his white pants and jacket, now badly in need of a wash and press. As he stood, he stepped into his loafers and pushed back the chair. "By the way, he wants to see you in Student Health at ten."

"Palmer?"

"He examined you in the emergency room yesterday."

"He was on duty?"

"No, I called him. I—"

"You were worried about me."

Reed felt his face redden and turned away. "After you fell asleep last night I called and explained how you'd 'checked out' of the hospital. He suggested seeing you as a follow-up. Student Health has your medical records, and he has clinic this morning."

Sammy sat up in bed. "You really admire him, don't you?"

Reed shrugged. "Actually, I hardly know the man. He's very private—serious. But I can tell you this. He's a brilliant researcher and a great clinician. I'm lucky to have gotten this rotation with him. If I don't screw up, I think I have a chance at the Mass. General residency."

Sammy smiled. "You? Screw up? Not a chance."

Reed sat down on the bed and gave her another gentle kiss—this time on the mouth.

Sammy threw her arms around his neck, burying herself in his embrace. "Have I ever told you what a *gitina shima* you are?" she whispered.

Reed sat back, wincing theatrically. "Why do I think that only means I'm a nice guy?"

"So?"

"So, I thought maybe after all this time, we could be more than 'nice.'" He shook his head. "Sammy, not all men are going to abandon you—just 'cause your father did."

"Since when was psychiatry your specialty?"

"Just trying to understand."

Sammy leveled serious green eyes at Reed. "Listen, I'm sorry I'm not—I can't. I'm just so overwhelmed right now. I don't know how I feel about us." She knew it was a poor excuse for her inability — or unwillingness — to deal with where their relationship was going. "I guess what I'm saying is I could really just use a friend right now."

Reed hesitated for a moment, then squeezed her hand. "Count on it." He rose from the bed.

"Reed?"

"Hmm?"

"Why didn't you tell me Bud Stanton was one of the students injured yesterday?"

"How did you — ?" Reed asked, then realizing the answer, said, "Well, of course, Ms. Super Sleuth. I should've posted a guard by your room."

"I would've climbed out the window," she returned, "and you didn't answer my question."

"I was advised by the FBI not to say anything," he explained. "They're investigating Stanton's possible involvement in the bombing."

"Bud? I don't think he was involved with the Taft people."

"Guess not." Reed shrugged again. "At least, that's what he told your friend Pappajohn."

"Not *my* friend." Sammy said. True, the man had saved her life and for that she was more than grateful. But it was hard to just put aside their frequent battles over the past two years. Sammy smiled to herself. If Pappajohn thought Stanton was part of this, she was sure he was barking up the wrong tree. She swung her legs over the bed and started to get up.

"Take it slow," Reed warned, watching her closely. "If you get up too fast, you'll get lightheaded. You could pass out."

"I'm fine. Really." Sammy was standing, though she had to admit, the floor seemed to be swaying gently beneath her feet. She was all right. She'd just been lying down too long. She raised and waggled her arms. "Look ma, no hands!"

Reed shook his head. "Look ma, no sense."

Sammy ignored the remark, as she inched unsteadily toward her nightstand. She pulled open the drawer to retrieve the photos

Mr. Brewster had given her yesterday. She held them out to Reed. "By the way, any of these people look familiar?"

Reed shuffled through the pile, stopping at one. "That's Katie Miller," he said, handing it to Sammy. "She's the student who was killed. I don't know the guy standing behind her."

Sammy stared at the girl in the picture. "She's the one who told me Taft planned to sabotage Nitshi Day."

"You're sure?"

Sammy nodded, stunned. So hard to believe Katie was now dead. Another person she'd touched, gone.

Reed slipped the photo into his jacket pocket. "I'll give this to the cops during rounds this morning."

"Sure." Her voice was thin, remote.

Reed glanced at his watch again. "Don't forget your appointment at ten."

"No, I won't."

At the door, he turned and added, "If you need me this afternoon, I'll be at the Nitshi Building. Dr. Palmer's asked me to check on one of his experiments."

Sammy waited until the door closed before allowing herself to cry.

Sammy was rinsing her red eyes in the bathroom sink twenty minutes later when her telephone rang. Grabbing a towel, she rushed to answer it. "Hello?"

"Hi, Bill Osborne here. Hope I didn't wake you."

"No, Dr. Osborne, I was up." Her voice sounded hoarse.

"Well, I wasn't sure you'd remember. Last night we made plans to meet this morning."

"Oh. Uh, yes." The truth was she'd just as soon forget most of last night.

"I have a cancellation at nine," Osborne reported. "How would that work for you?"

Sammy hesitated, considering all she had to do that morning. She planned to talk to Larry, then meet with the fire chief and

Pappajohn. She owed it to Brian to find out what happened — and why. "I don't know."

"Sometimes our hardest task is to give to ourselves," Osborne said, acknowledging her conflict.

If only I could, Sammy thought. A moment to unburden herself, to comfort herself, to rest. She checked the clock on the nightstand. It read 7:05. Still early. Perhaps —

"I guess I can make it." She surprised herself by agreeing to the session. In fact, the Psych Department was just around the corner from Student Health. She could see the psychologist at nine and still make her ten o'clock appointment with Dr. Palmer.

Two hours later, Osborne ushered her into his office.

The room was pin neat, its decor surprisingly opulent. *Definitely not university issue*. Framed Impressionist paintings covered pale blue walls. Thick, plush carpeting softened her entering footsteps. Several rows of psychology reference books were organized by author in a rosewood bookcase behind a matching rosewood desk and credenza. No papers or files cluttered the desk's polished wood surface — only a Mont Blanc pen and pencil set, letter opener, and letter tray, precisely arranged.

Sammy also noted the absence of the traditional family desk photos. Osborne probably wanted to keep his personal life separate from his professional world. That made sense.

"Please, have a seat." Osborne waved at several chairs and a couch opposite his desk.

Sammy chose a comfortable armchair across from him.

Osborne settled into his own high-backed leather chair. Clasping his hands, he touched his fingers to his lips and smiled at Sammy. "So, how are you doing?"

Sammy exhaled slowly. "Physically, I'm okay."

"And emotionally?"

"I'm fine," Sammy said, though her lower lip trembled.

Osborne leaned forward and looked across at her. "What happened yesterday was horrible. I know you must be hurting terribly."

Even as he spoke the words, Sammy could feel the ache rise within her, powerless to control it as her emotions took a free fall. "Yes," she acknowledged, expelling a fresh gush of tears.

Osborne reached over to his credenza, pulled a tissue from the box, handed it to her, and waited until she was composed again.

"Brian was a friend. A real friend."

"They're hard to find. And harder to lose. I know." Osborne's voice was almost a whisper.

Sammy looked at him. It seemed as if his eyes were glistening with unshed tears. Even therapists are human, she thought, realizing that he must have felt the same way about Conrad. "How do you stop feeling responsible?" she asked.

"Is that what you're feeling?"

She nodded. "Last night, I had this dream."

"What happened? Can you recall?"

Haltingly, she began to tell him what she couldn't seem to share with Reed. She was at Professor Conrad's home. "It was last Saturday morning," she began, "but this time, instead of finding Conrad dead, he was alive — hurt, bleeding, from his head." Sammy's hand touched the bandage on her own forehead. "His hands were stretched toward me. He was pleading for help. But I turned away. For just a second. When I looked back again, his face belonged to Brian McKernan — burning, like a candle."

She shut her eyes tight, hoping to erase the horrifying memory. "I started running toward him, but he just kept getting farther away. I kept running and running and finally, I was so tired." Sammy's voice cracked. "I couldn't do anything." She moved her finger up and down her forearm as if tracing an old scar. "I — it was my fault!"

"No, Sammy. Your mother was already dead when you found her. So was Professor Conrad and your friend at the station." The psychologist's voice was gentle, soothing. "You couldn't have helped any of them."

Sammy opened her eyes. There was a knot in her chest and she could barely swallow. "You've explained that, but —"

"But it will take time for your subconscious to accept what your conscious mind understands," Osborne interpreted. "For you to accept here," he tapped his breastbone, "what you understand here," he touched his temple. "You've held in your feelings about your mother's passing for close to fifteen years. That's a long time to build up walls, defenses."

"It still hurts. Here." She pointed to her chest. "I should be over that by now."

Osborne shook his head. "There's no schedule for survivors. And seeing a student your age and then a professor you knew take their own lives brings it all back again." Then he patiently went over the same ground he'd covered the other night at dinner. "You still have a great deal of unresolved guilt. You've survived, they haven't. You have to keep telling yourself that it's not your fault. Your mother, Sergio, and Connie all made a choice — their choice. There's nothing you could or should have done."

"I wish I could say that about Brian."

Osborne frowned. "The Fire Department feels his death was an accident. How could you have helped? The poor young man was just in the wrong place at the wrong time."

Sammy chewed on her lower lip, struggling to articulate the conflict within her. "But he wouldn't have been there if it hadn't been for me."

"Sounds like magical thinking, Sammy," Osborne said.

"What's that?"

"Very common among youngsters. You feel as though everything that happens is under your control — that you're directly responsible for other people's actions — and what happens to them. As adults, we know that's not true. We have little control over —"

"I just need to make sense of it all."

"Sometimes it all makes no sense."

"You think I'm off base to want other explanations?"

"Not if finding the answers will finally put your doubts to rest," Osborne assured her. "I am curious, though. I thought after we talked on Tuesday, you were comfortable that Dr. Conrad's death was a suicide."

Sammy took a deep breath. "Yes, but there's a lot I didn't tell you then, and a lot that's happened since."

"Can you tell me now?" he asked.

Sammy hesitated, then sensed that Osborne was the only one she could unburden herself to — a best friend who would understand — who could be a valuable ally in helping to bring Conrad's killers to justice. He would believe what Reed and Larry and Pappajohn passed off as "magical thinking."

"I don't have any proof," she began slowly. "Brian didn't get a chance to tell me what he discovered. But it's just putting everything together." Relieved to have someone to confide in, she quickly reported her near hit-and-run, the man with the mustache, the stolen photographs, the missing brown envelope, her primitive analysis of the static-filled tape. Describing her research trip to the office of Contracts and Grants, she laid out her theory about Taft and the Nitshi Corporation. "Brian discovered something on the tape I gave him that would have proven Professor Conrad was killed that night. And now," she shuddered at the thought, "now Brian's dead, too."

"Well, that's quite a story." Osborne leaned back in his chair. "Have you shared any of this with the police?"

"No, I — You'll probably think I'm really paranoid, but I'm not sure Pappajohn isn't part of a cover-up. Last year I researched Taft's organization. After the anti-abortion riots."

"I remember that well," Osborne commented. "A volatile concentration of antisocial impulses."

"Taft instigated the violence," Sammy said. "I was there." Her eyes narrowed. "Did you know that the one hundred fifty thousand dollars of property damage was amortized by a gift from several alumni — all members of Taft's congregation? And the OB nurse who got hurt and ended up in the ICU? I learned that someone from Taft's Traditional Values Coalition paid her medical bill."

"You don't say?"

"Uh-huh. You never heard about that, did you?"

Osborne shook his head.

"Neither did anyone else. I told Pappajohn about the connection. You'd think he would've tracked down my lead and blown Taft's machine sky-high."

"And he didn't?"

"Nope. He must've gone and told Taft everything. The next day, the Reverend's lawyers threatened to sue the university. If the chancellor hadn't smoothed things over, I'd be paying lawyers forever. Bad enough they took me off the air for the rest of the semester."

"Sounds as if it's wise to proceed with caution."

Sammy nodded, reminded of Larry's warning. "I don't think the administration will be as understanding this time."

Osborne sat up in his chair. "Tell you what. How about if I look into things a little? I might be able to open some doors without setting off fireworks. Meanwhile, don't do anything for now. Let's meet tomorrow morning and see where we go from here." He looked at his spiral calendar book. "Nine o'clock is free."

For the first time in days, Sammy felt a sense of release. Finally, there was someone she could trust who believed her. Rising, she took Osborne's hand, then, catching sight of his wall clock reading 9:55, dashed from his office and down the hall to Student Health.

9:15 A.M.

"Do you send every kid with chickenpox home, Doctor?" Pappajohn asked.

"Not necessarily," Palmer explained. "But the disease is highly contagious. If we don't isolate students, we could have a campus-wide outbreak. Sending Miss Peters home to recuperate seemed the most prudent thing to do." Closing the folder in his hands, he forced a smile.

"Why didn't you contact her parents?"

The smile disappeared. "She is a legal adult. She said she wanted to call them herself," Palmer said. "I did, however, tell her sorority sister and her boyfriend that she'd be leaving."

Pappajohn pulled a notepad and pen from his jacket pocket. "Names?"

"Is there some problem, Sergeant?" Palmer asked.

"Lucy Peters never made it home."

"Good Heavens." Palmer seemed genuinely puzzled. "Where do you think she might be?"

"Frankly, doctor, I don't have a clue. I was hoping you could shed some light on the matter."

Palmer's mouth compressed. "I wish I could, but I haven't seen her since Monday. I suggested the train because in a private compartment, there'd be minimal risk of infecting others," he explained. "She should've arrived by now."

"Did you know which train she took?"

The doctor gave an impatient shake of the head. "I don't have any idea. You could call Amtrak. There can't be that many trains leaving for Iowa."

"We'll track it down," Pappajohn stated. "Even so, that doesn't explain why she never called her parents."

"Now that doesn't surprise me at all," Palmer said. "The girl really wasn't that sick. Maybe she decided to take off with her boyfriend for a few days and didn't want to let Mom and Dad know. When you work with college kids —" The doctor held out his hands, appealing for understanding.

Pappajohn nodded. "I hear you, Doc. You know the boyfriend's name?"

Palmer opened the file once again and skimmed through it briefly. "Here we are, Christopher Oken. The sorority sister's Anne Sumner."

Pappajohn wrote down the information. "Okay." He looked at Palmer. "Is there anything else you remember that might be helpful? Anything she did or said?"

"I wish I could help you, Sergeant. But I've told you all I can." With a brisk nod, Palmer turned his attention to the computer on his desk and began typing — a clear signal that the interview was over.

Taking his hint, Pappajohn moved toward the door, allowing himself a brief glance at the monitor. Palmer seemed to be entering rows of numbers from a yellow pad next to his keyboard. Arcane medical data, Pappajohn figured. It was literally all Greek to him. Adding a polite "thank you," he quietly left the room.

Finally alone, Palmer's thoughts remained with Lucy Peters. That was a close call. He knew he was covered for the moment. Good thing he had the foresight to think of chickenpox. According to her medical history questionnaire, Lucy never had it as a child. He had to make sure no one found out she didn't have it now.

Palmer picked up his telephone and began to dial.

Larry Dupree stared at the burned out shell of his radio station, conscious of the lump in his throat. Last night, he'd watched as flames swallowed most of the rickety wooden structure. With the devastating fire, his dreams of creating a dynamic campus communications center had literally gone up in smoke. All that remained was the concrete foundation. The campus facilities men were already demolishing the tottering remnants of the walls. Charred papers lay among a tangle of blackened studio equipment and melted records. The shade trees that still stood by the structure were heavily scorched. It was clear W-E-L-L was out of commission. Even setting up temporary new quarters would take several weeks.

The hardest blow of all was the loss of his young protégé. Brian *was* W-E-L-L. He lived and breathed the station — and kept it alive. Larry couldn't begin to imagine how he would rebuild without the technical expertise and cheery optimism of his beloved engineer. Tragic irony that his fatigue — and those cursed cigarettes — would finally kill him.

"Find anything?" Larry flashed his station identification badge. "I was hoping we could salvage a few show tapes at least."

"Ground zero so far," the construction chief replied. "We're still cleaning away ash and debris." He wiped the sweat from his brow. "Not much could've made it through this one."

Larry nodded, "Yeah. Ah know." Even one of his favorite classic albums would be little consolation now.

"Look, we'll call you if we come up with anything. But don't hold your breath."

Larry forced a wan smile. "Ah'm too old to believe in miracles."

10:00 A.M.

"You're not here for another story?" Nurse Matthews groaned when Sammy entered the Student Health Center. The nurse waved a hand around the crowded waiting room. What had been a deserted clinic the last time Sammy visited was now teeming with patients. "There's no time to breathe today."

"Probably healthier that way," Sammy observed over the rasping coughs and loud sneezes of waiting students. "Actually, I'm here for a follow-up with Dr. Palmer."

"Right, you're on for this morning. Doctor said to squeeze you in." The harried nurse focused on Sammy's wounded head. "Terrible what happened yesterday. I've been on this campus nearly twenty-five years and I thought I'd seen everything. World's going crazy." Matthews touched the bandage on Sammy's temple with a gentle hand. "Dr. Palmer will re-dress this." She picked up a clipboard and paper and handed it to Sammy. "Have a seat over here." She indicated a bank of chairs not far from her station, adding, "and fill out this questionnaire while I pull your chart."

Sammy scanned the printed questions on the page. They seemed to cover everything from family history to sexual activity. "Is this form something new?"

Matthews shook her head. "Only for Dr. Palmer's patients. I wish other doctors were as thorough, but then you don't find many like Dr. P." From the proprietary tone of her voice, it was evident that Nurse Matthews held the physician in high esteem.

"He takes the data and enters it into his computer so next time you come, he's got it at his fingertips," she went on to explain. "Wish we had time to do it for every student, but it's hard enough to get some of our doctors to write legible notes."

Sammy nodded, reminded of Reed's chicken-scratch handwriting. "Oh, by the way," she said, "as long as you're off to the chart room, do you think you could bring Sergio Pinez's medical record?"

"Beg your pardon?"

"Well, I just wondered when Sergio was last seen." Sammy related what Reed had said on the radio about people often seeing their doctors shortly before committing suicide.

The nurse shook her head. "First of all, the chart has been sent to Sergio's family doctor in New York. Second, even if the chart were here, I couldn't let you see it — not without the family's permission. And third, I happen to know that Sergio hadn't seen Dr. Palmer for at least a month."

"Excuse me?" A willowy blonde leaned over the triage desk, vying for attention.

Matthews turned to her, efficiency personified. "Check in at station two, appointments at station three, then you come back here."

Ignored, Sammy retreated to the bank of chairs and located a seat between a sneezer and a cougher. She tried not to turn in either's direction, looking down instead, and concentrating on the questionnaire.

"No, you don't understand. I don't need to see anybody. I'm not sick," Sammy heard the girl at the station say. "I'm just trying to find out about my friend."

Nurse Matthews's tone was brusque. "Sorry, I can't release any medical information."

"No, that's okay," the blonde interrupted. "I don't want to know what she's got. I'm trying to find out where she is. Lucy Peters. She came in to see Dr. Palmer last Monday. We haven't seen her since."

Hearing Dr. Palmer's name, Sammy couldn't help eavesdropping.

"Lucy Peters?" Matthews repeated. "We see so many students."

"She's a blonde too, about my height. A little plumper. Freshman," Anne described her sorority sister. "She came in for a rash, it was chickenpox."

"Chickenpox? You sure?" the nurse queried, her brows arched in surprise. "I don't remember sending a Health Department notification." University policy required reporting contagious diseases, and Matthews was a stickler for following regulations.

"Dr. Palmer called me himself. Said he was sending Lucy home to recuperate."

"Well, then I guess maybe that explains it," Matthews replied. "He must have filled out the notification form."

"But she never got there," the girl replied.

"What?"

"Lucy's parents called me last night. They said Lucy never made it home."

Abandoning her questionnaire, Sammy focused on the conversation at the nurses' station. Yesterday, she'd heard Luther Abbott was missing. Now Lucy Peters. Both patients of Dr. Palmer. Perhaps just a coincidence, but the reporter in her was intrigued. She walked over to where Anne and Nurse Matthews stood. "Was your friend involved in Reverend Taft's group?"

"Not that I know of," the blonde responded. "Why?"

"Was she friendly with a student named Luther Abbott?"

Anne shook her head.

"You mean the young man bitten by the monkey?" Nurse Matthews intervened.

Sammy started in surprise. That's right! Luther Abbott had been injured at the animal rights demo. "Do you know what happened to him?"

"Had a terrible reaction to that bite," the nurse said. "My guess is he didn't take the pills Dr. Palmer prescribed. Passed out during a midterm and ended up at Ellsford General."

Not according to what Sammy overhead in the hospital elevator yesterday. "Do you know where he is now?" she asked.

Nurse Matthews shrugged.

"Look. I'm really sorry," Anne broke in, "but I'm here to find out about my friend. Is there any way I can see Dr. Palmer?"

"Sorry, he's booked tight this morning," the nurse remarked. "He's already running a half hour late for her appointment."

Anne turned to Sammy. "You mind if I come in with you — just to ask him —"

"Sure," Sammy agreed, thinking it might be a good way to find out what happened to the two missing students.

"That's out of the question," said Matthews. "We can't allow —" Her desk phone buzzed, interrupting her in midsentence. As she listened to the caller, her benign expression became a worried frown. "Yes. Yes, doctor, but, what about —? I suppose. Yes, we could. At least six. All right. Yes, doctor. Yes. Bye."

Hanging up, she turned back to the two girls. "Well, it seems that neither of you will be seeing Dr. Palmer this morning. He's had a sudden emergency." Nurse Matthews motioned to Sammy. "Let's go to the recovery room. I'll change your dressing."

"What happened?" Palmer demanded.

"Grand mal. She's out now. I don't know what function's coming back."

The doctor began to share his nurse's pessimism as she described Lucy Peters's sudden turn for the worse.

"We pushed twenty milligrams IV valium before the seizures stopped. I paged you right away."

Just like Luther Abbott, Palmer thought. A rapid downward course in a matter of days.

"I hung a Dilantin drip," the nurse said. "Should we get an EEG?"

Palmer stared down at his patient. With her eyes closed and the respirator gently rocking her chest, Lucy appeared peacefully asleep. The relentless beep of the cardiac monitor, however, was like an intrusive funeral march, reminding the doctor that the prognosis for the poor girl was hopeless. "No," he said slowly. "That won't be necessary. At this point all we can do is make her comfortable."

While Nurse Matthews re-dressed Sammy's wound, the young reporter was figuratively scratching her head. Two students, both patients of Dr. Palmer, had disappeared under mysterious circumstances. And Sergio. Another Dr. Palmer patient. Could there be some connection? Perhaps a visit with Palmer was just what the doctor ordered.

"It's all over."

"Huh?" Sammy looked up at Matthews.

"The wound looks pretty good. Should heal without much of a scar."

"Oh. Great." Sammy smiled. "Thanks."

"Just keep it clean and dry. You can change the dressing yourself from now on."

"Okay." Sammy rubbed her temples. "How about my head? Shouldn't I have Dr. Palmer check me?" she pressed.

"You look fine to me," Nurse Matthews said, "but if you like, I'll squeeze you in with Dr. Harris."

"Dr. Palmer's not coming back today?"

The nurse shook her head. "Some kind of emergency at Nitshi. I don't expect him back 'til closing."

Didn't Reed say he was working at the institute today? Sammy checked her watch — quarter to eleven. By the time she reached North Campus it would be close to twelve. Maybe she could wangle a lunch date with Reed. She wasn't so much hungry for food as for answers. And if Reed couldn't answer her questions, perhaps she'd have a chance to meet the elusive Dr. Palmer himself.

"Do you want to see Dr. Harris?" the nurse asked.

"Uh, no, I don't think so." Sammy gave her a perky smile. "As a matter of fact, I'm meeting my boyfriend up at Nitshi. He's a med student working in the lab —"

Before Sammy had a chance to finish her story, Nurse Matthews was out the door and onto the next patient.

Outside the clinic, Sammy pulled her peacoat tight to shelter her from the blistering cold. Her chest ached and her windpipe burned in the frosty air. Her gait was still unsteady, and she had to stop every few minutes to rest on one of the park benches.

After almost an hour, Sammy arrived at the institute's modern entrance. She looked back down at the grassy area fronting the glass-and-steel structure. Hardly a trace of yesterday's events remained. Every piece of trash and debris had been picked up. Even the chairs and what had been left of the podium had been removed. *How pristine.* The Nitshi people should be subcontracted to do the rest of campus.

"You coming in?" A security guard addressed her from beyond the electronically open doors.

"Uh, yeah." Sammy strode into the comfortably warm lobby as the doors glided shut behind her. "Dr. Palmer's lab?"

"Sorry, miss. No one's allowed on the fourth floor without clearance."

Surprised, Sammy said, "I just wanted to see Dr. Wyndham."

Frowning, the guard turned to a computer screen on his desk. "Wyndham?"

"Yes, he's a medical student from—"

"Immunogenetics lab. That's where they work." He pointed to the bank of elevators. "Third floor. Then turn left."

"Thanks." Sammy waved as she eased over to the elevators.

"Just a minute," the guard called. "You'll need to sign in and get one of these."

Sammy returned to his desk, signed her name on the daily roster, and collected a visitor's badge. You'd think she was entering Ft. Knox.

"Return it before you leave," the guard said, time stamping her entry.

"No problem." Sammy hurried into an empty elevator just as the doors automatically opened. Scanning the buttons, she punched "three." It lit up in a warm orange. As soon as the door closed, she reached over and pressed "four." Nothing happened. The button remained dark. She tried again, but it still did not light up. Probably burned out, she figured, as the elevator arrived at the third floor.

Sammy stayed on board and waited for the doors to close. The elevator immediately started its descent. Sporting a sheepish grin, she edged to one corner, out of sight of the security guard as the door opened once again on the ground floor. How did anyone get to "four"? Shrugging, she pressed "three" anew and made a second trip upstairs.

This time, Sammy exited on three and immediately felt as though she'd entered a hall of mirrors. Polished metallic walls reflected her somewhat disheveled figure in wavy rainbow colors. The mirror images followed her like guardian shadows as she walked down the hall on her left. Otherwise, she was alone.

Within a few yards, she passed what appeared to be doors on both sides of the hall, each labeled: VIROLOGY, BACTERIOLOGY, CHEMISTRY, SEROLOGY. Beside one marked IMMUNOGENETICS, Sammy paused and pressed a small security lever. The door whooshed open to reveal a huge, high-tech laboratory brightly lit by midday sunshine filtering in through wall-to-wall windows. Several white-coated technicians were quietly bent over microscopes.

Across the spacious room, Reed glanced up from his work and smiled. "What a pleasant surprise!" He pointed to the neatly wrapped fresh bandage on her forehead. "You actually took my advice and went to Student Health."

Sammy walked over and planted a quick kiss on his lips. None of the techs bothered to look up from their stations, she noticed. Shrugging, she reached for the nearest stool and sat down wearily. "I did, but I missed your Dr. Palmer. Nurse Matthews did the dressing. Some kind of an emergency here, she said."

"Really? I haven't seen him," Reed stood, surveying the room.

"I guess he's on the fourth floor," Sammy suggested.

Reed hesitated. "Maybe."

"Good. Can we go up and talk with him? I have a few—"

Reed's expression reflected disappointment. "And I thought you came to see me."

"Of course, I did," Sammy said. "I just thought while I was here, I could ask him about—"

"Absolutely not!" Reed raised his voice just enough for a few of the techs to look up from their work. He quickly reduced the volume to a bare whisper. "If he's got some kind of emergency, he can't be disturbed by a —" He turned to the nearest tech. "Slides are all cooking. I think that's it for me this morning."

The Asian nodded. "You go to lunch now?" he asked in a thick accent.

Reed checked the wall clock. Quarter to twelve. "I'll be back before one." He turned to Sammy. "How about grabbing a bite to eat?"

Afraid to upset him further, Sammy agreed. "Sure. Luigi's?"

"Fine with me." Reed led her to the door, and they exited to the sterile hallway toward the elevator.

"Look, I didn't mean to —" Sammy blurted. "I'm sorry if —"

Reed stared at her for a long beat as if trying to judge her sincerity. "It's okay," he finally said. "Maybe I overreacted. It's just that Dr. Palmer is very private about his research. When he's on four, he doesn't tolerate interruptions."

"The security guard said you need some kind of clearance to get upstairs?"

"There's a special elevator that goes straight to the fourth floor. And you have to have an access card," Reed explained. "Dr. Palmer has the lab for his AIDS vaccine up there. It's amazing. If you think these are high tech," he said, pointing to the labs on either side of the corridor, "you should see that place. Deep Space Nine."

"You've seen it?"

"Once. I helped with a case last week —"

"So he's got patients up there?"

"Patients? Uh, no." They'd reached the elevator. Reed pushed the "down" button. "It's just a lab."

"Then why all the cloak-and-dagger?"

"Synthesizing and testing new drugs is a multimillion-dollar business. A lot of companies out there wouldn't mind making a profit off Nitshi's discoveries."

"Industrial espionage?"

Reed nodded. "The stakes are high. That's why Nitshi's got such a high-powered security system. Human and technical. Protects trade secrets."

"I'm impressed. So they develop all their new drugs here?"

"Some. This site is the nidus of their antiviral research. But they've got labs, partners, and subsidiaries in Asia, South America, and Europe. And their corporate headquarters is in New York."

"Is this where they keep the animals?"

Reed raised an eyebrow. "What animals?"

"The chimps. You know, for experiments. When I was at the animal rights riot, the tech mentioned some of the chimps were from Nitshi."

Reed scratched his chin. "Must've meant Nitshi funded them or something. Gave them grant money to buy the chimps. All the animals are kept over in the Biology Building."

"I know," Sammy said, confused, "but somehow I was sure he meant something else. They're not doing any experiments with animals here?"

"Not that I know of."

"Nothing with infections or anything?"

"I don't know, Sammy." Reed sounded irritated again. "Why do you ask?"

"There's this guy. He was at the rally. One of Taft's kids. He got, uh, a little excited and tried to let the monkeys out of their cages."

"So?"

"Well, one of them bit him."

Reed didn't look surprised. "Is he all right?"

"That's the funny thing. Actually, he got sick."

"That can happen with animal bites," Reed explained. "Wasn't rabies, was it?"

"I don't think so."

His tone was casual. "Then all it takes are some antibiotics and he should be fine."

"But, Reed, I'm trying to tell you. He's disappeared. Luther Abbott's disappeared."

Reed frowned.

"Matthews told me he'd been admitted to Ellsford General, but when I was there yesterday, I heard a nurse say he'd been transferred to Nitshi."

Reed shook his head. "I think that concussion has made you delusional."

"I know what I heard."

"You know what you *think* you heard, Sammy. I can assure you there are no patients here."

"I suppose you don't know about Lucy Peters either?"

Reed looked totally lost. "Sorry?"

"Freshman. She got this rash. It was supposed to be chickenpox, but her roommate says she never went home. Now she's missing, too."

"And how are these two kids related?"

"I'm not sure. But they're both patients of Dr. Palmer."

Reed's expression darkened. "Yesterday you were sure Professor Conrad and your friend Brian had been killed by Reverend Taft. Now you think Dr. Palmer is kidnapping students?" Reed's voice was tinged with anger. "I'd be very careful about making such accusations if I were you. Maybe you don't give a damn about *your* ass, but I've got a career to think about."

"I never said Dr. Palmer did anything," Sammy protested. "I don't know what happened to these students, but if there *was* foul play —"

"Foul play?" Reed tapped his forehead with the heel of his hand. "Sammy, this is getting totally absurd. You're starting to see sinister plots and evil forces everywhere you look."

"Fine. Just forget it." Reed did have a point. Without proof of any wrongdoing at Nitshi, she had no right to threaten his relationship with Dr. Palmer, or his career. "I'm sorry. I guess I *am* overtired."

Reed gave her another long silent appraisal. "You mean that?"

"Sure."

The elevator doors finally opened. This time the car was packed. Reed and Sammy barely managed to squeeze on board. They stood silently staring at the floor number display as the car rode smoothly down to the lobby.

At the main desk, Sammy handed over her visitor's badge and signed out.

"So, what do you want on your pizza?" Reed asked, draping his arm around her shoulders and guiding her toward the exit.

"Excuse me," the security guard called after them. "Sammy Greene? There's a message here for you."

Sammy walked back to the desk. "A message for me?"

"Call from Police Chief Pappajohn." The guard checked his notes. "It says to be at his office at one. Or else."

Pappajohn? How did he know where to find her? Sammy turned to Reed with a shrug. "Guess this takes care of lunch." Not that she'd been hungry to begin with, but now she'd really lost her appetite.

For Pappajohn, the day so far had been a total wipeout. He had already talked with Chris Oken, Lucy Peters's boyfriend, and Anne Sumner, her sorority sister. Neither could provide any new leads. It was as if the girl had not only disappeared from Ellsford, but dropped off the face of the earth as well.

Edna entered his office carrying a sheaf of curly papers. "The ME's report on the Conrad autopsy."

"I thought we'd ordered that plain paper fax," he muttered as he accepted the unruly bundle.

"Budget cuts. Purchasing says we have to wait until next fiscal year."

"Funny how those university cuts never affect Chancellor Ellsford's salary."

"That's because Reginald Ellsford *is* the university," Edna said. Not waiting for a reply, she returned to her desk, leaving Pappajohn to sift through the material. From a cursory review, the medical examiner's findings seemed to support the prevalent theory. "Single gunshot wound, through the mouth. Twenty-two caliber. Death instantaneous from brain trauma. Consistent with suicide. Powder burns on left hand."

Was Conrad left-handed? He made a mental note to check.

The report on the site analysis yielded little more information. Blood on the sofa and adjacent floor matched that of the decedent. Number of prints in the house, some ID'd. Of course, the majority belonged to Conrad. They also found, surprisingly, Karen Conrad's prints. And, not so surprisingly, Sammy Greene's. Fine. There were also a few others that, so far, could not be identified. A crosscheck with the Tafties was negative. But, not everyone from the group was on file. Maybe the FBI report would be more helpful.

He read on. Only Conrad's prints were found on the gun. Now, this was unusual. Pappajohn frowned. There were no fingerprints on the suicide note.

Pappajohn leaned back in his chair and looked up at a corner of the water-stained ceiling. Why in hell not? Conrad's prints should've been on the note — unless he wore gloves. But, why would anybody wear gloves to commit suicide? They wouldn't care if their prints were on the note. The only person who'd care would be —

Much as he wanted to, Pappajohn could not deny the implication. *Damn.* He reached into his desk drawer for a new pack of antacids. Someone else was there that night. Someone who wanted to make sure it looked like suicide. Someone who helped Conrad. Or someone who killed him. Damn it to hell.

His eyes fell on the Taft flyer he'd lifted from Bud Stanton's apartment. He almost felt sorry for the boy. It'd be a shame to ruin his career. Fire and brimstone coming home to roost. He flipped over the paper and saw the list of phone numbers that had been posted on the athlete's refrigerator. Almost absentmindedly, he started to dial the first number.

"Hi, this is Tiffany," a breathy voice answered. "I'm not in, but I'd love to hear from you. Leave me a message, and I may even call you back." The message ended with the sound of a kiss. Shaking his head, Pappajohn continued down his list.

"Hi, this is Michelle and Jennifer and Shannon and Jessica. We're out and we love you." This message dissolved into peals of laughter before the abrupt beep.

The next three or four numbers also led to giggly, barely articulate young women. This guy had the bimbo concession for the entire university. Pappajohn debated not calling the last two numbers, but wearily decided to get it over with, and began punching in the digits. True to form, he got yet another answering machine. However, he was stunned by the name of its owner. Dean Jeffries. Pappajohn sat frozen for a moment before starting to dial the last number.

Sammy made a detour to Ellsford General on her way to Pappajohn's office. "May I come in?" She leaned into the spacious hospital room where Bud Stanton, bandaged from head to toe, lay against pillows, bookended by a pair of beautiful young women.

"Suit yourself," he said, patting a space on the bed, "there's room."

"No thanks." Sammy eased into a bedside chair. "I'm here on business."

"We have to go, Buddy." One of the girls planted a moist kiss on his lips.

Her companion nodded and kissed the athlete even more passionately, while Sammy studiously fiddled with her reporter's notebook. "Bye-bye, Bud," she breathed as she pulled herself away.

Stanton gave them each his most charming smile, lifting up a free right arm to wave. "Okay, babe."

His smile faded as the women left, and he turned to Sammy. "Looks like *you* survived all right."

"That's for sure. I guess you're feeling pretty lucky, too."

"Yeah, right." Stanton held up his left hand. "Call this lucky?"

To her shock, Sammy saw three fingers were missing. "Oh my God."

Stanton stared off at a corner of the room. "Yeah."

"Can you still play?"

"Sure. In the Special Olympics."

"I'm really sorry."

"You know, I had three pro teams after me. You should've seen the offer I got from the Celtics."

"You didn't take it?"

"I was holding out for a better deal. Now I'll be lucky to play in the junior varsity at St. Charlesbury High." Stanton's voice cracked.

Sammy felt uncomfortable. "I could come back."

Stanton's voice returned to normal. "Nah. Ask away."

"About Professor Conrad? Do you think — ?"

"Not again," Stanton exploded. "First the coach, then the feds. I even got the third degree from our very own chief of campus cops, and now you." He turned and faced her squarely. "Trust me, I didn't have to hurt the guy. The fix was already in."

"But Conrad wasn't going to pass you if—"

"I have friends over his head. Way over his head. Okay?"

"Oh." Sammy doubted any names would be forthcoming, but asked, "You wouldn't — ?"

"You got it. I wouldn't." Stanton's mouth set in a hard line. "Next."

Sammy looked down at her notebook. "Uh, what do you think of the Reverend Taft?"

"Taft? I checked him out. Maybe some of his stuff made sense, but man, he was over the edge." Stanton rolled his eyes. "Not my scene."

"Then why attend the rally?"

"Senator Joslin invited me."

Sammy was stunned. "Why?"

"Next year's elections. Thought I'd make a good physical-fitness spokesman during the campaign. Funny, isn't it? The guy wasn't even there. And now —" His eyes fell on his injured hand.

"I'm really sorry, Bud," Sammy repeated.

The athlete's famous confidence was nowhere in sight when he answered, "Yeah. So am I, babe, so am I."

Pappajohn was about to try the last number on the list when Sammy walked into his office.

"Okay, I'm here. Only five minutes late."

The police chief hung up the phone before the connection was made. His expression hardened and his voice was icy. “Sit down.”

“Thanks.” Sammy pulled up a torn leather chair. “How did you know where to find me?”

“Let’s just say the subject came up.” He nodded at Sammy’s bandage.

Nurse Matthews. Pappajohn must have tracked her down to Student Health. If only the old guy was as good at investigating murders.

“All right, I’ll come straight to the point. What was on that tape?”

Sammy squirmed. “Nothing.” Best not to mention the computer sound.

“Ms. Greene.” Pappajohn gave her a fierce stare. “Do you realize that you can be prosecuted for withholding evidence?”

“Evidence? I thought you said it was a suicide.” Sammy shrugged, affecting nonchalance.

“Don’t change the subject. The information on that tape belongs in our investigation. Thanks to your irresponsible negligence, it seems to be lost.”

Sammy threw up her hands. “I don’t remember.”

“Let’s see if I can jog your memory.” Pappajohn’s smile was cold. “Trespassing. Breaking and entering. Lying to my clerks and tampering with documents under false pretenses.”

“You going to have me arrested?” Sammy asked with an edge of sarcasm.

“Worse. I’ve got enough here to bring you up before the university disciplinary board. Guilty on any one of these charges and you’ll be out on your . . . own. So, if you want to graduate from Ellsford, you’d better start talking.”

Sammy seemed to have little choice. “Look, there really wasn’t much. Like I told you yesterday, the recorder was in my purse. It’s mostly static.”

“Well, what *did* you hear?”

"Most of the tape was my interview with the professor from Friday night. But after I left, he had at least one visitor."

Pappajohn sat up in his chair. "Who?"

"I couldn't make out the voices," Sammy replied. "From the tone, though, they could have been fighting."

"About what?" Pappajohn demanded.

"All I could tell were a few words here and there. Nothing that made sense."

Pappajohn banged his fist on the desk. "And that's it?"

"That's why I asked Brian to help."

Pappajohn eyed her dubiously. "Did you touch anything else?"

Sammy hesitated. No way could she risk telling him about the pill bottle now. If she survived his explosion, she was sure she'd end up on the receiving end of a court date. "Not that I remember. No."

"All right." He fixed his brown eyes on hers. "I have just one more thing to say. And let me say it in no uncertain terms. Stay out of my way. Or you'll be sorry."

Sammy had never seen Pappajohn so aggravated. She offered him a conciliatory smile. "Can I go now?"

He nodded. "And I don't want to see you again for a while. A long while."

"For once, Sergeant, you and I agree."

While Sammy had every intention of staying out of Pappajohn's way, she never planned to stop her own investigation of the Nitshi bombing. After striking out with Bud Stanton, she tried to locate and interview a few of the students she'd photographed from the animal rights protest. Poor Katie Miller's picture was the only one she'd given to Reed. The rest of the shots were still stashed in the bottom of her purse. It took two hours to match them up with the out-of-focus ID card images in their records at the Registrar's Office, but by late afternoon Sammy had tracked down the names and addresses of three members of Taft's Youth Crusade.

One refused to talk at all — literally slamming the door in her face. One had left the university for what her roommate termed a sudden "leave of absence." The third answered Sammy's questions with one irrelevant Bible quote after another. Sammy wasn't sure if the Scripture review was intended to hide information or ignorance about Taft and his motives. In either case, the student's loyalty to his "mentor" was unshakable.

By five-thirty, Sammy was convinced that if she wanted any information on the Reverend, she'd have to get it straight from the horse's mouth. Fifteen minutes later she was in St. Charlesbury, standing in front of Taft headquarters. She entered the brick building, knocked on the door to the Reverend's office suite, and walked into the reception area. Except for the thirty-something secretary seated at a desk in the middle of the room, the place was empty. Quite a change from Sammy's last visit. A year ago it was packed with anti-abortion protesters and press.

The woman rose and slipped on her coat. "Sorry. We're closed."

"But she may not be with us tomorrow," Sammy said.

"Sorry?"

"Edith. My great aunt Edith. She's very ill," Sammy improvised. "Surely the Reverend can spare a moment to pray for my dear sweet auntie. She never missed him on TV—gave him more than five hundred dollars last year for his Crusade. And now," Sammy manufactured a single tear and a sad smile. "And now we could lose her." Sammy hoped she wasn't laying it on too thick.

The secretary seemed torn. She looked back and forth from Sammy to Taft's inner sanctum. "I don't know. He's really not— Just a minute." The woman reached for her telephone and pressed the intercom button. "Reverend, can you squeeze in a fifty-eight?" She listened, nodded, then added, "Okay" before hanging up. "God has answered your prayers. The Reverend will see you right after he's done with his meeting."

The secretary picked up her purse and headed out the door. "Have a seat over there," she said, pointing to a folding chair along the wall. "He'll be out in a minute."

Alone in the reception area, Sammy wandered over to the secretary's desk, intent on some snooping. She was reaching for the center drawer when the door to Taft's office opened. She moved out of the line of sight, into the shadows. Two men in dark suits emerged, followed by an effusive Taft. Though not facing her, something about their profiles seemed vaguely familiar to Sammy. She wasn't sure, but they could be the same men she saw trying to get into Stanton's hospital room yesterday.

"It's all taken care of, no problem at all." Taft patted one of them on the shoulder, and Sammy saw him pull away as if in pain. "Sorry. Let's finalize things tomorrow. Call me by noon."

As the Reverend shook hands with each man, Sammy slipped into his office. She looked around the traditional New England study. Its wood paneling, leather chairs, cedar desk and bookcases sported a collection of texts on religion, history, and philosophy. Judging from the variety of titles, Taft's taste in literature was broader than she would have expected. Even more surprising, a high-tech media center with TVs, computers, and other communication devices filled the entire far wall. Some of the bank of television monitors were tuned to local news stations; others broadcast more international fare. Taft's ministry might preach nineteenth-century values but used twenty-first-century tools.

"God's word often needs man's voice. How may I help you?" The words resonated behind her.

Sammy turned to face the preacher whose plastic smile dissolved as soon as he recognized his visitor.

"Oh, no. Not you! What the hell do *you* want?"

Sammy struggled to keep her voice light. "Tsk, tsk. Language, Reverend, really. I'm here about the Nitshi bombing, of course."

Taft remained impassive as he walked over to a high-backed leather chair behind his large cedar desk. He gestured toward the armchair facing him. The minister sat down, placing his hands on the desk, fingertips together as if in prayer, and produced an ironic smile. "I assume you're not planning to confess."

Seated, Sammy realized she had been forced by subtle positioning to look up at Taft in his throne of power. "I'm Jewish. I only confess to my shrink," she admitted wryly, adding in a more serious tone. "What about you, Reverend? Do you have any idea who's responsible for the misfortune?"

"I'm afraid only Satan can be blamed for such tragic events," Taft said. "Terrible incident. Terrible."

"I'd call it more than an incident," Sammy said. "Tell me, Reverend, were you or your people responsible?"

Taft's eyes flashed anger, though he maintained his composure. "Don't think I've forgotten you, young lady. Trying to discredit me at every turn. You're no different than any of the damned media — printing or saying the foulest poison about the Traditional Values Coalition and my ministry."

"Look, I know you've been fighting the Nitshi Corporation from the beginning. You led the campaign against building the institute on campus."

"Ours is a holy crusade," Taft stated. "With only one goal. America for Americans. To recover the old-fashioned morality this country once stood for."

"Old-fashioned morality," Sammy observed. "That's your code for pro-life, anti-women, anti-gay, anti-foreigners."

"If you mean that we're against single people living together in sin, against women murdering their unborn, against the abomination of homosexuality, and, yes, against allowing foreign companies like Nitshi to take over our universities and businesses — you're absolutely right."

"How can you set yourself up as a one-man morality board? Our country was built on diversity of opinion and choice."

"Our country is dying and we have to save it. A smart girl like you should understand that."

"A smart girl like me understands that you're dangerous, Reverend. And I suspect you'd stop at nothing — including violence — to achieve your noble goals."

"Our sense of morality — despite your prejudiced impressions, Ms. Greene — would never condone violence. Something which, judging from your exposure to our pro-life counseling, I would have expected you to understand."

"Maybe violence isn't a part of your religion, Reverend," Sammy responded. "But can you guarantee that it isn't for some of your followers?"

"God speaks to us in different ways," Taft said. "Perhaps some misinterpret His word."

"So you admit it's possible that your people might be behind the—"

"I admit nothing of the kind!" Taft erupted. "Our mission is salvation. To rescue the unborn, to redeem the sinners. We give of our bodies, hearts, and minds. But we would not sacrifice the lives of our young people to do it!" He pointed to the door. "This interview is over."

"You've said enough." Sammy remained seated, slowly thumbing through her reporter's notebook. She added almost casually, "Then you deny that you've been targeting professors who are doing AIDS-related research as part of your anti-gay crusade?"

Taft appeared surprised. "What are you talking about?"

"I'm talking about the deaths of Dr. Nakamura and Professor Conrad. Could your battle plan have included getting them out of the way?"

Taft jumped to his feet. "Out of my office now, or you'll be hearing from my attorney. Again."

"Is that your answer?"

"Would you like me to call security?" Taft's finger was poised over the intercom button on his desk.

Sammy rose. "Thanks. I don't need an escort. I was just leaving." She sauntered toward the door, then turned. "One last question, though, Reverend. What did you do with Luther Abbott?"

The moment Sammy left his office, Taft picked up the phone. But he didn't dial his lawyer's number. Instead, he called the private line of the Republican Senator from Vermont.

"God dammit, Joslin," he shouted when the line was finally answered. "You're going to pay!"

• • •

"Ah believe this is the best pizza in town," Larry declared.

"It's the only pizza in town," Sammy laughed. The program director's exposure to Italian cuisine in Jackson, Mississippi, must have been limited. Luigi's only culinary gift was his cheap prices. Still, she'd missed lunch and she was starving. Sammy swallowed her first goopy bite of the double cheese dish. "So, when do you think we'll be up again?"

Larry shrugged. "Not for a while, ah'm afraid. Dean Jeffries is looking at one or two sites for our temporary quarters."

"And they are—?" She was well aware of the situation. University departments coveted their territory like real estate moguls. She wasn't optimistic.

"Y'all are not going to be happy. He's thinking about the basement of the History building."

Sammy groaned. "Jeez. No windows. And there's no room for us with all the roaches."

"We'll be lucky if we can get that."

"I know. I know." Sammy gazed down at her plate for a moment, lost in thought. "How are we going to set up without Brian?" she asked, fighting back tears.

"It won't be easy," Larry said. "He practically built the station from scratch."

"Guy could hot-wire a generator faster than you could say—Marlboro," she said wistfully. "A real mensch." She looked at Larry. "Anything new on the fire?"

"No. Arson squad's sure it was an accident."

"I don't know. It's too damn convenient if you ask me."

"Convenient?" Larry's frown was quickly replaced by a look of regret. "You're not brewin' another conspiracy theory, are you?"

Sammy's green eyes flashed her frustration. "I'm not paranoid. Brian found something on that tape, Larry. Something I think would have proven Conrad's death was not suicide."

Larry digested his pizza along with her assertion. Finally, he drawled. “Well, even if he had — and we really don’t know that for sure — the fire was unrelated. Everything around the studio was flammable — wood, paper, chemicals.”

“What chemicals?”

“Brian kept a supply of acetone around to clean his equipment. One of the firemen found the remains of an open canister in the debris.” He shook his head. “Ah don’t know how many times ah told Brian to keep those caps on tight. One smoldering ash from his blasted cigarette is it all it would take to light the place up.”

Sammy was about to suggest someone else could have opened the canister, but decided Larry was no more interested in her suspicions than Reed. Without proof. The tape. “By the way, you won’t mind my finishing the Sergio and Conrad stories once we’re back on the air, will you?”

“Something new you didn’t cover?” Larry asked warily.

“Just the friends and family angle. I’ve still got a few more people to contact when I go to New York.”

“New York?”

“Yeah,” Sammy replied, formulating her plan as she spoke. “I want to talk to Sergio’s doctor. Give me a little background as to why he was so depressed. And I’ll try to see the wife of Professor Nakamura.”

“Nakamura? How come? Wasn’t there talk about him killing himself because of some stress reaction from World War Two?”

“Uh-huh. He was Conrad’s mentor. Anyway, I think we should do a follow-up show on suicide, especially from a multicultural perspective,” she explained. “As long as we’re off the air for a while and I’m finished midterms, I might as well take the opportunity to fly down and get the interviews.”

“Okay, but it’s on your nickel,” Larry said. “All our petty cash went up in smoke. Literally.”

“No problem,” Sammy said. “I’ve got a ticket I’ve been saving all semester. There’s something personal I’ve been meaning to do. I guess this is as good a time as any.”

• • •

A few hours later Sammy was back in her apartment, wondering if she really was up to the trip. Her last visit back to Manhattan was so long ago — almost three years. After her grandmother died, there was no reason to return. Without family there, the city was no longer home.

Sammy had spent the summer between her freshman and sophomore year in Los Angeles with her father and his young wife in an unsuccessful attempt to mend their severed relationship. Sammy admitted the rift had been as much her fault as Jeffrey Greene's, but somehow she still couldn't forgive him for abandoning her as a child. She'd understand, her father had said at the airport, when she had a family of her own. Unlikely, Sammy thought. Her family goals, she swore, would be responsibility and commitment. Last summer she'd stayed on campus taking extra courses in American Lit. This summer — she didn't know.

Sammy looked at her watch. Almost nine. Perhaps it was not too late to call. She picked up the notepaper where she'd jotted down the address and phone number Karen Conrad had left on her machine. With a twinge of hesitation, she began to dial.

"Plaza Hotel."

"Uh, room fourteen thirty-six, please. Mrs. Mimiko Nakamura." Sammy drummed her fingers on the table as she waited for the connection.

"Yes? Hello?" The voice on the other end was soft and tremulous with a mild Japanese accent.

"Mrs. Nakamura? Karen Conrad gave me your number."

There was a moment's pause. "Yes?"

"I wanted to know if I might talk with you." Sammy explained that she worked for the campus radio station. "I'm doing a story on Professor Conrad."

Mrs. Nakamura's voice barely rose above a whisper. "So terrible, what happened to Barton. I just heard. A fine man."

"Yes, I know. I'm sorry. I'm planning to be in Manhattan tomorrow, and I wondered if I could stop by your hotel?" Sammy said nothing about her own belief that Conrad was murdered or her sense that somehow his death might be connected with Dr. Nakamura's. She'd wait until she met with Mimiko Nakamura face-to-face.

"Of course. Would one o'clock be all right?"

"Sounds good." Sammy jotted down the time on her notepad. "I'll see you then."

The call had been easier than expected. She hoped Mrs. Nakamura would be as open to her questions tomorrow. Reviewing her plans for the trip, Sammy realized she already had a full schedule: Dr. Ortiz at ten, Mrs. Nakamura at one. Her personal visit would have to wait until late afternoon.

She picked up the phone again and checked with the airlines. If she left on the first flight out of St. Charlesbury and caught an evening commuter back, she could accomplish all her tasks and still return to campus before ten. Maybe Reed would even meet her at the airport.

She dialed his number, hoping to speak with him, but reached his answering machine. "Hi, it's me," she began. "I've decided to fly down to New York tomorrow for the day. Larry asked me to finish my story on Sergio and Conrad and there are a couple of people I'm interviewing, so I'll be running around. But I'll call you sometime between meetings. Hopefully we can get together tomorrow night. Oh, and Reed?" she stopped for a moment, considering whether to add that she loved him. No question that she cared about him, that she enjoyed his company, but love? "Uh, Reed?" Beep. *Saved by the bell.* The machine allowed only a two-minute message.

Just before falling into bed, Sammy made one last call. She asked Dr. Osborne's service to tell him she was going out of town and had to cancel their session in the morning. She would reschedule sometime next week.

CHAPTER EIGHT

FRIDAY
7:00 A.M.

With the contrariness typical of New England in late fall, the weather had changed once again. The passenger compartment of the seven a.m. commuter from St. Charlesbury to Boston alternately filled with streaks of light and sudden blackness as it tossed and dipped, teased by a huge, low-lying nimbus cloud that seemed to resent the trespass of the twin-engine Cessna. One of a mere half dozen travelers rocking in the plane's cocoon, Sammy stared through beads of water marching across her window, anxiously listening to the straining engines that labored against the winds. She had no particular fear of flying. Still, she gratefully exhaled twenty minutes later, after the plane made a skittish touchdown at Logan Airport and rolled to a bumpy stop.

With only minutes to catch the six thirty shuttle to La Guardia, Sammy raced for her gate. She'd dressed up for the city in a green wool sheath dress and black leather pumps. It was the first time in months that she'd worn high heels, and she almost tripped several times as she navigated through the terminal's rush-hour crowd. Arriving, breathless, she handed the flight attendant her ticket and edged her way to the one empty seat on the 737.

Seat 24D was on the aisle next to a balding, middle-aged executive who reluctantly stowed his laptop computer for the upcoming takeoff. "Can't abide by talkers, I'll tell you right now." No sooner was the seat belt light turned off than the man had his shirtsleeves rolled up and was asking for a large cup of coffee. He switched on his laptop and began typing, stopping only to thank the flight attendant for the beverage. That was the last comment Sammy's seatmate made during the forty-minute trip.

Sammy didn't mind. She needed quiet time to think. Retrieving her spiral notebook and a ballpoint pen from her purse, she tried to review the incredible events of the past week by creating a list of what she already knew and what facts were missing.

> #1: Friday—Conrad warning something going on at the university, Sergio's suicide (Palmer's patient)
> #2: Saturday—Conrad found dead: suicide or murder? Brown envelope—Nakamura's gun

Sammy considered the facts pointing to suicide. Conrad had a history of depression, exacerbated by drinking. That was true. Then there was the medical examiner's conclusion favoring a self-inflicted fatal gunshot. Reed had explained that the paraffin test proved Conrad shot the gun with his left hand. Sammy had observed the professor writing on the chalkboard with his left hand. And, of course, there was the suicide note and no sign of a break-in or struggle. So, wasn't suicide the obvious cause of death?

The note could have been typed by anyone, she countered. It would be easy to place Conrad's hand on the paper to create prints—*after* his death. The tape recording proved Conrad had at least one other visitor that night. Who? And what was he after? And where was that brown envelope? What was so important that Conrad had labeled it CONFIDENTIAL? No one seemed to know or care. Also against the suicide theory were Karen Conrad's own doubts. For Sammy, Pappajohn's remark yesterday about withholding evidence created even more suspicion. "Evidence" meant an investigation. If he bought the suicide theory, why investigate?

What evidence did she have to prove murder? Not much. Certainly nothing substantial. Still, Sammy trusted her instinct, and it told her that Conrad's was not a self-inflicted death. Leaning back in her seat, Sammy reflected on the other suicides and what she'd discovered about them, starting a separate list on a new page.

#3: Nakamura — 3 years ago;
Conrad, Sergio — November, 1995

Two suicides in two days. Wait a second. Sammy sat forward. At Conrad's home last Saturday, didn't the paramedic tell Pappajohn there'd been *three* suicides that month? He couldn't have meant Dr. Nakamura. Then who? Sammy put a star by number #3. Once the plane landed, she'd stop by a pay phone and call Reed. Maybe he could find out for her.

She continued her summary of the week's events.

#4: Sunday — Taft sermon — Katie Miller, Luther Abbott there

#5: Monday — attempted hit-and-run, man with mustache

#6: Tuesday — pictures stolen — man with mustache

#7: Wednesday — Nitshi bombing — Katie Miller dead, fire at station — Brian dead — tape, Luther Abbott missing (Palmer's patient)

Next to Luther's name she added — bitten by monkey

#8: Thursday: Lucy Peters reported missing (Palmer's patient)

Then she studied the list. Four deaths. Two, maybe three, suicides. Two missing students. One bombing. One fire. One almost hit-and-run.

A week filled with violence and death.

A jigsaw puzzle of fact and supposition.

Were there really any unifying themes here? Or was her imagination working overtime?

She studied the list, trying out her theory about Taft and a possible vendetta against Nitshi. Yesterday's meeting with the Reverend convinced her she was on the right track. She added "Nitshi" next to each person on her list receiving grants from the conglomerate: Palmer, Conrad, and Nakamura. Grants sponsoring work that, however obscure, had some relationship to AIDS. Now, if you assumed the Reverend was mad and out to get anyone doing AIDS-related research, then maybe Taft did have Nakamura and Conrad killed. Two murders made to look like suicide.

But what about Sergio? Sammy had no reason to believe he hadn't killed himself. She crossed his name off her list for the moment.

Katie Miller and Luther Abbott were directly involved with Taft. That fit.

Lucy Peters was another possible red herring—although she and Sergio were both Palmer's patients. Sammy underlined Palmer's name. Was Taft so diabolical that he targeted the doctor's patients to somehow discredit Palmer? If you believed the Reverend could bomb the Nitshi ceremonies and murder Nakamura and Conrad, anything seemed possible—including setting fire to the studio. Taft must have learned that a tape existed—a tape to prove he was a murderer. A tape that Brian died for.

Sammy circled the word "tape" over and over, wondering how Taft knew.

The flight attendant's announcement over the loudspeaker interrupted Sammy's train of thought. "Ladies and Gentlemen, please fasten your seat belts. We'll be on the ground in five minutes."

Sammy's neighbor shut off his computer. Ping!

The sound reminded her of the engineer's words on her answer phone: *I figured out that ping at the end of the tape. It's the sound of a computer being turned off.*

Being turned off.

Wait a second. She remembered turning the Macintosh off and on at Conrad's home. She'd reached behind to—

That was it!

Behind the computer.

Not the way Conrad did it. His secretary said he always used the floor switch. If Conrad had turned it off that night, the back switch would never have worked for her.

But it did.

Which could only mean one thing: someone else had turned it off.

And if someone else turned it off, it had to be *after* Conrad died.

The implication stunned her. Her instincts had been right all along. Finally, real evidence that someone had killed the professor. Except for one thing. Without that tape, who would believe her?

The plane began its descent into La Guardia as Sammy considered. Through the window she could see that the rain had all but stopped, a few random droplets sliding down the glass like tears.

Tears for whom? Sammy wondered. For Barton Conrad? For Yitashi Nakamura? For Brian McKernan? For Sammy herself?

Without that tape, no one would believe her. She'd have to prove the killing some other way. But how?

"You gonna stay here all day?"

"Excuse me?" Sammy's seatmate stood over her, his laptop clutched in one hand, his briefcase in the other. The plane was already on the ground and had just taxied up to the gate.

"Sorry." Quickly, she stuffed her list back in her purse, gathered her raincoat and handbag, and joined the line heading for the exit.

"I'm sorry, Dr. Wyndham doesn't answer his page."

Sammy had been on hold for almost five minutes. "Can I leave a message?" she asked, her tone brusque.

"One moment." The Ellsford General operator connected her

with the resident voice mail. All medical students, interns, and residents on hospital call used it, so it wasn't private, but Sammy had no choice.

"This is Sammy Greene. I'm calling Reed Wyndham. Reed, I need some information on a third suicide on campus this month. Name, date, where, and why if you can." She checked her watch. "It's eight-thirty now. I'll check back. If you get the information, leave a message on my machine. Thanks."

Sammy hung up and turned to walk toward the terminal exit, unaware that the Asian man speaking Japanese into the telephone beside hers had just relayed her entire message to his boss.

Dr. Palmer stared at the laboratory analyses, letting the full impact of the results sink in. Since his first study subject had died, the doctor had been desperately searching for an explanation. He'd checked and rechecked each batch for contaminants, certain that by strategically deleting key viral genes, he'd eliminated any risk. But now he understood. The problem was not his genetically engineered vaccine. It never had been. The revelation came crashing in on him with the force of a tidal wave.

He turned back to the first page of the report, reading it through once more just to be sure. The virus isolated from Luther Abbott was the same HIV strain he'd originally used to inoculate the macaques, the same strain he'd used to painstakingly develop his AIDS vaccine. That was no surprise. What was completely unexpected was the fact that tissue samples from Subject #12 and Sergio Pinez were not the same.

The significance was almost too much to accept and yet the report left no room for doubt.

A different HIV strain!

The thought chilled him. The virus infecting these two subjects had somehow mutated!

And if it was different in these two, how many others, including Lucy Peters, might be incubating this new strain? The strain that seemed so rapidly fatal, so resistant to treatment. And to his vaccine.

Palmer's mouth grew dry. He felt an incessant drumming in his temples. Horrified, he could no longer avoid the real possibility that his work to save lives had created even more death.

9:40 A.M.

One of the delights of Spanish Harlem is La Marqueta on Park Avenue between 110th and 116th Streets. Sammy grabbed a breakfast burrito at the indoor-outdoor food market before hurrying to her ten o'clock appointment on Lexington.

Dr. Ortiz's office was on the second floor of a graffiti-decorated building. The first floor contained a liquor store whose few windows had been bricked in long before. An ad for cerveza $5.99/6-pack was hung on the front door. Sammy peeked into the shop. Only one wall sported shelves with sandwiches, boxed goods, and nonalcoholic beverages. It was at the far end of the large shopping area, past a gauntlet of wine, beer, and hard spirits. *Clever marketing.* Sammy walked up to the checkout clerk and asked, "How do I get upstairs?"

Without looking up from his girlie magazine, he mumbled, "Around the side."

"Thanks." Sammy walked out to search for the entrance to the doctor's office. She finally found the door, its broken panes of glass repaired with cardboard patches. One flight up, she heard the cries and shouts of children, and used them to guide her to a tiny crowded waiting area. Sammy stepped over a few toddlers and nodded to their young mothers and several seniors seated on uncomfortable looking bridge chairs lined up against the walls.

Behind a makeshift counter, Sammy spotted a gray-haired man dressed in a white lab coat as wrinkled as Reed's. He was probably close to seventy, she guessed, his face full of creases caused by years of worry over families who had more problems than money. Still, José Ortiz had a warm smile, and if the schedule posted on the front entrance was accurate, apparently enough energy to see an army of patients nine hours a day, six days a week.

"Dr. Ortiz? I'm Sammy Greene. I called—"

"Come." The general practitioner pointed to a side door. "I only have a few minutes," he apologized. He ushered her into an empty exam room. "I'm afraid I don't have a real office anymore. I needed all the space for patients."

He pointed to a counter attached to the wall. "Actually it's more efficient. I can see my patient, write my notes, and go on to the next case without breaking stride." He motioned to Sammy to take a seat on the exam table while he leaned against the wall. "Mr. Pinez said you were a close friend of Sergio's — from the university."

Sammy hesitated. Friendship was the ploy she'd used to see the doctor, but now she felt she had to qualify her association with Sergio. "I was a classmate. We took Intro Psych together." That certainly was true enough. "Unfortunately, I really didn't get to know Sergio better," she admitted. "He was a wonderful musician."

"We all thought the boy would be a star."

Sammy nodded. "I played one of his concerti on the air. We got more calls —"

"So where is this radio station, Miss uh —?"

"Greene. Sammy. At Ellsford." Sammy explained about her radio show and the impact of her recent program on suicide. "Actually, Dr. Ortiz, one of the reasons I came to see you was because Sergio's death has upset so many on campus. I'm trying to understand more about Sergio and what made him do what he did," she said. "Maybe keep others from following the same road."

"What is it you want to know?"

"Well, our guest expert said that people often visit a doctor shortly before committing suicide. I wondered if Sergio had come to you."

"You really think knowing that could help others?"

Sammy sensed that the doctor was uncomfortable. "I really do," she said.

"I'm in a difficult position," Ortiz finally answered. "Patient confidentiality, you understand."

"But didn't Mr. Pinez say you could talk to me about Sergio?"

"We spoke. Juan also wishes to prevent other such tragedies."

Abruptly he nodded, slapping his thigh. He left the room and returned shortly with two thin manila folders.

He flipped through the yellowed pages of the first. "Up to date on his shots. Chickenpox. Flu. Ear infections. Typical childhood illnesses. Hadn't really seen him much the past few years."

He moved to the end of the folder. "Fact is, the last time he was here was for his college physical. June twelfth. Everything checked out okay. He—" Ortiz seemed lost in thought for a moment, then snapped back to attention and pulled over the second folder. "A copy of Sergio's Student Health chart just came this morning. I haven't had a chance to look." He opened the record to the last few pages. "Let's see. There are a number of visits here. Most of them to Dr. Palmer. July fifth for immunizations. That's funny, we had him up to date on his shots."

Ortiz scratched his head. "Then twice in October, Palmer again. Sergio saw a Dr. Osborne in Student Counseling Services several times, too, but there's no doctor's note written. I guess they don't write much about counseling visits."

Sammy shrugged.

"More Dr. Palmer. Headaches, cough, and a rash. The last visit was in November. 'Chief complaint, severe headache' and," Ortiz said, turning the page, "Palmer states that Sergio was depressed about a girlfriend." Looking puzzled, he stared off at the corner of the room.

"Something troubling you, Doctor?"

Ortiz hesitated.

"Off the record." Sammy flipped closed her notebook. "I know that Sergio was gay."

"His family would be devastated if they knew."

"I promise to keep this between us, doctor. But I *am* curious. Did he talk with you about it?"

"At his last appointment. Sergio admitted to me that he was struggling."

"What did you say?"

"What could I say? We talked about safe sex. I wanted to be sure the boy would not get AIDS."

"Did he ever go out with girls?"

"He said no. But," the doctor chuckled, "it was hard to avoid them, since his sisters were always bringing friends around. The girls were crazy about him." Ortiz pulled out a photo from a manila folder: Sergio at fifteen. "He was a very good looking boy."

Sammy agreed.

"Such a tragedy."

Everything Ortiz told her jibed with Lloyd's recollection of his roommate. Lloyd had referred Sergio to Dr. Osborne to deal with his gay identity. So why the note about a girlfriend? Maybe Sergio was trying to go straight. Or, maybe he just didn't feel comfortable confiding in Palmer.

"Here's the autopsy report." Ortiz handed Sammy the typed sheet. She skimmed the data. Death was due to multiple trauma and massive hemorrhage. Toxicology negative. Slides of brain tissue had been sent to pathology for analysis, results pending. A shame that analysis couldn't show what Sergio had been thinking in his last few days as well, Sammy reflected. His chart had made the picture even more confusing.

"Could I have a copy of this, doctor?"

"I don't know how it will help other students, but I suppose it's okay."

Sammy again promised to keep that information confidential.

"If you can wait, I'll have my nurse make a Xerox."

Twenty minutes later, Sammy was back outside hailing another cab. When the driver pulled up, she directed him to the corner of Central Park South and Fifth Avenue.

1:00 P.M.

Originally built in 1907, the Plaza Hotel is a legend in its own time, a landmark that has hosted, among others, Zelda and F. Scott Fitzgerald, Teddy Roosevelt, and the Beatles. Solomon R. Guggenheim lived for years in the State Suite surrounded by fabulous paintings. It was Frank Lloyd Wright's New York City headquarters. Sammy hurried inside, stopping only for an instant at the entrance to admire the international flags representing the many countries of important foreign guests. Today, Japan's flag was among those waving in the breeze.

At the registration desk, a hotel clerk informed Sammy that Mrs. Nakamura was expecting her. "Room fourteen thirty-six." The young woman directed her to the far end of the lobby where she stepped onto an elevator filled with out-of-town tourists loaded down with shopping bags and cameras.

At fourteen, Sammy got off and wandered down a long hallway until she found Mrs. Nakamura's room and knocked. It was on the corner — probably had a great view.

A tiny Japanese woman in a blue silk Chanel suit opened the door. Her short black hair was streaked with gray and stylishly coifed. Her face was smooth skinned, almost creaseless, her eyes bright ebony. Sammy guessed her age to be a very well-maintained eighty. "Miss Greene?" she inquired.

Sammy nodded. Mrs. Nakamura's features looked surprisingly familiar. Sammy surmised she must have seen her photo in the *Ellsford Eagle*.

Mimiko Nakamura bowed her head. "Please come in." She ushered Sammy into a large sitting area with a floor-to-ceiling view of Central Park. The light morning drizzle had left the city with a scrubbed and shiny look — at least from this height.

"How beautiful," Sammy proclaimed. "And far above the madding crowds."

"Actually, crowds do not bother me. Like all Japanese, I am used to being surrounded by people." Mimiko spoke in flawless, lightly accented English. "If I'm not mistaken, you've spent many years among the crowds here in New York. I'd guess at least some in the Lower East Side."

"How did you —?"

"I received my master's degree in linguistics from Berkeley. Studying the American accent became a fascinating hobby. Or, should I say, accents?"

"Like Henry Higgins."

"Except I avoid the social judgments," she replied diplomatically. "My interest is purely academic." She waved at a lemon-colored loveseat opposite her own cushioned chair. "Please, have a seat."

A silver tea service had been laid out on the table between them. "I took the liberty of ordering tea," Mimiko said as she poured Sammy some of the steaming brew into a china cup. "It's not green tea, but it is pleasant enough."

"Thank you." Sammy waited for the older woman to serve herself, then both drank at once in a kind of ceremonial silence. Sammy found the taste of the tea a bit strange, but felt herself soothed by its warmth. Pleasant indeed, she thought, taking another long sip of the beverage. A "magic brew."

"How long have you studied at Ellsford University, Miss Greene?" Mimiko finally spoke.

"I'm a junior. And, please, call me Sammy."

"That is an unusual name, is it not?"

"I was named after my grandfather — my mother's father. He had a heart attack just before I was born. In the Jewish religion, children are often named after those who've died — so they'll live on through us." Sammy was surprised at herself. It was the first time she'd ever told anyone the real reason for her name. She'd usually make a flip remark — that her parents wanted her to be different, for example — probably because she'd always felt different. For the first time, as Sammy relaxed in the spacious hotel suite, she felt as if her name actually suited her.

"The spirits of one's ancestors require that they be remembered and honored by their descendants." Mimiko spoke softly. "It is that way for us, too." She looked off to one side for a moment, then quickly turned to face her guest. "Now, Sammy, how may I help you?"

Sammy put down her cup and took her notepad from her purse. "Professor Conrad was one of the best teachers on campus. The students respected him — even though they didn't always like him."

"That is usually true of the good teachers."

"I'd started interviewing him the day he received the Ellsford Teaching Award. Unfortunately, he—" Sammy searched for the right word, refusing to say suicide, "unfortunately, he passed away before I could finish the piece." She looked at Mimiko. "One of the things I've since learned was how much he admired your husband."

"Barton was like family in a way. Yitashi loved him as a son." The widow's eyes drifted over to several family photos placed on an end table beside the loveseat, focusing on one of a young Yitashi Nakamura with his wife and two children: a girl and boy. "Perhaps even more than a son," she added before turning back to Sammy.

"I understand your husband was responsible for bringing Professor Conrad to Ellsford."

"Yes. He offered him a position after Barton failed to gain tenure at Stanford."

Sammy started writing. "I thought Professor Conrad's research was considered top caliber. And he brought in grants. Why do you think he didn't get tenure?"

"The ways of universities are not always understandable to outsiders, but when it comes to tenure, there is often more than just academic talent to be considered. In Barton's case, I believe, the talents that made up his remarkable character may have led to his downfall."

"How do you mean?"

Mimiko took time to formulate her answer. "As you yourself have said, he was a brilliant teacher and researcher. Unfortunately, his enthusiasm was often misinterpreted."

"Passion over politics," suggested Sammy.

"There were some with whom he fell into disfavor, I'm afraid. It is an old story."

"Apparently about to be repeated. Professor Conrad wasn't a shoo-in for tenure at Ellsford, either."

Mimiko poured herself another cup of tea.

Sammy asked, "Any idea who his friends were at Ellsford?"

"It has been over two years since I visited St. Charlesbury. I have had no wish to return since my husband's death." Mimiko paused for a moment, eyes misting. When she spoke, her voice was barely a whisper. "I suspect Karen — his wife — was his best friend. It must have been difficult for him when they moved apart."

She narrowed her eyes, thinking. "And Dr. Osborne, the psychologist. From our Stanford days. Of course, Dr. Chandra, in biology, I believe — part of our evening discussion group — a very literate man. He had done a study of Hindu architecture and the Tamil influence that we found so intriguing. We would meet on Friday evening, you know, to talk of . . ." She waved a hand, searching.

"Yes, I know," Sammy said. "Karen told me. It must have been a really awesome group." Looking down at her notebook, she tossed out a casual question, "Did Professor Conrad have any enemies?"

"I fear Hamilton Jeffries was never very fond of Barton. At least that's what Yitashi always believed." Mimiko took a sip of her tea. "As chairman of his department there and a graduate of Stanford himself, Jeffries would have influence over the tenure committee."

Hamilton Jeffries? Sammy thought back to her conversation with the dean, recalling how deftly Jeffries had sidestepped her questions about tenure at Ellsford by saying that Conrad's death made the whole issue moot.

Was the dean, as Mimiko suggested, Conrad's enemy? Sammy contemplated a new scenario for a moment. Conrad had dialed Jeffries the night he died. He'd also had something ready to send him — in the brown envelope. Was Jeffries in when Conrad called? Did he ever get the envelope? If he did, and if it contained information exposing a scandal on campus — one that could destroy careers or even the reputation of the university itself — what wouldn't Jeffries do to stop Conrad? Hard to believe that such an eminent academician would resort to murder. Still, it was another piece to an already jumbled puzzle.

"All you all right?"

Sammy looked up, embarrassed. "Sorry, I was just thinking there's so much about Professor Conrad's death that doesn't make sense."

Mimiko raised an eyebrow. "How so?"

"Well, to be honest, Mrs. Nakamura, suicide just doesn't fit." Sammy shared her impressions of Conrad during their interview. She related the disparities between Conrad's circumstances and the typical suicide profile, mentioning Karen Conrad's assertion that her husband seemed incapable of killing himself.

"Sometimes we don't always know the men we love as well as we think we do," Mimiko said, her eyes welling up with tears.

Sammy realized she must have been referring to her own husband. "I'm sorry. It must be very difficult."

"Yitashi was a remarkable man." Mimiko's soft voice was filled with obvious sadness.

"It must have been quite a shock," Sammy said.

The widow stared straight ahead for a moment, then answered, "I had no idea that he was so depressed."

"He seemed normal to you?"

"Well, no. He was concerned. Worried about something. But I never imagined that he would—"

"Forgive me, but I read that he'd been interned in a camp during the war. Maybe—?"

"Posttraumatic stress syndrome? That's what they said, but it wasn't so," Mimiko insisted. "After such a terrible experience, we were stronger, not weaker."

"We?"

Mimiko lowered her eyes. "We met in the camps. I had recently been widowed. We helped each other get through those difficult years."

"I didn't realize you—"

"It's something neither of us spoke about. We went on with our lives."

Sammy looked over at one of the photos: Mimiko carrying a bouquet of flowers standing next to a smiling Yitashi. There was a small boy, maybe four or five, beside them. Sammy now recognized him as a younger version of the child in the other family portrait. Obviously, Mrs. Nakamura had a son before she married the professor. Another photo showed the older boy, his arm around his little sister and his parents at the beach. Seemed like an idyllic family. Why would Nakamura want to leave?

"Mrs. Nakamura," Sammy asked, "why do you think your husband—?"

The widow looked down at her hands and barely whispered, "Shame."

Sammy was confused. "What?"

Mimiko abruptly stood, her face impassive. "I'm afraid I must get ready for another appointment."

Sammy rose. "I've overstayed my welcome as it is."

The Japanese woman walked her to the door.

Sammy flipped her notebook closed as she followed. "One last question, if you don't mind?"

"Yes?"

"Do you have any idea why Professor Conrad didn't get any grants from the Nitshi Corporation or its subsidiaries after your husband died?"

This time Sammy caught the flash of hesitation. "I'm afraid I don't. As I said before, linguistics was my field, not immunogenetics." She opened the door, making it clear that she preferred to end the conversation.

The moment Sammy was gone, Mimiko Nakamura wondered whether she had said too much or whether she should have said more. Finally, she decided she'd made the right choice. No turning back now.

At two fifteen Sammy found a phone booth in the lobby of the Plaza Hotel and paged Reed at Ellsford General. After several minutes, the hospital operator announced that he wasn't answering his beeper. Busy with an emergency, Sammy guessed. Falling back on her contingency plan, she tried her answering machine.

Sure enough, Reed had left a message, "Sammy, I don't know what you're up to, but I hope you're being careful."

Sammy smiled to herself. Just like Reed to worry about her.

"There was a third suicide on campus this month," his message continued. "A psych grad student named Seymour Hollis. I remember him because he was admitted on my ER shift. The guy had AIDS and apparently was pretty depressed. He OD'd on barbiturates. Ironically enough, I just got a call from Harvey Barnes."

Sammy knew Reed's friend, Harvey, was a hospital pharmacist.

"About those tablets you wanted me to check out. Seems that Professor Conrad brought one to Harvey's boss two weeks ago asking the same question."

That was interesting.

"Turns out it's a new drug being tested for AIDS — developed by Nitshi. Dr. Palmer is the principal investigator. What's weird is number twelve on the label refers to the twelfth patient in the study — Seymour Hollis!"

Sammy did a double take. Nitshi again. And Palmer.

"And the strangest thing," Reed added, "was that —" Beep!

Oh no! Reed had run out the two minute message limit. "Reed!" Sammy banged on the pay phone. "Reed. Reed. Call back." Damn.

The machine had clicked off. That was it. No more messages. Frustrated, Sammy redialed Ellsford General, but got the same response from the operator. Reed was off beeper, although this time, the voice on the other end was less polite. Hanging up, Sammy considered the significance of what she'd just learned. The third suicide was someone with AIDS, someone receiving a drug produced by Nitshi.

Nitshi and Palmer and AIDS research.

It hit her like a lightning bolt. Would Taft stop at nothing to discredit the Japanese? Conrad must have made the same connection. A connection that cost him his life.

Someone tapped on the door of the booth. Sammy turned to see an impatient man pointing to his wristwatch. She held up one finger to indicate she'd just be another minute, then pulled the phone from its cradle and furiously punched in Manhattan information. "Nitshi Corporation. Please hurry."

• • •

Fifteen minutes later, a taxi deposited Sammy at Forty-fifth and Park, just in front of the Nitshi Tower. The company's corporate headquarters was housed in a building that looked even more high-tech than the Research Institute at Ellsford University. The fifty-five-story bronze mirrored-glass building was as sleekly contoured as a rocket ship. Sammy entered the lobby through hand-carved ebony doors and was immediately impressed with the chic blend of glass, black furniture, textured concrete, and a gurgling koi-filled stream. Only the tailored-suited men and women striding through with briefcases in hand gave an inkling of the intense activity on the floors above.

Unlike the Research Institute, there was no central island with camera monitors. Instead, Sammy noticed several uniformed guards strategically placed at various posts around the perimeter of the lobby — each with a handheld device that resembled a Sony Watchman. In fact, it was a combination walkie-talkie and sophisticated multistation TV network that played off of remote control video cameras throughout the building, allowing them to observe the comings and goings of anyone inside. Nitshi's security was just as strict, Sammy thought, observing that no one entered the elevators without a badge.

She searched the spacious lobby until she located an information area where a well-dressed Japanese woman was seated. "May I be of assistance?" the woman asked with a practiced politeness.

"Where is Mr. Ishida's office?" Sammy spoke with all the confidence she could muster.

"Suite fifty-two ten." The woman raised a sculptured eyebrow. "Do you have an appointment?"

"No," Sammy admitted. "But I need to see him."

"Without an appointment, I'm afraid that's impossible."

"If you could just call Mr. Ishida, I'm sure —"

The receptionist cut her off again. "I'm sorry." She quickly turned her attention to a bespectacled older man who'd just walked over and handed her his business card. "Yes?"

"Hal Winfield, Dean of Natural Sciences, L.A. University. I'm here for the presentation."

The receptionist checked the small pile of nametags on her counter. "Of course, Mr. Winfield." She handed him his badge and held up another one. "Is Miss O'Malley with you?"

"No, I'm afraid my assistant couldn't make it this trip."

The Japanese woman returned the assistant's badge to the pile. "The academic group will be assembling in the third-floor conference room in—" she checked her watch, "five minutes. Take the first set of elevators in the corner."

He hurried off in the direction she'd pointed.

The phone behind the receptionist rang, forcing her to turn away from the counter. Taking advantage of the woman's momentary inattention, Sammy grabbed Margaret O'Malley's nametag and clipped it to her dress. Seconds later, she had followed Dean Winfield across the lobby into the crowded elevator.

The guard posted near the lift waved her in when she flashed the fake badge. Once inside, she covered it with her coat and wedged herself in the back behind an overweight couple so that Winfield wouldn't notice her. At three, the group stepped off and headed down the corridor. Sammy came too, but lingered until they had all entered the conference room before taking a seat near the exit—just in case she had to make a quick escape.

Without any sign, the room darkened and on the wall opposite where everyone sat, a film began to roll.

"Good morning," boomed the anonymous announcer. "Welcome to Nitshi Corporate Headquarters. You've been invited here this morning to learn about how our company has grown in less than fifteen years, from a small chemical manufacturing firm to a sophisticated global multinational pharmaceutical conglomerate."

The screen filled with a black-and-white shot of the original plant in Kyoto where inside, industrious looking Japanese scientists were shown working in spacious, well-equipped labs. "Today we have factories and holding companies in over a hundred countries." A world map located each of sixty factories and a dozen research centers including Malaysia, Singapore, Sydney, Brussels, Johannesburg, Montreal, and Buenos Aires. The audience of academics couldn't help but be awed. Even Sammy was impressed.

"Most of you represent universities that have been the recipients of generous Nitshi grants. We believe that through these collaborative research alliances between academia and private industry, we can determine the etiology of Alzheimer's disease or the immune mechanism causing AIDS and develop new and more effective treatments and cures."

Over a montage featuring sleek edifices of sparkling glass and steel like the Research Institute at Ellsford, the voice told of Nitshi subsidiaries specializing in every major new scientific area from biotechnology to genetic engineering.

"At Nitshi, we are committed to long-term goals. For every new drug that works, there are about a thousand that don't. Some drugs are researched for as long as ten years and then abandoned. A single drug can cost as much as three hundred million dollars in R & D before we can bring it to market."

The film featured a modern manufacturing plant where empty bottles were carried in on a giant conveyor belt. By the time they had crossed the room, the bottles had been sterilized, filled with capsules, labeled, topped with cotton, and sealed. All done by automation.

"Through work initiated at Biotech Development Corporation, some twenty new biotech drugs are currently in clinical trials — several at your institutions."

Sammy sat up straighter. Biotech Development Corporation was one of the companies that had sponsored Conrad and Nakamura. She wondered if it was the same one that was testing the AIDS drug Seymour Hollis had taken.

"NuVax, Inc. and Virology Research Foundation —"the announcer was saying.

So Reed was right. They were all Nitshi subsidiaries. Until Nakamura's death, Nitshi had funded Conrad. Sammy already knew that Nitshi funded Nakamura and Palmer. Now she had confirmed the link to Conrad.

She had to talk to Mr. Ishida. Quietly, she slipped out of the conference room before the movie ended.

Once in the hallway, Sammy checked to make sure that no one had followed her, then headed for the elevator and pushed the "up" button. A few moments later, an empty car was whisking her swiftly and quietly to the fifty-second floor. Certain her stomach had shifted a few inches when the car finally braked to a rapid stop, she walked off, a bit shaken into a dimly lit, plush-carpeted corridor stretching in both directions. There were no signs indicating suite numbers and no one around to ask the way. Sammy decided to turn to her right for a first try.

After passing several doors, she realized she had traveled down an odd-numbered hallway. Returning in the other direction toward the even numbers, she finally arrived at Suite 5210. Gated by an unmarked walnut door, the suite number was engraved in small letters on a brass plaque that hung off to one side. Sammy looked around for a doorbell or buzzer. Seeing none, she decided to try the doorknob.

The door opened easily. Sammy stepped into a spacious, brightly lit, paneled reception room containing a small sitting area — empty — and a desk, behind which sat a very attractive secretary who could easily have been the twin of the woman in the lobby.

"May I help you?"

"I don't have an appointment, but I've got to talk to Mr. Ishida," Sammy spoke quickly, heading off an interruption. "It's a matter of life and death."

That got the woman's attention.

"Please, I won't take much of his time. Just tell him it's about the bombing at Ellsford University. I'm a student there. My name is Sammy Greene."

The woman examined Sammy's nametag and frowned.

"I borrowed this," Sammy started to explain. "Please," she said again, "ask Mr. Ishida if he'll see me."

"All right, have a seat." The secretary pointed to the cluster of comfortable chairs as she herself rose and moved toward the back door. "Mr. Ishida is on a trunk call. Let me stick my head in and see if he's free."

"Thanks." Sammy walked over to the waiting area and sat down as the woman disappeared into the inner sanctum. Scattered on a glass table were several brochures. She picked up one that was a descriptive public relations flyer about the Nitshi Corporation and slipped it into her purse. *Something to read later*. Several brightly colored pieces of paper in an adjacent trash can caught her eye. She fished out a few discarded old employee newsletters. They, too, went into her purse just as the secretary reappeared.

"Go right in," she motioned with a wave. "He'll be off the phone in a minute."

Sammy entered the room slowly, trying to shore up her courage. The corner office was dominated by floor-to-ceiling glass windows that allowed a panorama of Manhattan even more breathtaking than the view from Mrs. Nakamura's hotel suite. The one remaining wall was filled with original French Impressionist paintings. The floor was decorated with antique Oriental rugs.

In the center of the room behind an enormous hand-carved mahogany desk filled with a myriad of expensive looking computers and technical equipment, sat the CEO of Nitshi, dressed in a tailored silk suit, one manicured hand writing on a notepad as he spoke into the receiver held by the other. He waved for her to sit in one of the plush leather chairs in front of the desk.

"Yes, yes. It is already taken care of." The executive's voice was icy. "I'll be arriving late this afternoon. On the Gulfstream."

"Miss Greene," Ishida said smoothly to Sammy as he hung up the phone. "I understand you have some information for me."

"Where was it?" Larry Dupree asked the fire chief.

"Must have been under your engineer's workstation. Looks like it was the only thing of his that survived." He handed Larry a charred and slightly twisted rectangular metal box. "My men didn't even notice it until they'd cleared away most of the debris."

"Is this all you found?"

"Afraid so. A blaze like the one that hit your radio station doesn't usually leave much more than cinder and ash. Obviously, that container was fireproof."

Larry looked down at the object in his hands. So sad. All that was left of poor Brian's world. It didn't seem fair that the essence of one man could be reduced to a small metal box.

"Amazing," Yoshi Ishida commented when Sammy had finished. He leaned back in his sleek leather chair. He was a small man, but his round face had a sculptured look that over the years he had forged into a hardness that could be intimidating. Now, he forced himself to soften his expression. "I must say, you make a compelling case against Reverend Taft. I wish my own investigators were that thorough."

"You mean you believe me?"

"Actually, Dr. Palmer first alerted me to the possibility that Taft might be dangerous," Ishida confided. "Unfortunately it was only after this week's bombing incident that I paid attention. And, of course, now the FBI is involved."

FBI. That explained the two men at the hospital. The same two men who visited Taft yesterday. Obviously undercover.

Ishida placed the tips of his fingers together. "While we do feel the Reverend is responsible for the bombing, we still don't have enough evidence to prove that anyone else was murdered."

"But what about the fact that all the so-called suicides can be tied in some way to Nitshi?" Sammy asked. "I think Taft is trying to damage your company."

"It all makes sense, I agree, but it's still not positive proof." Ishida affected a smile. "At this juncture, Miss Greene, it is critical that we keep the investigation confidential. I'm sure you understand."

"Of course."

"Then I hope you will allow the proper authorities to do their job." The smile broadened. "Without interference."

"Oh, I would never do anything to undermine the FBI," Sammy said. "I'm just glad you're on top of things."

Ishida stood up and came around to where Sammy sat. He extended his hand. "It's been a pleasure, Miss Greene. I'll have my secretary show you out."

Sammy rose. "That's okay. I know the way." She removed her badge and placed it on the CEO's desk. "I guess I won't be needing this.".

Sammy exited the suite and headed for the double elevators just outside. Both arrived at the same time—one lit for "up," one for "down." Sammy stepped into the down car and turned to face forward just as the doors closed. She barely saw two men, each wearing Nitshi employee badges, engrossed in deep conversation walking down the hall. One man had his face turned away from her. The other? She wasn't sure, but the short, heavyset man looked familiar.

"I hope she didn't recognize you." Ishida was watching his own handheld TV monitor. It was tuned to Station #1, the lobby entrance. Sammy was just walking out of the building.

Peter Lang turned away from the monitor and shook his head. "I'm sure she didn't."

"And your friend with the mustache?"

"He's agreed to take a long vacation."

Ishida nodded. "Fine. Now you must concentrate on Miss Greene. She has proven to be a very resilient young woman indeed."

"At least she hasn't put it all together."

"But she will," Ishida said. "Unless, of course, we conclude her investigation." He stared at Lang for a long moment, before adding, "Once and for all."

It was after three when Sammy slid into the backseat of the dirty, dented cab and gave the man at the wheel her old address.

The driver, a recently immigrated middle-aged Indian, looked back at Sammy. "You sure you wish to go there? That is a very rough neighborhood."

"I used to live there."

The man shrugged, put the cab in gear, and sped toward FDR Drive.

Sammy listened with only half an ear as the cabbie chattered in nonstop musical English about the family he'd left behind in Bombay, his dreams for a better life, and his disappointment in this new country, which seemed to have such a voracious appetite for violence. "Sometimes I think maybe I will never live to see my wife and sons again."

Sammy mumbled a sympathetic response as they remained caught up in the slow-moving rush hour traffic on 3rd Avenue. They hit some gut-wrenching potholes near East 34th and narrowly avoided colliding with a crosstown bus, a sanitation truck, and a bag lady before pulling onto the expressway. At East Houston the man exited, driving down back streets to a run-down, crumbling area just twenty minutes from New York's Upper East Side.

"You wish for me to wait?" the driver asked, his voice tinged with concern.

Sammy reached for her wallet. "That's okay. The subway station is a few blocks away."

"You should be suiting yourself."

The moment the cab sped off, leaving her standing alone on the street corner, Sammy began to regret her bravado. A light breeze had sprung up, carrying a hint of more rain on its chill edge. Behind, in the east, the sky was darkening. Fighting a shiver, Sammy started down the cracked sidewalk toward Hester Street. It was early evening and the Lower East Side neighborhood where she was born was just now coming alive. Only the scene wasn't the way it had been in her childhood—the litter-free sidewalks and well-maintained brownstones had given way to crumbling buildings decorated with graffiti and gang signs.

When Sammy finally arrived at number 453, she found a scrawny Puerto Rican teenager dressed in a spandex miniskirt and thigh-high black boots pacing in front of the building, trying to attract men in passing cars. An unshaven old codger leaned in the doorway, drinking from a bottle wrapped in a paper bag. A group of young Asian toughs stood in the park across the street, exchanging packages for cash.

Sammy walked up the steps to the front door, hesitated for an instant, then entered the small foyer. A fly-specked, fifteen-watt bulb created feeble light, exaggerating shadows, obscuring corners. She shuddered, assaulted by the sour odors of stale urine and decay. The brown and red carpet had long been pulled up, leaving only filthy cement flooring. Paint was peeling from the walls, thick with grime.

A small boy, maybe eight or nine, sat on the stairs and eyed her with practiced toughness. "Whatcha doin' here, lady?"

"I used to live here." To her right was the closed door of the ground-floor apartment. Directly ahead were four flights of stairs.

The boy didn't seem convinced. "Which one?"

"Three B." She began her ascent, avoiding the greasy banister. Someone had written "Fuckit" on the wall. Otherwise the tagging was unintelligible to Sammy. When she lived here, the wall had always looked freshly painted. She could still hear her mother reminding her from the top of those stairs not to touch it with dirty hands.

As she reached the second floor, she was so overcome by the presence of old memories, she had to stop on the landing for breath before going on.

Playing hide-and-seek through these corridors with friends.

Her mother coming home, still wearing her white hospital coat.

Her father, handsome and young in his elegant custom suits, always smelling of cologne.

The past wrapped around her like a time warp. A brief, safe time almost two decades ago. Before—

"You okay, lady?" The boy was still shadowing her.

"Fine," Sammy said. Taking a deep breath, she continued up to the third floor. The relentless beat of hip-hop emanating from the apartment she'd called home for the first seven years of her life grew louder with each step. Back then the halls would have been filled with the sounds of Mozart and Bach.

"Gimme ten bucks. I'll show it to you."

"What?" Sammy turned to the boy. His face was earnest. "Someone's in there. I couldn't."

"Nah. They just playin' music. Looks like they're home."

"Excuse me?"

"So's they don't get ripped off," he explained. "Ten bucks."

Sammy pulled two fives from her wallet. "You have a key?"

"Nope. Just this." The boy took out a penknife, not unlike the one Sammy had used at Conrad's, and picked the tarnished lock. The door opened under his expert hands. Sammy was reminded of Vince DeFuccio, the teenager who taught her to pick locks at age eight. Some things hadn't changed.

Sammy glanced around the hallway with a guilty look as the boy motioned for her to enter. "Well, I'll only stay a minute." She couldn't resist a peek inside.

Ton-Lōc assailed her ears, the smell of urine and feces her nose. But it wasn't the different sounds or odors that overwhelmed Sammy as she walked from room to room. It was the fact that this apartment had a transient feeling, as if no one ever lived there any length of time, no one ever made it their home. The furniture was sagging and worn, the walls and shelves, paint peeling and cracking, devoid of any pictures or personal mementos. When Sammy had lived here the unit had been filled with books and family photos and music and, at times, love.

At least until the trouble started. And her father moved out.

At the end of a narrow, dimly lit hall was the room her mother had used as her office. Now it was someone's bedroom. The mattress on the floor was tattered, the sheet covering it, long in need of washing. As she gazed around the room, a kaleidoscope of images tumbled through Sammy's mind.

The day her mother died had been beautiful for November, and she'd dawdled coming home from school. When she'd finally returned to the apartment that afternoon, no one greeted her. There was only silence. She threw her books and coat on the living room sofa and headed for the back. Her mother lay peacefully on the daybed. Thinking she was sleeping, Sammy tiptoed in and stood over her. "Mommy," she whispered. "Wake up."

Sammy recalled reaching out to touch her, then seeing the note and the empty pill vial. A paralyzing fear gripped her. "Mommy! Wake up!" Sammy screamed and screamed until she was wrapped in the arms of old Mrs. Shapiro from next door who heard the cries and came and found them.

Sammy felt awash in a wave of guilt, as palpable now as it had been fifteen years ago.

If only she'd come home sooner.

My fault.

Dr. Osborne had called it survivor's guilt.

Your mother was already dead when you found her, Sammy. You couldn't have helped her.

She thought about his words as she stared at the space where the daybed once stood, where she'd found her mother. Already dead.

She wasn't responsible?

Your mother made a choice, Sammy. Her choice.

Sammy started as she felt something running across her foot. She looked down to see a small furry animal scurrying under the bed. A rat. Her mother would have gone ballistic if as much as a dust bunny had graced the room. And now—she looked at the dilapidated room—everything's gone.

Dr. Osborne was right. All these years she'd blamed herself for her mother's dying, and it wasn't her fault at all. Never had been. Neither had her father's leaving. She could feel the weight of all that guilt leave her shoulders. It was time to move on.

"Best be goin', Lady. They'll be home soon."

The boy's voice interrupted her thoughts. "Oh, yes." Sammy checked her watch: five fifteen. "I had no idea it was so late."

She followed the boy out into the hallway. The sound of the apartment door slamming behind them reverberated like a gunshot. Nervous, she mumbled a hasty "thanks" to the youngster and, without looking back, hurried off down the stairs.

Outside, the last embers of twilight were long faded. A quarter moon cast a wan pallor over the dark neighborhood, throwing the outlines of buildings into jagged relief. The already foreign-looking terrain appeared even more forbidding. The early morning's drizzle had returned with a vengeance, chasing most of the street-life parade indoors — or at least out of sight. Shivering, Sammy peered down the empty street, feeling very alone. Thank God the subway stop was only four blocks away.

Hunching against the raindrops, she hastened her gait, adrenaline rushing through her veins. In the middle of the first block she almost tripped over a derelict lying in an abandoned doorway. The homeless man mumbled a slurred complaint and she hurried along.

At the end of the second block she stepped into a deep puddle, soaking her feet to the ankles. "A *brokh*!" she cursed, as she tried to shake off the water. Now she had to walk with an accompanying "swish, swish" from the moisture in her shoes. The sound was unnerving. She felt as if a wet ghost shadowed her with each step. She looked up and down the alleyways, afraid of an unexpected meeting with her ethereal stalker. Damp, rain-slicked debris littered the sidewalk. She stopped for a moment, trying to sort out the sounds around her, giving each small noise an identity in order to allay her fears. The high-pitched drip, raindrops hitting a tin can, the "whoosh," distant traffic blocks away, the "rasp," her own ragged breathing. Calmer, she moved on, her footsteps slapping like a drumroll against the pavement.

By the third block, she was certain she heard a different cadence creating a counterpoint to her own footsteps. The beat was loud and invasive. Paced steps behind her. Though the night cold was piercing, beads of sweat broke out on her forehead. Her heart pounded against her chest. She glanced uneasily over her shoulder.

Only her own shadow stretched behind her. Nothing more. She laughed nervously and took a deep breath, trying to slow her racing heart.

A car swept past, perilously close to the curb where she stood, buffeting her with hails of spray. Its taillights disappeared into the misty curtain of darkness before she could react. "Shit!" Now she was really soaked, her hair damp against her ears, a worm-like cap of sleek ringlets.

One more block.

She picked up the pace to a jog, her pumps losing traction and slipping on the slick pavement. She didn't dare slow down, urging herself onward at a faster rate. *Come on, Sammy, one more block, you're nearly there!*

Focused on her goal, she was unaware of the man who came out of the darkness until he was directly behind her. He grabbed her by the belt, tossed a jacket over her head, and, before she could react, dragged her into an adjacent alley.

"Help!" But Sammy's cries were merely sounds within her. The pressure of her attacker's hand against her mouth made it impossible to scream. She felt as though she were suffocating as the man threw her on the wet gravel and crushed her with his weight.

"You're gonna pay!"

Terror seized her. *Oh God, he's going to rape me*. Struggling to resist the attacker's hand moving up her thigh, Sammy kicked one leg out. The leg missed its target, as the rapist grabbed her calf and sat down on her knee. Angry, he punched her hard in the stomach. "Damn bitch!"

Galvanized by the pain, Sammy pushed out with her other leg, aiming her two-inch heel at her attacker's private parts. This leg landed in the right place and the man, screaming in agony, rolled off of Sammy's knee.

"Run, motherfucker. Police!"

Sammy and her attacker both heard the distant shout. The sounds of a siren were growing louder.

"Police!" The voice was closer now, as was the moan of the siren.

Still groaning in pain, the man lifted himself up and hobbled off down the alley into the darkness.

Stunned by the blow to her abdomen, Sammy felt too weak to move. She lay in the alley for several minutes before opening her eyes. There was no trace of her attacker.

"You okay, lady?" The child who'd shown her the apartment stood over her.

"I'm —" her voice was barely a croak. Painfully she sat up. "I'm okay." She was cold and wet and covered with dirt, but at least she was alive. My God, she thought, how close she'd come to dying— again.

He held out a hand to help her up.

Slowly, pressing a hand into her stomach to contain the pain, Sammy struggled to her feet. "I'm okay." She gave the boy an inquisitive look. "Were you the one who yelled 'police'?"

The boy's eyes had a mischievous twinkle. "Yeah."

Sammy looked around. No sirens, no cops. "I thought I heard a siren."

Sporting a wide grin, the boy pulled out an electronic gizmo from his pocket. He pressed a button on it, and the alley echoed with the sound of a siren.

Sammy couldn't resist a laugh. "I'm glad you're here. Thank you."

Nodding, the boy extended his other hand. In it were Sammy's two bills. "Momma tol' me to give the money back."

"What's your name?"

"Darnell."

Sammy took the bills and stuffed them in the boy's pants pocket. "Well, Darnell. I think your momma would be very proud of you right now, and she'd say it was okay to keep a reward."

"Yeah," Darnell grinned. "Okay."

Off in the distance, the wail of a police siren once again was heard coming toward them. This one sounded real.

"I'm outta here," Darnell said, running off. "Cops."

"Wait!" Sammy shouted after him to no avail. The boy had disappeared into the alley before the squad car arrived.

At seven p.m. Dr. Palmer switched off the respirator. Exactly three minutes later, he pronounced Lucy Peters dead.

The Japanese man standing by the bedside waited until the doctor finished turning off the other monitors before suggesting they chat.

"What about?" Palmer asked, his voice cracking.

"About this accident," Yoshi Ishida answered quietly.

"What accident?"

Ishida fixed Palmer with a penetrating stare. "My company simply cannot afford any leak about these unfortunate . . ." he seemed to search for the right word, "side effects."

"But the autopsy?"

"There will be no autopsy."

"We must —"

Ishida held up a hand. "The family thinks you sent her home, that she was going to travel by train?"

"Yes." The doctor couldn't fight off a growing feeling of dread.

"Well, suppose she took the train, but somehow, during the trip, she managed to fall to her death — with a little help, of course," Ishida explained. "Her body was too badly mangled to be recognizable, let alone autopsied." He shook his head in mock sympathy. "Most unfortunate," he added. "Accidental death, multiple trauma. Wouldn't you say that's the most pragmatic way around this problem, Doctor?"

Pragmatic? Palmer looked at his hands. Though clean, he felt as if they were covered with blood. Pragmatism was pernicious; each step might be just a few simple inches, but the cumulative result could be horrific — the sight of Lucy Peters's lifeless body a silent reminder of just how much.

"Wouldn't you say?" Ishida repeated his question.

Reluctantly, Palmer nodded. Lucy Peters's death had put the final nail in the coffin for his soul.

• • •

"Pretty smart — going into a neighborhood like that alone at night," said the city detective from the Seventh Precinct. Lt. Hector Rodriguez was on his fifth assault case that shift. A thin, intense man, with a heavy five o'clock shadow and eyes as black as his hair, he could have been plucked right out of central casting. "Damn good way of getting killed."

"I'll keep that in mind," Sammy said, a sarcastic edge to her voice. It had been more than three hours since the two patrolmen had found Sammy. First they'd driven her to Mt. Sinai Hospital, where after a two-hour wait the examination showed only a few bruises, no serious injuries. Then they'd brought her back to the station where she was given a change of clothes — a floppy old NYPD sweatshirt and a pair of loose-fitting jeans. Shoes weren't part of the package — she was forced to wear her damp pumps. After another long hour, they'd handed her off to a couple of detectives for questioning. Lectures, she didn't need.

Rodriguez was not amused. "Assuming you didn't go down there to commit suicide, what the hell was on your mind?"

Suicide.

The mugging in the street had been bad enough. This barrage of questions seemed like a second assault. Weak and queasy, Sammy just wanted to go home. "I had to bury some old ghosts," she explained, her voice cracking. The surly detective's accusatory manner made her almost feel guilty.

"Looks like they almost buried you," said Rodriguez.

Sammy sat up straight, her eyes blazing. She was just about to respond when Hector's partner, Lt. Dave Williams put a comforting arm on her shoulder.

"He's had a rough day," Williams said, nodding at Rodriguez. The gray-haired detective drew up a metal chair, leaned forward, and asked gently, "Is it okay if I call you Sammy?"

Sammy nodded, though she didn't feel like talking to anyone. "That's my name."

"Would you like something to drink? A snack from the machine maybe?"

"No, I'm not hungry."

"I understand," the detective said. "Can you tell us why you were on Hester Street tonight?"

"I used to live there," Sammy admitted, fighting back tears. "I just wanted to see the place again."

"Give me strength." Rodriguez rolled his eyes upward. "You expect us to believe you were out sightseeing?"

"I don't care what you believe!" Sammy exploded. "Some maniac just tried to rape me — or worse. I want him caught and put behind bars!" Sammy clasped her shaking hands in her lap.

Williams silenced his partner with a wave of his hand. "Sammy, we want to get the guy that attacked you, too, but we need your help," he said in a soothing voice.

"I didn't see anything. I told you, he had a jacket over my head."

"There's nothing you remember? Did you see his hands? His legs? Was he white, brown, black?"

Sammy took a deep breath. "I don't know." She shifted uneasily in her chair. "White, I think."

"Do you have a sense of how tall he might have been? Was he big?"

Sammy shook her head. "He felt big." Her voice was plaintive. "But I don't know."

Rodriguez threw up his hands. "Swell. I don't know, I don't know, I don't know. How the hell are we supposed to find him? No ID, no suspects; no suspects, no arrests. Waste of time going through the motions."

His partner persisted. "Did the man say anything?"

"He called me a bitch." Sammy shivered as the sound of her attacker's abuse rang again in her ears. "A damn bitch. Said I would 'pay now.'"

"Pay? What do you suppose that meant?" Williams held her gaze. "You think maybe he knew you?"

Sammy hadn't even considered that possibility. Could she have been followed by one of Taft's people? Did he plan to kill her because she was getting close to the truth about him? She shuddered at the thought. "Oh, God."

"Come on, Williams, you're wasting your time. This is a local perp. Pure and simple."

"You think he knew you, Sammy?" Williams repeated, ignoring his partner.

Sammy looked at both detectives. Good cop, bad cop. She almost laughed. It was such a cliché. Did her attacker know her? It wasn't likely. She had been crazy to go down to her old neighborhood alone at night. As Grandma Rose would say, "Why ask for trouble?" That neighborhood was full of trouble these days. "No, I don't think so," she replied at last.

The door to the interview room opened, and a female officer poked her head inside. "Detective Williams?"

"Yes?"

"He called twenty minutes ago from La Guardia. He's on his way."

"Good. Thanks." Williams nodded, then continued with his interrogation, "Did he have some kind of accent?"

Sammy frowned. "Come to think of it, I'm not sure. I don't think New York." She shook her head. "It was only a few words."

"Any witnesses?" asked Rodriguez.

Sammy hesitated. Had the boy been close enough to see her attacker? Probably not. Even if he had been, would he talk to the police? In the law of the streets, wouldn't testifying be akin to sleeping with the enemy? She remembered how the boy had run away to avoid the squad car.

Sammy made her decision. How could she betray her savior? Besides, she knew nothing more than his first name. "I didn't see anyone around when he attacked me," she answered truthfully.

Rodriguez raised an eyebrow and gave her a piercing stare. "Then who called the police?"

Sammy was certain that he didn't believe her. "I must've screamed," she began when the door swung open all the way and slammed into the adjacent wall.

"Hell of a thunderstorm in Boston. I got here as soon as I could."

To her astonishment, Sammy looked over to see, standing in the doorway, a haggard Gus Pappajohn.

Two hours later, Sammy and Pappajohn boarded the last shuttle back to Boston. "My sister's got a guest room. You can stay there tonight. I'll drive you back to Ellsford tomorrow," the burly campus cop had said. Sammy had merely nodded in dull compliance.

It turned out that Pappajohn and Williams were both veterans of Boston's finest—and fishing buddies as well. Sammy was grateful that the nice New York detective had called his old friend. Pappajohn's entrance had saved her from Rodriguez' aggressive questioning.

Once on board the flight, fatigue seeped through Sammy like an anesthetic. She drifted in and out of an uneasy sleep. Gruesome, savage images floated through her consciousness in an incoherent muddle. At one point she choked back a scream as she pictured herself being smothered by a man with a mustache. Pappajohn's good arm on hers was calming, and gradually she lapsed into a deeper, less troubled slumber.

Only when the plane bumped down on the runway did she open her eyes. Around her there was a flurry of activity as passengers clogged the aisles, jockeying for position.

"Might as well wait," Pappajohn said. "My sister is never on time."

They sat in silence until most of the passengers had deplaned. Finally, Pappajohn unbuckled his seatbelt. Reaching up, he pulled his rumpled overcoat from the overhead bin, his substantial paunch tugging at the belt of his trousers. Sammy noted that sweat had plastered his once white shirt against his back like a giant Rorschach pattern. She stood, waiting for him to clear the way, then followed him past the smiling flight attendants down the movable metal stairs.

It was nearly ten p.m. The evening rains had cleared, leaving a crisp chill Sammy found surprisingly invigorating.

They walked briskly to the terminal, their footsteps in cadence. Sammy looked around the waiting area for a friendly face, but the sergeant, knowing better, plopped down on a row of scratched plastic chairs and motioned for her to sit next to him. Both seemed uncomfortable with conversation. Sammy looked off at the entrance, Pappajohn down at his hands.

Finally, Sammy cleared her throat. "Thanks."

The sergeant nodded. "You hungry?"

Sammy realized for the first time that she was. "Uh-huh," she said with more energy.

"Good." Pappajohn leaned back in the chair and yawned. "My sister's a damn good cook."

"Oh. Good. Thanks."

They both returned to their uncomfortable silence. Fifteen minutes passed before a woman with Pappajohn's build, but a softer, rounder face came rushing forward to greet them. Eleni Pascalides gave her brother a warm hug and put a comforting arm around Sammy, blessing her with the traditional Greek double-cheek kiss. "*Yasou.* Come on, let's go home. I've got a big bowl of avgolemono waiting for you."

"That's chicken soup," Pappajohn translated.

"Greek penicillin," his sister said, laughing. "Now come, some soup, then a hot bath and a good night's sleep. Everything will look better in the morning."

CHAPTER NINE

SATURDAY
NOON

The room was dark when Sammy opened her eyes. Thick linen curtains blocked all but a single ray of sunlight that dissected the brown wool blankets. Jolted awake, she sat up in the unfamiliar double bed, trying to get her bearings. *Where am I?* Of course, the memory returned. Pappajohn's sister's house.

Sammy quickly looked around the room. She began to make out the objects there, one by one: the bedside lamp with its pink plastic shade, the alarm clock at five past twelve, the four-poster bed that cocooned her in its warmth, and beyond, the sewing machine draped with unfinished dresses. A bureau piled untidily with magazines held a photograph of a slim Gus Pappajohn in his Boston police uniform, his hair pitch black, standing next to a pretty brunette and a small child. Must have been many years ago, Sammy surmised. The sergeant's hair was now more salt than pepper.

She lay back in bed and stared at the canopy, thinking about yesterday. The trip to her old home had helped rid her of past guilts. She was glad she'd finally gone. But after — the assault. She shuddered, remembering her fear.

You're gonna pay now.

She could still hear the man's words, still feel his hands groping her.

You're gonna pay now.

Pay? Whom? For what?

The sound startled her. She sat up, heart racing, and looked to the door. Someone knocked again, and a gruff voice followed with, "It's almost noon. You gonna sleep all day?"

Pappajohn.

Sammy pulled the blankets up to her chin. "It's open."

Pappajohn stood at the door, a brightly colored floral-pattern dress draped over his arm, looking slightly uncomfortable. His eyes wandered around the room, taking in the details, and at last fell on the photo on the bureau.

Sammy thought she detected tears in the corners of his eyes, but the gravel in his voice belied any underlying softness. "Eleni said this would fit you. We'll leave in half an hour." He took two small steps into the room and reached to drape the dress over an armchair.

To her surprise, Sammy realized she was disappointed that she wouldn't be getting another delicious meal from the police chief's sister. Last night's chicken soup and lamb stew had been just what the doctor ordered. Her stomach growled in protest as she, not wishing to seem ungrateful, answered, "Okay, thanks."

She'd barely gotten the words out when Pappajohn left the room. *Strange man.* She slipped on a cotton bathrobe his sister had laid out for her. Just like her father. *Very, very strange.*

"Hope you're hungry," Pappajohn greeted Sammy as she came down the stairs. Pacing impatiently by the front door, dressed in his down overcoat, he gave the impression of a large grizzly bear.

Sammy tried not to smile, instead brushing at her borrowed dress. "There's got to be a McDonald's around here. Do we have time to say good-bye to your sister?" She looked off in the direction of the kitchen.

"Here's something warm. That raincoat of yours is made of paper." Pappajohn tossed her a heavy leather jacket. "We'll meet Eleni there."

Sammy raised an eyebrow. "There? St. Charlesbury?"

Pappajohn jingled his keys as he stepped out the door. "St. Sophia."

Nestled in suburban Somerville, St. Sophia had been built to resemble its namesake, the famed Byzantine church in Constantinople with its tall towers at each corner and a central dome. Sammy's impression, as they drove onto the church parking lot, was of a large mosque somehow transported to the midst of bucolic Levittown.

Next to the parking lot, a giant circus tent covered most of the grassy grounds. As she stepped from the car, Sammy heard strains of Greek music — bouzouki and bagpipes — amidst the voices of hundreds of people. A banner fluttered from a card table ahead announcing: ST. SOPHIA GREEK FESTIVAL, SATURDAY, NOVEMBER 25, 1995 in bright red letters.

"*Costaki, yasou.*" A buxom gray-haired woman jumped up from the entrance table, shouldering through the crowd to greet them. She gave Pappajohn a warm bear hug, pressing a kiss on each cheek. Sammy found his obvious discomfort amusing as she watched him pull back like a schoolboy hoping to avoid the cheek pinch of an effusive great aunt. Seeing his injured arm, the woman demanded an explanation, "*Ti epathes, vre!*"

After some rapid chatter in Greek, Pappajohn extricated himself, paid the entrance fee for two, and slipped his wallet back into his pocket.

"Thanks," said Sammy. "Six dollars?"

"Includes food," he told her. "Let's get some."

She followed him inside the large tent, which housed several rows of brightly decorated booths. Pappajohn made a beeline for one advertising a roast lamb dinner, leaving Sammy standing near the entrance. She took a moment to catch her breath and surveyed the crowd pressing up to the booths. Young and old, families with children, all happily celebrating an autumn afternoon surrounded by Greek music, dancing, and food.

Sammy wandered by a table that displayed native scarves and

blouses, neatly embroidered with blue, red, and white designs. A poster overhead featured a pristine Greek island, bleached white cottages reflected in crystal clear azure seas. She closed her eyes, visualizing the warmth of the summer sun as she lay on a sandy beach.

"Well, come on."

"Huh?"

Pappajohn stood behind her, plate in hand. "Do you want spanakopita or tiropites with your lamb?"

Sammy gazed over at the next booth where Eleni was holding up another plate. "Home cookin'."

"From the best," Pappajohn said between bites of a second serving.

His sister blushed, pleased. "Don't you listen to him. Did you sleep well, dear?"

"Great, thanks." Sammy pointed to a casserole. "I'll try that."

"Pastitsio," said Pappajohn. "I'll take some too."

Eleni sliced off a tiny piece for her brother, much to his displeasure. "Come on, I'm a growing boy."

Eleni looked directly at Pappajohn's substantial gut. "You certainly are."

"Costa!" A middle-aged woman approached their booth. "Eleni, you didn't tell me Costa was here!" She eyed Pappajohn with sympathy. "You poor dear. You must miss Effie so much."

Pappajohn forced a wan smile before drowning his sorrows in a huge bite of moussaka. "You get used to it," he mumbled through a mouthful of food.

The woman peered at Sammy. "And Ana, how big you've grown. You must meet my son George. I know you two would hit it off."

Sammy was about to explain who she was when Eleni stepped in. "So how is George?" she asked, winking at Sammy.

"He's pre-med! Only twenty years old!" the woman bragged. "We're spending all month filling out applications. I want him to go to Harvard, of course."

"Of course." Pappajohn repeated.

Sammy couldn't resist a smile. On his home turf, Pappajohn was just like a rebellious schoolboy.

"Let's go see the dancers," Pappajohn whispered to Sammy while Eleni and her friend continued their animated conversation.

Sammy looked off at the male and female dancers dressed in bright native costume all in a row, kicking up their legs like an amateur Rockette line. Sammy noted with surprise that the men were wearing skirts too.

"I thought only the Scots—"

"They're evzones, male soldiers," Pappajohn explained. "And yes, they do," he added in response to Sammy's obvious unasked question.

She laughed. "The way they kick like that, for sure. How come some of the dancers aren't in costume?"

"Because they're people. Like us." He reached for her arm and led her toward the floor. "That's the great thing—everybody dances."

"But I don't know how," protested Sammy.

"It's easy." He slipped off his sling and with his good hand, broke apart two dancers in the outermost chain. Motioning Sammy in on his other side, he rested his casted arm over her shoulder. The circle reclosed, everyone's arm on his neighbor's shoulders as the tempo increased. Sammy made a valiant attempt to pick up the not-too-difficult steps, but her greatest surprise was in watching Pappajohn move like a true Zorba.

She also observed that several of the other attendees would wave or shout greetings at him. Pappajohn seemed to be spurred on by the attention, and soon made his way to the front of the line, leading the group while waving a soiled napkin with his free arm extended. After an exhausting round of dances, he finally moved back toward her, wiping his sweaty brow with the napkin shreds.

"Boy, am I thirsty." He shouted to a teenager manning a drink booth, "A bottle of ouzo, and hurry."

"Uh, no thanks." Sammy had once tasted the licorice beverage—to her dismay. "I'll just have a coke."

"That's okay, more for me." He handed her the soft drink, as he savored a long swig of the alcohol. "*Opa!*"

Sammy indicated the crowd. "You seem to be pretty popular around here."

"It's a small community."

"Effie was your wife?"

"Yes." Pappajohn gulped more ouzo.

"She—?"

"Died six years ago. Cancer."

"That must have been very difficult."

"We were married thirty-one years," he spoke with a touch of pride.

"Special lady, huh?"

"Very special." Pappajohn turned his head to watch the dancers who began the syrtaki.

"Why did you become a cop?" Sammy asked, unable to resist probing. Police work seemed such a risky profession for a family man.

Pappajohn shrugged. "Couldn't open a restaurant."

"No, really."

Pappajohn considered her question for a long time, as if delving deep into his psychological motives, but if he had, he chose not to share his insights. Instead, he tossed off a glib response, "I guess somebody's got to do it.

"Well, I'm glad you were doing it on Wednesday," Sammy said, hoping she'd conveyed her gratitude for his saving her life.

True to form, Pappajohn simply nodded.

"How's your arm holding up?"

"Still stiff after I sleep, but otherwise—" He shrugged again. "It'll be fine."

"I'm glad." Sammy turned to him. "Any idea who did the bombing?"

"Can't say."

"You mean you're still investigating."

"I mean, I can't say."

"Surely you have a gut feeling."

"Honey, I've stopped trusting my gut years ago."

"Don't call me honey."

"Oh sorry, I forgot, it's not politically correct." Pappajohn studied her face. "I could be your father, you know."

"You called your daughter 'honey'?" challenged Sammy.

Pappajohn's tone took a transient contemplative quality. "Not enough." He poured the last of the ouzo bottle into his paper cup and repeated, "Not enough."

Sammy didn't miss the gesture. "What's she like?"

"My daughter?" He looked directly at Sammy for a moment, then removed two dog-eared snapshots from his wallet. "She doesn't look like me," he said, handing her the pictures. "She's a beauty—like her mother."

Sammy considered the two dark-haired women in the photo. The older one radiated warmth with her broad smile, her features glowing, her eyes twinkling with laughter. The other, still in her teens, stood slouched facing the camera, sporting a sullen look. Sammy had one of those photos too. She was surprised to see how much Pappajohn's daughter reminded her of herself at that age.

"But she isn't happy," Pappajohn was saying. "It worries me—her bottomless appetite for misery."

"She's not here, is she?" Sammy asked, looking around.

"Hardly." Pappajohn snorted. "You'd never catch her at one of these things. Los Angeles."

"That's where they all go to find themselves, I guess. My dad moved there after my mom died."

"I'm sorry," Pappajohn said. "Has it been a while?"

"About thirteen, fourteen years. I grew up with my grandmother in New York."

"I didn't think that was an L.A. accent." Then he turned serious. "Was it cancer?"

"My mom?" Sammy looked down for a moment. "No. Suicide."

Pappajohn seemed genuinely saddened. "I didn't know."

She looked up again. "It's okay. Either way, it's still the pits." She raised her soda and took a large gulp as a pseudo-toast. "To survival."

Pappajohn's paper cup was emptying fast.

"Is your daughter all right?"

"You're asking me? I'm just her father."

"That bad, huh?"

"She's clean. That's all I care about." His response was unconvincing.

"Oh." Sammy knew so many friends who'd fallen into that trap. "What's she doing now?" she asked, before regretting the choice of words.

Pappajohn didn't seem to catch the double meaning, answering honestly. "She told me she'd decided to return to school. Maybe one of these days it will happen." His tone didn't sound convinced. "I e-mail her every so often, but that's about it."

"You think she'll ever come back East?"

Pappajohn shook his head. "No. No illusions. I guess if I ever have grandchildren, I'll have to visit by computer." He downed the last few swallows from the cup, crumpled it into a small ball, and pitched it perfectly into an almost-full trash bin. He was off to the beverage booth for a refill to fuel another round on the dance floor.

Larry Dupree sat in his apartment's living room, examining the shoebox-sized metal container the fire chief had given him yesterday, uncertain how to open it. The heat had twisted the metal and virtually melted the lock. He turned it over and over, about to give up when he finally noticed a buckled seam that had created a tiny space — probably less than half a centimeter — but room enough to insert a small screwdriver.

He rose from his chair and hurried into the kitchen where he stored his tools. Among the eclectic assortment of screwdrivers, he found just what he needed. Returning to the living room, he wedged the six-inch flathead under the metal, pushing down with all his strength until, at last, he pried the box open.

"Papers," Larry muttered, disappointed. He was hoping for some salvaged program tapes — the classics, anything — to help restart the studio library they'd just lost.

Defeated, he rummaged through the pile of burned crisps of

paper mixed with black flakes of the scorched interior. Brian's engineering license, FCC certification. A copy of his campus housing rental agreement. His car insurance. Brian was a real pack rat.

Then, a picture.

Larry blew the ash dust off the photo. It had been taken two years ago, right after they'd broken the facilities contracts story. Brian was sitting in his rickety chair, bookended by his two best friends, Larry himself and a grinning, almost childlike Sammy. His eyes welled up with tears.

He was about to close the container when he saw it — at the very bottom of the box, tucked underneath. Larry pulled it out and turned it over in his hand.

Well, ah'll be! Though the label was torn, he could make out most of the letters written in Brian's chicken-scratch penmanship: *Sammy's tape*.

Sammy was relieved when she finally left Interstate 91 and drove onto quiet Route 15. The radio talked about a five-car pile up near Bellows Falls with traffic backed up all the way to Brattleboro. They'd stayed at St. Sophia's well into the evening — only leaving after most of the revelers had called it a night. Pappajohn had had too much ouzo, so Sammy promised his sister she would drive them home.

Now snow fell like confetti and the roads were becoming more treacherous. Sammy was grateful Pappajohn owned a Land Cruiser. Though clumsy to steer, the behemoth four-wheel-drive vehicle rode solidly on the accumulating snow.

Sammy turned her head for a moment to look at her companion. Pappajohn was leaning against the opposite door, his head partially covered by a hunter's cap, snoring loudly in an irregular pattern. Sammy felt obligated to play chauffeur on the trip home — not only because the chief had had too much to drink, but because Sammy felt that her conversational questions might have gotten him in that condition. The poor guy. He was a real teddy bear at heart. But with his wife's death and his daughter's leaving, he had to fight his way alone. Sammy looked over at him again. It seemed she and Pappajohn actually had a lot in common.

"Damn it!" Sammy tugged hard at the wheel and the Land Cruiser swerved to the right, skidding smoothly in a circle, finally coming to rest in a small gully by the side of the road. She looked up to see the rear lights of a large limousine speeding down the roadway ahead in the distance. Her whole body shook as she took a few deep breaths to calm herself.

"Whutiz?" Pappajohn murmured, lifting up his cap.

"Nothing," Sammy shook her head angrily. "Some son of a bitch in a limo practically ran me off the road."

"Djgetalisuz?" he slurred.

"No. Didn't have time. They're gone." She started rocking the car back and forth out of the gully. "Sorry I woke you, go back to sleep."

"Rockabyebaby," Pappajohn mumbled as he drifted back into slumber.

Sammy nudged the car back into traffic. Looking off in the distance where the limo's taillights had been only a moment before, all she could see was the darkness, shielded by a curtain of snow.

Peoria, Illinois
8:00 p.m.

Tom Nelson was exhausted. Not to mention hungry, horny, and freezing cold. He couldn't decide which was the greatest of his miseries. The rookie cop had been on foot patrol for close to eight hours, and it had been snowing constantly. He glanced at his watch. Another twenty minutes and he could sign off duty. Then he'd grab a burger at Mickey D's—his bride of only three weeks was no cook—before heading for home. He thought about Patti in bed, her naked body waiting to warm his, and he smiled. Whatever skills she lacked in the kitchen were more than compensated for by her expertise in the sack.

The Amtrak whistle blew in the distance as the train steamed off toward its next stop. Nelson's beat included the Peoria neighborhood abutting the railroad yard. All along the crisscrossing tracks, inside abandoned cars or beside them, homeless men, women, and even a few children had set up temporary camps. The cop approached one ragged group standing around a burning oil can and warmed his hands over the flame.

"Officer!"

Nelson turned to see a man pointing to something lying in a mound of snow. Although several feet away, the cop sensed trouble.

"Officer, come quick!"

Nelson hesitated, his first impulse to leave it for the next guy. Less than five minutes to go, damn it. If this were anything requiring a report, he'd be hours doing paperwork before savoring burger, wife, or bed.

"Officer!"

Sense of duty prevailed, and Nelson hurried over to where the man was frantically signaling.

"Jesus!" His exclamation was involuntary. Worse, he'd lost all his appetites as he stood staring down at the ripped and twisted, now totally unrecognizable body of Lucy Peters.

Sammy left Pappajohn snoring in his bedroom and tiptoed out to the living room. Before falling back into his semi-stupor, he'd mumbled something about her staying over that night — "too dang'rous," he'd slurred — but as she checked out the sagging, food-stained sofa, she wasn't sure she could comfortably manage even a few hours sleep there. Besides, if there were anything to fear, Pappajohn would be of no use. He'd be out of commission for a good five or six hours at least. Sammy peeked out the living room window. Only a couple of inches of white covered the ground; the snowfall seemed to be tapering off. She shouldn't have too much trouble walking back home now that the worst of it was over.

Still wound up from the events of the past few days, Sammy couldn't resist wandering around the rooms of the small cottage. She went through all of them in less than three minutes, then stopped in the kitchen to wash a sink full of dirty dishes. When she was done, she walked back into the den and sat down in front of the computer sitting atop Pappajohn's cluttered desk. Maybe she'd use the time to modify her list of fact and speculation, adding what she'd gleaned from Dr. Ortiz and Mrs. Nakamura, as well as the question of whether yesterday's assailant might have been someone from Taft's organization. She could print it out on Pappajohn's dot matrix, then later fax it to Mr. Ishida in New York. It might help the Nitshi CEO focus on any missing pieces in his own investigation.

She retrieved the handwritten list from her purse and switched on the computer. Once the system booted up, she opened an untitled file and began typing, transcribing the original and adding the following:

> Six deaths: Yitashi Nakamura, Barton Conrad, Sergio Pinez, Katie Miller, Brian McKernan, and Seymour Hollis
> Four "suicides": Nakamura, Conrad, Pinez, and Hollis
> One fire and resultant death: Brian
> One bombing and resultant death: Katie Miller
> One almost hit-and-run and one assault: Intended victim: Sammy Greene
> Two missing: Luther Abbottt and Lucy Peters

Done. Sammy wadded up her handwritten sheet and tossed it in the trash can under Pappajohn's desk. Then she returned her attention to the computer screen, convinced that Taft was behind all the violence and death. A man so determined to discredit the global enterprise that he was willing to sacrifice anyone—including Sammy herself—to accomplish that goal.

Conrad had warned her that something was going on at Ellsford. He'd already discovered that Seymour Hollis, the third suicide on campus, was a Palmer patient and had been taking a new AIDS drug developed by a Nitshi subsidiary. Whatever other evidence he'd gathered must have been in the brown envelope addressed to Dean Jeffries. If in fact, Jeffries hadn't received it, it was likely that whoever visited Conrad Friday night, shot the professor and took the envelope. The tape would have proven that Conrad was murdered. That's why Brian was killed. That's why someone — someone sent by Taft — had been after her. Even in New York.

What if, as Lt. Williams suggested, the attacker knew her? Someone sent to kill her before she learned too much? Because she was starting to piece the puzzle together.

Sammy shut her eyes, absorbing this terrifying idea.

Eventually, her calm voice broke through. Unlikely that the Reverend would send his henchman after her all the way to New York. She opened her eyes and took a deep breath. Of course, it was absurd.

Relieved, Sammy punched the function keys for "Print." A few minutes later, she had two hard copies, which she folded and placed in her purse. Turning back to the computer, she pushed "Save" and waited for instructions to name the document. *Let's see. Guess "Greene" is as appropriate a name as any.*

"DO YOU WANT TO OVERWRITE? Y/N?" flashed on the screen.

What? Overwrite? There's another file with my name? Why? Sammy tried to access it, but only succeeded in repeatedly getting a prompt for a password. She tried the names of Pappajohn and his relatives to no avail, finally banging the desk in frustration. Irritated, she went back to check the directory for a clue. Among the multiple listings of games, communications services, and home tax and budget programs, she found files titled "Conrad," "Nakamura," "Nitshi," and "Taft." They, too, were equally inaccessible.

Sammy bit her lower lip. What the hell was going on?

Her pulse quickened as she considered the worst possible scenario. Whoever shut down Conrad's computer the night he died might not have realized that Conrad always turned his off and on using the master switch on the floor. But, he would have had to know how to use a computer.

And Pappajohn fit that profile, Sammy realized, feeling at once angry and betrayed. She'd been a fool to begin trusting the man. After all, if you're into university corruption, who better to have on your side than the campus chief of police?

A conspiracy.

Could she prove it?

She didn't know.

All she did know was that the more she learned, the more frightened she became.

Impulsively, she hit the "Delete" button on the computer, instantly removing the document she'd just created. Then she switched off the computer, grabbed her purse and jacket, and headed out of the cottage. It was still snowing. Falling flakes soon filled in her footsteps as if they had never existed.

Peter Lang was freezing. Parked outside Pappajohn's home ever since Sammy and the campus cop had arrived, Lang couldn't risk turning on the engine. He'd sat there without heat for what seemed like hours, without even a cup of coffee to warm him. Worse, he'd had to crack the windows a bit to prevent fogging and now gusts of icy wind blew across his face, burning his nose and ears.

Damn that Greene. So far, this assignment had been a disaster. His hired killer had screwed up badly—not only missing the girl with the car and at the bombing, but allowing her to get a look at him *and* his blasted mustache. If she ever made the ID, the authorities might connect him to Lang. After all, Lang had arranged the contract.

Ishida had been right not wanting to bring in an outsider, but Lang had persuaded his boss that it was necessary. Lang himself wasn't a killer. He couldn't even pull the trigger on Conrad.

Industrial espionage was Lang's game. Planting bugs, gathering dirt, spreading disinformation. He had no qualms about his undercover work—including double-crossing that idiot Taft. Murder, however, was another matter. That was why he'd backed off in New York, why he'd run the minute that kid had yelled "police." Now he'd been given only one more chance to stop Greene. Once and for all. Or else. Well, he thought with a certain resignation, he was in too deep to back out. There was no other choice.

He looked over at the house. Lights still burned in the living room and den. That meant at least one of them was probably awake. He held his hands up to his mouth and blew hot air on them, trying to coax feeling back into his stiff fingers. Shit! This was going to be a long night.

Lang was half-asleep when he heard the sound. He sat up to see a shadow emerge from the house and shut the door. It was Greene. Alone. The snow was falling more thickly now, so he wouldn't have to wait long before he could start his motor and follow. Damn, she was taking the walk path toward the university campus. He'd have to follow on foot. Cursing the foul weather, he dragged himself out of his cold car into the colder night. There was so little light that he had a hard time tracking her progress without moving in too close. He hoped the wind noise muffled the sound of his footsteps.

Fifteen minutes later, hidden in the shadows, he stood shivering outside the building where Sammy lived. She had just gone inside. He saw the lights in her apartment flip on. He checked his watch. The crystal had fogged, making it difficult to read the time. One a.m. It wouldn't be long before she'd be asleep, and he'd have a chance to make his move.

Soon, very soon, his duty would be fulfilled.

The moment Sammy locked her apartment door, she stripped off her clothes and jumped into the shower, turning on the water full force. Rotating slowly, she let the needle-like jets crash down on her head, rivulets of warmth running along her body, relaxing her muscles made tight by tension. She closed her eyes, emptying her mind of anything but the pure pleasure of the shower.

The sound of the telephone didn't register at first. Finally, she opened her eyes and listened. Another ring. Who'd call at this hour, Sammy wondered, shutting off the faucet. Hair dripping, she stepped out of the shower, wrapped a towel around her wet body, and padded into the living room. "Hello?" she spoke tentatively into the receiver.

"Sammy?"

"Dr. Osborne?" What in the world?

"I'm so glad you made it home safely."

"Me, too," Sammy said. *If only he knew the half of it.* "Didn't you get my message?"

"Yes, as a matter of fact. My service said you'd canceled our appointment because you were going out of town."

"Something came up and—"

"It's all right," Osborne reassured her. "I wouldn't have thought twice about it, but I ran into your friend Reed Wyndham today, and he told me you hadn't returned from New York. He seemed troubled—"

Oy vey, Reed! In the midst of all the turmoil she completely forgot to call him.

"And frankly," Osborne was saying, "after our chat on Thursday, I wondered if somehow Taft's people had gotten to you."

Sammy was touched by the psychologist's concern. More than that, she was gratified that he had believed her story about Taft before anyone else did. "Actually," she replied, "they almost did."

"What happened?"

Sammy began to relate the incredible events of the past two days. As she spoke, her eyes wandered to her purse lying on the chair next to the phone. She'd thrown the shoulder bag down when she came in earlier and somehow one of the Nitshi brochures she'd taken from Ishida's office had fallen out. "Jesus!" she exclaimed into the receiver.

"Sammy, are you all right?"

"Yes, I'm fine." She picked up the brochure and stared at a small unlabeled group photo on the back cover. "A man I saw Friday in New York—a man who apparently works for Nitshi." Sammy flipped through the brochure until she found him again—this time in a shot with Yoshi Ishida. She searched for a name in the caption. "Uh, here it is. Peter Lang. I couldn't place him when I saw him walk past the elevator, but now I remember," she said excitedly. "He was at the animal rights protest. My God, that means he's also working for Taft!"

"You're sure it's the same man?"

"I've got pictures from the demonstration." Sammy grabbed her purse and pulled out the photo of Luther Abbott. There, standing behind him, was the short, stocky man she hadn't recognized before. No question. That was Peter Lang. "This time I have real proof."

"Sammy, listen to me. You've got to be very careful with this information."

"I'm not going to talk to the police. I think Sergeant Pappajohn may be involved in some kind of cover-up. Or worse." She told him what she'd seen on his computer. "He even has a file on me!"

"Incredible," Osborne sounded shocked. "But if what you say is true, you could be in grave danger." His voice was laced with concern. "Sammy, you mustn't breathe a word of this to anyone."

"I have to get this out. We're talking about murder!"

Osborne's voice was calm. "We will. But we can't do anything in the middle of the night. I'll see if I can set up a meeting with Chancellor Ellsford sometime in the morning. Give me a call around ten. Meanwhile, stay home, lock your door, and try to get some rest. Whatever you do, don't go out. Oh, and you'd better leave the phone free in case of emergency."

"All right." Sammy was both frightened and relieved. Chancellor Ellsford could take care of things and her nightmare would be over. "But, what if something — ?"

"Take my number." He gave her the seven digits. "If anything happens, call me immediately. I'll call the state police and come right away."

She wrote the number down on a loose piece of paper and stuck it in her purse.

"Thanks," Sammy hung up the phone, too keyed up to sleep. She didn't know if she could take much more. What she did know was that she didn't want to be alone. Even if it meant facing Reed.

Sammy put on long johns and pulled on a pair of jeans and a warm sweatshirt. She slipped the brochure back in her purse and reached for her jacket. The blinking light on her answering machine drew her back. It was a message from Larry. He needed to talk to her. She checked her watch: 1:30. She'd call him first thing tomorrow.

Sammy bounded down the stairs, one eye over her shoulder, her ears cocked for footsteps. The only footsteps she heard were her own, echoing up and down the barren stairwell. As she neared the front entrance, Osborne's words came back to her. *Stay home, you could be in grave danger.*

She paused, then made a quick decision. The back door was unlit. She could sneak out, be in the woods in seconds, and still make it to Reed's relatively quickly. Without further hesitation, she ran to the back, and looking around to see if she was followed, stepped into the cold, snowy night alone.

Sammy wasn't the only one getting middle-of-the-night calls. The telephone beside Pappajohn's bed rang four times before he realized it wasn't part of his dream and picked it up. "Yeah?"

The man at the other end identified himself as Tom Nelson of the Peoria Police Department. "I'm afraid I have to report a death. One of your students at the university. Name of Lucy Peters."

Pappajohn sat up to full attention. "How's that?"

Nelson explained how he'd discovered Lucy's body in the snow near the track. "Best as we can guess, she must have fallen from the southbound train. Unfortunately, the northbound local was coming down the track where she fell. Her body was completely crushed. ME dispensed with the autopsy."

"How'd you make the identification then?" For Pappajohn, the news was an unpleasant surprise. He'd called the Amtrak office for a list of passengers from St. Charlesbury. Lucy's name hadn't been on the roster. Not that an oversight wasn't possible. It happened all the time.

"There was a student ID card a few feet from where she fell,"

Nelson explained. Hesitating, he added. "Uh, in fact, that's why I'm calling. I figured you guys would want to uh notify the . . . uh . . . next of kin."

"Yeah," Pappajohn said. "I'll take care of it." Who could blame Nelson for wanting to dump the call? He took down the Illinois trooper's number, then hung up and reluctantly dialed the Peters. Almost twenty-five years as a Boston city policeman and he'd never gotten used to this. But now as a campus cop, it was a part of the job he'd never counted on.

2:00 A.M.

"Well look who finally made it." Reed stood in the open doorway of his apartment dressed only in a T-shirt and jockey undershorts. At this hour Sammy knew she'd gotten him out of bed. "Miss your plane?"

"Reed, I—"

"I waited for you, you know. Three hours. At the airport."

"Oh, Reed," Sammy groaned. "You weren't supposed to come until I called."

"My fault. I forgot."

Sammy brushed at the snow on her jacket. "Can I come in?"

Shaking his head, Reed stepped aside to make room for her to enter. "I don't know why I—"

"Thanks." Sammy locked the door after her. She followed him to the bathroom, where he bent over the sink and splashed cold water on his face. "Look, Reed, I'm really sorry. If I could only explain."

"You're always sorry. That's not the problem." He turned off the faucet, but remained with his back to her, staring into the mirror.

Sammy studied his reflection, feeling a rush of tenderness. More than anything, she wished she could melt in his arms, feel his warm embrace. If only she could pour her heart out to him, tell him her thoughts and her fears, have him keep her safe.

"I was attacked in New York," she finally said with forced calm. "Almost raped." She watched Reed's expression carefully, trying to gauge his reaction to the information. His face was unreadable. "That's why I didn't call. I-I couldn't."

Reed turned around. "You're serious?"

Sammy nodded. "I've never been more serious."

"What exactly happened?"

Starting from the visit to her old neighborhood, Sammy quickly told him about the attack — including the fact that the clever youngster had saved her. "If he hadn't yelled, I'm sure —" her voice choked with emotion.

"Were you hurt?" Reed's tone was now solicitous.

Sammy shook her head. "Just a few bruises. I was lucky."

"That wasn't very bright — going into a neighborhood like that alone."

"That's exactly what Lieutenant Rodriguez said."

"Smart man."

She couldn't blame Reed for his reaction. Grandma Rose would have said the same thing. Instead, she blurted, "I think the man who assaulted me was one of Taft's people."

"Did you tell that to the police?"

"Uh, no. I didn't."

"Why not?"

"Well, because I didn't have proof. Not then."

"And now you do?"

"Yes." Sammy took the brochure from her purse and pointed out Peter Lang. "Lang works for Nitshi."

"So?" Reed frowned.

"So he also works for Taft. I saw Lang at the animal rights demonstration. That's why he had someone try to run me down. Lang knew I'd taken his picture, that I could connect him with Taft."

"Whoa. You said you were attacked. What's this about running you down?"

Sammy stopped, realizing she'd never mentioned the hit-and-run to Reed. "Uh, it was the other day, near Mr. Brewster's store." Now she related the incident.

"Why didn't you tell me about this before?"

"Mr. Brewster thought it was just an accident, and I wasn't really sure — not until I found out the man with the mustache stole my pictures."

"What man with a mustache?"

Again she explained how she'd caught sight of the driver — the same man Mr. Brewster described in his shop the next day. "Taft must have hired this guy to kill me and steal the pictures of Lang."

Reed ran his hand through his rumpled sandy mop. "I'm trying to keep up with this story, but —"

"It's what I tried to tell you the other day. If Taft can discredit Nitshi, the university will be forced to cut all ties with the company. He's trying to stop Nitshi's AIDS research. Targeting any professor even remotely associated with that kind of work — Nakamura, Conrad, now your Dr. Palmer."

Sammy's face was flushed with the excitement of unraveling a puzzle. "Look at this." She produced the list she'd created on Pappajohn's computer. "If you buy my hypothesis, then these deaths can all be linked to Taft." She took out Sergio's autopsy report. "Tomorrow I plan to talk with Dr. Palmer —"

"Enough." Reed 's voice was tinged with anger. "Sammy, you can theorize until you're blue in the face. Reverend Taft is a man obsessed with his view of morality, I'll admit. I'll even admit he's gone to some extreme measures to foist those views on others. But so far, you haven't convinced me that he's resorted to murder. If it turns out he's tied up with the bombing, then he might be held responsible for Katie Miller's death. At the moment even that link hasn't been proven. As for these other people," Reed cast the list aside, "you've made fantastic leaps, apparently taking all sorts of risks with your life — and my career, I might add — to come up with a whimsical explanation for what are clearly a series of unconnected, unfortunate incidents."

"What about Brian? He was killed because I gave him the tape. It would have proved —"

Reed held up his hands. "Facts don't seem to matter to you at all, do they? The fire chief said it wasn't arson."

"I don't care."

"That's right! You don't care—about me, about us, about anything."

"You know that's not true."

"Sammy, right now all I know is that I'm exhausted. I've been on call for two out of the last three nights. The third I spent waiting for you at the airport. I've got to get some sleep." He headed for his bedroom. "You—you do what you have to do."

Those calls never get any easier, Pappajohn thought as he hung up the receiver. Loss was a lousy part of life, but he couldn't imagine a harder one than losing a child. He thought of his own daughter. Far away. Who knew how safe? He dreaded someday receiving a call like the one he just made to the parents of Lucy Peters.

Pappajohn donned his bathrobe and slippers and shuffled into the kitchen. Maybe a cup of warm milk would help settle his acid stomach—not to mention his headache—and let him get back to sleep. Somehow he didn't think so.

Standing at the stove, waiting for the milk to heat, he gazed out the window at the moonlit driveway, covered with pristine white snow. The Land Cruiser resting against a snowdrift reminded him that it was Sammy who had driven him home from Boston, the reason confirmed by his aching head. They had had rather a good time—even if it *was* the ouzo that loosened his tongue. Pappajohn was glad he'd gotten to know her a little, had a chance to talk. Maybe the kid wasn't so bad after all. A lot like Ana.

Pappajohn took out the cocoa mix, added some to his milk and poured a second cup for Sammy. Cups in hand, Pappajohn walked into the living room. To his surprise, the room was empty, the pillows on the couch seemed undisturbed. Frowning, he looked up to see the light was on in the den. What the—?

He moved over to the den. Once again, he found the room empty. He set the cups down on his desk and looked around. Nothing seemed different or out of place. As he reached for his cocoa, his hand brushed against the computer. It was warm. Pursing his lips, he pulled up his chair and powered the computer on. Sure enough, Greene's footprints were all over his disk.

"Damn," he cursed. "God damn it to hell."

Peter Lang began to panic. Forty-five minutes had passed since he'd watched Sammy enter her apartment building and still the lights burned in her bedroom. What the hell was she doing? Pulling an all-nighter? College kids!

Standing in the cold, his hands and toes tingled, the tips of his fingers grew more and more numb. At this rate, he'd develop frost-bite before morning.

After several moments of indecision, he walked down the path to a pay phone just outside the building. Checking with St. Charlesbury information, he dialed Sammy's number and waited. It took three rings before her answering machine kicked on. "This is Sammy Greene, I'm not in right now."

Not in!

How'd she—?

Lang looked up toward the building. From where he stood now he couldn't see Sammy's apartment, but he did have a clear view of the entrance. Unless she'd gone through a window or out the back, she was still inside.

Lang checked his watch. Quarter to two.

She was probably sitting in her bedroom with the lights on, scared to death or, better yet, fast asleep. Time to make a move. Without a particular plan in mind, Lang trudged up the steps to the front door. Looking over his shoulder to make sure he was alone, he jimmied the lock with a credit card and slipped inside. Fortunately, at this hour no one was wandering about the brightly lit lobby area. Taking the stairs two by two, he quickly reached the third floor and found Sammy's apartment. For several moments he stood outside her door and listened. Not a sound.

He picked the lock in seconds and stepped inside. The tiny foyer and living room were dark, but light seeping from beneath the bedroom door helped guide him to where he expected to find his quarry. Heart pounding and breath coming in rapid bursts, the stocky man inched toward his goal, a .357 magnum in hand.

With one smooth motion he turned the knob, threw the door open, and pointed his gun toward the bed.

Sammy was not there!

Stunned, Lang scoured the apartment before convincing himself that she had indeed disappeared.

Goddamn that redhead. Defeated once again.

Recognizing he had no choice, Lang found the phone in Sammy's living room and began to dial his boss.

4:00 A.M.

Eureka!

Pappajohn had been studying Sammy's written list since he'd found it crumpled in his trash can almost two hours earlier. He only now recognized the pattern.

Padding into the kitchen, he poured himself a cup of strong black coffee with a three TUMS chaser. It had been a long night and would get longer still, he thought as he carried the steaming brew back into the den. Pappajohn yawned as he reached for the desk phone. "California information? Get me the number for Berkeley. Campus Police."

It took forever to reach his party. Bypassing voice mail to the night switchboard was an irritating obstacle. They said they'd get back to him soon, but Pappajohn knew better. The search would take at least an hour. As he waited for the call, he rebooted his PC, switched on his modem, and got on the university E-net site.

6:30 A.M.

Sammy sat bolt upright from a fitful sleep. Her eyes flew open, searching the not-so-familiar room for an orienting clue. She'd been lying, twisted like a pretzel, on a couch. Reed's couch, she thought as she rubbed the waffled pattern the cushion had left on her cheek. The memory of their argument swept over her now. Reed's storming into his bedroom, refusing to talk, her decision to stay in his apartment until morning, hoping to patch things up after he'd had a good night's rest.

She did a few arm and neck stretches as she walked over to the living room window. Outside, the snow had stopped. Dawn's first light revealed the kind of dazzling winter landscape Mr. Brewster captured in the scenic photos hanging in his shop.

Sammy tiptoed to the bedroom and peered in. Reed lay on his back, one arm covering his forehead, the other dangling off the bed. She smiled as she studied his peaceful repose, his mouth sagging in a soft snore. He'd be out for a few hours more.

She noticed Reed's lab coat thrown carelessly on the floor. As she stooped to pick it up, his Nitshi Research Institute ID badge fell from the pocket along with an unsealed envelope addressed to Reed. The return address read "Marcus Palmer c/o the NRI." Sammy opened the flap and found what looked like a folded letter inside and—

She frowned. Along with the letter was the picture of Katie Miller at the animal rights demonstration!

A spider of anxiety crawled up the back of her neck.

Reed never turned the photo over to the police! He'd promised to notify the FBI.

So why was the picture still in his pocket?

Maybe he just forgot.

Or maybe—

No, impossible. Reed?

Now she recalled her words: *I just wish I knew what Brian learned from that tape.*

And his. *Maybe you don't.*

And why not?

Because if you are right, that kind of curiosity might have killed your professor.

Could Reed, *her* Reed, be part of the conspiracy? Was that why Reed seemed to reject her theory, why he insisted that Brian and Conrad hadn't been murdered? Because he knew she was telling the truth?

I ran into your friend Reed Wyndham . . . he seemed troubled—

Osborne's words.

Troubled? By what? And yet Reed hadn't seemed so much troubled as annoyed when she'd arrived at his place in the middle of the night. Granted, he'd softened up when he heard why she was late, but—

Suppose he'd just made a show of his surprise and concern for her. Maybe he already knew.

No. Sammy shook her head. He wouldn't. He wouldn't—

Six deaths. And she was almost number seven.

A thought nagged and tugged at the edges of her consciousness until finally it struck her. All along she'd assumed Taft was the link, that he had to be the villain.

But what if all of the Reverend's denials were true and he had no involvement in this conspiracy?

Who then could be responsible?

Sammy recalled Yoshi Ishida saying that he too had considered Taft a suspect—*Actually, Dr. Palmer first alerted me to the possibility that Taft might be dangerous*.

Dr. Palmer. Trying to throw them off the scent?

Sammy looked down at the folded paper she still held in her hand and opened it. It was a letter of recommendation to the chief of Internal Medicine at Mass. General.

> Dr. Wyndham is not only an excellent clinician, but also an outstanding researcher. He would make a fine addition to your residency program.

Sammy realized with a sinking feeling that her conspiracy theory could just as easily implicate Palmer as Taft.

Palmer was conducting some sort of AIDS study for Nitshi. That much she knew.

And Palmer's patients were dying or disappearing.

She remembered what she'd overheard the nurse at Ellsford General say. *Once they go to Nitshi*—

They were gone.

Sammy thought for a moment. Suppose Taft somehow learned that Palmer's research was going wrong. He could use that knowledge to advance his anti-AIDS agenda. It would devastate the doctor's position and his career.

If so, Palmer just might be desperate enough to arrange the Nitshi Day bombing to discredit Taft and destroy his organization.

Was that the plan? And who else was in on it?

Palmer's assistants? His students?

From the doorway, Sammy watched the gentle rise and fall of Reed's breathing, trying to shake her growing paranoia.

Answer me, Reed? What part did you play?

I can assure you there are no patients here.

This man she'd held in her arms. And almost loved.

I helped with a case last week.

If Palmer was up to something, Reed might be willing to cover up for a man he admired. Especially with the promise of a prime residency and a successful future research career. Sammy knew Reed wanted that future more than anything. What price was he willing to pay for it?

The system is skewed to reward research, Conrad had said.

Disguised in the garb of academic excellence is a community of malcontents and thieves.

Palmer and Reed?

I've learned that sometimes it's better to let sleeping dogs lie. Stay as far away from this as you can.

No patients at Nitshi? Sammy was suddenly filled with doubts about Reed.

She examined the picture and ID in her hand. Exactly what kind of research study was Palmer conducting at Nitshi? She needed to know. Quietly, Sammy turned and tiptoed back into the living room. Clutching her purse and jacket and the lab coat, she left the apartment, careful not to slam the door.

It was only later that she realized she'd forgotten to bring along the Nitshi brochure with Lang's picture. *Wonderful.* A piece of hard evidence and she'd probably never see it again.

CHAPTER TEN

SUNDAY
7:28 A.M.

It was almost seven thirty when Sammy reached the Nitshi Institute. She left her jacket on a bench outside and threw Reed's white lab coat over her jeans and sweatshirt. Hoping to pass for one of the researchers, she strode confidently over to the information desk. An armed guard sat facing a large U-shaped bank of TV monitors. She flashed Reed's plastic ID badge.

"Dr. Wyndham," she said. "My boss, Dr. Palmer, asked me to check on some slides."

The guard, head buried in the Sunday sports section of the *Vermont Post*, barely looked up. "Just sign in, Doc."

Sammy clipped the ID badge onto the lab coat's breast pocket and scribbled "Reed Wyndham" on the roster, surprised to find a half dozen names already there. Reed was right on one count. Researchers were a dedicated group. She hurried past the guard and headed for the elevators, her heart racing. When the steel doors glided open, she stepped in and pushed "four." Just as the other day, nothing happened. The button remained unlit.

Afraid the guard might notice if she stayed on the ground floor too long, Sammy quickly punched "two." Seconds later, she was padding down the plush maroon carpeted halls of the second floor past several rooms marked as laboratories or faculty offices. Near the end of one wing she found an auditorium with a multimedia display center. Frustrated, she turned around and followed the same path back, pausing every few steps to listen for sounds of activity. The floor was as quiet as a mausoleum.

Sammy was trying to figure out a plan for getting up to "four" when she almost collided with a middle-aged woman wearing a blue cotton uniform and pushing a cleaning cart.

Don't blow your cover, now, girl! Concealing Reed's ID badge with her lapel, Sammy drew in a deep breath and offered her most officious smile.

"Sorry, Doctor," the woman apologized in a guttural accent.

"My fault." Sammy replaced a dustpan that had fallen from the cart.

The cleaning lady responded with a noncommittal grunt, then shuffled over to an elevator just a few feet away and punched the "down" button. Sammy watched her disappear into the arriving car, breathing a sigh of relief when the doors closed. It was only then that she noticed the elevator was marked PRIVATE. That's it. Now she remembered Reed said he'd taken a private elevator to the fourth floor.

Sammy glanced up and down the empty corridor, before strolling over to the elevator and pushing "up." When the car appeared, she stepped inside and tried to insert Reed's plastic ID badge in the card slot above the buttons. The badge was rejected. Damn. Reed did mention some sort of special card. Now what? She had to move quickly or risk being caught. On impulse, she pushed "three."

The elevator ascended upward as silently as a spider on a thread. At the same time, Sammy turned to survey the car, her eyes coming to rest on the roof above her. In the center of the tiled ceiling was a small rectangular service hatch. She paused for a second, considering options. Could she do what she'd seen so many heroes and heroines in the movies do? It was worth a try, she decided, taking a deep breath.

Balancing her weight on the metal bar handles on each side of the elevator, she pushed her shoulders firmly against the back wall. Like a mountaineer, she slowly inched her hands up the walls until she was able to lift open the hatch with the tips of her fingers. After several tries she managed to slide it aside. Light from the elevator shaft filtered upward through the dusty darkness, revealing the thick, supporting steel cable and guide wires overhead.

Determined, she hooked her fingers on either side of the opening and hoisted herself up with all the strength she could muster. She was halfway there when the muscles in her forearms began to cramp and she had to let herself down again.

Unwilling to declare defeat, Sammy shut her eyes, inhaling and exhaling several times. Then, like a gymnast, she pulled herself up and through the opening until she was balancing her weight on her abdomen, her feet still dangling into the car.

Come on, come on, Sammy!

With her last ounce of strength she swung her legs over the edge of the hatch and pushed the metal cover back into place.

So far, so good!

At that same moment, the steel elevator doors slid open.

Ishida stared at the monitor receiving from a tiny camera hidden inside the wall of the private elevator. "The girl is definitely resilient," he remarked.

"Obviously she wants to reach the fourth floor."

Ishida's smile was inscrutable. "Then, Doctor, I think we ought to give her what she wants," he said, flicking a switch that remotely closed the elevator doors again and stopped the car permanently on "three."

The next ten minutes were the longest in Sammy's life as she lay on top of the grease-coated cab roof, gripping its edges with clenched fingers. All light had been extinguished with the closing of the hatch and in the eerie darkness, magnified sound bounced off the concrete walls of the elevator shaft like cannon rounds.

Suppose the car started moving again? If her plan had even the slightest chance of success, she couldn't rest here. Slowly, she stood, blindly using the steel cable for support. It was impossible to see even a few inches above her. She had to guess the distance to the next floor. Four feet, five, at most.

She could do it.

She *had* to do it.

She stripped off her white coat, turned it inside out and tied it around her waist. Hopefully, this way she'd avoid looking like a grease monkey when she arrived at her destination. With measured breaths, she hoisted herself onto the cable and strained to pull her body upward, hand over hand, the way she'd learned in high school gym class. After the second advance, she clamped her thighs tightly against the cold steel for support, her arms already trembling with the effort.

"Can't give up," she whispered over and over.

Another strong tug upward and she found herself parallel with the fourth floor elevator doors. By now her eyes had accommodated to the dark. With the added ribbon of light filtering through the opposed doors, Sammy could see that there was a distance of about two feet between where she hung on the cable and the doors' opening.

Almost there, she thought, feeling a certain charge — though it was tempered with the realization that if she lost her grip now, she'd fall back on the car and have to start again.

She forced herself to relax, concentrating on her goal. Clutching the cable as tightly as she could, she swung her legs forward until her toes struck the three-inch ledge at the base of the door.

"Ouch!"

Ouch. Ouch. Ouch.

The involuntary exclamation of pain echoed against the shaft's concrete walls. Now she'd surely be caught. Sammy's heart hammered against her chest as she waited to be discovered, her petite body tautly stretched, her toes on the ledge of the doors, her hands grasping the support cable.

Even after the sound had died away, she counted to one hundred before deciding to continue.

Another few deep inhalations and she groped for the rubber edge of the closed elevator door with her left hand. Clinging to the bumper as tightly as possible, she let go of the cable and brought her right hand to the right door edge. As she caught hold, she pushed both doors aside with all her strength, propelling her body through the narrowed opening, and sprawling spread-eagled on the floor.

"Welcome to the fourth floor. My name is Carl. You will need a pass."

"Remarkable! She actually made it." Ishida shook his head, fascinated by the image of Sammy projected on his monitor.

"Shouldn't you go get her now?"

"Patience," Ishida responded. "That's something you Americans have never understood." He pointed to the monitor. "This floor is escape proof. We don't need to get her. She'll come right to us."

7:35 A.M.

Bleary-eyed and unshaven, Reed sat hunched over his kitchen table, sipping black coffee, trying to concentrate on an article in the *Journal of Immunology*. He'd awakened at seven a.m. to find Sammy gone. No note. No "I'm sorry." Not that he was surprised. She seemed to be forever running out on him, always preoccupied with her own concerns — never his.

He was reading and rereading the same sentence when he noticed the papers Sammy had left last night — actually thrown — on the bathroom floor when they'd argued. He'd picked them up, put them on the kitchen table.

Now he looked over Sammy's list:

> Six deaths: Yitashi Nakamura, Barton Conrad, Sergio Pinez, Katie Miller, Brian McKernan, and Seymour Hollis
>
> Four "suicides": Nakamura, Conrad, Pinez, and Hollis
>
> One fire and resultant death: Brian
>
> One bombing and resultant death: Katie Miller

One almost hit-and-run and one assault: Intended victim: Sammy Greene

Two missing: Luther Abbott and Lucy Peters

Reed shook his head. The girl possessed quite an imagination.

He pulled out a second sheet. It was the autopsy report on Sergio Pinez. Why did that name sound familiar? Of course, he remembered. Sergio was the student who'd committed suicide, the student with—

Wait a second. Something didn't make sense. The name was right, but the diagnosis was all wrong. This report gave cause of death as massive internal injuries secondary to suicide. No mention that the boy had AIDS. Why? Reed wondered.

And something else. Unless he was mistaken, the time stamp was off. Reed remembered that Palmer had summoned him to the Nitshi Institute during evening rounds—at least two hours *after* this final autopsy report had been filed.

Reed scratched his head. No doubt Sammy was way off base, but something wasn't kosher. He picked up the Nitshi PR brochure and found Lang's picture on the back cover. The short, stocky Lang stood next to a smiling Marcus Palmer. Most of the other people in the group shot were unfamiliar.

He studied the photo for a long time before he noticed. Just behind Palmer and Lang and slightly hidden was a dark-haired man sporting a well-manicured beard. Reed's eyes widened as he recognized the bearded man—someone he would never have expected to be there.

Grabbing his kitchen extension phone, he dialed Sammy's number.

"Hi, this is Sammy."

Somehow Reed wasn't surprised that she was out. Still, he left a message for her to call the minute she got back. "It's important."

After that, Reed showered, dressed, and headed for the Nitshi Research Institute.

• • •

Sammy stood up and faced the tiny silver robot that had introduced itself as Carl.

A tray emerged from within the machine. "Place your right hand here," the robot commanded.

Sammy hesitated, unsure what to do.

"I won't hurt you," Carl assured her in an Elmer Fudd voice. "Everyone on the fourth floor needs a pass. For security reasons."

Sammy unwrapped Reed's white coat from her waist and slipped it on over her now grease-stained clothes. She pulled off the medical student's ID badge, flashing it quickly in front of the robot. "I already have a pass. See? Dr. Wyndham."

"Sorry," the silver machine squeaked, now Bart Simpson. "That does not compute. According to my memory bank, Reed Wyndham is male, five foot ten, sandy hair, violet eyes. Fourth-year medical student, Ellsford University Medical School, 3304 Menlo Avenue, Apartment number 2B, phone number 617-555-9748. Social security number—"

"Okay, okay," Sammy conceded, hardly believing she was interacting with this R2D2 clone. She looked down the empty corridor, expecting an armed guard or two to appear, but there seemed to be no humans around. She might as well go along with Carl's request—obviously the little machine was programmed to act as security. "Here." She placed her right hand, palm down, in the tray.

Her prints were instantly copied and processed. "Sammy Greene, third-year communications major, Ellsford University, 213 Thayer Street, Apartment number 3A, phone number 617-555-6090. Social security number 555-42-7186."

"How did you do that?" Sammy marveled as seconds later, a plastic card with her information appeared on the tray.

"Keep it with you at all times." The robot ignored her question. "Follow me."

"ID badge please." The Nitshi guard looked up from his newspaper and smiled. "Oh, hello, Doc." He'd greeted Reed almost every day for the past week. "Getting a late start?"

Reed shrugged. "Sunday morning. Thought I'd sleep in."

The guard nodded and turned his attention back to the football scores.

Reed checked his pocket, realizing he'd run out without grabbing the badge from his lab coat. "Listen, I forgot my ID. I'm only gonna be a minute. Gotta check on a few slides."

Without looking up again, the guard motioned to the sign-in sheet on the counter. "Just leave your X. It'll be okay this time. I know you."

"Thanks, I owe you one." Reed scribbled his name on the roster and hurried to the main elevator. He passed a couple of research assistants on the third floor — all Ellsford University grad students, driven to working brutal hours by hopes of moving up in the academic hierarchy. They were too engaged in their own projects to offer Reed more than a head-nodding acknowledgment.

Luckily, the immunogenetics lab was empty when he entered. He'd have to hurry, though. Reed made a beeline for Dr. Palmer's desk in the far corner and tried to open the middle drawer. It was locked.

About to give up, he spied the professor's coat slung over the back of the desk chair. Recognizing the slim odds, Reed reached into the pockets and dug around until his fingers found a metal object at the bottom of the left one.

The key fit!

He slid the drawer open and pulled out a cardboard packet marked VACCINE. STUDY PATIENTS. Sitting down at a large workbench with a microscope, he began checking names. The twenty-four glass slides were in chronological, not alphabetical order, so it took several minutes to find the ones he was looking for.

His hands shook as one by one he removed four slides.

Seymour Hollis.

There was a third suicide on campus this month. What's weird is #12 refers to the twelfth patient in the study, a new drug being tested for AIDS — part of a Nitshi study. Palmer was principal investigator.

Luther Abbott.

Luther Abbott's disappeared. Nurse Matthews told me he was admitted to Ellsford General, but when I was there yesterday, I heard one of the nurses say he'd been transferred to Nitshi.

Lucy Peters.

I suppose you don't know about Lucy Peters either? Freshman. She got this rash, it was supposed to be chickenpox, but her roommate says she never went home. Now she's missing too.

Sergio Pinez.

Massive internal injuries secondary to suicide.

No mention of AIDS.

Reed flipped on the light beneath the microscope, picked up Sergio's slide and placed it on the stage. It was a cross section of the boy's brain. Magnified a thousand times, the microglial cells scattered throughout the gray matter and smaller areas of demyelination surrounding veins in the white matter were evidence of subacute encephalitis. Reed had aced pathology. He knew this was consistent with a diagnosis of AIDS.

He checked the other three slides, not surprised to find identical pathology.

Two students "missing." Two student "suicides."

Hollis, Pinez, Peters, and Abbott.

All four dead.

All four with AIDS.

All part of a study. Marcus Palmer's study.

Vaccine Study Patients

Reed's mind whirled with conflicting doubts and emotions. What did this mean? Palmer never mentioned testing an experimental vaccine in human subjects.

Now he recalled Sammy's words: *I don't know what happened to these students, but if there was foul play —*

Hearing voices and muffled footsteps coming nearer, Reed quickly replaced the slides and returned the case to the drawer. Then he put Palmer's key back in the pocket of the lab coat and switched off the lights.

• • •

Sammy followed Carl down several sterile hallways, stopping to sneak a quick peek into a few of the rooms they passed. All seemed to be high-tech laboratories staffed by robots. She still had not encountered one human. And certainly no patients.

The silver security robot was about to turn a corner when Sammy noticed a single sign that read PATHOLOGY in Japanese and English. She pushed a button on the wall, opening an electronically controlled door. Stepping inside, she stood a minute, orienting herself. The fluorescent-lit room lined with counters, shelves, and sinks appeared to be some kind of operating theater. But the sharp smell in the air was formaldehyde, not antiseptic, and the soapstone bench in the center of the tiled floor was no ordinary surgical table.

Sammy froze as she eyed the white sheet covering a human-sized mound. Slowly, she edged forward. It was more than the room's chill that had raised goose bumps on her arms. Hesitating, she pulled up the sheet just enough to see two bare feet. The skin was the color of beeswax. Swallowing hard, she moved to the other end of the body, gently unfolded the white cloth, forcing herself to examine the face.

Luther Abbott!

His eyes were closed, but the expression on his pale face was anything but serene.

Sammy's stomach plunged. Overcome with nausea, she leaned against the table, willing herself not to vomit.

Another patient of Palmer's to die.

She had to tell someone. Now! Frantic, Sammy searched the room until she saw a phone on the far wall. Osborne. She'd call the psychologist. He'd know what to do. Sammy reached in her purse for the slip of paper with his number, then picked up the receiver and dialed. A few seconds later she heard the first ring. *Please be there.*

"Hello?"

"Dr. Osborne, I'm at the Nitshi Institute. I'm in trouble."

A hand shot past her face and punched the disconnect.

Sammy whirled to see a gray-haired man in a white lab coat standing behind her. His face was distorted with rage. Even without the nametag she knew he was Dr. Palmer. She thought he was going to hit her.

"You don't know what kind of trouble you've gotten yourself into, young lady."

"Oh there you are, Miss Greene." Carl swept into the open door behind the researcher.

Palmer grabbed Sammy's arm.

"What are you doing?"

"I'm taking you to Mr. Ishida. I'll let him deal with you."

Ishida rose as Palmer and Carl escorted Sammy into the CEO's office. "Hello again, Miss Greene," he said.

"Mr. Ishida. I know I shouldn't be here, but . . ."

The Japanese man ambled over to Sammy and patted her arm. "No need to explain." He motioned her to a seat in front of his desk. "Please."

Sammy looked at Palmer still hovering by the door, his face firmly set in a scowl. "Could I talk to you in private, Mr. Ishida?" she whispered.

"Of course. Marcus, leave us alone for a few minutes. I shall call you in if we need you."

Palmer exited without protest, closing the door behind him. Carl, Sammy noted, had already disappeared.

She sank into one of two comfortable chairs facing Ishida's massive walnut desk. Her heart was just beginning to slow.

Ishida walked across the room to a stylish wet bar that included what looked like a high-tech hot plate. "Now, Sammy — May I call you Sammy?"

"What? Uh, yes, of course."

"I know you've just had a terrible shock." He poured from a carafe into two mugs. "Why don't we have some tea," he said, placing one mug on his desk for Sammy, "and talk about what you've learned?"

Reed's heart thumped wildly as he stood still in the darkness of the lab, listening. Finally, after what seemed like an eternity, the voices and footsteps began to recede. Whoever it was had proceeded down the hall toward Chemistry.

Reed waited another five minutes before he felt safe enough to leave and head for the elevator.

Sammy was in way over her head, he realized. And so was he. He had to warn her as soon as possible, he thought, as the car neared the lobby. First, he would stop at her apartment and apologize, and then they were going to the authorities. Together.

"Green tea." Ishida watched Sammy take another sip from her mug. "Quite soothing, don't you agree?"

Sammy nodded as the warm liquid slid down her throat. It was slightly more bitter than the tea she'd shared with Mrs. Nakamura, but already she was beginning to feel a calmness settle over her. Her pulse had returned to normal, her breathing had slowed. She took a moment to survey the room. The CEO's decor here was slightly less elegant than his corporate office in New York — walnut instead of mahogany, expensive prints instead of original French impressionists.

"I'm sorry you had to see that body," Ishida continued. "What happened to the boy was most unfortunate."

Sammy eyed Ishida over her mug. His expression reflected genuine regret. "I know Luther was bitten by a monkey, but I don't understand why he died. I mean he was treated at Student Health right after the injury."

"You are obviously a bright young woman and a very resourceful one," Ishida said, smiling. "So I'm going to be very frank with you, Sammy. The monkey that bit Luther was infected with a deadly virus."

"Virus?" Sammy's eyelids drooped as she felt a torpor stealing over her. She was totally exhausted, but she forced herself to sit straighter in the chair. She sipped another mouthful of tea and tried not to think of Luther's corpse.

"Two years ago Dr. Palmer began testing a new vaccine to combat the AIDS virus. He was using an approach developed by another Ellsford University professor."

"Dr. Nakamura," Sammy said sleepily.

"Why, yes. Of course," Ishida agreed, raising an eyebrow. "But Dr. Palmer significantly refined the original technique." Ishida paused and took a sip of his tea. "The early trials with pigtail macaques showed great success, and frankly, we would have continued using monkeys if not for Reverend Taft."

"Taft? I don't think—" Sammy couldn't remember what she was going to say.

"The Traditional Values Coalition has lobbied quite hard to stop animal research. They have even tried to buy influence among those of a political persuasion."

Ishida's smile seemed somehow odd to Sammy, who tried vainly to suppress a yawn. She felt very, very tired.

"Perhaps with enough time and money, we could have overcome the opposition in the public arena. But it seemed prudent—given the significant financial potential for Nitshi if we were first to develop the vaccine—to simply proceed to the next phase. Human trials."

Sammy was puzzled. "I'm not sure I follow."

"All the infected monkeys were ordered destroyed. Unfortunately, Dr. Palmer allowed one newborn to survive. That was the pigtail that bit Luther Abbott." Ishida drank once again from his tea mug before proceeding. "Truly a pity. By the time he realized the boy was infected, it was too late. We know from students already tested that the vaccine only works as a preventive measure."

"Students?" Sammy frowned, trying to concentrate on the conversation. "Lucy Peters, Seymour Hollis, Sergio Pinez are students—"

Ishida nodded. "A shame the vaccine did not protect them. But I assure you, their sacrifice was for the greater good."

"Sacrifice? Greater good?" Despite the hazy cloud she felt settling over her thoughts, Sammy began to grasp what Ishida was saying: Lucy, Seymour, and Sergio had been part of a study. They'd been infected with the virus and now they were dead. Palmer had killed them and Ishida had given the corrupt doctor his blessing.

"You know, this tea is my mother's favorite."

Sammy focused on Ishida's lips for several moments, fascinated by how slowly the words were forming in his mouth.

"See? Here we are together in Kyoto."

Sammy followed his fingers to a small photo perched on his credenza. Ishida stood next to a beautiful Japanese woman dressed in a traditional kimono. Sammy stared at the picture, then back at the Japanese executive sitting in front of her. A chill of alarm spread through her veins an instant before full comprehension settled in. The truth was there before her all the time. No wonder the woman's features seemed so familiar that day in New York. "You're Mimiko Nakamura's son."

"If I hadn't had you watched, I'd never have known you visited Mother," Ishida said. "For some reason, she didn't tell me."

Sammy's mind raced as the significance of Ishida's true identity registered. She felt a mixture of disgust and fear.

Sometimes we don't always know the men we love as much as we think we do.

Sammy assumed Mimiko had meant her husband, but the long-suffering woman had been referring to Ishida. She shivered, certain of one fact: Dr. Nakamura never committed suicide. "You killed your own father," she gasped as she struggled to stand.

"Yitashi Nakamura was not my real father," Ishida declared. "Fifty years ago he married my mother. I was five years old."

Sammy slid back down in her chair, confused. "But your accent sounds Japanese."

"When I was eleven, Yitashi convinced my mother to send me

to Japan to 'complete' my education. He called me a '*nisei*.' Second generation. Too American. I never forgave him for that. I took my mother's name back. I *became* Japanese. After graduating university, I joined Nitshi Pharmaceuticals, starting, as you say, at the bottom. As administrative associate, I reviewed all scientific proposals submitted for funding. One was from my stepfather. I understood enough immunology to recognize that Yitashi's early work was visionary. A word to the director of program development was sufficient."

"Huh?"

"My stepfather was invited to work for us. A very productive association at first. I was promoted. Yitashi had all the financial support he needed for his vaccine project and, in exchange, Nitshi would own the patent." Ishida produced a bitter laugh. "But Yitashi was always such a pedantic moralist at heart. He believed private funding could corrupt researchers, compromise their objectivity. He eventually wanted out, and that would not have been good for either of us."

Sammy's head hurt as she tried to focus on Ishida's words.

"I was sure a little pressure from above would force Yitashi to change his mind, so I went directly to the chancellor. Reginald Ellsford was only too happy to accept our yen. When we proposed the institute, he was delighted."

"But you're — Yitashi?"

Ishida's voice was icy. "Yitashi tried to block the venture, to hide his research. That's why he had to go. He was standing in the path of science. Of progress, of —"

"You were his son," Sammy said quietly.

"I was never his son."

No, Conrad, not Ishida was his son, Sammy thought, remembering her conversation with Mimiko:

Yitashi loved him as a son. Perhaps even more than a son.

"You killed Conrad." The words tumbled out slowly. "You were jealous."

"Jealousy is a useless emotion." Ishida shook his head. "He just managed to get in the way."

Sammy struggled to keep her eyelids above her pupils. It took all her strength. "Of what?"

Ishida finished the last of his tea before responding. "Conrad learned we'd progressed beyond animal studies. Somehow he'd plugged into Palmer's database so he knew about our work. He planned to tell the dean and the board of regents."

"Dean Jeffries . . . brown envelope . . ." Sammy's words were slurred.

"My, you have done a bit of detective work. Pity that no one else will ever know."

Sammy's mind recoiled. Her tongue struggled in vain to express the horror at what she'd just heard. "I . . . don't . . ."

Ishida picked up Sammy's mug. It was empty. "More tea?"

". . . don't feel so well . . ." Sammy slumped over in her chair.

Ishida shook his head. "A very bright young woman," he said. "We might have benefited from your talents. A real shame." Picking up his desk phone, he buzzed Palmer. "You can come in now."

Pappajohn's home fax hummed as the machine produced the Berkeley University records he'd requested hours before. Twelve pages dating back over a decade were sent. Some of the typing had faded and was difficult to read. He sat at his desk and skimmed through the papers until he came to the report he was looking for: Faculty Senate minutes, June 1986. Reading the journal carefully, he knew he'd discovered the last piece of a complicated puzzle.

A black-and-white yearbook picture had been included in the faxed materials. Pappajohn gazed at the photo of the bearded young man, wondering whether the decision to sell his soul had come easily. Temptation had crossed his path many times during his own career, but Pappajohn had never stepped over the line.

Why? It was a question he wanted to ask the man when he caught him.

Now Pappajohn lifted the receiver on his desk phone and dialed Sammy's number. He didn't care what time it was. He needed to talk to her.

"This is Sammy Greene. I'm not in."

Damn it. Nothing but — what was it — *tzoris* — trouble — from that girl.

About to dial another number, his attention turned to a new message flashing on his computer screen. He'd been searching through Marcus Palmer's files via the E-net when the fax had interrupted his search. Someone was making a new entry. At this hour?

Across the terminal came the words, row by row:

NRINET UPDATE: 0257 GMT
ADMITTING PHYSICIAN: M. PALMER
DATE OF ADMISSION: 11/29 /95
STUDY PATIENT #24: SAMMY GREENE

Pappajohn frowned. What the hell was going on? The terminal source was NRI. That mean it was located not at Ellsford General Hospital, but the Nitshi Research Institute.

"*Ghamo to!*" he cursed out loud.

Without a second thought, Pappajohn jumped up from his desk, grabbed his coat and his gun, and bolted out the door.

Sammy dreamed she was lying in a hospital bed, but she couldn't remember how she'd gotten there. Her head throbbed with pain. Had she been in an accident?

Voices buzzed back and forth around her. She strained to listen.

"It seems to me that this is rather an inappropriate time for you to begin setting moral standards for yourself, Doctor."

Sammy recognized Ishida's voice.

"But giving her the virus. You might as well kill her."

That was Palmer talking, Sammy realized, forcing herself to concentrate.

"That is unavoidable. Would you prefer she tell her story to the police?"

A pause.

"I didn't think so."

Another pause.

"In fact, go ahead and give her the vaccine. That way she'll be another subject for your study. We can keep her in the institute until she contracts the disease."

"But you don't know. It could protect her."

"Hardly, Doctor." Ishida's laugh was filled with contempt. "Haven't you figured it out yet? After all those deaths?"

"It's got to be some kind of mutation producing a different, much more virulent strain."

"A different strain, yes. But not from some random mutation. You'd be happy to know, my people used your techniques to alter the virus."

"You did this?" Palmer's voice was strained with shock. "Why?"

"In the words of the Roman philosopher, Seneca, 'Most powerful is he who has himself in his own power,'" Ishida answered calmly. "Today's friends are tomorrow's enemies. What better tool than a deadly virus that no one can cure — not even you, Doctor."

"You're mad!" Palmer screamed. "Absolutely mad."

"Do not even think about running," Ishida said. "Or you will meet the same fate as our patient."

Sammy felt a rush of panic. Ishida was trying to kill her!

"She's more alert. Look, her lids are fluttering."

Sammy slowly opened her eyes. Colors spun like a psychedelic light show across the ceiling. Struggling to move, she sensed something binding across her chest and thighs. They'd strapped her down.

"Don't worry, Sammy. They're just safety belts. We didn't want you to fall out of bed."

That voice sounded strangely familiar. "Thirsty," she croaked.

A hand lifted her head gently and held a glass to her lips. She gulped it down, then turned to focus on the face.

"Dr. Osborne." With her head, Sammy motioned for him to approach so she could whisper in his ear. Even in her sluggish state she noted how out of character he seemed. His blue blazer was missing a button, his cotton shirt was poorly tucked, his tan slacks wrinkled. "You found me . . . Have to get out of here . . . Not Taft . . . Ishida wants to kill me." She strained against the straps, but they held tight and she lay back on the pillow, gasping.

"I'm really sorry."

Something in his tone disturbed her. She gaped up at him with alarm.

"You had to be so persistent, didn't you?" His face grew bleak. "If you'd just stayed in your apartment as I asked."

"Peter Lang would have made your end much more pleasant than I'm afraid it's going to be now." Ishida had come over to stand behind Osborne.

"Help me!" Sammy appealed to Osborne.

Osborne looked away. "It's out of my hands."

"There's too much at stake to let you leave the institute alive." Ishida's statement left Sammy numb.

Sammy was unable to breathe. Her whole world was collapsing. Osborne? The man whose eyes had been so kind, whose wisdom and understanding had helped her to open up her heart and reveal feelings she'd kept buried for so long. Could this same man be part of such evil? She turned to him with a look of despair and strained to speak. "You? You're involved?"

"From the beginning," Ishida confirmed as Osborne turned away. "How do you think we picked our best subjects?"

Reed rushed from the Nitshi Institute as Pappajohn pulled up the driveway in his Land Cruiser.

"Hold it right there." Pappajohn leaped out of his truck and ran up to him.

"Look, I'm sorry, but I have to go."

"I'll bet you do. Where's Sammy?"

"Sammy Greene? I was just on my way to her apartment. I—"

Pappajohn nodded at the building towering behind them. "She's somewhere in there." He described the disturbing message that had flashed on his computer screen.

Reed looked genuinely surprised. "No way. There're no patients in the —" His voice trailed off as he spotted Sammy's peacoat lying on a nearby bench.

Luther Abbott. Nurse Matthews told me he was admitted to Ellsford General, but when I was there yesterday, I heard one of the nurses say he'd been transferred to Nitshi.

My God! He'd never considered that Sammy might be right. Luther and Sergio sent to the institute. To die.

It was too horrible to believe. Palmer conducting some kind of AIDS vaccine study that had gone terribly wrong? And if Sammy *was* in there, she could be in the gravest danger. Reed's face reflected his panic. "We've got to get her out!"

"Back-up's on the way."

Reed shook his head. "There may not be time!

It's a big building. She could be anywhere."

Reed peered up at the institute. "I think I know where they may be keeping her."

Pappajohn only hesitated a moment before reaching into the truck for his gun. "All right," he said as he strapped on the holster and replaced his jacket. "Let's go."

"Now. Inject it now!" Ishida ordered.

Trembling, Palmer approached Sammy's hospital bed, clutching a syringe filled with clear liquid. When he was just a few feet from her, he turned and faced Ishida. "I can't," he said. "I'm not a killer."

"Do it!" Ishida pulled a .22-caliber handgun from his suit jacket and pointed it at Palmer. "Fitting, don't you think?" he asked as Sammy watched the drama with growing horror. The effects of the chloral hydrate Ishida had slipped into her tea had nearly worn off, leaving her senses raw. "My stepfather's gun."

"How did you get it?" Sammy tried to keep her voice steady, fighting to retain control of her fear — and her rage.

"Lang stole it from the police property room." Ishida said. "Keeping it in the family, so to speak." He laughed at the irony.

"You're crazy!" Sammy appealed to Palmer. "Please!"

Palmer shook his head, then suddenly lunged at Ishida, his arm sweeping down in an awkward karate stroke aimed at the gun. But his attack was too slow and far too weak. Without hesitation, Ishida pointed the semiautomatic at Palmer's mid-chest and fired.

"No!" Sammy screamed.

Palmer fell backward, collapsing on the floor.

The uniformed guard reluctantly led Pappajohn and Reed to the private elevator, and, using a special card, reached in and turned off the override that prevented access to the top floor. "I'm gonna lose my job," he complained.

"You'll lose a lot more if you don't," Pappajohn threatened as he punched "four." "Stay here and wait for my back-up. Send them up as soon as they arrive," he ordered. Pointing to the portable phone the guard carried on his belt, Pappajohn added as the car doors closed, "And stay the hell off that phone."

Osborne bent over Palmer's body, assuring himself that the doctor was indeed dead.

"You killed him!" cried Sammy, her eyes flaring with anger at a frighteningly calm Ishida. The CEO still held the gun, but he was no longer pointing it at anyone.

"No, Sammy, you did," Osborne replied, standing. "Your obsessive investigations are responsible for his death. In the end, Marcus couldn't face his own deal with the devil." He glanced at his Japanese co-conspirator.

"And what about yours?" Sammy accused.

Osborne's smile was patronizing. "You should've studied your Shakespeare, my dear. 'The devil hath power to assume a pleasing shape.' Palmer's only error was letting compassion overcome common sense. I won't make the same mistake." Osborne removed a syringe from his blazer pocket, at the same time moving to Sammy's bedside. "I suggest we dispense with the vaccine now."

Ishida nodded. "It's your call."

Sammy was stunned. Sergio Pinez, Seymour Hollis, and the

others — all innocent victims who had gone to the psychologist for help. And he'd led them to their deaths. Now he planned to give her the virus — to murder her too. "What kind of monster are you?" she cried.

"It's the natural characteristic of man to do everything he must to ensure his own survival," Osborne said as he slipped off the plastic cap from the syringe, and, holding it up to the light, squeezed out the air bubble and a drop of the clear liquid. Then, he bent down and moved the syringe toward Sammy's bound arm, about to prick the skin.

"Don't anybody move!" Pappajohn yelled as he threw open the doorway. Reed stood right behind him.

Ishida pivoted and fired his semiautomatic at the campus cop, but the shot went wide, hitting the doorjamb. Pappajohn aimed and returned fire. Ishida grabbed at his right shoulder as he reeled backward and dropped to the floor.

"Help!"

Sammy's scream startled Osborne, who jerked back with the syringe. Reed dove, grabbing Osborne's arm, twisting it, and sending the syringe flying to the far corner. He kicked Osborne sharply in the groin at the same moment, driving the heel of his hand upward into the man's nose. An expulsion of air, the snap of bone, and Osborne was groveling on the floor.

"You have the right to remain silent," Pappajohn said, his gun aimed at Osborne.

Two St. Charlesbury policemen and three campus deputies ran in, armed with rifles. Behind them rushed the Nitshi guard and the two EMTs Sammy had seen last week at Conrad's home. The medical technicians turned their attention to Ishida and Osborne while Reed rushed to unstrap Sammy.

"You all right?"

"I am now." She lunged into his arms and clung tightly to him, as if she couldn't hold him close enough.

"Ow!" At Reed's cry, Sammy let go. His hand was already swollen and discolored.

"Guess I should brush up on my karate," Reed said with a crooked smile.

Sammy gently kissed his injury. "I never knew you were such a hero."

"There's a lot you still don't know about me."

"I'd like to learn," Sammy said as she melted back into his arms.

Four hours later, Sammy and Reed sat in the emergency room at Ellsford General Hospital, expecting the ER doctor to return with results of Reed's X-rays. Down the hall, in a curtained cubicle, two deputies guarded Osborne, who awaited admission for his injuries.

"Once I recognized Osborne in the Nitshi brochure, I knew you were in trouble," Reed said, rubbing his sore hand. "How do I say I'm sorry for not believing your conspiracy theory?"

"The distrust was mutual," Sammy admitted. "How did you figure out where I was?"

Reed pointed to Pappajohn, who approached them carrying a manila folder. "He hacked into Palmer's computer."

"Impressive," Sammy said. "What made you suspect the good doctor?" she asked Pappajohn.

"I didn't put it all together until I found that list you'd made," Pappajohn confessed. "Every student who died had been a patient of Palmer's. Actually, I'd been tracking Taft on this one."

"That explains the "Taft" file on your computer," Sammy said.

"Figured Taft was stirring up trouble with Nitshi. But I couldn't tie him in with Conrad," Pappajohn continued. "When you insisted your professor was murdered, I thought I'd nose around in Conrad's files. Somehow he'd downloaded Palmer's study data."

"We know Conrad called Dean Jeffries the night he was killed. Probably wanted to tell him what he'd learned about Palmer's work," Sammy said.

"He also called Osborne. Obviously, he didn't know his old buddy was on Ishida's payroll." Pappajohn produced the faxed pages he'd scanned a few hours earlier. "Pulled a few strings with my counterparts at Berkeley to get this confidential file. Seems Osborne was caught falsifying research data as a postdoc. The public story was that he left the university for personal reasons. It's likely that's all Conrad knew."

"How did Osborne end up at Nitshi?" Sammy wondered aloud.

"Ishida must have dug up this dirt and blackmailed him," Pappajohn said.

"So that car, those clothes—"

"Obviously not on a professor's salary." Reed finished Sammy's thought

"In any case," Pappajohn went on, "Osborne was in too deep to afford exposure. I suppose that's why he shot Conrad."

"Osborne shot him?" Sammy registered shock. "I thought it was Peter Lang. I mean, didn't Osborne call Conrad from New York?"

"Maybe New Brighton or anywhere else within an hour or two of St. Charlesbury. Dave—Lt. Williams—found the rental car records for a John Darsee at La Guardia."

"Darsee." Sammy frowned. "Darsee and Somerville! I think I saw those names in the Osborne file on Conrad's computer."

"Darsee and Summerlin," Reed corrected. "Two genetic researchers with stellar careers caught falsifying data. Ironic, he'd pick that name."

"*Ivris*." Pappajohn agreed. "Hubris in English. He drives up and kills Conrad on Friday night, back in New York by Saturday morning. We calculated the mileage from the odometer."

"So Osborne confessed?" Sammy asked.

"Not yet. My men are still questioning Lang. Given that he's facing a felony murder charge, I expect him to be very cooperative. If not, we have this." Pappajohn pulled out a cassette tape.

Sammy jumped up. "My tape!"

"Larry Dupree dropped it off this morning after he didn't hear from you. Your engineer friend saved it from the flames."

"Poor Brian. He always came through."

"We'll have a voice expert from Boston identify Osborne and Lang as the two men with Conrad when he was killed. It should make for pretty convincing evidence."

A deputy was waving for Pappajohn. "They're ready to take Dr. Osborne upstairs."

Pappajohn turned to Sammy and, smiling broadly, saluted her with the tape. "We made a good team," he added as he walked off.

Sammy watched Pappajohn leave. The old man wasn't so bad — all bulk and bluster.

Reed saw her look away. "Penny —?"

Sammy turned back, embarrassed. She gazed up at him. "Remember you said I was jinxing our relationship, that I was afraid you'd abandon me like my father did?"

Reed shook his head. "Amateur psychobabble. I was way off base."

"No, you were right." Sammy insisted. "The trip to New York made me see that. I blamed myself for my father's leaving. I thought any man who got close to me would leave, too. I know now I was wrong to feel that way. My parents made their own choices. I wasn't responsible. Funny." She peered off in the distance. The psychologist was being loaded onto a gurney for his trip to the locked ward. "For that insight I have to thank Dr. Osborne."

The emergency room doctor walked over to them holding up X-rays of Reed's hand. "Nothing's broken. All it needs is some ice. Looks like you can still be a surgeon. Or an ER doc, if you're up to the pressure."

"Actually, I was looking for an easier specialty. Anything's got to be less draining than research." He reached out for Sammy and tousled her red hair. "But for the next week or so, I'm going to specialize in Sammy."

EPILOGUE
NEW BEGINNINGS

Ellsford University
January 1996

It was a perfect day for a celebration—and new beginnings. One week after New Year's, the afternoon had brought unseasonably warm weather and crystalline Vermont skies. Inside borrowed space in the new Ellsford Sports Center, twenty or so WELL staffers along with assorted faculty and friends crowded around a brimming potluck buffet table and caught up on what was now known on campus as "the Nitshi Disaster."

Reed read the latest buzz from a copy of *The Vermonter* magazine. "Lang plea-bargained murder one down to second degree in exchange for his testimony. Looks pretty bad for Osborne and Ishida. Lots of lawsuits down the road. Preliminary trial date is set for March."

"There go spring midterms," Sammy said.

"You don't have to cover the trial," teased Reed.

"Neither snow nor hail nor midterms—" Sammy retorted. Nothing could keep her from that story.

Pappajohn pointed to the eggplant casserole heaped up on his plate. "Not bad, Greene."

"Thanks, you should try the tiropites."

"Since she ate your sister's food, Sammy's really gotten into Greek cuisine," Reed patted his stomach. "I've gained five pounds."

Pappajohn brushed crumbs off of his own ample gut. "I didn't get this from doughnuts."

The ER doctor who'd treated Reed walked over to say hello. "By the way, regards from Bud Stanton."

"I heard he'd withdrawn for the semester," Sammy said. "Where'd you see him?"

"He had a follow-up with our hand surgeon. Bud's doing really well in rehab."

"Think he'll be able to play?" Reed wondered aloud.

"Probably not pro, but apparently he's gotten into something new. He wants to be a physical therapist."

"If only Reggie Ellsford could see his star forward now," Sammy said. "The chancellor had been strong-arming Conrad to pass Stanton. Didn't want to lose those generous alumni donations."

"How do you know?" Reed asked.

Sammy gestured to Pappajohn who told them how he'd found Ellsford's private phone number in Stanton's apartment. "When I dialed, the chancellor answered. It didn't take long for the old man to break."

"Whoever thought the great-great-grandson of our university's founder would resign in disgrace?" Sammy asked. "Though I hear Ellsford's niece is a straight arrow."

Pappajohn nodded. "The new chancellor has promised to clean house. Full disclosure from here on out. She'll be working closely with the feds and the CDC on their investigations of the whole affair. The Nitshi Institute will become a university-owned-and-funded facility."

"Not such an easy task," Reed observed. "Good research costs big bucks."

"Reginald Ellsford brought in millions from all kinds of questionable sources, including Nitshi," Sammy said

"Think he knew what Ishida was up to?" the ER doctor asked.

"Not according to Lang's sworn statement," Pappajohn reported, "though Ellsford did admit to burning the brown envelope. Claims he had no idea Conrad had been murdered for it."

Sammy shook her head. "At least Conrad's message got through in the end."

"Hey, did you see this?" Someone in the crowd held up a page of the magazine. "An ad for Taft's Senate campaign."

"I'll bet Joslin's pissed his old ally's running against him," another chuckled at the irony.

"Serves him right," Sammy said. "Senator Joslin was playing both sides. He convinced Taft he opposed foreign investment, at the same time he collected huge campaign contributions from Nitshi."

"Is it true Peter Lang used to be a Joslin staffer?" the ER doctor asked.

"That's how Lang came to work for Ishida," Pappajohn explained. "He was paid to keep tabs on the Reverend. Lang even set up the bombing. Tried to point the finger at the Traditional Values Coalition."

"Taft running for Congress?" someone else piped up. "That should be a religious experience."

Much of the humor rippling through the room was tempered by fear that the man might win.

"Seriously, if an actor can become president, why not a televangelist, senator?" Reed asked.

Sammy rolled her eyes. "Heaven forbid."

"Good news!" A breathless Larry Dupree burst in with Dean Jeffries. "Ah just came from the new chancellor's office. Looks like we're going to get that new building."

"To start off her tenure, Eunice Ellsford has earmarked construction funds for the new station," Jeffries announced.

"All right!" Sammy punched her fist up in the air. "Not Nitshi money, I hope."

Larry smiled. "Nope. These funds'll come the traditional way. Rich, vain, alumni donations." Even Dean Jeffries laughed.

Amidst the chuckles, Larry produced a serious look. "The building is going to be the cornerstone of a new communications program. And," he paused, his voice cracking, "we're going to name it after Brian."

"Mazel tov." Sammy's eyes filled with tears.

"And," Jeffries continued, "we wanted to let you know that we have established two scholarships remembering our students in the Departments of Music and Natural Sciences. The Sergio Pinez Performance Award will provide opportunities for students from underrepresented minorities to pursue studies in music, and the Lucille Peters Honors Grant will offer full tuition for an outstanding student in Biology."

Sammy let the tears fall without restraint.

"All right, gang, it's almost six," Larry announced. "We gotta get on the air. Don't want to be late for our grand reopening." The entire crew followed him into another small room set up as a makeshift studio.

From one corner, Larry powered up the temporary transmitting equipment. Across the room, Sammy sat down in front of the microphone. As the clock struck six, the program director smiled and delivered Sammy's cue. Sammy flipped on her mike switch, grinned at her studio audience, and began:

"Hello, I'm Sammy Greene. Corruption, Greed, Murder. Wall Street? Washington? No, right here at Ellsford University. That's tonight's topic — on *The Hot Line*."